"A deft satire on the excesses of contemporary America."
—Greg Johnson,
Chicago Tribune

"Matthew's journey from soup to nuts, though disquieting, is salutary, because Eric Kraft has a moral vision. His target is those who take nothing seriously but themselves, and his artful, bitter portrait of a man without compassion makes the best possible argument for that quality."
—Malcolm Jones Jr.,
Newsweek

"Boy, does Eric Kraft have the tone of contemporary American life and concerns down perfectly. . . . [His] premise is unique and beautifully realized."
—Frederic Koeppel,
Memphis *Commercial Appeal*

"A merciless sendup of contemporary American pretensions. . . . Eric Kraft can pack more wit into a sentence about grilled pork tenderloin than a lot of authors can fit into an entire book, which is just one of the things that makes *Reservations Recommended* fun."
—Janice Harayda,
Cleveland *Plain Dealer*

"I recommend this novel without reservations."
—*Los Angeles Times*

Also by Eric Kraft

Herb 'n' Lorna

Little Follies

Where Do You Stop?

What a Piece of Work I Am

At Home with the Glynns

RESERVATIONS RECOMMENDED

ERIC KRAFT

Picador USA
New York

For Mad, Scott, and Alexis

Grateful acknowledgment is made to the following for permission to reprint previously published material:

Beldock, Levin & Hoffman: an excerpt from lyrics to "Once in a Lifetime" by David Byrne and Brian Eno. © 1980, Index Music Inc./Blue Disque Music, Inc./E. G. Music, Ltd. Reprinted by permission of Beldock, Levine & Hoffman, attorneys for Index Music Inc.

Coward, McCann & Geoghegan, Inc.: an excerpt from *The Man Without Qualities*, by Robert Musil. Translated by Eithne Wilkins and Ernst Kaiser. Copyright © 1953 by Coward-McCann, Inc. Reprinted by permission of Coward, McCann & Geoghegan, Inc.

Thanks to Alex and Rita Shaknovich for the snatches of Russian in Superior Indian Cookery.

Library of Congress Cataloging-in-Publication Data

Kraft, Eric.
  Reservations recommended / Eric Kraft.
      p.   cm.
    ISBN 0-312-13597-1
    1. Middle aged men—Massachusetts—Boston—Fiction. 2. Food writers—Massachusetts—Boston—Fiction. I. Title.
  [PS3561.R22R4   1995]
  813'.54—dc20   95-34775
                                                        CIP

First published by Crown Publishers, Inc.

First Picador USA Edition: November 1995
10 9 8 7 6 5 4 3 2 1

Midway along the road of life,
I found myself within a shadowy forest,
For I had lost my way.

Dante
Inferno

... by the time they have reached the middle of their life's journey
few people remember how they have managed to arrive at themselves, at their amusements, their point of view, their wife, character, occupation, and successes, but they cannot help feeling that not
much is likely to change any more. ... Something has had its way
with them like a fly-paper with a fly; it has caught them fast, here
catching a little hair, there hampering their movements, and has
gradually enveloped them, until they lie buried under a thick
coating ...

Robert Musil
The Man Without Qualities

You may ask yourself,
"Well, how did I get here?"
And the days go by ...

David Byrne and Brian Eno
"Once in a Lifetime"

'Tis plain, these useless toys of every kind
... little can relieve the laboring mind ...
... every man o'er works his weary will,
To shun himself, and to shake off his ill;
The shaking fit returns, and hangs upon him still.

Lucretius
De Rerum Natura

The ungrateful greed of the soul makes the creature everlastingly
desire varieties of dainty food.

Epicurus
"Epicurus's Exhortation"

Preface

For years I have spent a good part of every day living apart from the present moment, living in my memory or in my imagination. In those hours I have found some of the greatest pleasure in my life, but I've also found pain there; sometimes memory and imagination gang up on me, and they become monstrous, ferocious, not a gift but a curse.

For example: about a year and a half ago, I was body-surfing and caught a wave badly. I came up spluttering and choking, with the salty taste of death by drowning, and found myself thinking of my old schoolmate Matthew Barber. I hadn't thought of him for years, but I found that once he had re-entered my mind I couldn't *stop* thinking about him until I had written this book.

I had lost track of Matthew many years earlier; in fact, after we graduated from high school we never saw each other again, although we exchanged letters a couple of times during college, and he telephoned me one night in our senior year, not long before graduation. He sounded drunk, which struck me as odd, because I'd never seen him take a drink and couldn't picture him drinking enough to lose control of himself.

"How are you, Matthew?" I asked.

He answered, automatically, "Oh, fine," but from that "Oh, fine" he took a step downward to "Well, not so hot, to tell the truth," and that began a descending recitation, from disappointment to doubt to disillusionment, disaffection, darkness, depression, doom, despair.

"They only taught me *things*," he complained. "They didn't divulge any secrets. I thought they would. But they didn't. No divulging. No divulging at all. So—what was the point? If this wasn't the first step on the path to that vast and verdant plain of understanding where once I hoped to graze, then what was the point of my coming here?"

"Well—" I said.

He went on without a pause: "Having expected to start out on the way to enlightenment, I have found only—a deepening dark-ness— a widening abyss of misunderstanding."

"Gosh," I said.

"Some days I don't see the point of getting out of bed."

This remark brought to my mind, with astonishing vividness, a weekend I had spent with a clever red-haired girl from my molluscan biology class, but I knew that this wasn't the time to bring it up.

"Oh, wait, wait," he said. "I did learn something. You ready?"

"I'm ready."

"You might want to take notes."

"I'll remember."

"Okay. Here goes. You know what a frustrated system is?"

"Yes!" I said proudly. "I do."

I waited, but he said nothing.

"Well?" he said after a while.

"Oh. Sorry. It's a mathematical system, a matrix, say, in which the elements or the relationships among them or both are defined in such a way that not all the conditions can ever be met. For instance—"

"That's all right. That's all right. You've got it. Well here's a frustrated system for you. You ready?"

"Still ready."

"It's the attempt to do more than two of the following three things. You ready?"

"I'm ready. I can't do more than two of the following three things."

"Yes. You. Me. One. One cannot do more than two of the following three things: Live in the world, be happy, and have a conscience."

He lapsed into a phlegmy laugh that made me think he might have been drinking for some time.

My body-surfing scare had reminded of an episode in my childhood friendship with Matthew, one that I would much rather have forgotten. In the following days, he kept popping into my thoughts like an advertising jingle. Almost against my will, I found myself wondering about him, and then trying to construct a likely life for him, based on the boy I had known: a dour little fellow, pale and fretful, convinced that most people are contemptible, that most things will turn out badly. It didn't take long for me to develop a profile for him as he might be in the present: a businessman, vice president of something, recently divorced, graying, obsessed with sex but sexually frustrated, a man with dreads and regrets dogging his heels.

I asked myself, "Where would a guy like that live?" Somewhere, I decided, where living is a struggle, where the weather keeps misery always in the air, somewhere like Boston.

At the library, I checked the Boston telephone directory. No number was listed for Matthew Barber. This intrigued me. Did it mean that I'd been wrong, that he wasn't living in Boston, or did it mean that he was living in Boston but had an unlisted telephone number? Why would he have an unlisted number? Was he involved in something that might invite crank calls?

Then the thought struck me that he might be living under an assumed name. Why would he do that? If he *had* taken an assumed name, what name was he using? Some twist on his own name would appeal to his mathematical mind. I tried looking under Matthews, but didn't find anything there. I wondered what I had expected to find. Something like Barbara Matthews? It wasn't likely that he would suppose he could get away with masquerading as a woman—unless he'd had a sex-change operation or something. Had he? Had Matthew undergone a sex-change operation in Denmark? It didn't seem likely, but it's best to keep an open mind when conducting an investigation of this sort and not turn away from any alleyways of inquiry until one is quite sure that they lead nowhere.

Maybe he would choose a false name that was an anagram of his own. I tried a few, but didn't find any of those in the telephone directory either, so I gave it up.

Still, I wondered what might have happened to him, and finally my curiosity demanded satisfaction, so I drove to Boston and spent a couple of weeks there—just to see what life *would* be like for him if he *had* settled there. I even thought that there was a possibility— remote, I admit, but still a possibility—that I might run into him on the street or in a restaurant, so I spent most of my time either walking around or eating. I was sure that if by any chance he did happen to be in Boston and I did happen to run into him, I would recognize him, even after all these years, even after the sex-change operation, if he had had one. I'd know him anywhere.

I ate in some interesting restaurants, including one that claimed to serve real honest-to-goodness New England food; I read some fascinating graffiti on my walks, very neatly printed expositions of a personal philosophy, a kind of twisted Epicureanism too deep or mad for me to fathom; and I marveled at the beauty of Boston women; but I didn't see Matthew. He may have been on vacation. Maybe he was in Denmark.

Perhaps I should have stayed longer, even if it felt like persisting in a folly, but, one otherwise lovely autumn day, the first wind of winter blew in. Funneled by the buildings, it pummeled me, and it seemed to moan, "Memento mori." The next day all Boston was wearing galoshes and the spring in their step was gone. They trudged along, heads bent, repentant. I got out of town.

I hadn't found Matthew, but I had developed a feeling for the kind of life he might be living there in Boston and I think that, as a result, I understood him better. Of course, there was still much more I wanted to know. I wanted to know how he spent his time, day to day, minute to minute. I would stand in my workroom looking out into the fog on the bay and ask myself, "What will become of him? What is he doing right now? What watchwords does he live by? What are his favorite foods?" Wanting to know those things led me to the writing of this book.

Every book is a means of discovery. I discovered things that I would just as soon have left hidden, but I wasn't really surprised by what I found. Along the way, I felt myself trying to reach Matthew, to show him that he didn't have to be living as he was. To the graffitist's neat messages I added some of my own, trying to echo his style but also to show—as Erasmus tried to show—that the true Epicurean isn't a bibulous glutton, but someone trying to understand the nature of things and to make out of his share of it all a life of happiness, goodness, the pleasures of the mind and heart—but who understands that, since a guy's got to eat and drink along the way, he might as well enjoy himself.

Often, while I was writing, I felt that I was struggling with Matthew, trying to pull him in a direction he didn't want to go, and finally I gave up and let him go his own way, just as I had had to do those many years before, in the episode I mentioned earlier. It happened one summer when we were boys at summer camp together. There we took a course of instruction in lifesaving. Matthew was not a strong swimmer. I was. In the final test, each boy had to swim from shore to the middle of a small lake and bring back a victim, another camper who had paddled out in a canoe, thrown himself into the water, and begun thrashing convincingly. The instructor impressed on all of us the likelihood that the victim would resist help, and he urged the boys playing victims to resist fiercely, to work themselves up to a witless panic. Matthew played victim to my lifesaver. By the time I reached him, treading water had tired him. The panic he simulated was very convincing. He fought me with a furious irrationality that I couldn't tell from the real thing. I couldn't get a grip on him, but he certainly got a grip on me. He pulled me under, and I was taken by surprise, caught without a breath. When I fought free of him and regained the surface, I was gasping, spluttering, and humiliated. A maniacal fire flamed in Matthew's eyes, and he reached for me again. I turned away from him and swam back to shore. The instructor pulled Matthew into his rowboat. Neither of us ever got our lifesaving certificates.

Peter Leroy
Small's Island
June 23, 1989

1

The Alley View Grill

Matthew never takes notes in a restaurant. That's one of his cardinal rules: Never take notes. He's worried that if he were seen taking notes he'd be identified as a reviewer, and it's important to him that he not be identified. He's also a little worried that if he *were* identified as a reviewer there would be some kind of scene, a row. He knows that that's not *likely* to happen, but still it does worry him at times. Worries aside, he enjoys feeling that he's not himself when he's reviewing. He signs his reviews B. W. Beath, a short version of Bertram W. Beath, an anagram of his own name, Matthew Barber. No more than five or six people in the world know that Matthew is B. W. Beath, and there's no reason why anyone who doesn't already know would connect a toy company executive with a restaurant reviewer. He's rather proud of his pseudonym; there is no apparent connection with his own name, but, if he chose to, he could easily demonstrate their correspondence.

The assumed identity, the disguise, is part of the pleasure. He has a theory that most of us are in disguise much of the time, a theory not original with him, but one he came to independently and therefore feels a proprietary affection for. His version goes like this:

"We spend much of our time not as our true selves, but disguised— to suit our occupations, or to appear to be the people our friends or relatives or spouses or lovers expect us to be, or to appear to be what we *wish* we were. The last is the important one, because when we disguise ourselves as what we *want* to be, we're doing it to hide what we think we are."

He uses himself as an example: "I used to be a fat boy. *Really* I'm still a fat boy, but now I'm a fat boy disguised as a fairly slim, fairly good looking, not-yet-middle-aged man, an interesting man, if you took the time to get to know him." For quite a while now he has been working to perfect this disguise. Currently he's concerned that he has been a little too subtle about it, that the disguise errs on the side of anonymity, so he has been trying to make himself a little more noticeable, to bring the inner, interesting man a little closer to the surface. He has begun to dress with a certain flair. He still buys his suits and shirts at a conservative shop—a department store, to tell the truth—but he's buying his socks and ties at a little place with marble floors and brass doors, where everything is imported, up-to-the-minute, and breathtakingly expensive. He doesn't buy anything that really stands out, only things that are a little out of sync with his conservative suits. The combination is intended to make him look a little out of the ordinary, but the other day the worrisome thought struck him that he might be making himself look even *less* remarkable than before, that the new mix of dull and chic had made him more generalized, spread him out all over the culture: a graying toy designer, moonlighting as a restaurant reviewer, in a conservative suit with an interesting Italian tie and startling socks, at heart still a fat boy, a suffering fat boy, for all fat boys suffer, are *made* to suffer, tormented by slim boys, teased and tormented by girls.

Sometimes Matthew uses the routine about disguises at cocktail parties or dinners, including the part about his having been a fat boy, but omitting the business about his still being a suffering fat boy at heart. He keeps a great deal to himself. He doesn't want to seem to be whining.

When he was concocting anagrammatic pseudonyms, he came up

with two women's names: Beth W. A. Bertram and Martha T. Webber. At first he was strongly attracted to them, but eventually he decided against them. For one thing, although he might have been better concealed behind a woman's name, he wasn't comfortable hiding behind a woman's skirts. It made him feel like a sissy, reminded him of the time in the sixth grade when he let his mother break up a fight he was losing. For another, he couldn't seem to make himself sound like Beth or Martha, but he found that he sounded exactly like Bertram W. Beath on the first try, and his, or *their,* reviews were a success from the start. Matthew has been reviewing as B. W. Beath for a couple of years now. He thinks of his alter ego as "BW," what BW's friends would call him if he were able to have friends, which he can't, because he must remain concealed. When Matthew's out doing a review, he's disguised as B. W. Beath, the well-known restaurant reviewer, almost a celebrity, who, because he must not be recognized as a celebrated restaurant reviewer, is disguised as Matthew Barber, a nearly anonymous man, a stand-in, a shell who lends BW a pseudonym to use when he makes his reservations, who is disguised as BW, and so on, round and round in a circuit of disguise, each self concealing another, each hiding within another. It's an idea that Matthew enjoys playing with, as he does with the notion of BW as an older brother, whose background is identical to Matthew's, but who is more worldly, whose tastes are so sophisticated that he can find the shortcoming in any experience. Sometimes Matthew has the feeling that BW is watching him, as if Matthew were his creation, not the other way around, watching his performance from an elevated position, a superior point of view, judging Matthew, reviewing him, looking for his shortcomings. *BW* probably takes notes. He doesn't have to worry; he knows that no one can see him. He's well disguised.

Matthew arrives home from work in a terrible mood. Christmas is coming, and it makes him nervous, even more nervous than it makes most people, because it's the time of year when all his ideas are put to the test. He's vice-president for new product development at Manning & Rafter Toys, where he is sometimes referred to, even to his face, as Vice-President for Sensible Toys. Every year, before the year is out, he must present his proposals for next year's line. The time for that ordeal is only a couple of weeks away, and Matthew fears it. He spent the afternoon in toy stores, checking to see how the toys he championed last year are doing, and they don't seem to be doing well.

Tonight he'll be reviewing the Alley View Grill. He knows he shouldn't arrive in a bad mood. The wise thing to do would be to shower and change his clothes right away. That really would be the wise thing to do. Fresh clothes, a shave—that might change his outlook. Instead he makes a drink, a martini, a Bombay martini. He sits in his living room with the lights out and drinks his drink and just looks out over the city for a while.

He has a beautiful view. It was the reason he bought this apartment. His living room looks out over the poorest sections of the city. He knows nothing about these areas at first hand; the newspapers tell him that black people live there, the illiteracy rate is high, children sell crack from their front steps, banks try to avoid writing mortgages there, many of the adults are unemployed or have jobs that don't pay well—food-service jobs, for instance—but from his living room it looks beautiful. The buildings are old, many of them brick Victorian town houses, and their roofscape is charming, by day or by night, but especially at sunset, when the red sun makes the red brick glow. A woman once told Matthew that it reminded her of Paris. He'd like to get Liz, his ex-wife, up here to take a look at the view sometime. He's sure she still thinks of him as Mr. Suburbanite, still the man he was until she left him fourteen months ago, but this apartment would be quite an eye-opener for her, a *penthouse,* the best apartment in the whole building, with lots of glass, a Parisian view. The building is new. It "wraps traditional elegance in a contemporary package," according to the sales brochure. *That's me,* thinks Matthew. *Traditional elegance in snazzy socks.* Everything in the apartment is black or white or glass or chrome. Matthew sits here at night with jazz playing and he feels like Fred Astaire in an old movie. Liz would be amazed to find him living here. *She'd be amazed.*

The apartment isn't perfect. There's a mysterious odor. The black lacquer cabinets that lined one wall have been moved to the opposite wall, in front of another bunch of black lacquer cabinets, the dining table has been pushed against them, and a hole, about three feet long and a foot high, has been cut in the wall so that workers can search for the source of this offensive odor.

Sitting there, looking out, he can't stop thinking about the toy stores, where his offspring seemed to sit forlornly on the shelves, as unwanted as ugly orphans. He can't understand why parents are so stupid about the toys they buy for their children, why they buy the junk they do, especially those video games, why they don't buy toys that do something more than just shut the kids up for a while, why they don't buy *sensible* toys, like the building sets he dreamed about when he was a boy. He once suggested that Manning & Rafter use guilt in their advertising, but the suggestion was taken as a joke and he laughed along with everyone else.

Matthew lets himself start feeling blue, *encourages* himself to feel blue. He hasn't done this to himself for quite a while, but he's a past master. He cultivated this kind of self-abuse in high school, when he used to sit in the dark, evening after evening, listening to jazz and learning to feel blue. He got good at it, and he thinks the skill served him well in college. He felt intimidated by his roommates because he didn't seem to have any talents that measured up to theirs. He began to brood. His roommates would come home from the library late at night and find him sitting in the dark, in a corner, listening to jazz and brooding. They began to think that he was deeply troubled, possibly dangerous. He enjoyed something like respect for this moodiness. He has brought with him from that period a bittersweet affection for the big, breathy saxophones of Coleman Hawkins, Chu Berry, and Ben Webster.

He's finished his drink. He hops up and dresses in a hurry. He's a little late.

In the hall, when he presses the elevator button nothing happens. He's not surprised. Among the "world-class luxury amenities" in the building are elevators that haven't worked right for months. Every morning two representatives of the elevator manufacturer arrive, disable one of the elevators, and begin leafing through an enormous repair manual. Because they work in the building *every* day, they've come to seem like part of the regular staff. They greet Matthew when he passes them in the morning, and Matthew smiles and says "Good morning" to them. Often they're still working when he comes home at night, still turning the pages of the manual. Matthew smiles, nods, and says hello. He never criticizes them. He doesn't want to cause trouble, to seem to be complaining, doesn't want them to think that he thinks they're doing anything less than the best they can, because he knows that it's important not to offend tradespeople when they're working for you, lest they give up on you, but he can't help asking himself where on earth the elevator company got these clowns. Are they men who actually know how to fix elevators, or were they sent here for on-the-job training? Every evening, when they leave scratching their heads, the super announces, "So ends another episode in the Adventures of the Hardy Boys and Their Amazing Electric Elevator." Matthew sketched an idea for a toy elevator that breaks. It would come with a troubleshooting manual, spare parts, and tools. He suggested that this launch a series: washing machines, cars, television sets, anything that breaks. The proposal was greeted at Manning & Rafter with a silence that Matthew took for repressed amusement. Even while he was presenting the idea he realized that it was too blue-collar to sell today. He was living in the past.

At last the elevator bell begins to bing. The left car is coming up, but from somewhere far below the alarm bell from the right car begins to sound. Then Matthew hears a small voice calling "Hello?" in the apologetic tone that people who, like Matthew, don't want to *cause* any trouble use when they find themselves *in* trouble. There is a long pause. "Hello?" There is another long pause. "Is anyone there? Can someone get me out of here?" More ringing of the alarm bell. The left car arrives. It comes up to Matthew's floor, hesitates for a second, and then heads down again, without ever opening its doors. He considers giving up. He thinks of going back into the apartment, calling Belinda, explaining that it's impossible for him to leave the building because the elevator isn't safe, heating up a goat-cheese pizza that he has tucked away in the back of the freezer for an emergency like this, opening a bottle of wine, putting on one of his Coleman Hawkins tapes, and phoning the girls down the hall to see if one of them wants to come to dinner, any one. It sounds like a great plan for about a minute, but then he remembers that he's too old to interest the girls down the hall. Besides, the elevator comes back up, and the doors open. He takes it as a sign.

In the lobby, one of his neighbors, a man of thirty-five or so, someone he knows only as Robert, is screaming at the girl behind the desk. (This girl is not a full-time professional concierge. She's a student. In fact, she's the prettiest of the girls who live down the hall from Matthew.) Robert's dressed almost entirely in black, including a black fur coat and black-and-white patent-leather saddle shoes. His date is standing behind him, with his arms folded, trying to appear uninterested, but his eyes betray him—they're afire with the thrill of watching Robert make a scene. He too is dressed in black. He has a rhinestone pin on the lapel of his coat.

"This is absolutely inexcusable!" Robert is shouting. "Fifteen minutes! Fifteen minutes we waited for the goddamned elevator. In-ex-*cus*-a-ble! Inexcusable."

Matthew tries not to chuckle. It sounds like a spelling bee. He can't keep himself from spelling, mentally, i-n-e-x-c-u-s-a-b-l-e.

"I don't *ever* want this to happen again, do you hear me!" Robert stamps his foot.

The girl is on the verge of tears. Matthew loves the way her hair falls over her shoulders, fine and straight, light brown, with a little red in it. For the first time he notices that she has freckles.

Freckles, he says to himself. *My God.* And he asks himself, *How old is this girl? Twenty-two? Eighteen? Twelve?* He has no idea. He can't tell. It occurs to him, just then, that he's well on his way to becoming an old fart, or a middle-aged fart, anyway.

The girl has a textbook of some kind open on the desk in front of her. She pushes some hair back behind her ear in that lovely, heartbreaking way girls do and runs her finger under her eye, wiping an incipient tear. For an instant Matthew considers snatching the vase of flowers from the lobby table and smashing it over Robert's head.

Then he remembers himself as not the sort of person who would do something like that.

"You understand that I have nothing to do with this," the girl says. She's trying to be calm, but her lip trembles a little, and there's a catch in her voice.

"All I know is this," says Robert. He heard that little catch in her voice, and he's pressing his advantage. He jabs his finger at her. "I never want this to happen again. Do you understand me?"

She frowns and nods, barely.

"Do you understand me?"

"Yes, I understand you, but—"

"Good! That's all I have to say about it." He turns on his heel, and his friend opens the door for him. They walk out and start off down the street, talking animatedly, flinging their arms.

The girl puts her elbows on the desk and lets her chin drop into her hands.

"He has no right to talk to you like that," Matthew says. He wonders if this is a good time to ask her if she'd like to drop in for dinner sometime.

She looks up and smiles at him, weakly. "I called the elevator company," she says. She blinks, and she brushes her hands across her eyes.

Matthew thinks again about staying home, just hanging out in the lobby, perhaps, chatting with her, helping her study, sending out for whatever girls her age eat. He pulls his stomach in and stands up a little straighter, is immediately struck by the fact that he thinks it's necessary to pull his stomach in and stand up a little straighter, and loses his nerve. He gives her a crooked little grin that he hopes she'll consider conspiratorial. "What more can you do?" he says.

She shrugs. For a moment he thinks she's going to ask him something. Maybe she's going to ask him why he didn't speak up in her defense, or maybe she's about to say, "I noticed you were considering hitting Robert with that vase. Why didn't you?" Whatever she thought of asking she thinks better of it, he guesses, because she just shrugs. She probably knows that he knows that she has three roommates, two more than the building allows, and she doesn't want any trouble from him. It has occurred to her that he must be about her father's age, and he probably has the same touchiness about rules as her father. She smiles at him, the very smile she smiles at her father when she wants his support but doesn't really want to talk to him.

The elevator alarm bell begins ringing again. "Hello?" calls the tentative voice. Matthew shakes his head and leaves, wondering what she'll do after he's gone. Will she call a friend and chat? Will she call the elevator company again? Will she stick her earphones in her ears so she won't hear the little voice calling from the elevator? Will she slip into the mailroom and efface the unhappy incident with cocaine? Maybe she'll say to herself, "He's kinda cute, that Mr. Barber. I'll bet he's pretty interesting when you get to know him."

Outside, Matthew sees Robert and his friend walking ahead of him, still talking and waving their arms. A short, heavy woman in a green coat is walking toward them. She looks like a gumdrop. As she approaches them, Matthew sees that she's saying something, almost shouting. They stop and put their hands on their hips; for a moment, they are a pantomime of homosexual umbrage. The gumdrop woman is *really* shouting now. They shout back, and the exchange escalates in volume until finally Matthew can make out what the woman's saying; in the singsong voice children use to taunt one another, she's saying, "Animals suffered agony to make your coat."

"Your mother suffered agony to make you, sweetheart," Robert's date shouts. Matthew laughs. The whole scene strikes him as funny, these people in various stages of coming unglued. Liz used to think he had no sense of humor, and at the time she may have been right, but he has a sense of humor now—he's sure he does, it's one of the many ways he's changed, as she would be amazed to see if she would take the trouble to look. He's learned this: a sense of humor is the best defense. He spent a whole childhood moping because he didn't have the defensive shield of a sense of humor. He has *cultivated* this sense of humor that he has now, and he believes that he mopes for only a small part of the average day.

He gets a cab at the corner, gives the driver Belinda's address, and then sits in silence. Whenever he's alone in a cab, it seems to him that he should talk to the cabdriver, but he never does unless the

driver speaks to him first. Cabdrivers, he knows, are supposed to
have a wealth of information, a repertoire of amazing stories, but
they rarely speak to him, and he never knows what to say to them.
This behavior isn't really a reluctance to talk to cabdrivers as such—
he has the same problem with anyone he doesn't know well—but
he's not usually riding alone in a car with other people he doesn't
know well, so it's most apparent with cabdrivers.

He rides to Belinda's without saying a word, and by the time they
arrive he's sure that the driver thinks he's the kind of supercilious
shithead who wouldn't deign to talk to a cabdriver, so he overtips.
This makes him feel like a sap.

He rings Belinda's bell.

Belinda is not her real name. Her real name is Linda. Almost a
year ago, not long after she and Matthew began having dinner together a couple of nights a week, she decided that Linda, as a name,
had had its day. She said to him, "Try calling me Belinda for a
while." He tried it that evening, and an amazing transformation
occurred. He had known Linda for years. She was married to a
friend of his, and Liz was a friend of hers. He and Linda were friends
by extension. When they began going out to dinner together, he still
thought of her as his old friend Linda. When he began calling her
Belinda, he found that this woman Belinda seemed a lot sexier than
his old friend Linda, and at the end of the evening they went nuts,
making love on the sofa and rug in Matthew's living room until they
were exhausted. After all those years, they were suddenly lovers—
well, not lovers, to tell the truth—something more like sex fiends. It
didn't last. Perhaps friendship is stronger than sex. They are back
to being friends, friends who have sex once or twice a week, after
dinner or the movies or the theater—still on the couch or the rug, but
with something missing. Matthew keeps hoping that she'll decide
to change her name again.

Snow has begun to fall, a pretty sight in the warm yellow light
that spills from Belinda's windows. It's a charming place, two floors

of a town house on Marlborough Street, a very desirable location, very pretty in the snow, and it should seem inviting, yet Matthew hesitates before ringing the bell. Why? He finds Belinda's daughter unsettling. Her name is Leila. She and Belinda say "Lay-la." He would say "Lie-la," but he supposes people should be able to decide how they want their own names pronounced.

Leila is fifteen. She's a girl of heart-stopping sexiness, with brand-new breasts that erupted from her chest as if overnight not long ago. Matthew can't seem to pin down just when they appeared. He remembers her as a girl without breasts, but he can't recall any slow blossoming of the disconcertingly assertive, boastful, taunting, teasing things that she's equipped with now. Whenever he sees her he has to work to keep himself from staring at them. With the addition of breasts, Leila now looks much more like her mother, and Belinda somehow looks much more like her daughter. This makes Matthew feel like a pervert, a highly specialized pervert: a seducer of the mothers of young girls. He suspects that Leila thinks he's exploiting her mother. She might be right, but she might be completely wrong— her mother might be exploiting him. He has wondered whether Leila regards him as a potential stepfather, and he has often wondered what she says to Belinda about him, constructing imaginary conversations, like this one:

"So, now that you changed your name, what's next? Are you going to marry Matthew? 'Belinda Barber,' won't that be great."

"No, I am *not* going to marry him. Matthew and I just go out together now and then. We're very happy with that arrangement. We have a good time together, and *that* is *that*."

"Do you fuck?"

He supposes that Leila would ask that, exactly that way. He thinks he can see it in her smile, that sarcastic, wise-child, know-it-all smile.

Leila answers the door; she usually does. Her hair is wet. She's wearing something that looks like an athletic undershirt her father might have left behind. "Hey," she says. "How ya doin'?"

"Fine," says Matthew. Leila's breasts fill all the space between them. Matthew gives her the half grin he has developed to avoid showing his yellowing teeth. "How about you?"

"Okay. Come on in. Where're you guys going tonight?"

"I thought we'd go to a new grill not far from my place. It seems interesting."

"Then back to your place to fuck, right?" She doesn't say that, of course. "Sounds nice," is what she actually says, and smiles—sweetly and, Matthew thinks, possibly sarcastically. "Do you want me to make you a drink?" It's a trick that her father—once a friend of Matthew's, now gone—taught her. She can mix just about anything, and pretty well, too, though she tends to use too much vermouth.

"Sure, that would be fine."

From upstairs Belinda calls, "We don't have time. I'm ready."

Matthew shrugs.

"Another time," says Leila. Is there an odd little lilt in her voice, not quite appropriate? Is she flirting with Matthew? Is she mocking him? Belinda comes into the room, dressed like an accountant. Belinda is head of new-product development for Zizyph, a computer software company that had six employees a year ago, has a hundred now, and at this time next year may have six hundred or may be only a fuzzy memory. Belinda is smart and attractive, but she dresses like an accountant. Though they have such similar jobs, she and Matthew never talk about work. Matthew thinks that this is because they are both embarrassed by his working on toys. (Years ago, at a party, Matthew was telling someone what he did, and Liz—they were still married—came up beside him and rumpled his hair. She smiled at the woman he was talking to and said, "Matthew never grew up." She meant it to be a compliment, that Matthew had kept his childlike innocence and charm, Matthew supposed, but he couldn't be sure that she hadn't meant something else. He still wonders just what she did mean.)

Belinda says, "Bye, honey," to Leila. She gives her a kiss and a pat. "Don't you stay out too late."

"You either," says Leila. She gives Matthew and her mother another smile. Matthew gives her another half grin. As she closes the door behind them, she says, "Have fun, you two." Again, her tone may not be quite appropriate.

The Alley View Grill *is* on an alley. This isn't Matthew's first visit; he has already been there for lunch, to look the place over. That's his usual procedure: visit for lunch to get a general idea of the place and decide whether it's worth reviewing. If it is, he makes a mental list of things to look for at dinner. No notes. His reviews are always based on one lunch visit and one dinner visit—unless a place doesn't serve lunch, in which case he reviews one dinner visit—and that's that. He is only reimbursed for a lunch visit and a dinner visit, one meal at lunch, two at dinner, one cocktail at lunch, two at dinner. He's familiar with the argument against reviewing in this way: suppose the chef is having an off night? B. W. Beath and Matthew's editor agree on this: it doesn't matter, or it *shouldn't* matter. Here's BW articulating his stand on this issue, in response to a heated letter from a reader:

Dining is like going to the theater. Cooking for the public is like acting. The show must go on. If the chef's mother dies, we should not taste tears in the béarnaise.

BW endorses this attitude without reservations. Matthew isn't so sure.

The Alley View is crowded when Matthew and Belinda arrive— jammed, in fact. This is often a bad sign, since it may mean a deliberate appeal to mass taste or current fashion, or as BW once wrote, "far worse, it may mean an *unthinking* appeal to mass taste or current fashion." They are greeted by a man who would make a good wrestler. He's bulging out of an expensive double-breasted suit, a silk-and-wool blend. From dark roots, blond hair cascades in ringlets to his shoulders. He's holding a huge pair of chrome-plated pliers with blue rubber grips. He gives Matthew and Belinda a big

smile, displaying dozens of paper-white teeth. Matthew takes an
immediate dislike to him. "Here for an extraction?" the wrestler
asks.

That can't be what he asks. He must be asking whether Matthew
has a reservation. "Barber," Matthew says.

"Uh-uh," says the wrestler, shaking his head. Another big smile.
"Guess again."

Maybe we should leave, thinks Matthew. *This might be leading
to some kind of serious trouble.* He has learned that one never knows
when one is going to run into a psychotic and rub him the wrong
way with an innocent remark. An apparently simple-minded, baffled
smile seems the safest response, certainly safer than words. You
just can't tell about words. The remark you make may turn out to
have been the psychotic's mother's last words or some other hair-
trigger tripper.

Matthew smiles a simpleminded, baffled smile.

"Dentist!" the wrestler says, raising the pliers in front of Matthew's
face.

"Oh, is *that* what you said? 'Extraction.' I *thought* that was what
you said, but it didn't seem likely, so I thought you must have asked
if I had a *reservation.* Extraction. Sure. *No,* I mean. No thanks. I
do have a *reservation,* though. Barber. The name is Barber." He
feels like an idiot.

"Barber. *Mister* Barber. We'll have a table for you in just a few
minutes. Would you like to have a drink while you wait?"

They would, so they go to the bar. The crowd is lively, almost
entirely composed of people younger than they. Matthew tries out,
mentally, a string of adjectives that BW could use to describe them
in the review. He comes up with *attractive, well dressed, talkative,
ebullient, vapid.* The last isn't a fair assessment. These people are
upsetting him because they're young, attractive, well dressed, talkative, ebullient. Most of them seem to know one another; Matthew
feels that he's an outsider, that he and Belinda have been given the
once-over, fairly discreetly he has to admit, identified as outsiders,
dismissed as uninteresting, and are being tolerated, though they aren't

really welcome, as if they were trying to elbow their way in, taking up space that would be better occupied by someone more attractive, better-dressed, more talkative and ebullient.

Matthew elbows his way to the bar. Over the bar a neon sign spells "Champagne" in green script, a prompt for neophyte drinkers. *Work on that idea,* Matthew tells himself. *BW can use that.* He orders a couple of Bombay martinis. The bartender takes the glasses and the Bombay from a freezer under the bar and pours the gin directly into the glasses. At no time does Matthew see vermouth. He doesn't mind this, really—he likes a frozen Bombay now and then—but this glass of gelid gin is not a martini; it's a joke at the expense of the martini, a sarcastic remark about the martini. Matthew takes it personally.

When he was young, Matthew developed an affection for the martini well before he ever drank one, an affection that came in part from watching William Powell and Myrna Loy down them in the Thin Man movies and in part from his careful study of *Esquire,* the text from which he hoped to learn sophistication. The martini seemed to be an essential item among the equipment of a sophisticated adult. When Matthew began drinking them, at Harvard, he was still only an *aspirant* to adulthood, and by the time he had actually *attained* adulthood the martini had become something of an anachronism. For quite a while the young didn't drink them, didn't even aspire to drink them, as, perhaps, they no longer aspired to sophistication or adulthood. Matthew began to wonder whether, if the martini was an anachronism, sophistication was also an anachronism, adulthood wasn't, too, and Matthew as well. Now, however, according to what Matthew reads in newspapers and magazines, the martini is making a comeback, and the testimony of his own eyes tells him that it's true, but his ears tell him that the martini revival is something of a joke. People always seem to be ordering gag martinis, with a jalapeño pepper or a *cornichon* instead of an olive or a twist of lemon, and when he orders a martini with "an olive" he usually gets three, but at least he no longer feels as conspicuous ordering one. He wouldn't feel conspicuous at all if he didn't think that his graying hair marks him as a member of an earlier generation of martini drinkers, a humorless bunch.

Though the room is crowded with people who are all gesticulating animatedly, he doesn't spill a drop in carrying the drinks to the outskirts of the crowd, where Belinda's standing in front of an arrangement of enormous obscene flowers, bizarre-looking things with penile elements and great leaves shaped like escutcheons of pubic hair.

"Are these real plants?" Matthew asks.

He has been amazed by the biological emulation he sees in the creatures that star in fantastic movies, so he wouldn't be surprised if that kind of high-tech weirdness had reached the fake-plant business. He touches a leaf with his little finger, gingerly. He can't decide whether the thing feels real or not. It has a waxy quality that doesn't seem botanical, but it moves like part of a real plant, shudders when he brushes it, and the penile member bobs gently over his forehead.

"Do you know what these are called? Do you think they're a product of genetic mutation? Maybe they're bred exclusively for the restaurant trade. Maybe they're given drugs to make them grow outlandishly. What do you think?" He's making witty chatter.

Belinda isn't listening. "Hmmm?" she says. "Oh. Sorry, Matthew. I wasn't listening." She leans closer to him and lowers her voice. "I was watching two guys behind you. Take a look. Go ahead—they're not looking this way."

He turns and looks.

"Are they *too* handsome or what?" Belinda asks.

Matthew sees two young men at a table of the kind that would have been used in a diner when he was a boy—chrome legs, a plastic top—but the plastic has a zebra-stripe pattern. They look like male models, the rugged, well-muscled type of male model. Matthew turns back toward Belinda, feeling that old feeling of adequacy coming on. Formerly, he called this feeling mediocrity, but he decided he was being too hard on himself. Adequacy is bad enough.

He suffers from the least noticed but most widespread of modern emotional afflictions of men his age—an adequacy complex. Among its symptoms is the lack of prominent symptoms. Consider Matthew as a fairly typical case: not unattractive, not unintelligent, not unsuccessful, not unhealthy, not even, at a random moment—this one, for example—terribly unhappy. He thinks of himself as adequate, but only adequate, stuck at the adequacy level, and sometimes the bitter taste of his adequacy rises in his throat like heartburn. He's the sort of person a witness to a crime would have a hard time describing. "Well, he was about average height, average weight, kind of normal-looking, no distinguishing marks, wearing sort of run-of-the-mill clothes. Come to think of it, though, he had kind of unusual socks, but that's all I remember."

When he wants to punish himself, he points out to himself that not even in his reviews does he reach or even reach *for* the top-notch. BW isn't a critic, after all, just a reviewer, a reviewer of *restaurants*. Restaurants. His reviews appear in *Boston Biweekly*, "Home of the Free-Ranging Critics," a large-format publication on slick paper that reviews everything from books to restaurants, with most of the space going to music and movies, and prides itself on giving critics "their head," as long as they have "a distinctive voice" and their work is "interesting to read." Matthew's editor has said, in a memo to Matthew and his colleagues, "I don't care what you say about what you review, so long as people will want to read it." Matthew once complained to Belinda that the magazine didn't have a serious attitude toward food. He stopped and asked, "What am I saying? A serious attitude toward food! Can a thinking, feeling person *have* a serious attitude toward food? Other than, say, working for famine relief? A serious attitude toward food? They don't even *care* about the food. They don't want brilliant descriptions of the flavors and textures, the presentation, that sort of thing. What I'm supposed to do is 'capture the experience' of being in the restaurants I review. The food is only supposed to be part of it—and not even the most important part. God! How do I live with myself, Belinda? How do I live with BW?"

Belinda said, "I don't know," in an attempt to turn the whole thing

into a joke, but the truth was that she didn't think it was a question
worth making that much fuss over, though she understood the source
of Matthew's uneasiness.

There is more to Matthew's uneasiness about the magazine than
that, though, something else that bothers him. No one connected
with *Boston Biweekly* has ever uttered a word about it, but all the
writers know that there is supposed to be an attitude behind their reviews, an attitude of superiority. The ideal reaction of a reader of
one of the *Boston Biweekly* reviews would be, "My God, what a
lousy book [play, movie, concert, restaurant]! But what a percep-
tive, witty, scintillating, provocative review!" This attitude is, of
course, a defense against the mediocrity complex—adequacy complex—that is endemic at the magazine. Matthew is ashamed of the
fact that he has made an effort to teach himself to take this attitude.
He hasn't been entirely successful, but he's working on it. For example, take the two handsome guys Belinda is still staring at over
Matthew's shoulder. Matthew's supposed to feel superior to them,
though he finds it easy to imagine that one is a genius sculptor, the
other runs an international famine-relief organization, and they've
met here in the bar at the Alley View Grill to discuss a benefit to
relieve famine somewhere in Africa or India or Asia, while *Matthew*
is here to collect information for a review that will damn the place
and its patrons with backhanded praise and acerbic wit, demonstrat-
ing thereby that B. W. Beath, *Boston Biweekly,* and all its free-ranging critics are superior not only to the ground-veal-and-*pancetta*
hamburger, but to the people who come here to eat it, including, of
course, the two guys behind Matthew, who are not only a genius and
a saint, but gorgeous.

"Your table is ready, sir," says the wrestler.

"Good. Fine. Good," says Matthew. As they walk off he mutters
to Belinda, "Is it just my imagination, or has *sir* become a sarcastic
remark?"

On the way to the table, Matthew begins to get to get an idea for
an angle on the place, an approach for BW to take in the review.

Here it is: Despite all the effort put into making the place up-to-the-minute, there's a kind of reactionism visible in the glorification of an old-movie sense of style and in the adoration of the low-tech gadgets of the past. In the bar there is an old neon-encircled clock, and conspicuously atop the little lighted table where the reservation book is kept sits an old telephone, with no dial, just like the phone Matthew's mother had at home when he was a boy. The wonderful thing about that phone was that whenever Matthew lifted it an operator spoke from it and said, "Number, please," and she was always there, at any time of the day or night. It was like having someone else in the house. Sometimes, when Matthew's mother was at work downstairs, in the secondhand shop she called Lydia's Antiques, he would lift the receiver just to hear the operator's voice.

"Look at that," Matthew says, "that old phone. We had one like that when I was a kid."

"A classic," says Belinda. "That odd matte finish they had. It always seemed worn-looking, as if it had once been shiny, but the polish had worn off. It was almost porous—probably absorbed the sweat from people's hands. Those phones give me the creeps, really. They always remind me of *Dial M for Murder*."

Matthew doesn't point out that this phone has no dial. Since shortly after Liz left he has been trying to keep himself from correcting people.

"Yeah," he says. "Or *Sorry, Wrong Number*. There *is* something sinister about those phones, isn't there? Something very *film noir*. Oh, that's good. That's good. I can use that. *Film noir*. They'll love it. Remind me."

"Do you want me to write it down?"

"No, no, no. No notes. No notes. I'll probably remember it anyway."

Belinda looks at Matthew for a moment, deciding whether to ask something, and then she does. "What were you like as a boy, Matthew? When you had a phone like that? What were you like?"

"Oh, I don't know. Normal. I don't think much about that time. I didn't have much fun as a kid. My mother was a widow. We didn't have much money. It wasn't a great childhood."

He looks at the menu.

He could have said this:

"When I was eleven or twelve, a rumor was spread about me, in school, that I never took a bath or a shower, never bathed. But *rumor* isn't really the right word. Not everyone believes a rumor. Everyone believed this. 'Of course Matthew doesn't wash—we always knew it,' that was the way they reacted. Boys claimed to have seen how filthy my underwear was when we undressed in the locker room. One of them had great success with a little routine about having to wrestle me in gym class and being disgusted by my stink. It was all false, of course. I was a fastidious boy. I'm a fastidious man.

"One day I came out of the shower in the locker room—that humiliating locker room, humiliating shower. I came out of the shower and hurried to my locker to pull on my underwear, and I found that they—some of the other boys—had smeared feces—

"'Feces'? What am I saying? Not 'feces.' *Shit.*

"They smeared shit on my underwear, in the bottom of my Jockey shorts, in the armpits of my undershirt. To this day, I'm uncomfortable if I'm far from fresh underwear. I need to know that I can change if I have to, if I want to. I keep clean underwear at the office, in the bottom drawer of my desk, at the back, in a Jiffy bag. You want to know an interesting result of all this? I could never spend the night with a woman at her place, just spontaneously. It would be too disgusting to have to pull on my day-old underwear in the morning. It would be too shameful to have her see it. You see? The persecution of a fat boy never ends. What you do to him while he's young stays with him. They made me into a man who hides underwear in his desk. But here's the question I ask myself. Weren't the girls who giggled at me disgusted by those boys? *Why* weren't they disgusted by them? They could handle shit, they could take a turd from the toilet, they could spread it on someone's underwear, and still *they* weren't regarded as disgusting, the girls didn't think they were disgusting. It was me they found disgusting, the victim. Why? Why should that be?"

He doesn't say that, though, and it's probably better that he doesn't. It wouldn't make him look good.

Belinda's studying her menu. Matthew's giving the appearance of studying his, but actually he's studying the room. Since every dish on the menu is, according to *Boston Biweekly* dogma, supposed to be an equally good representative of the quality of the food, what he orders is never terribly important to the review. It's more important that he be aware of the context. Right now he would like his immediate context to include a waiter. He wants to order another martini. There are waiters in sight, but none is looking in Matthew's direction, and none seems to regard Matthew and Belinda as his responsibility. Here is BW on waiters who do not deign to wait, from his review of Miranda's Verandah:

> They belong to the school of waiters and waitresses who take as their motto, "Circumstances may have forced me to take a job as a waiter, but I'll be damned if I'm going to lower myself to the point of actually serving anybody." Waiters of this school chat among themselves most of the time, and then, when they are good and ready, amble over to your table and drop by to see what you might want, manifesting in their manner the suggestion that they *might* exert their influence to have some lackey bring it, *if* you are found acceptable. Often they arrive at our table still chuckling over the witticisms of their fellows, and sometimes they share these bons mots with favored patrons, with whom they join in happy rounds of table hopping. To be accepted as worthy by a waiter of this ilk is to be considered one of the few patrons as bright and chic as the waitpeople and busfolk. Where this attitude prevails, it is *much* stronger on weekends, when outré suburbanites swarm.

Those suburbanites *do* swarm on weekends, congregating in mur-

murous throngs at restaurants BW has reviewed, regardless of whether he praises the places or damns them. They will go to a place that BW has liked because they expect to enjoy it but will go just as eagerly to a place BW has ridiculed, because they expect to enjoy feeling superior to it. They seize the opportunity to assume BW's attitude toward it, to wear his sophistication, thus to savor, if only for the space of a meal, a life lived with the savoir-vivre of *Boston Biweekly* and B. W. Beath. The casual observer, seeing that these vandals wear the clothes that *Boston Biweekly*'s fashion critic has endorsed and take the attitude toward the restaurant that BW has endorsed, might mistake them for sophisticated adults, but BW wouldn't be fooled. He often takes a swipe at suburbanites in his reviews. It increases his readership. They all think he's writing about their neighbors.

Seated at the table to Matthew's left is a trio of young women. One is very young, a girl, still in her teens, delicate and lovely, dressed in a boxy black dress. She has pale, pale blond hair, almost white, long, smooth, and even, with a black velvet bow in it. On a banquette beside her is a small woman, Chinese, her black hair short on one side, shoulder length on the other. She's wearing an oversize silk jacket, black, and her brow is furrowed with apparent worry. The third woman is sitting across from the other two, at the seat corresponding to Matthew's. She is a redhead, large-boned, wiry, striking. She is tearing bits from the edges of the paper napkin under her drink. The tiny table keeps them close enough so that they could hold hands or touch knees if they wished.

This is what Matthew thinks about them:

The redhead seems annoyed. She must be jealous. She wants the delicate girl for herself, but the Chinese girl is winning her away. The redhead is strong, independent. At one time, the delicate girl was attracted to the redhead's strength. She needed someone to lean on. But time passed, and the delicate girl grew tired of being dependent on the redhead, being under her thumb. She wanted to be the strong one for a while; she wanted someone who needed her. Along came the Chinese girl. The Chinese girl wanted the delicate girl, and she saw that the delicate girl wanted to feel that someone needed her, so she used a pretense of frailty to win the delicate girl from the redhead. The redhead had no defense. Maybe, in her own way, the redhead needed the delicate girl as much as the delicate girl needed her, but the delicate girl was convinced that the redhead was strong and independent and didn't need her at all. That's probably the way it was with Liz. I would have been playing the redhead, Liz the delicate girl, and someone I don't know would have been the Chinese girl. It must have been something like that. There must have been someone else, despite what Liz says.

If B. W. Beath agreed with Matthew, he would find some brisk way to sum it up, something like this: "We all need someone to lean on, but we all *want* someone who needs to lean on *us*." Something like that.

With the neighbors all figured out, Matthew turns his attention to the menu. The food, he knows from his lunch visit, is interesting and good.

"The hamburger is good," he says. "The veal-and-*pancetta* hamburger. I had it for lunch—delicious." Belinda doesn't seem to hear him. "Belinda?"

"Hm? Oh, I'm sorry. I was—ah—daydreaming. The truth is, I just can't get my mind off those guys. They're so gorgeous." She pauses. "Matthew?"

"Mm?"

"Do I look dowdy?"

"Dowdy? No. Not at all. You look wonderful."

She does. The drink has relaxed her. The light is good for her. She looks her age, but she looks good, and, to tell the truth, every now and then Matthew sees a little Leila in her and it makes Belinda seem to him youthful and naïve. This isn't something that he thinks it wise to say to Belinda, so he says, "I was saying that the hamburger is good."

"Oh, but I don't want a hamburger. I want something a little more—grown up," says Belinda.

"I'm just *so* depressed," says the Chinese girl. She lets her head fall onto the shoulder of the delicate girl, and the delicate girl strokes her hair. "Just *everything* is upsetting me now, you know? It's like I can't even drag myself out of bed, I'm so frightened. Everything just *frightens* me. Like today I was afraid of the ozone layer? The ozone layer, you know? It's like a torn curtain. It used to protect us, but now it's being like dissolved by gases and exposing us to all these harmful things, rays from the sun and like that? I just think we're all going to get these like awful cancers. Everyone will be so hideous. It makes me feel so awful, just so awful. I know I probably sound ridiculous, but it just makes me aware of how like *vulnerable* we are."

"I'm going to the bathroom," says the redhead.

A waiter arrives. More accurately, a waiter who happens to be passing stops at the table to see how Matthew and Belinda are doing.

"Hi," the waiter says. He smiles. "How you doin' tonight?" He could be an old pal who spotted Matthew on his way to the men's room and stopped to chat, but Matthew is virtually certain that he's a waiter because he's dressed as a waiter and is holding an order pad.

"Fine," says Matthew.

"We have some specials tonight," the waiter says. "As an appetizer, we have a salad of grilled wild duck and papaya on a bed of braised endive, and that's served with a mustard vinegarette." Matthew winces at this mangling of *vinaigrette*. "For an entrée, we have a grilled pork tenderloin, and that's served with an onion relish and a kind of a garlicky mayonnaise—"

"*Aïoli?*" Matthew asks.

"Excuse me?"

"Is it *aïoli*? The garlickly mayonnaise?"

"I'm not certain. I'll have to ask. That's also served with a melahng of sautéed vegetables."

Another wince.

"Are you all set for cocktails?"

"Do you want another drink, Belinda?" Matthew asks.

"Not as strong as a martini," she says. "Do you have sherry?" she asks the waiter.

"Just Amantadillo," he says. Uh-mon-tuh-dill-oh.

"Ah-mahn-tee-ah-doh," Matthew says, slowly, sighing.

"No," the waiter says with a smile. "Sorry. Just Amantadillo."

"I'll have that," says Belinda. Only her eyes laugh.

"I'll have another martini," Matthew says. "Bombay, straight up, with an olive. Just one olive."

"Very good, sir," says the waiter.

There it is again, Matthew thinks, that use of *sir* as a code word for *shithead*. He believes he can hear in the waiter's voice, see in his eyes, that he considers Matthew an old poop with yellowing teeth—so *derrière garde* that he isn't familiar with Amantadillo sherry and can order a martini without irony—whose tie and socks betray a hopeless struggle against age, a pitiful yearning to be young.

"I'll be right back," says Belinda. She leaves for the ladies' room. Matthew tries a mental draft:

> The waiters mispronounce the names of the foods they serve, and the menu misspells them. Perhaps this is all that contemporary sophistication amounts to—the conviction that one knows more than one does.

No, that's not quite it.

> Perhaps this is all that contemporary sophistication amounts to—ignorance denied.

That isn't it, either.

> Quite possibly the Alley View represents the height of contemporary sophistication, which is to say the flaunting of ignorance as if it were a virtue. The staff here doesn't really know anything about food or service or dining or the luxe life to which they pretend; all they've done is replace their parents' paltry small-town ignorance with a paltry urban ignorance.

It needs work, Matthew recognizes that, but now he has a theme, and that's the key.

When Belinda arrives in the ladies' room, the redhead is standing at the sink, wiping her face with a wet paper towel, snarling at her

reflection in the mirror and saying "Bitch!" and "Cunt!" Belinda
scoots into a stall, locks the door, and pees as quietly as she can.

The redhead begins whining, imitating the Chinese girl. "I'm *so*
worried about the *ozone* layer," she says, and then in a louder voice
she calls out, "Can you believe that dyke?" Belinda knows that she's
talking to her, but she says nothing, pretending that she thinks the
redhead is just asking a rhetorical question. The redhead knocks on
the door of Belinda's stall and says, "Hey! Did you hear me? You
must have heard what she was saying. The ozone layer? All that
shit?"

Belinda says, "Well, I—did hear something about that—"

"Yeah, you'd have to. You're sitting right next to her. I'm surprised she hasn't tried to grab your knee." She waits a moment and
says, "She hasn't, has she?"

Belinda laughs. It's a nervous, forced laugh.

"Just kidding," the redhead says. "You're probably not her type.
I say 'probably' because I think she's omnivorous."

Belinda laughs again, because she thinks it's expected of her. She
hopes the redhead will leave, but the woman wants to talk. She says,
"Do you believe that, that crap about the ozone?"

Belinda sighs. "I don't know," she says. She decides that she
might as well come out of the stall, figuring that if she washes up
and makes some agreeable noises, she may be able to get out quickly.
She's trembling a little. She tells herself, as she has before, that she
shouldn't be so uncomfortable with lesbians, but she's always afraid
that they will say or do something that will embarrass her, specifically that they might make jokes about her that she doesn't understand, making her feel ignorant and horrible. Every now and then,
she thinks that perhaps she should go to bed with a woman just so
that she'll know something about it, so that she'll be protected from
feeling ignorant.

She flushes the toilet and pulls herself together, takes a deep breath,
and comes out of the stall. The redhead is gone. Belinda washes her
hands and looks herself over in the mirror, though she tells herself
that this is probably a mistake. For the last year or so, whenever she
looks in a mirror she feels almost sexless. She has been finding it

difficult to imagine that she's still attractive, or even interesting-looking, to men—or to women, for that matter. This isn't exactly a problem of aging; in fact, it strikes her as funny that she sees her young self more and more in the mirror, that the face she had when she was a girl is there, with some not-so-welcome new details—wrinkles, lines, spots—but still there, the same girlish face, and it amuses her sometimes to notice how incomplete Leila's face is, a pretty face, but characterless, like an apartment with white walls and no pictures, something like Matthew's apartment.

She decides to do something with her hair. She brushes it all over to one side. The effect strikes her as pretty odd, but she knows that odd is a look, and it seems somehow livelier now than it did before. She likes it. It makes her smile. It's kind of crazy.

When she emerges from the ladies' room, the redhead is talking on the pay phone in the hallway: "I'm just *very* worried about her, Mrs. Chu. Very, very worried. I've never seen her so crazy. Do you understand what I'm saying? She's just—she's *really* irrational. She's going on and on about how she's worried about the ozone layer? In the sky—in the atmosphere? The ozone layer? It's some kind of gases—"

She nearly blocks the narrow hallway. Belinda couldn't get by without rubbing against her, so she says, "Uhm, excuse me."

The redhead turns around. Her face is blank for a moment, but then she winks at Belinda and points to her hair and raises her eyebrows and grins, still talking into the phone, saying, "She's *irrational*, Mrs. Chu. I really think you should come down here. She's been like this before, but never this bad. It scares me, I mean it really scares me. I just don't know what she might do. I can't take responsibility for her. I *really* wish you would come down here and take her away. Take her home. She needs help, Mrs. Chu. She really does."

Belinda returns to the table, the waiter arrives with the drinks, and, in a moment, the redhead returns to her table. All this traffic in a small space occasions some confusion, jostling, stepping aside, shuffling of chairs, asking to be excused. The waiter stands to one side, holding his tray, aloof from the fray, frowning through a thin smile. Belinda seems upset. She's trying to smile, but her forehead's furrowed, and her smile slips, now and then, down to a frown.

"Is anything wrong?" Matthew asks.

"Oh, no, no," she says. She looks up at him and smiles, but she rolls her eyes in the direction of the three women in black. Matthew can't tell what that roll of the eyes means. He notices that Belinda has done something to her hair. Most of it is on one side, with just a few wisps dangling on the other. He thinks she looks wonderfully sexy, in an out-of-date way, like the bad girl in an old movie. He gives her a roguish look—a smirk, a raised eyebrow, a wink—like the gigolo in the same movie. He raises his glass, she hers. They clink. They drink. For a while they chat, but then the salad arrives, the meal has begun, and Matthew turns his attention exclusively to the food.

He prefers not to talk while eating. When he and Liz ate at home, he liked to watch television during dinner because television permitted him to be alone with his food and his thoughts. Unlike living human dinner companions, television doesn't insist that you actually pay attention to it, and Matthew feels that the surroundings in which one eats are best when, like television, they permit one to ignore them. Interesting surroundings and an engaging companion are fine, even welcome, while he's having a cocktail, but when the food arrives, that's all he cares to pay attention to. In this, he and B. W. Beath are in complete agreement; here's BW on the subject:

> When the food arrives, shut up, everyone, please. Dim the lights. Drift off, companions. Vanish, waiters. Return when we have finished, or when we need you, not before. Don't intrude. Please, please, don't come back to ask, "Is everything okay?"

Matthew has never managed to complain about that is-everything-okay intrusion or to respond to it with a snappy retort because the waiters always ask the question when his mouth is full, perhaps deliberately, to ensure that he can't complain or deliver a snappy retort, only smile or nod or say "Mmmmm," but he has thought of

several snappy retorts after the fact and, disguised as BW, claimed
to have made one:

> We paused with our fork, our full fork, before our mouth. We
> turned upon our waitperson a hangdog look. "Is everything
> okay?" we repeated. We set our fork down. "Well, no. My
> wife is leaving me because, after fourteen years of marriage,
> she claims to have discovered that she has never loved me.
> What do you think of that? She said, 'I just don't love you. I
> feel sorry for you. I know you're going through a rough time.'
> *That* was certainly an understatement. My mother had just died.
> That was the time my wife chose to leave me. How do you
> like that? 'I know you're going through a rough time,' she
> said, 'but I've decided that I don't love you, I've never loved
> you, and there is little likelihood that I will ever come to love
> you. I don't want to live the rest of my life with someone I
> don't love, so I'm catching the next flight to anywhere. I hope
> you understand. Have a nice day.'" Here we shrugged and
> said, "But, heck, that's my problem. How's everything with
> you?"

Matthew samples Belinda's pork, the sauce, the *aïoli* (it is *aïoli*),
the vegetables, the rice. While they're having coffee, he consoli-
dates his mental notes as he sometimes does, by reciting to Belinda
important judgments he hopes to include in BW's review. This
postprandial draft is a risky business. Since he looks to Belinda's
response not so much as a test of his observations but as an affirma-
tion of them, he only tries it when he's feeling confident. Belinda
finds it a trial. Matthew tries to speak softly, but he has to speak
loudly enough for Belinda to hear him. He imagines that diners
nearby sometimes think he's mad, and he is not displeased to think
that thus he distinguishes himself from the crowd. He's saying, "Both
the diners and the flowers tend toward the exotic and showy—and
there's a kind of lush, tropical sensuality to the place—fecundity—a
warm fecundity—dew-damp pistils and stamens—bizarre varieties
of vegetable sexuality—and animal, too."
The redhead gives Belinda a look, a raised eyebrow, a twisted

smile. She might be asking Belinda whether Matthew is crazy. The delicate blonde is spoon-feeding to the Chinese girl a dessert listed on the menu as "chocolate decadence." The Chinese girl is pretending to resist this cosseting. She keeps her lips closed when each spoonful arrives, like a child fighting puréed lima beans, but at the first touch of the tip of the spoon she parts them ever so slightly, yielding, and the spoonful of chocolate slips into the tiny oval orifice she creates. She parts her lips farther as the delicate girl slips the spoon into her mouth, just the slight bit needed to accommodate the bowl, and then closes them until only the handle protrudes from her pursed lips. Then, slowly, the delicate girl begins withdrawing the spoon, and with it, slipping out between her lips, comes the Chinese girl's tongue, streaked with chocolate, pursuing the bowl of the spoon to lick the last of its residual decadence.

"Want some?" the delicate girl asks the redhead.

"Fuck you," says the redhead, very softly, very sweetly. She gets up and goes off in the direction of the ladies' room again. Discreetly, Belinda and Matthew watch her go, noticing, individually, what an alluring body she has. Belinda leans across the table and says to Matthew, "I've *got* to start going to aerobics every morning."

Matthew realizes that he hasn't checked the men's room yet. On the way he takes careful note, without seeming to do so, of the other diners—their apparent satisfaction or dissatisfaction, the contents of their plates, their leavings. The men's room has peacock-feather wallpaper.

When Matthew comes out of the men's room, the redhead is standing at the phone, with her back to him, saying this: "You'd better come right away—it's—oh—it's terrible. She's dead—she's *dead*. She *killed* herself, Mrs. Chu. Mrs. Chu? Hello? Is this *Mr*. Chu?"

Beyond the redhead Matthew can see that everyone in the dining room is behaving as if nothing remarkable has occurred. Is he witnessing a grisly demonstration of contemporary indifference? A woman has killed herself and people go on munching their *raddichio*? As he makes his way across the leopard-spot carpet back to the table, he can see that in fact nothing has happened, and then he understands what's going on, and he decides that it would be best to get out of the restaurant before the Chus arrive. He finds the waiter chatting with some other waiters, giving a lively account of something. "Just unbelievable," he's saying, "just unbelievable!" *What?* Matthew wonders. *A concert, a movie, a love affair?* He catches the waiter's eye, and the waiter frowns.

"Excuse me," Matthew says. "Would you bring us our check? We're in kind of a hurry."

"Certainly, sir. I'll be right over, just as soon as I've finished with these people."

In a few minutes the waiter does come by with the check, sets it in the no-person's zone exactly midway between Belinda and Matthew, and says, "I'll take that whenever you're ready."

Matthew has learned that, in the lingo of waiters, "whenever you're ready" means "whenever *I'm* ready," so he says at once, "I'm ready," and hands over his American Express card.

Matthew and Belinda leave the restaurant, walk to the end of the alley, and turn toward Matthew's apartment, which is only two blocks away. Matthew says, "The most incredible thing happened when I was coming out of the men's room. That woman who was sitting at the next table, the redhead, was on the phone—"

"Oh, I know," says Belinda. "She was on the phone when I came out of the ladies' room, and I think she must have been talking to the Chinese girl's parents. She was saying 'Mrs. Chu'—"

Before they are halfway up the block, they are startled by the sound of screeching tires. They turn to see a black Toyota come to a halt at an angle to the alley. A young Chinese man leaps out and rushes into the restaurant.

"Her brother," says Matthew.

An older man gets out, then a young woman, and then an older woman, helped from the car by the young woman.

"Her parents. And a sister, I guess," says Belinda.

"The redhead told them that the girl killed herself," says Matthew, watching the wretched trio. "There, in the restaurant."

"Oh, my God."

"Let's get out of here."

"She was jealous," says Belinda after a moment.

"Oh, I'm sure of it," says Matthew. "She wanted that little blonde."

"She *was* a beauty," says Belinda.

When they arrive at Matthew's, Belinda goes into the living room, and Matthew goes into the kitchen to fix himself a drink. Belinda rarely wants one after dinner.

"Matthew, what on earth happened here?" she asks.

"Oh, I forgot. I should have warned you."

He pokes his head around the corner. Belinda is looking into the hole.

"There's a smell, an odor coming from somewhere," he explains. "In fact, I can smell it in here and in the den, too. It's not quite the same in the den, not quite the same smell. They've been looking for it for a couple of days. The manager brought in a vice-president from the construction company and some sort of jack-of-all-trades. They came in here, moved the furniture around, and pulled the carpet back, and then they—we—all got down on our hands and knees and started sniffing. Nothing. Couldn't smell a thing. So they asked me if they could open a section of the wall to see if it would come wafting out. I said that was all right, and they made a little hole." With his hands he indicates a hole the size of a magazine. "They poked around and peered in with flashlights, and sniffed, but they couldn't get anything. So they made the hole a little larger. Then they had a little conference, and they made the hole a little *larger*. Then they conferred some more, and sniffed some more, and enlarged the hole some more, and they kept on conferring and sniffing and enlarging until three o'clock, when they all packed up and went home."

"They don't know what it is?"

"Not yet. I'm supposed to smell it under various conditions to see—well, to see what I see. Or what I smell."

"So these are your notes?" She's reading penciled notes on the wall.

12/6—OPENED WALL, NO APPARANT ODOR,
PULLED CARPET BACK, NO ODOR

12/7—6:00 PM, NO ODOR
12/8—7:15, SHARP ODOR, ALMOST HURTS MY NOSE,
AS IF SOMEONE WERE BURNING ORANGES

"Yeah. Well, not the first one. The guy from the construction company—my fellow vice-president—wrote that. You see he misspelled *apparent*. I figured that if he wrote right on the wall like that he must intend to have it painted, so now I just write on the wall, too."

He returns to the kitchen, pours himself some cognac, pours Belinda a lemon-flavored water, though he knows she won't drink it, takes a condom from a carton in the drawer where he keeps coupons, rubber bands, pencils, and other odds and ends, puts the drinks and the condom on a black plastic tray, and carries the tray to the living room. Belinda has picked out a compact disc and put it on the player. She's stretched out on the sofa.

"What did you think?" she asks.

"I liked it. I even felt comfortable there, odd as that sounds. Well, almost comfortable."

"We were the oldest people there, I think."

"No, we weren't, not at all. You're letting your feelings blind you. I checked everyone out, and there were several people older than we are. They were just wearing young disguises."

"Really? Where do they get those disguises? I'd like one for myself."

Matthew puts his hand on her breast, caresses it, lightly, affectionately. Belinda stretches luxuriously. "Let me have a sip of that," she says.

"It gives you a headache," Matthew cautions.

"A whole glass does, but a sip won't bother me."

He tips her head up and brings the snifter to her lips, wets them with cognac. She licks her lips, savors the flavor. Matthew sets the snifter down. Belinda gets up and slips her shoes off and puts them under one of the chrome tables, takes her blouse off, folds it, and hangs it over the back of a chrome chair. Matthew hangs his jacket on the back of another chrome chair, removes his tie and drapes it over the jacket, removes his shirt, folds it, and sets it on the seat of the chair. Belinda removes her bra and hangs it over the arm of her chair, takes her skirt off, folds it, and drapes it over the seat of the chair, pulls her panty hose off and tosses them under the chrome table, onto her shoes.

"Floor or couch?" she asks.

"Floor, unless you prefer the couch."

"No, the floor is fine."

"You're sure?"

"I'm sure." She settles onto the floor. "Come on."

Matthew pulls his briefs off and drops them onto his shoes. He tears the condom wrapper open, removes the condom, and rolls it down over his penis.

A week after Liz left, Matthew decided that he might as well go out and try his luck at finding solace between the legs of other women; at once the question arose, at first only hypothetically, whether he ought to use condoms. He was, at that time, afraid of getting herpes, but it seemed awfully timid to be afraid of herpes, and he didn't want to admit to the fear. Then along came AIDS, and in a way AIDS has really been a godsend to Matthew. Now that so many people are afraid of death by sex, he can use a condom without feeling like a coward, and he can avoid herpes. He has never brought this matter up with Belinda. The first time they made love, he didn't use a condom. He had a lot on his mind, and he tried to concentrate exclusively on the pleasure of the moment, but he couldn't help himself—he worried a bit; even his sexual fantasies include periods of concern about disease. For her part, Belinda had a fleeting fear of pregnancy, but they were both so surprised and happy to find themselves making love to each other that they didn't want to spoil it. The second time, Matthew used a condom. He didn't say anything about it; he just put it on. He's sure they both feel much more secure this way, and he suspects—in his case he's certain—that there's an element of excitement introduced by the condom, because it implies that Belinda isn't Matthew's only lover, thereby making him seem a little more interesting, a man who has sexual adventures. It makes him feel virile, too, since he might, of course, be using the condom to protect Belinda from an unwanted pregnancy, though he suspects, and has some reason to believe, that there's little danger of that. He also supposes that the condom is an emblem of his affection for Belinda, his concern for her well-being, since her assumption must be, if she has inferred properly from the implication in his wearing the thing, that it is she who must be protected from the possible consequences of his adventures. He also feels that if Liz should come back, if she could be persuaded to come back, he could offer these condoms as evidence of his essential loyalty, a distance that he kept between himself and Belinda. All these thoughts and feelings reside in a condom, so many ideas in such a small thing.

When they're finished, they lie for a while on their backs, looking at the night sky through the skylights. They hold hands, but otherwise their bodies do not touch. After a while Belinda asks, "What time is it?"

Matthew sits up and looks at the clock on one of the chrome tables. "Nearly midnight," he says.

"I have to go. I'm taking Leila skiing tomorrow."

He calls a cab. "I'll call you during the week," he says at the door. He waits until the elevator arrives, blows Belinda a silent kiss, then waits at the door a while longer. He hears no elevator alarm bell, so he locks up. He collects his folded clothes from the living room, hangs his pants and jacket, puts his shirt into the bag of things to go to the cleaner, drops his socks and underwear into the laundry basket, gets into bed, and falls asleep quickly.

In the night, he's awakened by sounds from his neighbor's apartment. A thumping and knocking drag him out of sleep, and when he's awake he hears cries, four sharp cries. He has heard these cries before, just this way. He can't tell whether the guy is having a nightmare or an orgasm. He listens for a while, but after the four cries there's nothing more, and Matthew still can't tell what inspired them. He goes back to sleep.

He has a dream in which he and Belinda are picnicking in a pretty spot, in a woods somewhere, their blanket spread out in a mossy glade, a brook flowing nearby, just the sort of idyllic spot one always hopes to find for a picnic. In the glade the sun is shining bright and strong, but woods and shadows surround them. Then, all at once, but without any sense of suddenness, in that unannounced, unheralded way that people arrive in dreams, no snapping twigs, no rustling branches, another woman is with them, and she sits down on their blanket as if they had invited her.

Have they invited her? Matthew isn't sure, but he has the feeling that he and Belinda know her, know her well, in fact. Yes, she's a friend of theirs. They're glad to see her. The three of them are relaxed together, relaxed as one ought to be on a lazy day at a picnic in an idyllic spot like this. Even though they know this other woman so well, Matthew can't quite tell what she looks like. Her face is indistinct. It's quite a while before he realizes that she looks like, that she is, Liz.

Then the little glade is charged with sexuality. Liz stretches and settles onto the blanket. Rapid dream time takes over, and in almost no time at all Liz is completely undressed. There she is, all of a sudden, naked, luxuriating in the soft air, the sun, on the blanket cushioned by the moss. Matthew has dream-sharp, dream-fuzzy impressions of her smooth skin, the dark triangle of her pubic hair, her small breasts, tight nipples. And then Belinda, to Matthew's great surprise, begins undressing, too, but Belinda undresses in slow dream time. Matthew is surprised that Belinda is being so bold. It isn't like her; even in the dream Matthew recognizes that it isn't like her, and this makes him aware that he's dreaming, because he has to admit that it's incredible that Belinda would be stripping to lie naked in the sun in a woody glade with him and Liz—who has never looked better.

Now the weather seems to have gotten a lot warmer. Both Belinda and Liz have tans, though they were rather pale when all of this began. Matthew didn't really notice how pale they were at the time; he realizes it only now, now that they're brown and oily. Liz raises herself onto one elbow, looks at Belinda for a moment, and then caresses her breast. Belinda, with her eyes closed, stretches, savoring the caress as she had been savoring the sun. Then Liz kisses her.

"I don't think I'm ready for that," says Belinda. She isn't annoyed. She's almost apologetic. She seems to be suggesting that she might be ready at another time, even in a little while, perhaps, but that she isn't ready just now.

Matthew drifts up from sleep, out of the dream, almost to wakefulness. He has developed a notable erection, one of his stiffest, largest, and most pleasant. The entire dream episode has made him very happy. It has made him feel that he is potentially a party to a more exotic life than the one he's currently leading. In a while, he sinks back into a deeper sleep. He won't remember this dream when he wakes in the morning, but the idyll will return to him later, when he sits with his coffee to make his notes, as if it is new, and it will return again from time to time for the next couple of days, whenever he works on his review of the Alley View Grill.

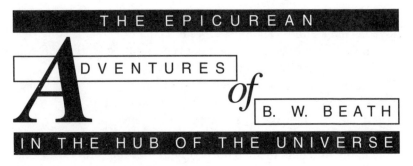

The Alley View Grill

We really enjoy the **Alley View Grill**. Honest. We do. Whenever we get a late-night craving for goat-cheese pizza or a veal-and-*pancetta* burger with some tomato *coulis,* it's almost the first place that comes to mind. Oh, sure, we know it's a frenzied, schizoid place, with one foot in Mom's kitchen back in bucolic Kansas and the other in New York's arty SoHo, but what the heck, we're probably a little schizy ourselves.

The décor—ah, the décor. Faux-zebra Formica, faux-tiger upholstery, faux-leopard carpeting, faux-peacock wallpaper. Our companion thought she had stumbled into an old Busby Berkeley musical—something like *Decorators on Safari.* But we like it. And since we've always favored gigantism in floral arrangements, we adore the Brobdingnagian bouquets. We don't even blush at their showy sexuality, the way they flaunt their whopping pistils, their stupendous stamens. We keep an open mind. We tolerate lubricious vegetation in all its bizarre varieties. We don't even blink at the gigantic buds of shell ginger, which seem to us so very like the spent and drooping members of enormous armadillos.

In a way, the Alley View Grill is a mom-and-pop eatery brought up to date: the décor is dada-deco, and the food is *nouvelle* Mom—a type that we have begun to see more and more in cutting-edge restaurants. Restaurateurs seem to be savoring anew their memories of Mom's kitchen. Suddenly they're nostalgic for the food they ate before they came to the city, learned to speak another language, began ridiculing their parents, and tried to hide their small-town naïveté. They don't serve up their nostalgia straight, of course; it's seasoned with the sophistication they've acquired away from home. So every remembered dish must be treated with face-saving contempt. Each is made the butt of an elegant, and sometimes quite delicious, joke. So the Alley View Grill offers Dad's favorite—grilled sirloin—but it's smothered in nasturtiums, not the onions Dad preferred. It arrives looking like a ritual sacrifice to Kong—grilled thigh of virgin, perhaps. There's grilled pork tenderloin, too, but it's served rare, flouting everything Mom said about pork. The apple pie is made with six varieties of apple (three American, one French, two Australian) and dusted with chopped macadamia nuts. There is even a burger, but it is the afore-mentioned veal-and-*pancetta* burger, with tomato *coulis,* about which Mom and Dad knew from nothin', we bet. (Even Dad's martini gets the snicker treatment. It's just a frozen ginsicle, minus the touch of vermouth that would elevate it from an anaesthetic to Nick and Nora's favorite tipple.)

The service. Well. Our heart is warmed by the sight of waiters and waitresses enjoying themselves, and here they certainly do. On some eve-nings our heart has been so warmed by their happy chatting and chortling that we have scarcely noticed that they have scarcely noticed us. Apparently the owners have quite an enlightened atti-tude toward what in the old, benighted, classist days of dining used to be called "service." Nor does the enlightenment end there. The Alley View Grill has, apparently, a hiring practice that favors waiters and waitresses with striking good looks and a total ignorance of food. We say bravo! These people have to start somewhere, don't they? Let them practice on us! We can attest to the fact that the Alley View gang learns quickly. They've already mastered indolence, indifference, and ignorance, the three essentials of contemporary sophisticated service. But does the place have style! The waiters mispronounce the names of the foods with impressive panache, and the menu misspells them in handsome deco-revival type. The golden-tressed fellow who will tell you, when you phone for a reservation on a Friday or Saturday, that he can't possibly fit you in for four weeks will be speaking to you over an old black telephone straight out

of an uncolorized *film noir* (perhaps that should be a *film noir-et-blanc*). The neon sign over the entrance once flashed beside a motel somewhere on the banks of the Connecticut River, the Valley View. Rescued from a salvage yard, it flashes again, all but the first *V.* And the ne plus ultra: above the bar, in pale green neon script, is the single word *Champagne.* Now if that's not *style,* we sure don't know what is.

Of course we adore the ebullient, well-dressed clientele. They're a vastly diverse group, representing every shade of sexual preference, sporting the latest garb smuggled in from New York. You'll get to know them well, thanks to their indefatigable table hopping, the ex-travagance of their greetings (are they performing for hidden cameras?), and the fact that the management has had the foresight to put the tables close enough to one another so that your neighbor (soon your chum!) is nearer (soon dearer!) to you than your dinner com-panion. Beware, though, of the week-ends, when the truly trendy are squeezed out by poseurs from the 'burbs, who have come in to see what they should be wearing and find out what arugula tastes like.

—*BWB*

The Alley View Grill
221 Rear Bartleby Street, 555-6100.
American Express, Visa, MasterCard.
No checks.
Handicapped: handicapped restrooms.
Lunch 12–3, Tuesday–Saturday.
Brunch 12–3, Sunday.
Dinner 6–11 Tuesday–Sunday.
Reservations recommended weekdays, a must weekends.

2

Flynn's Olde Boston
Eating & Drinking Establishment

Matthew's toting a bag of groceries in each hand, those bags made
of thin, improbably strong plastic. He carries groceries home successfully in these bags several times a week, but he always expects
them to break. Today he has too many bottles of spring water, the
only water he drinks, because the water in his apartment smells of
fish. Stretched thin, the handles of the bags dig into his hands.

In front of the library two boys are fighting. They are small and
thin, one black, the other Vietnamese. The larger boy is clutching
the smaller one's neck. He has a look of odd detachment, shows no
anger. The little one is choking. About forty adults are watching,
waiting for a bus.

Matthew feels that he should do something. He walks over to the
boys, saying, "Hey, hey. Cut that out," speaking with the voice of
reason, as a peacemaker. The boys ignore him.

A large man, who strikes Matthew as quite likely a high school
football coach, walks up to the boys and bellows at the larger, "You

little shit! Get your fucking hands off him!" He smacks the boy on the head, and the boy releases his choking grip. The smaller one drops to his knees and retches into the gutter. "Get out of here!" the coach shouts at the larger boy. He takes a fearful step backward and seems about to cry, but pride toughens him, and he tries to look defiant. More quietly, but with real menace in his voice, the coach says, "Get the *fuck* out of here." The boy runs away.

Matthew's about to say that his method would have worked, too, when the coach looks at him and snorts. Matthew's certain now that the man *is* a coach, because this is the same snort Matthew's high school gym teacher used to make when Matthew handed him a note asking that he be excused from gym with an upset stomach. Now that Matthew has seen a little of the world, he knows that bulls and even bison snort this way. From coaches, this bull snort means, approximately, "Stay out of my range, you fuckin' pansy."

Matthew walks on, but at the corner he makes another stop, to read some work of the writer he calls the Neat Graffitist. The Graffitist leaves messages all over Boston, printed in small, precise capital letters. He always uses a black marker, and he favors smooth surfaces free of other graffiti. He's especially fond of the metal boxes that house traffic light controls, but sometimes he uses the sides of newspaper vending boxes. His work combines elements of a personal philosophy, pronouncements exhortatory and cautionary, snapshots of contemporary life, and bits of autobiography. The result is varied, intriguing, and mad. This is the message that stops Matthew:

> NEVER FEAR PAIN. TIME DIMINISHES IT. BUT
> AVOID BOSTON CITY HOSPITAL. NURSES
> THERE WEAR USED UNIFORMS PURCHASED
> FROM BURGER KING, TREAT PATIENTS WITH
> FATALISTIC DETACHMENT.

Considering this on the way home, with the plastic handles digging into his hands at each step, Matthew decides that the heart of the message is the business about fatalistic detachment. That must be what's really bothering the Graffitist, not the used uniforms purchased from Burger King.

Matthew has been collecting the works of the Neat Graffitist for some time, memorizing them in the field and writing them down when he gets home. (He wouldn't like to be seen copying them on the street.) His current theory is that the Graffitist is someone well educated who snapped at a period of high stress—in the middle of the oral defense of his doctoral thesis, say, or while expounding a marketing plan for a toy Burger King franchise. (Not a bad idea, it occurs to Matthew—movable action figures for the manager, teenage crew, off-duty nurses eating lunch. Uniforms sold separately. Tiny burgers, buns, fries, and shakes—also sold separately.) *Why does he single out Boston City Hospital?* Matthew asks himself. *Maybe he was a patient there. Maybe he worked there as an orderly. Maybe he was a doctor there, a brain surgeon, driven mad by the escalating cost of malpractice insurance. That's a long shot, but certainly isn't impossible.*

Several themes run through the Graffitist's oeuvre: the paranoiac fretting of someone who feels he's being watched, criticized, harassed; loneliness and a desire for friendship; and the everyday indignities visited on the vulnerable. At times, he seems to be giving advice for good living, from one who has failed to live as he hoped he would.

> ON THIS CORNER AGENTS OF THE
> INTERNATIONAL LADIES GARMENT WORKERS
> UNION OBSERVE SOCIAL DEVIANTS. THEY
> MAKE NOTES, AND TAKE PICTURES. I DON'T
> THINK THEY HAVE A PROPER RESPECT FOR
> THE CHARACTERS OF OTHERS.

> DRIVE OUT THE BAD HABITS THAT HAVE BEEN
> DOING YOU HARM. EVEN IF YOU ARE A DRUG
> ADDICT, YOU CAN BE TRAINED TO GROW
> PAPRIKA IN MINES. NOBODY WHO SEES EVIL
> WOULD DELIBERATELY CHOOSE IT.

> UPS STRONGMEN SLEEP IN THE PAULIST
> CENTER, WHICH IS NOT A CHURCH, BUT YOU DO
> NOT HAVE TO BE AFRAID OF THEM. (YOU DO
> NOT HAVE TO BE AFRAID OF THEM.)

TWO PINKERTONS BIG BULLIES STOLE A
LETTER FROM MY SISTER NOW LIVING IN
WISCONSIN. THIS WILL NOT BE ENOUGH TO
SATISFY THEM. WHY WOULD THEY DO AN EVIL
THING?

TO HERBERT: YOU WERE BORN ONCE AND NOT
TWICE AND WHEN YOU ARE DEAD YOU WILL BE
DEAD FOREVER. GIVE ME BACK MY WATCHES.
THEY WILL NOT MAKE YOU HAPPY. THEY ARE
NO DEFENSE AGAINST DEATH.

NEVER LAUGH AT SOMEBODY WHO IS CRYING.
(YOU KNOW WHAT I MEAN.) DON'T DRINK IN
FRONT OF SOMEBODY WHO IS THIRSTY. DON'T
EAT IN FRONT OF SOMEBODY WHO IS HUNGRY.

DORA STOLE A SANDWICH AND TWO SOCKS
FROM ME AND I SAID NOTHING. YOU HAVE TO
BE READY TO DO EXTRAORDINARY THINGS FOR
THE SAKE OF FRIENDSHIP. EVERYBODY NEEDS
A PAL.

There is no concierge on duty when Matthew reaches his building. He sets the bags down, gets his key out, opens the door. A sign on the desk reads "Concierge on Break." This sign appears several times a day, whenever a concierge abandons the post. To Matthew, it seems an invitation to burglars. He said as much to the manager of the building, who listened with a puzzled smile, said, "I hadn't thought of that," and then chuckled. The sign has continued to appear, and Matthew supposes that the staff now regards him as a paranoid crackpot.

The elevator arrives. The door opens, but Matthew waits a moment before entering. He wants to be certain that the floor isn't going to leap up at him or vanish. Nothing alarming happens, so Matthew steps in, presses the button for his floor, and ascends without incident. It annoys him that he should feel relieved each time he succeeds in getting from the lobby to his apartment.

A piece of paper has been shoved under his door, a memo from the head of the condominium board, a contract lawyer with a great affection for capitalization. She writes: "As many Owners may al-

ready know, the Building was burgled sometime during the day today. The Individual or Individuals apparently gained access from
the Roof. . . ." Matthew fights the impulse to chuckle. He turns his
radio off and takes a quick look around. His apartment hasn't been
entered. Leaving the radio on, as he always does, worked. From his
foyer table he takes a point-and-shoot camera. He returns to the hall
and snaps a picture of some scraps of paper on the carpet just around
the corner from the door to his apartment. Then he carries his bags
into the kitchen and fixes himself a drink. He turns the lights on in
the dining room and looks into the hole in the wall. The insulation
has been removed; Matthew can see the metal framing in the wall
and, beyond it, the brick facade of the building. In the cavity are
several paper coffee cups from Dunkin' Donuts. *Were these part of
the original construction,* he wonders, *or were they left behind by
the smell-search team?* One of the workmen has written on the
wall, "Can't smell anything. Until we smell it, there's nothing we
can do." *The motto of the building,* thinks Matthew. He sniffs around
a bit to see if the odor is still there. It is, but it's in its quiescent state,
subtle enough for the workmen to be able to ignore it. On the wallboard beside the hole, he prints:

> TUESDAY: ODOR PERSISTS, BUT WEAK.
> SOMETHING BURNT? INSULATION? ROTTING
> SNACK FOODS?

Should I put my unit on the market? he asks himself. Matthew
has been living in the building for a little more than a year; he has
probably thought of selling once a week, on the average. The building is wearing him out. It embarrasses him. He's sure that he made
a mistake in buying into it. He hides this feeling for the sake of his
self-respect. He usually doesn't tell anyone about the slovenly way
the building's managed and maintained, and most of his guests don't
notice what he notices. They wouldn't notice, for example, the con-
stellation of paper scraps on the carpet in the hall outside his door.
These scraps haven't been vacuumed up in eight days. This particular bit of neglect gives Matthew a certain satisfaction, because he
has been snapping pictures of the bits of paper, one picture a day,

with his point-and-shoot camera, bought for this purpose, a camera that imprints the date and time on each photograph. He intends to display these photographs at the next owners' meeting, as evidence of the attitude problem he perceives in the management company that runs the building.

He goes into the den to check the messages on his answering machine. The first is a nonmessage, or an antimessage: the machine's go-ahead-and-talk whine, a silent hesitation at the other end of the line, the clunking of a handset hanging up, the dial tone, the whine again. Matthew surmises that this was the burglars calling to see if he was at home. He can imagine them coming to his door, hearing the radio, tiptoeing away, and burglarizing his neighbor, the one who cries out in the night, in ecstasy or fear. He can't help smiling at this thought; he knows he shouldn't, but he can't help it. The second message is from the superintendent.

"Mr. Barber? It's Benny. The super. The guys were in your place again looking for that smell, and they brought someone with them from the contractors again, too. They still aren't sure where it's coming from, but they think if they can open the wall up a little more, they might be able to find it. Also they want me to tell you they would like you to give them permission to cut away some of the carpet, because they think it might be mildew or something in the pad. They say they'll be able to put it back so you won't even notice, but I wouldn't let them do it without you being there, so they didn't do anything except pull out some of the insulation. They want to know if you could meet with them tomorrow to talk about opening the hole up some more and cutting the carpet back. So let me know, okay?"

The third message is from an old friend.

"Hey, Matthew. It's Jack. I'm going to be in town day after tomorrow—Thursday—and I'm hoping we can get together. I want to have dinner at Flynn's. You know. 'Flynn's—the taste of old Boston.' Or 'the scourge of old Boston.' Whatever. Will you set it up, make the reservations and everything? See if you can get hold of Effie. I'd really love to see her. But get her to leave dickhead at home, okay? I'll be in sometime in the afternoon, but I've got meetings, so I can't get to Flynn's until about eight. Make a reservation for nine, and I'll meet you in the bar between eight and nine. I hope this is all okay. You're not in Vermont or something, are you? If you don't get this message, and you're not there at Flynn's, I'll never speak to you again." Clunk of hanging up, silent stretch, dial tone, whine, snap of the machine shutting off. No more messages.

Matthew goes to the living room and sits looking out over the roofscape, sipping his drink, wondering why Jack would choose Flynn's. It isn't the kind of place he would ordinarily enjoy. It's big and noisy, popular with out-of-towners looking for what the Flynn's ads call "The Flavor of Olde Boston," and the flavor of olde Boston is not one of Jack's favorites.

Twenty years ago Matthew and Jack were in graduate school together, working toward degrees in teaching. They were great friends. They thought of themselves as bohemian, beat, hip, and they were seriously committed to improving the quality of public education. They may even have been *passionately* committed. All of that seems like a joke to Matthew now. The memory of it makes him feel naïve and foolish. He was recruited by the Harvard Graduate School of Education. Now he sometimes feels that he was conned, but at the time he and Jack—and their pal Effie—really considered the public schools the best long-term hope for the downtrodden and desperate. Each of them taught for a couple of years, and each of them left teaching disappointed and angry. Jack and Matthew *have* kept some interest in the development of young people, though. Matthew supplies them with toys that expand their imagination and hone their motor skills (though such toys don't appeal to them half as much as jingo killer dolls and long-legged plastic housewives that look like hookers). Jack makes television commercials that teach them how to act when they drink, drive, deodorize, and go into debt. Jack's work seems glamorous to Matthew, but Jack claims that it isn't glamorous at all, that the stars treat him like shit, and that he wants to make videos instead. Matthew thinks this is false modesty, intended to make him feel better about his own work and compromises.

Effie. Ah, Effie. Effie may have been a terrible teacher by every objective measure, too full of pep for her own good, so eager to give what she knew that it spilled out of her as if through a burst dike, making her seem disorganized, confused, and ill prepared in front of a class, but Matthew and Jack decided that she was the best natural teacher of all of them, and since she was also pretty in a flyaway sort of way, they took to her at once. She lived alone in a small apartment not far from Matthew's. She had a car—a battered Volkswagen—and gave Matthew rides to the school where they did their practice teaching. She knew rock musicians and folk singers, and that made her life seem thrilling and bold to Matthew, risky. Sometimes, when he arrived in the morning, he smelled marijuana in the apartment. The idea that he knew someone who smoked marijuana with her morning coffee was thrilling. Usually he would get to her place early, and she would be running late. From the first, she was only partly dressed when he arrived. He would pour himself coffee while she bustled around, and he would ignore her limber little body, on principle, because he believed, or managed to make himself believe, that not making any sort of advance was cool, that the chummy, sexless domesticity they shared for half an hour showed how sophisticated and modern they were, the vanguard of a new social order, in which the brightest and best would teach the poor and sad, in which men and women could work together without fucking, without even thinking about fucking. He never touched her, never tried.

Actually, Matthew was too intimidated by her to make advances. He believed that she was an extremist, politically, socially, culturally, that she spent nights in smoky rooms debating politics, planning strikes, printing leaflets—that is, when she wasn't up till the small hours in clubs, after the clubs had closed, when the real music happened, when everyone got stoned and snipped away at the fabric of conventional society. He supposed she must be an extremist sexually as well, and that, if he ever did make an advance, what she would want or expect from him might be something he didn't know how to deliver. He told himself that there was no sense risking a friendship by trying to turn it into something else, and he admitted to himself that there was no use risking an embarrassing failure, either.

But what a crush he had on her, and what fantasies he entertained! One morning she was still in bed when he arrived. She called out from the bedroom to say that she couldn't get up. "I don't think I'm sick," she said. "I just can't get out of bed, you know? I do this to myself. I wear myself out. I just can't do it today." Matthew made coffee and toast. She sat up in bed when he brought it to her. She wasn't wearing anything. When she sat up, she pulled the bedsheet over her breasts, but it kept sliding down and she didn't pay much attention to keeping it up. He tried not to look at her little breasts, because he couldn't decide *how* to look at them, what attitude to take toward them. She didn't seem to care whether he looked or not. He sat on the bed, they talked for a while, and he began to grow annoyed at how completely at ease she was. Some crumbs of toast fell onto her breasts, tiny bits like grains of sand, and for a moment he thought that he wouldn't be able to keep himself from brushing them off. Then he thought that he might ask her if he could brush them off. Or maybe he might mutter, "Crumbs," as a prefatory justification and then brush them off. Or perhaps it would be best not to touch her, just to say something about the crumbs. Maybe that would be enough, since it would make her aware that he had noticed the crumbs and she would figure out that he must therefore have noticed her breasts, too, and there would be a suggestion that he was concerned about her welfare, at least to the extent of not wanting her made uncomfortable by crumbs on her breasts, and that might be the start of something. He could say something like "You have some crumbs on those lovely breasts," or even just "You have crumbs on your breasts."

What he did say was, "You're getting crumbs on you." Effie looked at her breasts, flicked the crumbs away with her hand, and went back to eating. Nothing else happened, nothing at all. Later, Matthew drove to school in Effie's car, wondering whether she had wanted him to try anything. No, he decided. They were friends, that was that, and a friendship like theirs was certainly something wonderful, something worth preserving, worth making sacrifices for, even the sacrifice of sex. Still, the thought kept returning that surely she must have *some* feelings like his. If so, why hadn't she given him some sign? She wouldn't have had to invite him into bed with her, but she could have said something just a *little* provocative. "Are you sure *you* feel like going to school today?" Something.

He was depressed as hell by the time he reached school. Everything annoyed him—the children, the other teachers, everything. He began to think that teaching wasn't for him.

Effie recently finished law school and has been doing volunteer work, defending indigents and championing hopeless causes. She has never lost her sense of outrage. Matthew hasn't seen Effie in nearly a year, but every month or so he gets the urge to call her, always during the day, when, he assumes, her husband is not around. It is, partly, an urge to talk about important things—issues, ideas— but Matthew recognizes that there's another motive behind these calls that are never made, and that recognition is the reason they're never made.

Thursday evening, at eight o'clock, Matthew and Belinda are waiting in the lounge at Flynn's. Matthew's nervous. So is Belinda. She has never met any of the people she's about to spend the evening with. In fact, she has never met any of Matthew's friends; that is, she has never met anyone who is a friend of his alone, not a friend of Liz and Matthew, that former couple. The lounge is crowded, noisy with conversation.

"Why is this place so popular?" Belinda asks.

"It's mostly popular with tourists," says Matthew. "It's probably listed in every convention package and in all those guidebooks you find in hotel rooms."

"Why is that, I wonder?"

"You mean, who's being paid off? Why doesn't one of the more interesting restaurants get the business instead? I don't know. Maybe this is really the sort of thing tourists expect. Maybe they'd be disappointed by something better, or something different, anyway. They *want* beans cooked to mush, fried fish, Indian pudding. But why did *Jack* choose this place?"

Belinda shrugs.

"A gag, probably," Matthew suggests.

"All set for drinks here?" asks the waitress, grabbing up empty glasses, napkins, plastic toothpicks. Matthew orders two more martinis.

He and Belinda chat, but Matthew keeps checking the lobby for Jack or Effie, mostly for Effie. There is already a long line of people waiting for a spot in the lounge, where they will wait for a table in one of the dining rooms. Later in the evening there will be a line of people outside, waiting to get into the line of people waiting inside. Many of the waiting people have children with them, and many of the children are wearing sweatshirts that tout Boston, the Celtics, the Red Sox, the Boston branches of Tower Records and the Hard Rock Cafe, and Flynn's itself.

Matthew spots Effie as soon as she walks into the lobby. She stands on her toes, looking over the crowd. She looks much the same as she did when he last saw her, and in the essentials much the same as she did twenty years ago when she stood in front of a classroom full of kids and tried to tell them everything at once, as if electrified. She and her husband, Richard, are just back from two weeks on a chartered sailboat in the Caribbean. She has a great tan, and she's wearing white. Her hair has always been very light; now there's some white mixed with the blond, and that makes it lighter still, like the exaggerated bleached-blond that Matthew has noticed on much younger women.

She looks great, he thinks, *just great, a little bundle of energy, bouncing on her toes.*

She doesn't see Matthew in the line, so she comes into the lounge, wary and curious, as if this were the first cocktail lounge she'd ever entered. Richard is behind her, wearing a puzzled look.

He always has that look, puzzled by Effie, Matthew thinks, *by the way she makes her way through life. She must wear him out. There's just too much coming from her all the time, too much energy, too many ideas, too many words. I'll bet she wears him out in bed, too. It's her body type: those thin, wiry ones just never stop.*

Matthew has had two cleaning ladies of that type—ectomorphs—and they astonished him with their energy. The vacuum seemed to run on a higher speed when they used it. What an exhausting pleasure a night with Effie would be! Matthew's heart would be racing like a bird's, and he'd be panting by the end, goofy with pleasure and fatigue.

"Matthew!" Effie calls when she sees him, as if she were at a high school picnic. "Hey, you look terrific. How's the war-toy business?" This is one of their jokes; it's the first thing she says when she sees him once a year or so.

"Excellent!" he says. He's ready for her. "Never been better. I'm getting good responses to a new idea: generic insurgents." A go-ahead grin. "Blood 'n' Guts Action Figures, I call them." The introductions ought to occur here, right here, Matthew realizes; he ought to introduce Belinda now, but he doesn't; he and Effie are having their banter, and Matthew doesn't want to interrupt it, doesn't, in truth, want to end it at all.

"They're little action figures," he goes on. "You know, toy soldiers. Dolls. But they're sort of racial mongrels—they can be just about any race, religion, or nationality the kid's nasty little mind wants them to be. And, with the appropriate Guerrilla Garb Kit— sold separately—the kid can dress the miniature fanatics in the garb of the guerrilla movement of his or her choice."

"No kidding."

"No kidding. We've got the trappings of all the lunatic religions, political movements, and other terrorist groups. Actually, though, the market tests show that the *parents* are going to buy the garb of the guerrilla movement of *their* choice, but what the heck. We're even thinking this could boost sales in the long run. The kids will start buying *more* figures and dressing them up to mount a force in *opposition* to the force their parents are backing. Soon—it's war! Great potential for escalating profits. Unlimited, really."

"I'm impressed."

"I'll let you in on my best idea of all." From the corner of his eye, he sees that Belinda is watching this performance with something like tolerant surprise. She doesn't know about Effie, and she has never heard Matthew joke about his work.

"Mmm? What's that?" asks Effie.

"Weapons. International weapons. The next big thing. A whole arsenal of weapons. Perfect replicas of the best sellers in the international arms trade. Full size. Can't tell them from the real thing. All the deadliest stuff from China, Russia, Israel, South Africa, and, of course, the U. S. AK-47s, Uzis, Stingers. That sort of thing."

"Terrific."

"Watch for 'em at Christmas," Matthew says. He turns to Richard. "Hi, Richard. How are you?"

"Fine, Matthew," says Richard. "Just fine." It seems to Matthew that there is always a certain coolness in the way Richard speaks to him. He has wondered whether Richard thinks that he and Effie were lovers, and because he likes the idea, he tries to encourage the suspicion by giving Richard a wry grin and a little wink whenever they meet. The wink is not *exactly* a wink, more a blink of one eye that could be *interpreted* as a wink, the kind of fleeting wink that might be exchanged by men who have enjoyed the same woman—if men who have enjoyed the same woman exchange fleeting winks like that. Matthew hasn't the slightest idea whether they do, but such a wink seems like a token of the sort of camaraderie that's supposed to exist among guys, coach types. Matthew doesn't pal around with any guys of that type, so he doesn't know what kind of sign to look for in a guy who has enjoyed any of the women he has enjoyed. Liz, to name one. She hasn't remarried, so Matthew supposes that quite a few guys have enjoyed her, though he doesn't know. On the rare occasions when he and Liz have gotten together since the divorce, they haven't discussed their romances. Matthew is curious, but he guesses that he's just as happy not to know. He does wonder whether *Liz* is curious, though. He has looked for evidence of curiosity—in her eyes, around the corners of her mouth—but he can't be sure what he has seen there, can't decide whether she has any interest in his sex life or not.

"I want you to meet Belinda Sadler," Matthew says at last. He puts a hand on her shoulder. "Belinda, this is Effie Parker and this is Richard Parker."

"All set for drinks here?" It's the cocktail waitress again. She wears a tight little satin skirt, and Matthew decides, after a quick review of his mental notes, that she has the most beautifully shaped bottom he's seen in weeks.

Richard looks up at her face, but then he moves his eyes up and down her body without tilting his head. Matthew can see this, but Effie can see only the steady back of his head, angled upward. When Richard's eyes reach the waitress's again, he smiles at her with great warmth. "What's the most popular drink here?" he asks.

"Probably a Paul Revere's Ride."

"What's that?"

"Supposed to be based on something the original Colonists drank. Rum and applejack." She reaches across Richard to pick up, from the center of the table, a card describing the drink. Matthew notices that, although her breasts do not brush Richard's face, they come close enough so that, if he had chosen to, he could have stuck his tongue out and licked them. She hands the card to him, and he glances at it.

"What about those drinks with obscene names?" he asks.

"'A Sloe and Comfortable Screw'?"

"Right. Or 'Sit on My Face.'"

"Not in this bar," she says, and she bursts out laughing. "We get a lot of families, you know. Tourists."

Richard orders a round of drinks, and the waitress wiggles off. Richard and Matthew watch her bottom move, and Matthew's embarrassed to find that it fetches the memory of an afternoon during college when he was delivering laundry to earn spending money. The boozy man who drove the laundry truck, watching a girl in a tight skirt cross the street, took a long drag on his cigarette and said, "Two piglets in a sack." When Richard turns toward Matthew, there's a look in his eyes that makes Matthew decide that all is not perfect with the Parkers. Perhaps Effie really is too much for Richard, and Richard has begun fooling around to shore up his ego. Immediately Matthew wonders how he would fare with Effie, not someday, but this evening, if Richard's flirting with this waitress becomes intolerable and Effie turns to Matthew suddenly and asks him to take her home. Would he be up to her, tonight? If whatever might happen between them tonight were to turn into something more, if Matthew said all the right things in the cab, if Effie asked to stay at his place, then surely a congenial divorce could be arranged, very quickly, so that everyone could be happy as soon as possible. He wonders if it would be all right to call a separate cab for Belinda if Effie asks him to take her home.

The drinks arrive. Matthew notes that this is his third martini of the evening and resolves not to have another.

"So tell me what you've been up to, Effie," he says.

"Oh, I've got myself set up with a nice little office at home, and I've been doing a lot of *pro bono* work, and I've done some 'regular lawyer stuff,' real estate mostly, enough to pay for my office equipment, and more than enough to convince me I don't want to do any more of that than I have to. I leave that to Richard."

Richard's a successful lawyer with a respected old firm, not one of the largest, but one of the oldest. His income makes their easy life possible, Matthew knows, but he also knows that Effie pays her share, and he knows that her needs aren't great. If she were living alone, she wouldn't charter a boat in the Caribbean every winter, but since Richard wants to, she goes along, and happily. What Effie wants for herself, she earns and pays for, and often all she wants is time, time to do what she wants to do, good works. Sometimes Matthew can't help thinking of her as saintly. He has begun to allow himself to say to himself, "I'm in love with her," and it seems as if it may be true, but he isn't sure. Perhaps he has always been in love with her. Perhaps not. Perhaps he just admires her.

I bet she'd be great in bed, though, and I bet we'd have a wonderful time in a cabin in Maine, snowbound.

The conversation splits, as conversations in foursomes often do, and Matthew finds himself talking to Richard. He never has much to say to Richard. He asks about the children, because he thinks people who have children are flattered to be asked about them, since they're investing their hopes in their kids, but then the thought strikes him that perhaps this isn't really so. Maybe people with children are actually envious of them, feel that their kids are getting a much better deal than they got when they were young. *In fact,* Matthew decides, *they're probably annoyed when they're asked about their children.* Now he feels uncomfortable about having asked Richard about the children. There is also the intriguing possibility that Richard might be haunted by the suspicion that one of them is Matthew's. Or both. The boost Matthew gets from imagining that suspicion comes not only from the pleasure it implies but from the implication that it's possible. He suspects that it isn't, or at least that it's unlikely. When Liz didn't become pregnant after three years of trying, her gynecologist suggested Matthew have a sperm count done. Matthew made an appointment, but as it approached he dreaded it more and more. He couldn't stand the idea of masturbating on demand, in a toilet with girlie magazines. Then there was the possibility that he wouldn't be able to. What if he couldn't get an erection under those circumstances? He'd have to face nurses, wouldn't he? He'd have to walk through a waiting room full of other men, and he could imagine them snickering as he passed. Matthew decided that he probably did have a low sperm count. It was a good explanation; why not just accept it without verifying it? He canceled the appointment but told Liz that he kept it. A couple of days later he reported the results, which he fabricated from *Taber's Cyclopedic Medical Dictionary* and *Our Bodies, Ourselves*: a low sperm count, low percentage of motility, high percentage of abnormalities. Liz was understanding.

While Richard talks about the children—something about school, television, shoes—Matthew is distracted by the conversation between Effie and Belinda. It seems to be entirely about work, but he keeps thinking—hoping—that they're about to start talking about him.

The lounge is getting more and more crowded. Matthew is amazed at how dark it is here. Everything is dark—the wood, the upholstery, the lighting. *Most restaurants aren't this dark anymore,* he thinks. *Does it have something to do with historical authenticity?*

More likely, he seems to hear BW say, *they are afraid that in bright light we would notice the authentic antique grime.*

The cocktail waitress materializes out of the dark with *another* round of drinks. The group is surprised.

"Did we order these?" asks Richard. He pauses, grins a lubricious grin. "Or can you read my mind?"

"'No' to the first one," says the waitress. "Your friend Jack ordered them. He said to tell you he'll be right with you."

"Is he here?" asks Effie. Her head swivels, like an action figure's.

"He must have ordered these by telepathy," suggests Richard. "Can you read his mind, too?"

A smile for Richard from the waitress. Matthew never realized before that Richard was the kind of guy who exchanges banter with cocktail waitresses. *If he were alone, would he pick her up?* he wonders. Matthew has often wished that he could make small talk. He realizes that you can't pick up women in a bar without the skill, for one thing. He has observed that in bars where picking-up seems to be going on, everyone is good at that nonsensical chat, that cotton-candy talk, but he can't seem to master it. When he tries, he begins perspiring across his upper lip.

"He called," the waitress says.

"He called?" asks Matthew. "He ordered drinks for us by phone?"

"That's Jack," says Effie. "He's probably in a limo with a car phone."

Matthew wonders how Jack identified the group for the waitress. He can imagine a conversation like this:

"Should be a group of three," says Jack. "An adorable little blonde, bouncy, full of life. A dull guy, her shithead husband, looks like a lawyer, probably tried to pick you up. And kind of a nondescript guy in his forties, most likely drinking a martini, the kind of guy you wouldn't pick out in a crowd."

"Well," says the waitress, "there is one group like that, but there's another woman with them, and the nondescript guy is wearing kind of surprising socks."

No. That's not it, Matthew tells himself. *He knew the reservation was in my name. He just asked if the Barber party was there.*

Suddenly there's Jack, putting his arm around the waitress and asking the group, "Is Luanne taking care of you?" as if he owns the place, immediately in charge, as he always was. *How did he find out that her name was Luanne? Did he just say, "What's your name, honey?" or what?*

Matthew's name is called over a loudspeaker before Jack has a chance to sit down: "Barber, party of six. Barber, party of six."

"Party of six?" asks Jack.

"I didn't know whether you'd be alone or whether you might bring someone."

Jack just grins. *Is he offended?* There was an edge to Matthew's voice; he was a little annoyed at being put in the position of social secretary.

The group rises and goes into the scuttling around that comes after one's name has been called at a place like this, trying to get the cocktail waitress to bring the check. Where is she? Where has Luanne gone? How can she have disappeared so quickly? Did she run off as soon as she realized they'd been called? She has come over to the table often enough to ask if they wanted more drinks, but now she's nowhere in sight. Richard volunteers to wait for her while the rest of them go to the table. Jack thanks him and reaches for his wallet. Richard puts his hand up, and Jack smiles, nods, puts his wallet away, and offers Effie his arm. Matthew observes all of this, and it seems to him that, over the top of Effie's head, just as Jack turns and heads for the dining room with her on his arm, Jack winks at him. He can't be quite sure. It might have been nothing more than a blink of the eye, but it might have been more. *Has Jack slept with Effie?* Matthew wonders. *Does he think I have?*

The section of Flynn's in which people eat, as opposed to the part in which they drink and wait, is huge and rambling. There are several rooms, added one by one as the restaurant has grown over the last two hundred something years, linked by passages that turn at unpredictable places and rise and fall wherever the growing Flynn's burst through the wall of an adjoining building. The dining rooms are brightly lit, blinding in contrast with the lounge, as if a sharp moral distinction had been made between eating and drinking, a New England attitude imposed: drinking, like sex, is a furtive, dirty occupation, to be done in the dark, but eating is wholesome, and, as long as you do it neatly, you may do it with the lights on. After an hour in the lounge, when one moves into the light one is apt to experience what BW has called

> . . . the penitential squint exacted from the daytime drinker, the squint that we make involuntarily when we've been drinking in the afternoon at that little spot on Newbury Street we favor and come out into the low winter sun and are made to feel that we have been doing something wrong, that this painful squint and its accompanying unwilled rearward jerk of the head are what we deserve, and we hang our head, a head already beginning to pound.

A group of ten is being seated at a long table. The five facing Matthew are obviously related. One of them is the grandmother of the clan, it seems, and Matthew guesses that she's being feted. They look to him like the sort of family that doesn't get together unless there's a reason, an obligation. All of them have the grandmother's curly hair, and all, male and female, wear it at nearly the same length. They all have her bulbous nose, too.

People come to Flynn's for celebrations, as this group has done, because they regard it not so much as a place to eat as a place to be experienced, and the experience is supposed to be shared with friends. Everyone's supposed to get together just like old times—it's been so *long* since we've gotten together—and have a hell of a good time. Matthew has never liked going out under such circumstances. There's always a false heartiness in the conversations, something too boisterous, like the false intimacy of salesmen who call him Matt or the phony camaraderie among people who work together but have nothing else in common.

At the table, they are greeted by a waitress who makes a show of bustling around, to establish right off the bat that she's responsible for the feeding of dozens of people, not just this paltry sampling of humanity, and that she will not tolerate long periods of pondering and hesitation. A breezy "Hi, folks. Welcome to Flynn's. All set for drinks here?"

They get themselves on her wrong side right away by exhibiting some indecision, since they have been doing various amounts of drinking in the lounge. She puts her hand on her hip and frowns while they hem and haw.

"Sure," says Richard finally. "I'll have a Jack Daniel's on the rocks."

"A glass of chardonnay," says Effie.

"Anderson's Denver Beer," says Jack. He doesn't *quite* shout it.

"I'll have that, too," says Belinda.

"I'll have a—"

Matthew stops himself. If he has a martini, it will be his fourth. That would be a mistake.

"—a Dewar's and soda," he says, making not as great a mistake, perhaps.

"Okay," says the waitress, "let me tell you about the menu. We're out of swordfish, the soup of the day is split pea, and the special dessert is tapioca pudding. Would you like a few minutes?"

"Oh, definitely," Matthew says.

The waitress bustles off, and Belinda almost snickers, which pleases Matthew.

"Jack," he asks, "why did you want to come here? Of all the places we might have gone, why are we in a place where—unless I'm just having a nightmare—the special dessert is tapioca pudding?"

"Ahh," he says. "Because I'm looking for a place to shoot a beer commercial. It has to be someplace that says 'Boston' to the rest of the country, and that's why I chose this. There's going to be a whole series of these commercials. They'll have famous people who're supposed to be hanging out in their favorite pubs, taverns, lounges, restaurants, whatever. That's why I wanted to come to Flynn's. What do you think?"

"Well—"

"'Well?' What do you mean, 'Well'? It's great. Fits right in with the whole marketing concept, which is so devious, so fiendishly brilliant, that I drop to my knees in front of it every morning and kowtow. Figuratively speaking. Complete this sentence: The grass is—"

"Always greener on the other side of the fence," says Belinda in a rush, as if there were a prize at stake.

Jack bangs his spoon against his beer bottle. "I knew you were the smartest one in the bunch," he says to Belinda. "I could see it in those sea-green eyes. Mmmm. Where was I? Oh, yes. Anderson's." He holds up his bottle. "'If it's Anderson's it's pure and sturdy and tasty, and if it's pure and sturdy and tasty it must be Anderson's! Anderson's Original Denver Beer.' Or Anderson's Original Anywhere Beer. Even as we speak, Anderson's is in the process of building small regional breweries all across this great nation. And before the year is out, they'll be brewing Anderson's Original San Antonio Beer, Anderson's San Francisco Beer, Chicago Beer, New Orleans Beer, Memphis, Atlanta, and so on. And soon, Boston."

A chorus of uh-huhs. He's got them all listening.

"They're all franchises, turnkey operations. Now here's the thing, the genius part. You can't buy Anderson's in the city where it's brewed. You can only buy it someplace else. So you can buy Denver Beer in Boston, but when the Boston brewery is in operation, you'll have to go to Denver or someplace to buy Boston Beer. You see? You get it? Because it's brewed in Denver, people in the East think of it almost as imported. Exotic. The beer from distant Colorado. It's got that Denver cachet, and that means something."

"And Boston Beer is going to have that Boston cachet?" asks Richard.

"Sure! Sure! See, that's the attitude, right there. The grass is greener. You don't think Boston's anything special, because you live here, but they'll be suckin' down Boston Beer in Denver, because it's got that Boston cachet. Of course, they'll also be sucking down a lot of Manhattan Beer and Memphis Beer and so on. *Chacun à son cachet.*"

"But Jack, why this place?" Matthew asks. "I thought people were interested in all the changes in Boston. Vitality, booming economy, high-tech, waterfront development, that kind of thing. Why not pick a place full of young, gorgeous people whose pockets are stuffed with disposable income? Aren't they the target?"

"Oh, yeah. Definitely. They're the target. The people you described, young people with money to spend, they're the target, but young people with money to spend *who live in Boston* are not the target of *this* ad. They're the target of the ads we film in San Francisco, New York, New Orleans, Chicago. Right? See what I'm getting at?" He leans across the table and takes Matthew's chin in his hand. "Aren't you *listening* to me, Matthew?" he asks. "How many of those Scotches have you had?"

"This is my first," says Matthew, emphatically.

"Well, then pay attention, will you? I fly all the way out here just to explain this to you, and you can't get your mind off Luanne's sweet little ass."

"I wasn't thinking about Luanne's sweet little ass," says Matthew. "I swear to God I wasn't." But he reddens, since the image of Luanne's bottom and the memory of two piglets in a single sack return together.

"This is the whole concept," says Jack. "Anderson's does *no* national advertising. It's all regional, and it's all based on the idea that most people think they'd be happier someplace else. If we shoot here, in Flynn's, you can be sure the place will be full of young beautiful types, and when we run the ad in Cleveland or Missoula, it's going to look like 'Oh, yeah, that's Boston, that's just the way I thought it would look, and look at all those hip, gorgeous Boston people getting rich on high-tech whatever and drinking Anderson's Boston Beer.' You see? It's genius. I'm not going to be modest. It's genius. I mean, look around you. What do you see? Everybody here but us is from Ohio. Except for these Japanese guys." He gesticulates toward a table at which two Japanese men in business suits are tying lobster bibs around their necks. His gesture catches their eye. "Ohio?" he says, nodding. "Ohio?" They nod and smile. "Well, them, too," says Jack. "So you see? Everybody in Ohio wants to live in Boston. And that's what we're selling. We're selling a young, successful life-style, and we're selling Boston or Denver, and we're selling every other city in America that anybody wants to live in."

"What about beer? Aren't you selling beer?" This comes from

Richard, and there might be an edge to it, though he's smiling in the boyish way he has.

"Hey. Of course I'm selling beer. And it's good beer. I'm not kidding. It's good beer." He looks to Belinda, who nods enthusiastically. "Have you tried it?" he asks Richard.

"Oh, sure," says Effie. "A few times. I like it, but it's not that easy to find, you know."

"Yeah, well, right now the Denver stuff is all you can get, all there is. But you wait till next summer. It'll be Anderson's from coast to coast. Let's all have some. Waitress! Miss? Hoo-hah, waitress? Bring us some more of that dee-licious Anderson's Denver Beer, will you? Bring five of them, okay? I want my friends to try it." To them he says, "You're going to like this. I wouldn't push the crap if I thought it *was* crap."

They all laugh at this, and he grins. "Well, maybe I would," he says. "Who knows? Got to keep gas in the Porsche, right? Oh, but listen, listen. I have had this *great* idea. Great idea. I'm talking art now, social commentary, and an excellent way to write off a month's vacation. I'm going to tour America, *in* the Porsche, and I'm going to visit a McDonald's wherever I stop. Or a Burger King. Whatever."

Matthew thinks of mentioning the graffito about used uniforms from Burger King. Not now, of course, but when Jack finishes. They might find it interesting, they might be interested in the whole idea of someone who goes around town writing these careful messages about himself and his life. *When Jack finishes*, he tells himself.

"And I'm going to interview the help," Jack is saying. "Teenage kids, managerial trainees, housewives, golden geezers, whoever's working there who will talk to me. Well, anybody who's an interesting type, anyway, interesting looking. Interview them all in their McDonald's uniforms, and get them to talk about what makes this part of the country, wherever I happen to be, this town or city, or region, whatever, *different*. Why is it *special* here? And I'll shoot each McDonald's as if it were the only one in the fucking world, you know? 'Here we are in Muncie, Indiana.' Title under the pimply face of some kid: 'Muncie, Indiana.' Maybe no voiceover. Maybe

I'll stay out of this completely. Just the people speaking for themselves. 'Muncie is, well, gee, it's just so *swell*. I can't think why anybody'd ever want to live someplace else, like one of them cities.' Or maybe the kid doesn't say that, maybe he says, 'Ah, Muncie sucks. Nothin' ever happens here. I wish t' hell I could get 'nough money together to get to New *York*.' Then cut to New York. Black kid in his McDonald's uniform. 'Man, New York is the *place*. It is the *only* place.' Mmm, I don't know. That might be a little too manipulative. I don't think I want to make the points as heavily as that, you know. Maybe just start in L. A., and drive. Shoot fifty Mickey D's in order, and leave them in that order. I don't know. I'll have to see what comes up. I'm thinking of writing up a proposal for a grant for this. I'm not shitting you. I can see this on cable. Or public television, brought to you by a 'grahnt from the Mowbil Oil Cawpawration,' or maybe even a grahnt from McDonald's. Or Anderson's."

Matthew isn't sure what he thinks of this idea. It does sound like an interesting commentary on something, the homogenization of American life, the changing aspirations of American youth, the assumptions underlying the Anderson's commercials, or something, but he isn't sure whether Jack is serious.

"I think it has possibilities," says Jack. He seems serious, but Matthew has been fooled before.

"So do I," says Richard. "I really do. I think it makes a statement about the homogenization of American culture. Maybe about the survival of regional differences. Individuality. I think you've got something. I really do."

Jack nods gravely. For a moment, Matthew wishes he'd spoken first. He's sorry that he let Richard get in ahead of him with praise for Jack's idea. Then Jack says, "Should be a great way to nail a lot of teenage girls, too."

Effie punches him, Jack laughs, Richard frowns, and Matthew chuckles, glad that he kept his mouth shut.

"Effie," says Matthew, so loudly that he surprises himself and everyone else; they all turn toward him suddenly.

"Matthew!" says Effie, just as loudly as he did.

"What's happening with that woman who spent her rent money for tuition?"

"Oh. Didi." She looks at Jack and at Belinda and says, by way of explanation, "I'm defending a woman who was being evicted from a housing project because she hadn't paid her rent for two months. In fact, she *had* paid part of it, but not all of it. She spent the rest to pay a tuition bill. How did you know, Matthew?"

"I saw the article in the *Globe*."

"Oh," says Effie. "It was a while ago," she says to the others. "She was ambitious. She enrolled in a couple of courses at the Harvard extension school, and she was about to be evicted because she'd stretched her budget a little too far. You know, she had been so foolish as to spend her rent money on her future. Well, she tried to explain that she would catch up over the next couple of months. They ignored her. She called Legal Aid. I got the case."

"And bingo!" says Richard. "The woman's all over the papers!"

Matthew remembers. For a week or more she was always there, sometimes beaming, sometimes sniffling, an attractive black woman, with darling Effie by her side, the little guys against the heartless bureaucracy. Now, sitting here at Flynn's, smiling at Effie while she goes on, recounting her struggles, he remembers reading the story, remembers the circumstances exactly. He was sitting alone in his living room, after work, drinking a martini. He thought of doing something for the woman, sending her some money. He must have been on his second martini. She only needed a couple of hundred dollars to make up the back rent she owed. It would have been simple to write out a check, and Matthew would hardly have noticed the money, but he put the newspaper aside and began pacing the floor, drinking, thinking. He began thinking beyond this one woman, he—

Uh-oh. Matthew is about to speak. The urge to speak has come upon him, and he's a little too drunk to fight it.

"You know," he says in a tone that announces his intention to say something important, interrupting Effie, "I remember reading the story about that woman. In the *Globe*. I remember the circumstances exactly. I was sitting alone in my living room, reading the paper. And when I read that story, it just struck me that she only needed a couple of hundred dollars. It just struck me. So little. I put the paper aside and started pacing the floor."

For a terrifying moment, Matthew realizes that he's about to get up out of his chair and demonstrate this pacing; to his relief, this passes. "I began thinking. Beyond this one woman, you know. To the struggles, the terribly hard time that I know so many people have." *Jesus, I sound like an idiot*, he thinks. "Just getting by, of course. But more than that. Breaking through! Getting *out* of a pattern of poverty and failure. I wondered how many of them could do it, *break out*, for just a couple of hundred dollars. You know what I mean?"

This question is answered with grave noddings of the head.

"Somebody wants to open a little shop or start some small-scale business. Doing landscape work or something like that. All he needs is a couple hundred dollars. To get started. And so I came up with this idea. We give poor people two hundred dollars apiece. No questions asked."

He makes a sweeping gesture with his hands, brushing aside the questions.

"Some of them just spend it. So what? It goes right back into the economy, doesn't it? Some of them just stick it into the bank. So what? It's available for loans. But *some* of them use it to start small businesses. Somebody in a ghetto where banks don't want to open up starts a small bank. You know, on the scale of a check-cashing service, something like that. Another guy opens—oh, I don't know— a shoe-repair business. All these people need supplies, right?"

They nod with some enthusiasm. They are a kind bunch, indulgent. *These people are my pals.*

"Pens and deposit slips for the little street-corner bank. Pieces of leather and rags and polish and tools for the shoe shop. They buy this stuff. They're fueling the economy, right?"

Matthew pauses; he liked the nodding earlier, the little smiles, and he's asking for more of that. His pals give it to him.

"And then when their little businesses begin making money, they begin spending it. They buy better cuts of meat. Flowers for the wife. Shoes for the kids. *Toys* for the kids. Beer imported from *Denver*, for Christ's sake."

Matthew stops here, thanks to some residual self-censorship, but at home, when he had read the article, when he was alone, he ran on with the impressive logic of his idea. He wondered why no one had seen this logic before. Why hadn't anyone understood that if the poor had money, everyone would be better off? He began running that over in his mind, making a slogan out of it.

If the poor had money, everybody would have money.

If the poor prosper, everyone prospers.

If you want to get rich, invest in the poor.

Lift the least and you lift yourself.

If the poor were rich, you would be, too.

He laughed at himself. *This must be an incredibly naïve idea*, he thought. *Not the idea of a grownup. A child's idea.* He made himself some dinner. He watched a movie while he ate. He had another drink. By the time he went to bed he had lost the urge to send some money to the woman Effie was defending. He even felt a little foolish for having thought of doing it. It no longer seemed like what an intelligent, thinking adult would do with his money. It was what a kid would do. However, he had not quite forgotten the woman's plight. He had incorporated it into a new bedtime fantasy. In this one he did send a check, to Effie, for the woman, a large check, and he asked Effie to dole the money out on a monthly basis over the next year, while the woman was finishing school, with the stipulation that her benefactor was to remain unknown to her. He derived an almost tactile pleasure from the thought of writing *benefactor* and meaning himself. When Effie called to thank him, he suggested lunch or dinner. She said, "I'd love that," in a voice that was oddly hushed, as if she were embarrassed that he had read her mind, at last, after all these years.

There is a moment of silence at the table after Matthew finishes

outlining his proposal. Then Jack says, slowly, very seriously, nodding as he speaks, "You know, Matthew—" He draws a breath, grim-
aces as if with the gravity of the moment. "You are *shitfaced*. I
mean, you are *really* drunk."

Laughter. Matthew joins it, and he makes a show of pushing his
glass away.

"So, Effie," says Jack, "what was the upshot of the whole thing?"

"Nothing," says Effie. "Zero upshot. The story in the *Globe*
brought in some money. Not a fortune, but enough. She paid her
back rent, and the agency let the matter drop."

"Good," Matthew says. "Good." He's aware of what he's doing,
and he's aware that he ought to be ashamed of himself for doing it,
but he's doing it anyway: nodding and smiling in a way that suggests he was one of the people who sent money. He thinks of saying
something more. He can imagine himself saying just a little something more, something like "That's what I hoped," and before he can
stop himself he has said it. *Sometimes*, he thinks, *my mind is my
worst enemy*.

Effie looks at him with a quizzical grin that quickly widens into a
smile. Matthew should feel like shit, but he doesn't, not at all. He
basks in that smile. "Matthew," Effie says, drawing his name out.
"You doll."

He raises his hand, shrugs, frowns a little, all to say, "It was nothing." Which, of course, it was.

Effie goes on, getting worked up. She sounds just the way she
used to sound twenty years ago, when at some point in any discussion she was sure to begin talking about injustice of whatever kind
she currently found most outrageous. Outrage was always there, the
way a grudge is always there for some people, an undercurrent to
every other emotion, even happiness, even lust. Matthew has missed
part of what she said, but now he hears her saying, "You know, don't
you, that any bread we leave in this basket will go to the Pine Street
Inn?"

"What's that?" asks Jack.

"A shelter for homeless men."

"Are those the guys my mother used to call bums?" asks Jack, wearing a look of mock naïveté. Matthew wonders whether he has any idea how dangerous is the ground he's treading.

"Probably so, Jack," says Effie. "Probably so." There's a bitter, stiff smile on her face.

"I'm sorry," says Jack, and he means it. "Go on."

"Oh, it's nothing," Effie says. "It's just that it's, well, it's just so *queer*. I mean, the poor eat our leftovers. I mean it. Really. Not what's actually left on our plates—though I did read a letter to Dear Abby from some old woman who said she and her husband could never finish the meals they got in restaurants and she wanted some group or other to send their leavings to the poor. God! Scrapings! But, you know, it's not such a big step from what really happens. I represent this outfit called Boston Gleaners? They collect food—leftovers, literally—and distribute it to soup kitchens, rehab centers, shelters. You'd be amazed at what they get. Anything that isn't actually put onto a plate, that kind of leftover. Fancy bakeries will *not* sell day-old goods, you know. Heaven forbid. At the end of the day they take away trash bags full of rolls, bread, *croissants*, for God's sake. This is our social welfare system! The poor eat the crumbs from under our table. Hey, I'm part of it, you know? I'm helping to make this ass-backwards system work. I'm a fucking sucker. We all are. I have this fantasy—of a little cocktail-party conversation?" She juts her chin out, locks her jaw, and burlesques the voice of a moneyed matron. "'You know, *Bradley* and I have found the most *wonderful* way to help feed these people one sees on the street.'"

Jack takes the cue at once; he responds as the matron's moneyed friend. "'Oh, *really*? What is that, dear?'"

"'Well, *Bradley* found out that if one doesn't eat all the *rolls* that are served to one, they go to the *poor*. So now, whenever we're served a basket of *rolls*, we make a point of leaving one or two un-eaten.'"

"'Is *that so*?'"

"'Oh, *without fail*. It seems such a small sacrifice. But that's not all. You know Bradley is *so* clever. Once he caught the spirit, there was just no *stopping* him, and now he's come up with something *else*. Every morning, on his way to the office, he drops our empty *cans* and *bottles* into the trash can on the corner so that these people can root them out and cash them *in*.'"

"'What a *clever* idea!'"

"'*Isn't* it though? These people can gather up those cans and feel almost as if they were actually *working* for their money instead of just *begging* on the street. I'm *sure* it gives them a sense of personal dignity.'"

"'Oh, *so am I*, dear. *So am I*.'"

They raise their glasses to Effie's performance, and she allows herself to laugh.

Matthew's attention is drawn again to Grandma and the group of ten. They're getting a little rowdy. He wonders how long they spent in the lounge. Grandma's clutching a drink of some kind, with a napkin wrapped around the bottom of the glass. The others seem to be urging her to order a lobster regardless of the expense. Five are facing Matthew: a man, Grandma's son, wearing Grandma's hair like a wreath around a bald spot on the very top of his head; a young man, certainly the first man's son, sullen, interested in the food but not in the event; a boy, bright, showing off, talking a lot, always informing the others about something, often correcting what he takes to be their misimpressions about things; Grandma herself, wearing a corsage, slightly bewildered, pleased, but worried about the cost of all this; her daughter, a worrier, a manipulator, wearing an expression of aloofness, almost disdain, though she smiles continually, seated at an angle to the table, her chair out a bit from it, sitting straight up on the edge of her chair. Across from those five are, Matthew feels certain, though he can see only their backs, the in-laws, matched to their mates, the balding guy's wife seated across from him, and so on. These five are a mixed bag. One of them glances around the room now and then, probably because she's embarrassed by the others; she is clearly the daughter of the woman who wants to be in charge, a girl, or young woman, in her twenties, the best-looking person at the table. She has some of Grandma's features, but on her they look good. She's playing at being "different," complaining that some rock club she went to with friends was too loud and crowded. When the waitress arrives at their table, everyone but Grandma orders right away—lobster. Grandma still fusses. "Bring her a goddamned lobster," says the pretty girl.

"What's new in toys, Matthew?" asks Jack.

Matthew wonders why that question must always sound like a joke. He's sure Jack isn't trying to be funny, doesn't mean to seem to be trivializing Matthew's work. He couldn't mean to do that. Matthew feels quite certain that Jack has as much respect for Matthew as he has for himself. He recognizes in Matthew someone who has made the same compromises he has, someone who has ideals, or at least had ideals, but who has, partly by decision, partly by accident, partly because of need, stepped to one side of them—hasn't exactly walked away from them, just stepped to one side of them. For one reason and another, Jack's making beer commercials. Matthew would never joke about that.

Matthew glances at Effie, and she grins. She expects him to give Jack the same string of gags he gave her. Matthew grins back. He has more up his sleeve than that.

"Well," he says, "we're coming out with a line of whore dolls. Hester Hooker and Her Pals." As soon as he mentions the whore dolls, he realizes that he really is getting drunk. The whore dolls are one of his jokes on himself, part of one of the mental discussions he sometimes has with himself. He has imagined himself being interviewed by a ghostwriter for his as-told-to autobiography, after he has become president of the company. The writer is a young snot who thinks Matthew is an idiot. Gradually Matthew feeds him, deadpan, his line of parody toys, as if they had actually been produced, were part of the history of the company, the secret of Matthew's success. At first these fake toys are just a little odd, but as Matthew goes on they grow odder and odder, become funnier and funnier, until the kid's rolling on the floor with laughter. The book they write together is a hilarious parody of corporate life, and it redeems all the years Matthew spent in toys. The writer develops a boundless respect and admiration for Matthew, and they become pals. Everybody needs a pal.

Matthew is amused by this discovery that he's as drunk as he is. He feels detached from his drunk self, a little superior to him, disapproving but indulgent, as if he were BW watching Matthew and saying to himself, "Oh, what does it matter? He hasn't gotten good and drunk for ages. Let him go." It's true. Matthew hasn't gotten good and drunk for a long time, not since Liz left. He got drunk that night, but it wasn't good; it was a sullen, lonely, feeling-sorry-for-himself drunk, and he hated it. Since then he's been drinking steadily and regularly, too much, he knows, but only in the evening, and never at a rate that gets him out of control. He's over the line now, though, he can tell, and he's glad. He feels like having a fling, feels like letting himself go with these old friends, these pals. He knows they'll take care of him. He takes another sip of his drink to seal the pact with himself. *Self*, he says to himself, *we're going to get plastered.*

"By the way," he says aloud. "You may be interested in knowing where I got the inspiration for Hester and her pals."

"We probably are," says Jack.

"Well," says Matthew, "I got the inspiration from a trip I made, when I was in high school. To Juarez. Mexico. I was the recipient of a grant. From the— Hmm. The what? Some agency. I forget. Some agency that was supposed to encourage science study among youth after Sputnik. The National Science Foundation, that's it. So I went to the New Mexico Institute of Mining and Technology for the summer. I was fifteen. I'm not making this up. I was the smartest kid in my high school class."

At that time, Matthew wanted to be a theoretical physicist, but after a year in college he discovered that, although he probably understood physics better than all but a few thousand human beings, he would never enter the small circle of people who really understood, understood well enough to advance the science. If he kept at it, he might keep chipping away at the flinty bit he didn't adequately understand, but he didn't want to be a plodder. There was nothing else he wanted to excel at, and so it no longer mattered what he did. Like a man in a rowboat who meant to row across a bay but finds himself exhausted in the middle, he let himself drift. In time, certain things came floating his way, and, drifting, he bumped into some flotsam now and then, and that was what had passed for progress since the day of his grand disappointment, the day when his real aspirations ended.

"Anyway, one weekend some of us took a trip to Juarez. Specifically, to Irma's. This whorehouse. We walked in, and there were the whores. Just, bang, there they were. I don't know what I'd expected, I guess I thought they'd be hidden or something, not just right out there waiting for us. But there they were. The first whores I'd ever seen. Dozens of them. Lined up along one wall, like a row of chorus girls. Or like a bunch of waitresses, for that matter. And what struck me right away was how different they were. How different one was from another. I'd never seen, or never noticed, such *diversity* in women. The girls I knew were all sort of alike. Or at least they seemed alike. Here was the whole *catalog*. Short ones, tall ones, big ones, small ones, just like the song. Some were so *adult*—not old, exactly, but *women*. Others looked like girls. Most of them were not pretty. They wore too much makeup for my taste, and they were—coarse somehow. Except one. One, I think, was quite pretty. But you know, as soon as I say that, I'm not sure if it's right. Was the pretty one at Irma's or was she at a strip joint we went to?"

"Matthew!" says Effie. "What revelations! Whorehouses? Strip joints? I never heard any of this before."

"I've been saving a lot of stuff for my authorized biography. Anyway, I can't remember just what this cute one looked like very well, which is kind of weird, because I remember other things from that night much better. There was a cop car chasing another car right down the main street, a big old Hudson. And there was a huge crash. I mean, the chase ended in a crash. Right in front of us. And we ate some chicken at a little restaurant, and it was kind of rare. Sort of green in the joints. And we bought western hats, straw. But none of that, none of those memories, comes back to me on its own, you know? It's always this memory of the lineup of whores that comes back. The *availability* of all those women still sort of *haunts* me, as an idea."

"And did you choose the cute one?" It's Effie who asks.

Matthew raises an eyebrow, grins his half grin. "I told you, I have to save some things for the authorized biography. But get this. One of the other kids— You won't believe this. He wired home for money on the spot, from this whorehouse, and spent the next four days there. At Irma's. I swear to God. The rest of us covered for him, said he was sick, did his homework." A pause. "So, anyway, Hester Hooker. But that's not all." Is there any stopping Matthew now? "We're coming out with a line of handicapped dolls, because we think that kids will grow up to be more tolerant of deformities if they get used to handling them on a small scale. And a line of warriors who actually bleed, lose limbs, die, decompose."

"Matthew," says Richard.

"Ooops. Sorry. But wait, I have one more. A little pet project of mine. And I think it's going to be a huge hit. A lifelike vinyl penis that little girls can strap on, sort of like a garter belt. It's hooked to a water tank that fits in the small of the back, so girls can piss like boys." He looks to Jack and Richard. "You remember those macho pissing contests when you were a kid? Now girls can enter! Not only enter, but win!"

"Pricks for Chicks," says Belinda spontaneously. Matthew is stunned. She stepped on his punch line. Not that what she said was exactly his punch line. It was better. Belinda laughs at her own joke, and Matthew realizes that she too is drunker than she ordinarily gets.

"Do you realize," he asks the whole table in a lowered voice, "that we're all bombed?"

"It's unavoidable," says Richard. "They keep you waiting so long."

"Do you think the waitresses notice?" asks Jack. "Do they wonder why most of the people in here keep bumping into the walls?" He touches Effie's arm and asks, as if in the voice of one of the waitresses, "Mary, did you ever notice anything about these people who eat here?"

Effie glances around the room and answers as another waitress. "Nope," she says.

"Well, they're all drunk, dearie. Schnockered. Plastered. Blotto."

"Well, yeah, you know, I *have* noticed that."

"Why do you suppose that is, darlin'?"

Effie inclines her head and thinks. "It must be that a lot of drunk people come here to eat fish because there's some myth about fish being good for warding off a hangover."

"No kidding!" says Jack. "'Warding off,' you say! Warding off! Is that it, 'warding off'? What the fuck would that mean, exactly, honey?'"

"Oh, shut up. Maybe fish is supposed to sober you up. The flaky fish flesh absorbs the alcohol or something like that."

"'Flaky fish flesh'?" says Richard.

Jack deals him a stern look, still in character, and says, "Now you keep out of this, Charlene, darlin'. Mary and I are having a serious discussion about the inebriation of our clientele. You just go off in a corner somewhere and practice saying 'flaky fish flesh,' okay?"

"Fish is brain food, too, you know," says Effie.

"So?"

"So maybe, I'm only saying *maybe*, these people think that eating fish while they're drinking will restore the brain cells that the alcohol destroys."

Nobody laughs.

Richard asks, "What do you do, Belinda?"

Belinda says, "I work for Zizyph. Zizyph Software? It's a computer software company." She bursts out laughing. "Of course it's a computer software company. That's why it's called Zizyph Software." She laughs again and shrugs and looks at Matthew, and he realizes again how nervous she must be, meeting his pals. Then another look crosses her face. She looks puzzled. It occurs to Matthew that she might be wondering why on earth she should be nervous about the impression she makes on his old friends, wondering something along these lines:

Why should I be trying to impress them? Why should I be trying to impress anyone? *After all, I'm vice-president of a company with a snazzy logo and up-to-the-minute office decor, not a hidebound toy company. Maybe Matthew and I have been going out too long.*

I'm beginning to act as if I'm serious about him. I'm behaving like a prospective second wife. Soon one of these people is going to ask me if I have children. They'll want to know whether my children would be a burden to Matthew.

"I don't know if you've heard of it," Belinda says.

"Oh, I certainly *have* heard of it," says Richard. "I wish I'd bought some of your stock when you went public. You guys are a howling success."

"Well, the company has grown," says Belinda, nodding her head, "very fast. It's—exciting." Matthew can see that she's flattered. She looks down and smiles a modest smile, but when she raises her head that odd look comes over her again for a moment, and Matthew wonders again what she's thinking.

"What do you do there, Belinda?" asks Jack. His tone is polite, but this is beginning to seem like an inquisition.

"I work in new-product planning."

"She's *head* of new-product planning," Matthew says. The pride in his voice surprises him; Belinda, too.

"Well, that's not so much," says Belinda. "When I began working there, I *was* new-product planning. I was also the customer service department. And personnel. And I helped in accounting. They used to keep their receipts in cardboard cartons. It was insane."

Richard: "You're kidding! They weren't using their own software to run the company?"

"They didn't *have* an accounting package then. They used—ah—a competing product."

Matthew says, in a tone much like a proud papa's, "Belinda actually designed the accounting software—"

"No, that's not really true. I—"

"It really is true," he insists. "I don't mean that she wrote the program, or anything like that, but she wrote out a set of requirements accounting software ought to meet—"

"I was really just reacting to the shortcomings of what I'd been using."

"—and that became the manifesto for ReCount. Zizyph commissioned somebody to write it, and it's now their most successful product. They would have been a one-product company without Belinda."

"Well—"

"And were you involved in the development after that?" asks Jack.

"A little."

"A little!" Matthew is out of control. "She organized all the field testing. She really guided the development of the whole product. Don't be so modest, Belinda."

A smile from Belinda. Matthew thinks she's secretly quite happy to have him trumpet her this way while she hangs back modestly.

"That's great," says Effie.

"Do you have any children, Belinda?" asks Richard.

Before Belinda can answer, the waitress, now accompanied by a couple of assistants, arrives with huge trays of food and begins delivering it with dispatch. Only the one who took the orders knows who ordered what, so the efficiency of this trio is low. The lieutenants stand around wearing the looks of friendly concern they were taught during employee training.

"What the heck is this?" asks Jack.

"Food," says Matthew.

"Did we order food?"

"Once upon a time," says Richard.

None of them can, with complete certainty, remember what kind of potatoes he or she ordered, and the waitress in command seems not too certain, either. For the few moments that the delivery takes, the five of them watch, helpless, befuddled by this sudden rapid activity. They try to gather their thoughts, focus them on the food, notice whether they're getting what they want and what they ordered, and then suddenly it's over. The waitresses are all gone, and the group is left to itself again. The table's crowded with dishes large and small. Where a moment before there had been nothing, there is now a heap of food, bounty, plenty.

It's a traditional sort of plenty, probably just what a bunch like this would have ordered ten, twenty, forty years ago: clam fritters about the size of golf balls, a Flynn's trademark, served in a basket lined with a napkin translucent with grease; prime rib; fried scallops; fried haddock; baked stuffed shrimp; french fries, baked pota-

toes, Delmonico potatoes; coleslaw, carrots, green beans, beets, baked
beans; a platter of onion rings for the table; a basket of corn bread,
rolls, and sticky cinnamon buns; celery, carrot sticks, sweet gher-
kins, olives; and salad for the table served in a huge crockery bowl,
another trademark.

When they've begun to eat, Jack says, "Hey, where's my lobster?"

He begins lifting the baskets and napkins and bowls in front of
him, looking for his lobster. "Anybody see it?" he asks. "I've got
my french fries here, my coleslaw, corn bread, onion rings, salad,
pickles, and all this other shit. I've got my lobster basket and I've
got this lobster-ripping thing and this cracking implement. I've got
my bib here—"

"It's got a *picture* of a lobster," says Effie.

"Yep, it's got a picture of a lobster, and it's got this Flynn's logo
on it. I've got a stack of napkins, and a condom—"

"That's a moist towelette," says Effie.

"No kidding?" He examines it. "Uh-oh," he says. "I may be in
some trouble back home. Anyway, I've got all this stuff, but I have
got no lobster."

"Maybe there just wasn't any room for it," Richard says.

Everyone begins lifting things as Jack did, as if hunting for the
lost lobster, snorting and giggling like naughty kids.

The trio of waitresses returns, bearing lobsters for Grandma and
the group of ten. Matthew and his pals follow the trio with their
eyes, their heads swiveling as one.

"You know something?" says Jack. "I'll bet one of those lobsters
is mine."

"I'll go get it for you," says Effie. "Which one is it?" She actually gets out of her chair.

"Effie," says Richard. There isn't a touch of humor in his voice.
Only caution.

Jack looks at Matthew. When he sees that he's caught Matthew's
eye, he mouths, "Dickhead." Belinda sees it; she snorts again.

All of a sudden the waitress is back again, looking baffled, holding a tray with a mammoth old lobster on it. "Anybody missing a

lobster here?" she asks. It strikes four-fifths of the table as the fun-
niest thing they have ever heard.

Matthew has had far, far too much to drink. The wise thing, as
soon as Jack finishes his lobster, would be to say his good-nights,
get into a cab with Belinda, and head for home, but he's a drink or
two beyond reason, and he seems to be having such fun, they all
seem to be having such fun, they all seem so clever and talented, that
Matthew doesn't want the group to break up. He wants them to
come back to his place. At a couple of points in the evening he has
almost spilled the beans about being B. W. Beath, and he knows,
somewhere in the back of his mind, that if he persuades the whole
gang to come to his place for a last drink, he's sure to tell them, and
then he'll stand out even within this superior group.
   "Listen," he says a little too loudly, "as soon as Jack finishes that
lobster, let's go back to my place for a cognac. I just bought a great
CD of old Coleman Hawkins stuff. 'Body and Soul'? Perfect for
cognac sipping. And I want you to see my place, and my view."
   Objections are raised by Effie and Richard: it's late, the kids are
with a baby-sitter, and so on, but Jack is eager, and together he and
Matthew persuade Effie to call the sitter, find out if the girl can stay
overnight, and come along for one drink.

They make their way outside in four styles of wobble; only Jack
walks with certain steps. The fierce wind, funneled by buildings,
makes them hug themselves. Cabs are waiting at the door, since
Flynn's is a perfect spot to find fares to downtown hotels. Jack steps
up to the first one, opens the door, motions Effie and Richard in, and
calls out to Belinda and Matthew, "Come on. We can all fit. Belinda can sit on my lap. Come on, come on." He's waving, puffing
frozen breath.
   "I don't think they can take more than four," says Belinda.
   "That's right," Matthew says. "He'll give us a hard time."
   "Why should he care?" says Jack. He slides in and pats his lap.
"Come on, Belinda. Matthew can sit in front." Belinda grins and

shrugs and settles herself on Jack's lap. Matthew opens the front door. The cabdriver, a woman, says, "I can't take five. I can't do it."

"It's not far," Matthew says. "And it's so cold. Can't you just take us?"

"No."

"But they're already in. Just go, okay?"

"Look, it's not my rule. I'm telling you, I can't do it. One of you has to get out."

Matthew looks back through the plastic partition. It's all laughs and good times back there. He has the impression that they aren't even aware that the cab hasn't started moving. He knocks on the plastic. Everyone looks at him.

"She can't take five," he shouts. "Maybe Belinda and I should—"

Jack makes a rubbing motion between his thumb and forefinger, and he mouths the word *money*. He looks at Matthew as if he should know that money's the answer.

Matthew has never done anything like this. He has never offered a bribe for a favor, for special treatment, never tried to get a rule bent, never even slipped a maître d' a folded bill to get a table. He wonders if it works, if it will work now. He takes his wallet out and looks into it. *How much?* He pulls out a ten. He looks at the driver.

"Here," he says.

She takes the bill, flips the flag down, puts the cab in gear, and drives off. Matthew feels absolutely wonderful for about a block and a half, but then he begins to wonder whether he could have gotten her to take them for *five* dollars, and then he begins to wonder about paying the fare. *Should I tip on top of the bribe? What's the etiquette here?* The driver asks about the restaurant, whether it's still "as good as it used to be." *She must think I'm a tourist.* Matthew comes close to telling her that he's B. W. Beath. When they arrive at his building, he adds a dollar to the fare.

By the time Matthew has brought out cognac and liqueurs, he has the feeling that each of them has come to the independent conclusion that coming here was a bad idea, but none of them wants the evening to end on a wrong note, so they are all making a big effort to try to enjoy it.

He stands beside Jack at the windows, looking out at the lights.

"You have a great view, Matthew," says Jack. Matthew wonders whether there is a social comment lurking in that remark.

"It's pretty, isn't it?" he ventures.

"Sure is," says Jack. "Must be the best view of the *get-toe* available. You ought to invite the black folks up, let 'em see how good they look from a distance."

Matthew laughs uneasily. He wonders what Jack thinks about the whole question of race now that he's a *rich* black guy.

"What's with the hole, Matthew?" asks Richard.

"Hole?" Matthew says. "What hole? This hole? This hole represents the unstinting efforts of our management company, Ingalls and Nelson, known affectionately as Ignore and Neglect, to discover the source of—ah—" He's embarrassed to say it. The idea that his apartment stinks is as embarrassing as the idea that he might.

"Leaks?" asks Richard.

"Yeah," Matthew says. This seems less painful to admit. He glances at Belinda. She looks surprised. He shrugs. The idea that his friends now think his apartment leaks begins to embarrass him, but not as much as their thinking it stinks would, and not as much as, say, having to admit that *he* has begun to leak, that he's started dribbling after urinating, like an old man. "Let's not talk about it," he says.

"Okay," says Jack. "Let's have a drink and put on some music and put out the lights and look out over the city and watch the cops hassle my people."

Matthew pours and Belinda hands the drinks around. The story of Jack's missing lobster is told again. Richard mimics Jack's looking for it under the plates of food. Belinda asserts that she and Effie could have talked the people at the next table out of one of theirs. Jack snickers and rubs his hands together and vows to get even somehow in his commercial. Matthew chuckles and says, "Don't worry, I'll get even in my review."

"Are you writing restaurant reviews?" asks Effie.

Matthew looks over at Belinda and grins. "Shall I tell them?" he asks.

"Up to you," she says.

"What do you think? They're not going to spread it around. Why not?"

"I don't know, Matthew," says Belinda.

"Maybe I'd better not," he says.

"Well, you have to now," says Effie. "Whatever it is, you have to tell us now."

Matthew looks to Belinda again, gives her a questioning look.

"Matthew," she says, "I don't have anything to do with this. If you want to tell them, then tell them."

"Oh, it's no big deal," Matthew says. "I write for *Boston Biweekly*. Restaurant reviews. 'The Epicurean Adventures of B. W. Beath'?"

"We read that!" say Richard and Effie almost simultaneously.

Matthew could hug them.

"Oh, I can't wait to see what you say about Flynn's," says Effie.

"I can't wait to see what you *remember* about Flynn's," says Jack.

"Maybe it *is* time to call it a night," says Belinda.

She's looking at Matthew. He realizes that he had fallen asleep for a moment.

"They keep you parked in that damned lounge so long," Matthew says.

No one responds. They begin to go. There are visits to the bathrooms, the getting of coats. Matthew gathers glasses, begins cleaning up in a desultory way. Effie helps and takes the opportunity to whisper to him, "That was a nice thing you did."

For a moment Matthew has no idea what she means. He runs through the events of the evening. Was there some little kindness that he's forgotten? Around the corner from the kitchen, where they're out of everyone's sight for a moment, Effie kisses him, quickly, impulsively. It isn't much of a kiss, but it is a kiss, and when she pulls away and looks at him, something lively flickers in her eyes and she repeats the kiss, just another peck, but a kiss. Matthew remembers what she means, why she's kissing him, and he's ashamed, but he hazards a return kiss anyway, and she accepts it and squeezes his arm. He's glad that he's been so regular at the health club.

Then suddenly everyone's at the door, and then out the door, waiting for the elevator. Belinda's leaving, too, and Matthew doesn't ask her to stay. He's not too drunk to know that he's too drunk for sex. He might as well save himself the humiliation of failure. She blows him a kiss and says she'll call him in the morning, and they're gone. Matthew weaves in the doorway for a moment, and then he shuts and locks the door and goes to bed.

He lies on the bed in his clothes for a minute, but then he's disgusted by the idea of falling asleep drunk and dressed. He sits on the edge of the bed and pulls his things off, tosses them onto the floor. He pulls his wallet from his jacket and takes the bills from it. He counts them three times and decides to believe the third count: fifty-seven dollars. He puts the money on the bedside table. He promises the memory of Effie's heart-shaped face that he'll take it with him on his way to the health club in the morning and give it to the beggar who stands at the corner every morning and asks, with downcast eyes, "Anything today? Anything at all?"

However, when morning comes he will have the vague, unsettling feeling that he made a fool of himself. He'll remember Hester Hooker, and the idea of distributing money to the poor, and he'll be embarrassed. He'll put the bills back into his wallet, and when he sees the beggar, he'll keep his head down and pass without pausing.

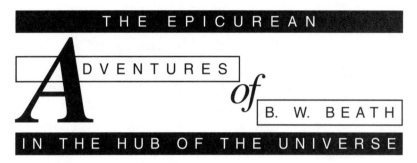

THE EPICUREAN

ADVENTURES *of* B. W. BEATH

IN THE HUB OF THE UNIVERSE

Flynn's Olde Boston Eating & Drinking Establishment

Sometimes, when a bit of undigested mutton awakens us at night, we lie in the dark, musing. You know the sort of thing. What is the point of life? What has become of our old pals? Do any olde Bostonians ever go to **Flynn's**? Recently, we decided that we had to know the answer to at least *one* of these questions, so we called some old pals who have spent the last few years seeking the point of life in Ohio, invited them for a visit, and took them to Flynn's.

We squeezed past the little stand selling T-shirts, beer mugs, baseball caps, and coasters emblazoned with the legend "Flynn's—A Taste of Olde Boston," and joined a small mob of people from states in roughly the same neck of the woods as Ohio until we were invited to wait in the lounge.

At this point, we would like to say something on the subject of parking. Did you know that on Beacon Hill a parking space costs more than a one-bedroom condominium? It's enough to keep you awake at night, isn't it? Actually, though, that's not the sort of parking we mean. We mean the practice of making one wait for a table in

the bar or lounge so that the establishment makes a larger profit on liquor. At Flynn's, parking is a tradition. It is even supposed to be part of the fun. One never knows whom one will meet while waiting at Flynn's (though one can be pretty sure that he will be a bathroom-fixture salesman from one of the many states that seem to be located in the Ohio region). Most diners are drunk as skunks by the time they lurch out of the lounge and into the dining room. Presumably, this is, like everything else at Flynn's, a tradition.

The lounge looks like the setting for a beer commercial—in fact, all of Flynn's looks like a beer commercial. It's a big, noisy place that, like it or not, says "Boston" to the rest of the country, as do, presumably, codfish cakes, scrod, chowder, lobster, roast beef, baked beans, boiled budayduhs, and Hahvud beets, baked apples, Indian pudding, corn bread, and sticky buns. One of the famously brisk serving wenches tosses the sticky buns onto the table as soon as everyone has ordered another drink, so that when your pals return to the nation's buckeye zone they will be able to say, as proof of their having tasted the *real*

Boston, "Isn't it *queer* the way they serve you sweet rolls before the meal?" (By the way, we can't help wondering whether another expectation about Boston isn't confirmed at Flynn's. The dining room is a sea of white faces. The occasional black, brown, or beige diner is as surprising as pumpernickel would be in the breadbasket. We spotted a single black diner on our visit. The only other nonwhites were Japanese, a group of businessmen who, in a touching moment of international cliché exchange, snapped pictures of one another wearing lobster bibs.)

And now, we have something we would like to confess. Forgive us, Father, but we were brought up in N*w Y*rk, raised on the clam chowder known hereabouts as M*nh*tt*n. Our first impression of what Bostonians consider the real goods, chowderwise, was that it must be a tonic for ulcer victims. We have, since then, found some wonderfully creamy examples that made us like the stuff, but what we got at Flynn's is not one of them. This is the Wonder Bread of chowders.

Visitors expect things Bostonian to be olde, and Flynn's satisfies that expectation, too. We're not talking only about the lobsters, either. Flynn's really *is* an old establishment, the Flynn family having opened the doors in 1785 (to, we suppose, a group of Cleveland Indians on a package tour). But to *be* old is not enough. To fulfill the expectations of the tourist, the place must *look* old, and Flynn's has accomplished this supremely well, through the simple expedient of, apparently, not cleaning the place for the last hundred fifty or so years. (We may be wrong about this. It *is* possible that the stains darkening the floors and walls have been sprayed on for effect.)

A warning: Quite suddenly, late in the evening, just when you are beginning to think that it must be about time to go home, a gang of famously brisk waitresses will arrive at your table and serve food. By this time, you will have been consoling and distracting yourselves with alcohol for so long that the idea that food might be served will have slid into the dark area of your brain where most of the cells are dead. Your pals are apt to be confused, even frightened, by this horde of waitresses bearing huge steaming trays of stuff. Assure them that it's traditional, one of the quaint ways of Olde Boston.

Based on what we can remember of our investigation, we can say, without fear of contradiction, that people who reside in Boston don lobster bibs at Flynn's only when hosting out-of-town pals. Beware! The pals may decide to get even. They may press you to visit them, and then make you eat buckeyes or something. Permit us to make a suggestion. Mail this review to your pals. Perhaps they'll decide to visit San Francisco and eat cioppino.

—BWB

**Flynn's Olde Boston Eating
& Drinking Establishment**
16 Tetford Street, 555-3232.
American Express, Visa, MasterCard, Diners Club, checks.
Handicapped: difficult access.
Lunch 12–3, Monday–Friday.
Dinner 6–11 Tuesday–Sunday.
Reservations are not accepted, never have been accepted, and, in the interest of tradition, never will be accepted.

3

Dolce Far Niente

Because Belinda's birthday fell in the middle of the week, when she and Matthew were both too busy to celebrate it, they agreed to celebrate this evening, Friday. When Matthew arrives at Belinda's, he asks his cabdriver to wait and dashes up the stairs. The toothsome Leila lets him in. In her eyes Matthew sees more coy sparkle than usual.

"Come on in," she says. "Mom'll be down in a minute. She's got a surprise for you, and I'm supposed to brace you for it."

"Brace me?" Now this is provocative; a surprise, and not just a run-of-the-mill surprise, but one for which Matthew must be braced. What might that be? A weasel of a thought crosses his mind, darting from cover to cover, shamefully: the virginal Leila has asked Belinda—no, begged Belinda—to ask Matthew to initiate her in the famous joys of love. He imagines mother and daughter, blushing, stammering, beating around the bush until they finally come out with it, and then the awkward march to the bedroom, the nervous jokes. Mother and daughter, lying side by side, awaiting him, while he folds his clothes. How thrilling! How flattering! How unlikely! The thought slinks off, but not far; it's sure to return when he's alone. Disappointed by the thought that whatever the surprise might be, it isn't likely to be that, he hangs his coat in the hall closet. Leila disappears into the living room, and almost at once Matthew hears her stirring a martini.

"Is that a martini I hear?" he asks. As soon as he's said it, it strikes him as the wrong kind of line—too old. He just can't find a way to talk to Leila. He wishes he could, but it's hopeless.

Leila presents the drink to him, holding the glass by the stem, with both hands, as if she were elevating a chalice. She's giggling.

"You can tell a martini by the sound?" she asks.

"Ahhhh, yesssss," Matthew says, drawing it out. He's trying to imitate W. C. Fields. "A very useful skill in the event of a black-ouuuuut. Enables one to find his way to a haven of safety and comforrrrrrt." *Not bad, really not bad,* he tells himself. He's delighted that the bit came to him so quickly—and the words, too. *"A haven of safety and comfort"—that really sounds like W. C. Fields,* he thinks. He's feeling pretty loose tonight; he doesn't feel half as ill at ease with Leila as he usually does. Her breasts are hidden under a heavy sweater, which helps, and— Uh-oh, there's a blank smile on her face; she probably didn't recognize W. C. Fields, probably doesn't even know who W. C. Fields was; nothing in her expression suggests that she does. But wait! Another humorous routine has occurred to Matthew. *What the heck,* he thinks, *I might as well go ahead with it.* The girl probably thinks he's an addled old duffer anyway, maybe he can boost himself up a notch, possibly to funny old coot.

He says, "It really *is* an unmistakable sound, the mixing of a martini. When I was a kid, radio stations used to have these sound quizzes. They'd play a sound, and if they called you up, you'd try to guess what it was. A toaster popping up, something like that. Rock 'n' roll stations used to have these." *Ha! That'll show her.* "My *mom's friend—my mom has this cute boyfriend—and he was in on the birth of rock 'n' roll."* He makes a mental note to tell her about lying in bed with the measles and hearing "Rock Around the Clock" for the first time. *Mmm, maybe not.* Measles might suggest that he was a sickly child, make him seem weak. He throws himself into the routine that inspiration has thrust upon him, beginning with the voice of the radio announcer: "All right, Mrs. Edward Dingle, for a *complete set* of waterless cookware, *what* is this sound?"

Will she know what waterless cookware is? he wonders. *Oh, shit, the cab. I should go out and tell the cab to keep waiting. But if I stop this now, I'll look completely ridiculous. I hope he waits. I hope he doesn't come to the door or something—make me look ridiculous.*

He makes the sound of a martini being stirred, and the gesture of stirring a martini, too, so that Leila will be sure to get it: "Linkala-plinkala, linkala-plinkala, linkala-plinkala."

Am I making a fool of myself? he asks himself.

In his own voice he continues: "Well, I would recognize that anywhere. It's a martini. Somebody stirring a martini, but Mrs. Dingle hasn't the faintest idea."

In the voice of Mrs. Dingle: "Um, uh, ah, oh, gee."

In his own voice: "A *martini*."

In the voice of the announcer: "Fifteen seconds!"

His own voice: "A martini, damn it, a *martini!*"

Leila laughs. *At the routine, or at me?*

Mrs. Dingle: "Somebody stirring tea—"

Matthew: "A martini, Mrs. Dingle, you ignorant teetotaler!"

Mrs. Dingle: "No, not tea—"

Matthew: "Ah! Finally!"

Mrs. Dingle: "*Coffee!* No—*tea*. Somebody stirring a cup of tea."

The announcer: "Oh, I'm *sorry*, Mrs. Dingle —"

A wavelet of unhappiness washes over Matthew now that he's finished. His shoulders sag. "Well," he says. "Something like that." He can't believe that he's just done what he's just done. He's not like this. He doesn't act out. *I'm behaving like a lovesick ado-lescent. In a minute I'll be crushing beer cans with one hand. No, that's not a feat anymore—all the beer cans are made of aluminum.*

"I—uh—have to go tell the cabdriver to keep waiting," he says. "I'll be right back."

Trudging back up the steps to the house, Matthew wonders whether those radio quizzes still exist. He hasn't heard one in years. Perhaps he would if he listened to talk radio or rock 'n' roll stations, but he doesn't listen to that sort of thing much anymore. He does listen to rock music now and then, but he can't enjoy listening to it for any length of time; the oldies make him feel old, and the new stuff makes him feel silly. Usually he starts the day with a dose of public-radio news, and then he listens to the first hour of a classical music program before he leaves for the office. He used to regret that he didn't have time to listen to the whole program, which continues until noon, but then on a holiday he listened all the way through and found that with each succeeding hour the music was less and less to his liking—the crisp architecture of Bach, the mathematician's fa-vorite, gave way little by little to things looser and, it seemed, nas-tier; Bach soothes him, Beethoven worries him, Shostakovich terri-fies him. By the final hour, the show seemed to Matthew to have become a hodgepodge of clangorous anger and self-serving inter-views that he neither understood nor liked. This discovery that the program wasn't all Bach led Matthew to the realization that for most of his life he had thought that he was missing something, in the sense that what he was missing was better than what he had. Now he was confronted with the possibility that that assumption was en-tirely wrong. Perhaps there was no reason to feel that he was miss-ing something better than what he had, no reason at all. Perhaps what he was missing was in fact worse than what he was getting, nothing but the various equivalents of jangling music and carping braggarts. There was certainly no reason to covet that. What a lib-erating idea this was at first, but, after a little time and thought, what a depressing idea it became. If what he was getting was the best there was, and it seemed none too good, then what was the basis for hope? It is a curse of the mind inclined to sadness that, given time, it will find the rotten spot in even the ripest, most promising idea.

"What's the surprise?" Matthew asks.

Leila only winks. She's not going to say anything about it. "Try that drink," she says. "See if it's any good."

He tries it. She's been mixing martinis for him nearly half her life, ever since her father taught her how, and Matthew's never had the heart to tell her that she uses too much vermouth. "Excellent!" he says.

For one lightning moment, he thinks of making a flirtatious remark, "You can mix my martinis anytime," but it sounds obscene to his mind's ear, so he doesn't say it—or anything else. Silence hangs in the air for a moment, and he begins to feel awkward, so he decides to go ahead and say it. "You can mix my martinis anytime," he says, but to show that it's a joke, merely a joke, he says it in his W. C. Fields voice. Too late, he realizes that if Leila doesn't know who the hell W. C. Fields was, then he must seem hideously goatish making such a suggestion in such a voice. He seems to be getting deeper and deeper into trouble. Maybe he should just go home.

"So," he says, "you're not going to tell me anything about the surprise?"

"Nope. Can't tell." Shrugging, she makes a girlish display of secrecy. This shrug, with her hands clasped backward in front of her pubes, her arms stretched straight, her shoulders hunched forward, makes her breasts balloon beneath the sweater. *Is she inviting me to tickle the secret out of her?* His composure's slipping.

"Are you ready, Matthew?" calls Belinda from the top of the stairs.

He takes another swallow of the drink, throws a grin at Leila. "Now I am," he says. "Shall I close my eyes?"

"No, no. I want to make an entrance."

So it's clothing, Matthew thinks. *A dress, probably, something daring that she wouldn't ordinarily buy herself. Good. Great.* He has often wished she would wear something slinky now and then, and this is the perfect night for it.

She steps into view at the top of the stairs wearing a white fur coat. She stands there a moment, with her hands in the pockets, striking a model's pose, making cat's eyes, sucking her cheeks in. Then she begins walking down the the the stairs, vamping.

The coat is startling. The skins are dyed mink, sewn in such a way as to create the effect of vertical stripes, white on white, and the collar and cuffs are ermine, softer and fluffier than the mink, with the slightest hint of black at the tips of the hairs. It's a staggering, breathtaking coat.

"Wow," says Matthew, and Leila giggles.

Belinda lets her face relax; it assumes a look that says, "Haven't I done something silly?"

"I got it on sale," she says. "I'm not going to tell you what it cost. I won't even tell you what it *would* have cost."

Belinda takes Matthew's arm, and they walk down the steps. The cabdriver, who has been watching for them, gets out of the cab—it would be fair to say that he *leaps* out of the cab—and comes around to open the door. This has never happened to Matthew before in his life. The driver begins sweeping at the seat with his hand, and saying something in so low a voice that Matthew can't be quite sure what it is, but it sounds to him like "'Scuse me, 'scuse me. Sorry, sorry. Dirty, dirty." Matthew and Belinda get into the cab, astonished. They look at each other, raise their eyebrows, struggle to keep themselves from laughing.

"If he were wearing a cap," Matthew whispers, "he would have touched it. And if he weren't bald, he would have tugged his forelock."

Dolce Far Niente is in the area where Belinda works, an area of spanking-new office buildings housing young companies engaged in microelectronics, computer software, genetic engineering, and any number of things involving lasers, many of which are offensive. Matthew looks around. "This whole section of town is all so new," he says. "What was here before—I mean, before all this?"

"Almost nothing. It was just a blank between two highways."

"Oh, yeah," says Matthew, recalling. "The only thing I remember about it is a lot of trucks. This is amazing. Last year it was a parking lot, now it's Houston."

He has the uneasy feeling that in one of these handsome buildings strange microscopic beings, the like of which have never been seen on earth before, are at this moment engineering their escape from a petri dish. *Do genetic engineering outfits use petri dishes?* he wonders. *Do they raise their manufactured microbes on agar, or are agar and petri dishes hopelessly out of date?*

"Do genetic engineering outfits grow their creatures in agar?" he asks. "In petri dishes?"

"What?" says Belinda. "What on earth makes you ask that?"

"I—" It seems too much to explain. "I don't know. I just wondered. Probably not. They've probably engineered some new stuff to feed the newer stuff. Something bred to be eaten. The perfect diet. Salvation of the planet. Feed the starving. Allow more breeding."

"Wow. Is it my coat that got you onto this?"

"What?"

"My coat made you bring up the subject of hunger?"

"What? No! Oh, no, not at all. I love your coat. You look spectacular in it."

The restaurant is in a building that used to be a service station for the trucks that were kept here. It seems a small and frightened thing, cowering in the presence of the towering. It has been decorated, inside and out, at great expense, to look like a ruin. Here and there are artful imitations of patches of peeling stucco, baring brick beneath. One window has been painstakingly painted with some clear goo to make it look as if there are bullet holes in it. Just inside the door a safe stands crazily, one corner embedded in the floor as if it had fallen from a great height. A section of one interior wall has been torn away along a jagged line, the vacancy covered with glass, so that the plumbing and wiring and heating ducts show. It reminds Matthew of his apartment.

Belinda's coat has done something to her; she strides into the restaurant with an assertiveness that Matthew has never seen in her before.

Almost as soon as they have entered the room, a voice from the bar calls, "Matthew!" Matthew turns at the sound of his name and recognizes Harold, chief of the engineering department at Manning & Rafter Toys, a man Matthew has some contact with nearly every week, with whom he has worked closely on the development of a new toy, a plastic press for molding bricks of sand. At this moment, taken by surprise, he can remember this man only as Harold. "Hello!" Matthew says brightly, far more warmly than he would if he were able to remember Harold's last name, very much as if he had been hoping that he might run into Harold here. *What the hell is his name?* he asks himself. It won't come, won't come at all. Harold's motioning to him, making large loops in the air with his hand, inviting him into the bar. With Harold is his wife, whom Matthew has met several times. He cannot remember even her first name. He decides not to bother with introductions; he'll say a quick hello, and he and Belinda will retreat into the dining room.

Harold and his wife make ecstatic noises inspired by the coat. Belinda obliges them by doing her model's turn, making the coat flare as she whirls.

"It's a birthday present," says Belinda.

"We're here to celebrate," says Matthew. He begins to back away, taking Belinda by the arm.

"Well, so are we!" booms Harold. "It's Gwen's birthday, too." *Gwen. Of course.* "Let us buy you a drink!"

Neither Matthew nor Belinda is good at saying no in situations like this. Neither of them can say the truthful thing, that they would rather go to their table and eat their dinner alone. Instead they say, "Oh," and, "Well," and before they know it Harold has summoned the bartender, who stands behind the bar and regards them expectantly, waiting for their orders. What can they do? They order.

"So the coat is a gift from you, Matthew?" asks Harold.

"No," Matthew says. At first he's surprised that Harold would think he had given the coat to Belinda, but then he realizes that of course it must look that way. It's Belinda's birthday, Matthew brought her here to celebrate, and she's wearing a new fur coat; therefore Matthew must have given it to her. Logical thinking is the source of so many errors. "Belinda bought it herself," he explains. "I gave her a necklace." ("Necklace" is a little grand for the simple gold chain Matthew gave her, a nice enough gift, but not one that made much of a statement.)

"Oh, yes," says Belinda, "Matthew gave me a beautiful chain." She throws the coat open, spreading her arms wide, and there is the chain, gleaming against more of Belinda's chest than Matthew has ever before seen displayed in a public setting. He is astonished, but he is very pleased with himself to find that he does not say "Wow," or "Gosh."

"Wow," says Harold. For an instant there's the strong possibility that he may reach out and hook his finger through the bottom curve of the chain, which lies almost out of sight between Belinda's breasts, but he thinks better of it, and to ensure that he doesn't lose control of his hands, he puts them in his pockets. "That's lovely," he says. "Really lovely."

"Let me check the coat," Matthew says. He realizes that he has said "the coat," not "your coat." He slips it off Belinda's shoulders and is startled to discover that her dress, which has so little front, has no back. Black crepe falls from Belinda's shoulders in languid folds to an arc below her waist. *Catenary arc,* he thinks, and because he has little control left he says, at last, "Wow."

He checks the coat. The young woman who is both coat-check girl and greeter takes it from him as if it were a child and smiles in a way that seems to suggest that if there are fur coats like this one to be had, she might be interested in seeing more of Matthew. He is, he realizes, almost certainly a victim of wishful thinking in so interpreting that smile, but he gets a nice lift from it anyway.

"We've invited you and Belinda to join us," says Harold when Matthew returns. He's smiling, trying to look relaxed, and trying, really trying, not to look down the front of Belinda's dress. He's losing both struggles, Matthew notices. Droplets of sweat dot his upper lip, and his eyes keep darting to Belinda's cleavage. The headwaiter is holding menus, ready to show the four of them to a single table; there seems to be no escape. Matthew and Belinda resign themselves, allow themselves to be led. *Maybe,* each thinks on the way to the table, *this won't be so bad. It might even be fun—who knows?*

They are shown to a table beside the glass-covered portion of wall. As soon as they sit down, Gwen takes a look around the room and sends up a wailing complaint: "Oh, everyone here is so *young.*"

So much for the possibility that it might not be so bad, thinks Belinda, but she's grateful to Gwen for not actually bursting into tears or thumping her breast.

Matthew can't keep himself from surveying the other diners to see whether Gwen is right. He's pleased to find that, with the exception of a child of six or so at the next table who has just knocked his water glass over, they don't seem so terribly young to him. Harold and Gwen must be about ten years older than he and Belinda, he decides.

"Do you realize how much effort has gone into making this place look like a wreck?" he says.

"Oh?" says Harold, as if he hadn't noticed. "I hadn't noticed." He looks around. "Reminds me of my childhood home," he claims.

Matthew gives him a chuckle, as a gift. He wonders how much truth there is behind the remark. At the office, Harold—what *is* his name?—always conducts himself as if he comes from wealth, his manner a pretense to upper-class disdain, but the truth is widely known: he's the son of immigrant parents who are still living, still speaking with embarrassing accents. Matthew has marveled that Harold apparently doesn't realize that everyone recognizes that he's only an aspirant to the genuine article, merely a snob.

"Oh. Look at that," says Matthew. "I hadn't noticed the leak stains over there. See? On the ceiling? They're probably painted on, aren't they? Trompe l'oeil leaks. They really look kind of attractive, the way they spread out that way."

"Like a topographic map," suggests Harold, after a moment's hesitation.

"Yes!" says Matthew. "And then the way they continue down the wall in sort of graceful waves."

"Like high-water marks along the shore," Harold offers, following a period of desperate invention.

"Mm-hm," says Matthew.

"Or the folds of Belinda's—ah—neckline," says Harold, responding to a genuine flash of inspiration. Having mentioned it, he seizes the opportunity he's given himself to glance down it, smiling as he does so a satisfied, oleaginous smile.

"Very good, Harold," says Matthew.

"He could be a writer," says Gwen. "I keep telling him he should write a book."

"You know," says Matthew, quite deliberately ignoring Gwen's remark, "this whole place gives me reason to take heart. You see," he says, addressing Harold and Gwen, "my apartment has a mysterious—odor." He tells the whole story, but this time there's a different quality to his telling. Under the influence of this setting, his trial has become a story. "So you see," he says after telling it, "this place has given me an idea. I've been looking at this problem in the wrong way. My thinking has been all wrong." He smacks himself on the forehead. "I've been thinking that I have to fix the place up when they finally get rid of the smell. I thought I had to bring it back to the condition it was in when I moved in. Make it brand new again. But now that I look around here, I see I don't have to do that at all."

"Ah-ha!" says Harold. "Here you have an entirely new aesthetic."

"Exactly."

"*L'esthétique du mal*," says Belinda.

"Very good," says Harold. "And if you embrace this *esthétique du mal*, it will save you a great deal of trouble and expense."

"You bet. Why repair the damage? I could just put some clear plastic over the hole in the wall—"

"Why bother?"

"Right. Why bother? Glue the old pieces of carpet back in place."

"Forget it. Leave the pad exposed."

"Good. Good. Very good." Matthew takes another look around, on the lookout for decorating tips. Something is missing, something that would be the perfect touch: one of the writings of the Neat Graffitist. What would fit here? He'll have to look through his collection and see, but here's a possibility, selected from the writings Matthew has copied into his notebook:

> ON SATURDAY, I WAS EATING SOME CHICKEN
> HERE, AT THIS SPOT, AND IT WAS PRETTY GOOD,
> BUT I GOT A BITTER TASTE IN MY MOUTH AND IT
> SPOILED EVERYTHING. THIS IS HOW IT IS.

A busgirl arrives at the table and deposits an earthenware vase, in which there is an arrangement of a single calla lily and a number of lengths of a skinny, twisted bread of a kind unfamiliar to all but one of our happy quartet. At the table next to them, the boy who spilled his water is now banging one of these loaves on the table.

"So what have we here?" asks Harold.

"My God," says Matthew. He pulls a length of bread from the vase. "Do these remind you of anything?"

"DNA?" suggests Gwen. She takes one.

"Oh, no, no," says Harold, working, straining, yearning to be funny. "Some kind of flora from Venus." Gwen wonders, as she has so many times before, why Harold feels this need to be amusing. It isn't in his nature. He's a serious man. He'd be much more successful in the company of others if he were content to be a serious man. It seems to her that if he would only admit to himself what he is, and work at being that, he could be regarded almost as a sage, but instead he wants to be a clown. *Why should that be? Is it this Belinda now, tonight, making him act the fool? She's so young! Those breasts! That dress! And the nerve, the wonderful nerve, just having the nerve to wear her hair that crazy way.* Gwen finds that she can't envy Belinda. She likes her. Gwen laughs at Harold's feeble joke and wonders again why she laughs, why she has stayed with him so long, too long, so that it seems too late now to leave.

"No," says Matthew. "That's not it. This bread is just like the stuff we made in the Boy Scouts, or I should say *tried* to make in the Boy Scouts. Bread baked on a stick? Weren't you in the Boy Scouts, Harold?"

"No. I went to a camp every summer, but I wasn't in the Boy Scouts." He's lying; there was never enough money in his family to send him to camp.

Of course not, Matthew thinks. *How could I have been so stupid? The Boy Scouts would be too plebeian for you to admit to.*

"Well," says Matthew, "one of the things a good Scout attempted to cook over an open fire was bread-on-a-stick. Or—wait a minute—maybe it was biscuits-on-a-stick. Whichever it was, you stripped the bark from a stick, and then you dried it out, I guess."

Right here, at this moment, just as he's beginning to describe the making of bread-on-a-stick, Matthew is struck by his strongest memory of Boy Scout camp. It isn't bread-on-a-stick; it's the memory of standing in a group of a dozen or more boys, in a hot canvas tent, watching one of the younger campers give a blow job to one of the older ones. Now and then, when Matthew recalls one memory or another from that period of his life, this memory pops up as well. He reacts to the memory exactly as he reacted to the original experience, with disgust and fascination. Witnessing this act was his first experience of sex between a couple, his only other experience having been solo experiments in his bedroom, at night while his mother sat up alone, in the tiny living room, just a door away, watching television.

"You made the batter," he says, "or the dough. I wish I could remember whether it was bread or biscuits. Maybe there were ways to do both. Anyway, you made the dough, let's say, and then you stretched it out—no, no—you *rolled* it out, like clay when you were making those bowls in grammar school. And then you wrapped it around the stick. Then you held the stick over the fire, and in a *remarkably* short time the dough became hard and black and tough as rope."

This is a success. Belinda and Gwen laugh. However, Harold feels that he must be more amusing, that he must take Matthew's success and build a greater one on top of it. He says, "Those were the precise instructions in the Scout manual, I imagine? 'Wrap dough around stick. Hold over fire. Cook until hard and black and tough as rope.'"

"Right," says Matthew. He chuckles. He breaks a piece from the bread and tries it. It's quite delicious. "Mmm," he says. "This is great. I wonder if this is the way it was supposed to come out in the Boy Scouts?"

"How do you think they make it here?" asks Gwen.

"They probably have Italian Boy Scouts in the kitchen, baking over an open fire," suggests Harold.

A waiter arrives to see if they want more drinks, and Gwen asks, "How do you make this bread?"

"The dough is wrapped around a stick—" the waiter begins.

Everyone bursts out laughing, except Matthew, who holds himself back because he doesn't want the waiter to feel that he's being insulted. He shrugs for the waiter's benefit, implying that his friends are hysterical or drunk. At least the waiter will know that the guy who brought the woman in the white mink isn't the kind of guy who makes jokes at the expense of waiters.

"—and then they bake it," says the waiter, pushing right on. It might seem that he's cloaking himself in the thinnest of dignities— overlooking what would otherwise vex him—but in fact it is the true dignity of the superior and self-possessed. This fellow is an Italian graduate student, studying physics at MIT, where he's near the top of his class. He is a cousin of the owner of this restaurant and pitches in now and then when a waiter doesn't show up for work. He likes the work, on the whole, and treats his waiting as a performance, but he has never enjoyed a night at the restaurant as much as this one, for he's quite smitten with Belinda.

"Over an open fire?" asks Harold.

"No, in a brick oven," says the waiter, smiling but cool. "Tonight it came out very well, I think." He pauses just an instant. "Usually it's hard and black. And *tiglioso*. Like a *fune*."

They are startled but recover quickly, Harold first. "*Fune*," he says. "Rope," as if he knew.

"Roper," Matthew mutters involuntarily, recalling Harold's name at last.

Drink orders are placed, and Gwen makes a point of not ordering alcohol. "Nothing with alcohol for me," she says. "Bring me anything, as long as it doesn't have alcohol."

"Perrier, Ramlösa, Evian, Pellegrino, Poland Spring, Saratoga, Lethe?" asks the waiter. Belinda catches it, and only Belinda. She looks at the waiter and shows a surprised smile. He grins.

"Oh, it doesn't matter to me," says Gwen. "Just as long as there's no alcohol. Perrier, I guess."

When the waiter has gone, Gwen says, in answer to a question no one has asked, "I haven't had a drink for a month or more. I think I was becoming an alcoholic."

"Oh," says Matthew. Belinda looks at him; it's a look that says, with no possibility for misinterpretation whatsoever, "Get me out of here."

"She took a quiz in a magazine," says Harold.

"I haven't missed it, really," says Gwen. "It's been fine. Just fine. I don't fall asleep so early, for one thing. I'm getting a lot more done."

"Don't you find that you're awfully tempted to have a cocktail when you go out?" Belinda asks. She raises her drink, sips it, raises her eyebrows, gives Gwen a questioning look over the rim of her glass.

"Oh, she has that solved completely," says Harold. "We don't go out anymore. If it weren't Gwen's birthday, we wouldn't be out now. We used to have friends, at least I seem to recall that we did, but they were all—*drinkers*. So of course we don't want to know them. They kept falling down stairs, sticking lamp shades on their heads, laughing at jokes that weren't half-funny, vomiting into their soup—disgusting, really. I don't know how we ever put up with them." This is delivered as a joke, of course, but Matthew and Belinda can tell that it's not a joke at heart, that Harold has lost something, has given up much more than he got in exchange. This thought chills Belinda, and it reminds Matthew of his former neighbor, Vic. When Matthew and Liz lived in Lincoln, Vic would telephone now and then, when he wanted drinking companions. Vic was a prosperous building contractor who had moved his wife and family from Brockton to Lincoln, thinking to give them the gift of the executive idyll, two acres of lawn in the best of the emerald suburbs; but his wife had wanted more from the move, a complete break with their past, which meant, specifically, that she didn't want any of his old cronies coming around, and she didn't want him stopping at his former haunts after work to drink with them. He was an executive now, living among executives, and he should get to know his executive neighbors and do his drinking with them, at home. Because Vic had met Matthew the day they moved in, Matthew was the only neighbor Vic ever invited over. The invitations always began with the same preliminary; Vic would say, as soon as Matthew answered the phone, "Hi. It's Vic. What're you doing, nothing?" Even after Matthew came to understand that this was only a conversational tic, he was offended by Vic's assumption that he wasn't doing anything, especially bothered by the fact that Vic had an uncanny knack of calling when, in fact, Matthew *was* doing nothing, at least nothing important enough to make it easy for him to say no to the invitation to come over for a few drinks. Because Vic's wife was a willowy blonde who thought the toy business "interesting" and Matthew clever, Matthew usually went. Sometimes Liz went along.

"So how are things with Mr. Matthew?" asks Harold. "I haven't seen much of you for the last couple of weeks." Matthew is almost certain that he had an interminable conversation with Harold only a couple of days ago, but perhaps it was in fact weeks ago. "Have you been up to anything interesting?" Matthew can hear in his tone the expectation that Matthew will say no, just as he used to hear it in Vic's.

"No!" shouts the boy at the next table. Our quartet glances over there.

"Well, he's right," says Matthew. "No, nothing much."

"Been skiing?"

"No. No, not yet. I'll go in February. *We'll* go in February, I hope." Matthew puts his hand on Belinda's. "I always go skiing in February. It's a tradition."

Always is an exaggeration, but for six seasons he has been going skiing in February. For five of those, he went with Liz. The winter after she left, he went alone to the same town in New Hampshire, where he stayed at the same inn, skied the same trails. He felt brave and independent making the reservation, and he was exhilarated driving up. He entertained fantasies of romantic encounters on the slopes, flirtations around the fire, but he didn't meet anyone. During the four days he spent there, before he gave up and left, he didn't see even one woman who seemed to him definitely alone, unambiguously alone enough for him to offer her a drink or to try to strike up a conversation. In fact, there were many, but Matthew didn't see them. The truth is that he was looking for Liz. For days before he had left for the inn, he had entertained the possibility that she might have had the same idea he had, and he had allowed himself to grow apprehensive that he might run into her on the slopes. It was she with whom he imagined a chance encounter, good-hearted teasing, a fireside flirtation, love under a comforter, but he never saw a sign of her. Recently he has been trying to get Belinda to go skiing with him, and he has found that the idea of their going to the same resort that he and Liz used to go to has great erotic potential. Belinda has been willing to go, as a favor to Matthew, because he seems to want it so much, even though she's a much better skier and prefers more difficult slopes than the one near the inn Matthew has in mind, but she's wary of leaving Leila at home alone. The thought has crossed Matthew's mind that he might suggest that Leila come with them. They could rent one of the time-share condominiums next to the lodge. Now *there's* an idea with erotic potential. What a cute little family they'd make!

"Seen any good movies?" asks Harold. This is almost a taunt.

"No," confesses Matthew.

"Plays?" asks Harold.

"Not lately." Matthew grins and shrugs.

Harold grips Matthew's shoulder, as if he were comforting him.

"Say, Matthew," he says, "you don't get out much, do you?"

"It seems that way," Matthew says.

"Read any good books?"

"Well—"

"Magazines, cereal boxes?" This is approaching cruelty, and Matthew's becoming annoyed.

What do I do with my time? he asks himself. Every month, when the cable television guide comes in, he reads through the descriptions of movies and makes a list of the ones he wants to tape, noting the channel, the dates, and the times when they will be shown. Most evenings he has his drinks, eats his dinner, watches one of the movies he has taped, programs the VCR to tape another, goes to bed, and falls asleep reading a magazine from the stack that accumulates on his bedside table. In the morning, while he's drinking his coffee and listening to the news or that classical music program, he checks to see that the movie was recorded successfully and, if it was, labels a three-by-five card with the title. By writing the titles along the ends and sticking the card sideways into the videocassette case, so that the name of the film projects above the case, he can get the titles of four films on one card before he has to discard it and use a new one. This hardly seems the stuff of interesting conversation.

"Oh, I know," says Matthew. "I've been—well—*playing* something interesting." He smiles at Belinda.

"Playing?"

"On my computer."

"A computer game," says Harold.

"Not a game," says Belinda.

"Not a game," says Harold, shaking his head at Gwen as if she had mistaken whatever it is for a game.

"It's something Belinda is developing. 'Picture Frame.' It's partly a mystery," says Matthew.

"More like a mystery," Harold says, again to Gwen.

"Not really," says Belinda. "It does have things in common with a mystery or computer games, adventure games, but it's really not a game. You don't win, you know? I mean, you don't even try to win, winning is irrelevant, just not in the picture. So it isn't like a game. And you don't try to solve anything, so it isn't like a mystery. You just find things out. You find things out about characters, and ideas, and things that have happened to people, so it's more like, well, *snooping*, spying on someone."

"More like snooping," Harold informs Gwen.

You jerk, thinks Belinda. "I'm not really ready to talk about it," she says. "It's still rough. Matthew's just been trying it out."

"I'm not getting it," says Gwen.

"Well," says Belinda. "Just to give you an idea—imagine that you're looking at your computer screen."

Gwen shudders theatrically. "The prospect terrifies me, but go ahead."

"You're a computer-phobe?" asks Belinda.

"Definitely," says Gwen, "but go on."

Belinda's estimation of Gwen drops very low indeed. "Hmm," she says. "That's interesting. Well, if you can do it without making yourself sick, imagine that you're looking at the screen and there's a page of text on it. But some of the words and phrases are *active*. If you click your mouse—"

"Oh, dear. I was afraid we were going to hear about the dreaded mouse. Just the idea of clicking my mouse sounds obscene."

"You click your cursor, then—"

"A curse on cursors!" cries the witty Harold.

"—on one of these active words," continues Belinda without a pause, "you go immediately to some *other* text. Okay?"

"Is it okay, Gwen dear?" asks Harold. To Belinda he says, "You have to excuse her, she's quite the little Luddite. It's part of her charm." Belinda decides that she despises Harold, utterly. Nothing he could possibly do could change her opinion.

"The text you jump to," Belinda continues, determined now not to be stayed, "is related to the word you clicked on—in some way. It adds something to it, or it takes you somewhere that's related to it. I'm not doing a very good job, am I?"

"Is this what happens in theory," Gwen asks, "or what really happens in the game?"

"Uh-uh-uh," cautions Harold.

"Sorry," says Gwen. "The—whatever you call it."

"I want you to understand *how* it works," says Belinda, "before I get into the game itself. Oh, shit, now I'm doing it. Call it a game—who cares? Suppose you click on the name of a character—*zip*—you're into something about that character's childhood. You find out that he"—an instant's pause—"was an orphan, or something like that. But it's not all text, you see, there are illustrations, too. And *they* have active elements." With her finger, she draws on the tablecloth. "You might have a drawing of this table, from above, with Harold here, me here, Matthew here, and Gwen here. We'd all be active elements. Click on Harold, and some text might appear on the screen, or a new picture, anything. But it would tell you something more."

"Like what?" asks Gwen.

"Oh, that his hand is on my knee, or whatever." A pause. "Just kidding," she says.

"Why the name?" asks Harold. "Picture Frame?"

"Ah!" says Belinda. "Well, when you start playing—'playing'— I don't believe I said that. Maybe it *is* a game. Anyway—when you start, you think you're in someone's apartment, and you work your way around in it, checking things out—you can look into her diary, listen to the messages on her answering machine, read some of her mail, look at the art on her walls, and so on. So you learn a lot about her. But the best thing you discover is that she's got a computer. You start it up, and there's a lot more you can discover about her there. But one of the things on her disk is Picture Frame. This game. When you open it up, though, it's not the same. You're not in the same apartment. You're in someone else's apartment." Belinda's a little breathless. This is the first time she's explained her game to someone she doesn't know. She's excited and anxious.

"And I'll bet he's got a computer, too," says Harold.

"She. But you're right. And much later, after you've been here and there, you find out that when you first started you weren't *really* in an apartment at all—you were wandering around in a *picture* of an apartment. A snapshot that's lying in a desk drawer in a room in an inn on an island. And so you can go right back to the beginning.

So the question is, when have you been in the picture, and when have you been in the frame?" She's done. She reaches for her glass and is surprised to find that her hand trembles.

"This would drive me back to drink," says Gwen.

"Probably," says Belinda, with a venomous smile.

"But why do you do it?" asks Harold.

"Oh, I just started fooling around," says Belinda. "I *have* played a lot of computer games, and I thought it would be interesting to try to do something that was set in this time, instead of the usual medieval epic—"

"No, I mean why does the *player* do it—keep playing?"

"Hm?"

"I mean, what's the point?"

"Well, it's intriguing—I hope."

"Forgive me, but I think I can give you some advice. You know, you're touching on my business here. Mine and Matthew's. So I think I can give you some help. You've got to have something to keep up people's interest. Put yourself in the position of somebody who might play this Picture Frame. Somebody who might buy it. Now suppose that's me. Why should I care about this? Why should I spend my time on it? What do I get out of it? Usually, if I'm going to sit at a computer, I'm going to be doing something practical. But you're asking me to sit there just out of curiosity. I'm not going to make more money by playing this. I'm not going to improve myself. So why should I bother? You see what I'm saying? You need some mystery or something to keep my interest. Throw in a body. A dead body. That's what you've got to have. Keep up the interest."

Belinda is hurt. She has been working on Picture Frame for months, and she's proud of having elevated it above the level of a game. She's annoyed with herself for not having done it justice, and she can feel in her throat the possibility of tears if she tries to speak. She would be grateful if Matthew would say something, do something, anything to end this torture, change the subject, rescue her. He doesn't, but the waiter does.

"Excuse me," says the waiter. "Am I interrupting?"

Belinda takes a deep breath, shakes her head.

"Would you like to order? Or would you like some more time?"

"More time," says Harold. "I haven't even looked at the menu yet." Harold picks up his menu, barely glances at it, and asks Matthew, "Have you been to Italy?"

"I've never been anywhere," says Matthew. And he thinks, *It's true.* He hasn't been anywhere. He and Liz spent a weekend in Montreal now and then, and Matthew has traveled on business, but he doesn't feel as if he has really been anywhere. He makes visits to Hong Kong and Taiwan and Mexico to check on the manufacturing of toys, but they are like inspection tours of a huge plant, not like traveling in foreign cultures. Suddenly he misses what he never had, the footloose travel of a young man, afoot in Europe, a student wandering around, having experiences that he would never forget.

"I hear that Italy is extremely expensive now," says Gwen. "When we were in Italy, I think we probably never spent more than three dollars on a meal—"

"Really?" says Harold, as if astonished. "Were we traveling together?"

"Oh, come on, Harold," says Gwen. "It's true—"

"Well, it's almost true," says Harold.

"All right. We never spent more than *five* dollars."

"*That's* true."

Belinda finishes her drink. She looks around for their waiter. She would like to eat and run.

"And for that we used to have wine," says Gwen, "and *huge* meals. I mean, I thought they were going to charge us extra on the plane, for the weight we'd gained."

"Or *duty*," says Harold. He's almost bouncing on his chair. To Belinda, he looks like a boy who has to go to the bathroom, but he's merely full of something he thinks is funny. "Say," he says in a tone of official suspicion, "isn't that Italian fat you're carrying there?" He makes a tummy-poking gesture. Matthew gets it, after a moment's uncertainty: Harold is supposed to be a customs officer interrogating Harold and Gwen on their return from Italy. Matthew laughs, after a fashion; to be precise, he smiles and makes a snorting sound. He too looks for the waiter.

Harold doesn't quit. "Why, ah, yes, ah, the missus and I really tucked into the pasta—" Now Matthew's confused again. Harold can't be playing himself. This must be a parody of what Harold supposes a middle-class Midwesterner to be like. Belinda's fascinated now. She wonders why Gwen has stayed married to this bloated buffoon. *Maybe he has a giant cock,* she tells herself, and she giggles. Her giggle encourages Harold.

"You're going to have to declare that, you know," he continues. Now Gwen is giggling, out of all proportion to the humor of Harold's routine, giggling like a crazy woman. *She seems to think Harold is hilarious,* thinks Belinda. *Is he? I can't tell. I must be losing my perspective on what's funny.*

"Oh, Harold," says Gwen. "You're crazy. But anyway, our friends Edith and Dan just came back from a week in Italy, and they said they spent a hundred and forty dollars on lunch. Lunch!"

"But we went when we were *kids,*" says Harold. "We only *had* five dollars to spend on a meal."

"But a *hundred and forty dollars* on *lunch.* Are things that expensive, or are Dan and Edith just gluttonous?" She laughs at this; she's surprising herself. She's usually content to leave the wit to her husband. Perhaps she's feeling a little loose because it's her birthday. Maybe she should have one drink. Well, maybe not. "I mean, maybe they spend a hundred and forty dollars on lunch all the time. I don't know. Can you do that?"

"Sure," says Matthew.

"We don't eat out that often," says Gwen, "but Harold keeps track of restaurants. He reads the reviews and so on. But I don't think you've come across many places where someone would spend a hundred and forty dollars on lunch, have you?"

Harold pulls a face. He is about to speak as an expert. "Oh, it certainly is possible. If a person is determined to spend money. Order a good bottle of wine, and—"

"Oh, of course, wine," says Gwen. The thought of a drink flits across her mind again, lighthearted as a debutante. "But you would know, wouldn't you, Matthew? You eat out quite a bit, I'll bet."

"Oh, a bit."

"Could two people spend a hundred and forty dollars on lunch?"

"At *many* places," Matthew says. "Seasons, Aujourd'hui, the Ritz—"

"Here?" asks Gwen. "Have you eaten lunch here?"

"I *did* come for lunch, last week. I got out for considerably less than a hundred and forty dollars."

"Casing the joint, eh?" suggests Harold.

"Well, yes, in a way."

"Oh, that's sweet," says Gwen. "You wanted to make sure it would be good enough for Belinda's birthday?"

Matthew just smiles and shrugs. "You were saying that you read the reviews?" he asks Harold.

"Gwen said that,"says Harold. "I don't know where she thinks I get the time for—"

"Oh, cut it out, Harold," says Gwen. "You know you do. You read all those reviews. He reads them out loud. When he comes home, while I'm getting dinner ready, he reads reviews. We used to have a drink then, you know, but now that we don't drink, Harold reads restaurant reviews. You know, I was thinking that I might have one drink. Since it's my birthday."

"Waiter!" Harold calls at once. The waiter comes to the table, and Harold orders Gwen a Kir Royale.

"Do you read these reviews every night?" Belinda asks.

"Yes!" says Harold, as if astonished to find that this is true. This is one of his odder affectations, delivering answers to questions about himself as if they startled him, as if he were crying "Eureka!" to discoveries about his life. Matthew wonders whether he thinks that this makes him seem more interesting. Then, as if a new thought has struck him, Harold says, "Well, no, not every night. Some nights I give demonstrations of positions in the Kama Sutra, some nights I read the comic strips, some nights I play the guitar and sing old Motown hits—"

"Oh, Harold, you do not," says Gwen, laughing again.

"I didn't know anyone actually read restaurant reviews," Matthew says, fishing.

"Which ones do you read?" asks Belinda. "Have you found any that are reliable?" Under the table, Matthew presses his knee against hers. She smiles a conspiratorial smile for Matthew, though she is facing Harold.

"Oh, I think they're all a bunch of nonsense," says Harold. "I'm sure there are payoffs involved—"

"Really? You mean that?" Matthew asks. "You think the restaurants pay for good reviews?"

"Oh, not directly," says Harold. "But I'm sure restaurants that advertise in a magazine or paper get better reviews than those that don't."

"You really think so?" asks Belinda.

"Of course," says Harold. "Don't be naïve."

Matthew glances at Belinda but isn't sure what he sees in her expression. She may be getting angry. *Why on earth did I let us get stuck with these people?* he asks himself. *Why are we spending time with them? Belinda's trying, really trying, I can see that. I wonder how long she'll be able to sustain the effort. How do I get us out of this?* It would be a grand gesture for him to get to his feet abruptly and announce that he has really had enough of all this, and that he wants to take Belinda back to his place and make love to her. It isn't the sort of gesture Matthew's likely to make, but it would be grand if he did.

"I hate this!" announces the child at the next table, smacking his fork into a plate of fusilli Bolognese.

"What do you do, Harold?" Belinda asks, still the good sport.

"Oh, nothing much," Harold says.

Belinda smiles, but she's thinking, *"Nothing much?" Why do you say that? Why are you acting like this? Do you want me to think you do something you can't talk about? Or are you just trying to make yourself "interesting"? You are, aren't you? That's the reason for the ridiculous clothes you're wearing, isn't it? You want to look like an eccentric. You're probably fifty years old, but when you take your wife out to dinner—her birthday dinner, for God's sake—you wear a tweed jacket and corduroy pants, the kind of outfit*

you wore in college when you had to throw on a jacket and tie to get
fed in the dining hall. I get it. We're supposed to say, "That Harold,
what an individual!" And your wife. She looks as if she hasn't
bought any clothes in years. Something's all wrong with her.
Maybe she's crazy. Haven't you noticed, you asshole? Why else
would she laugh so much at everything you say? And why can't you
stop trying to be funny? You're trying so hard, and you're really
nothing but a bore, Harold, just a bore.

"Harold is an engineer," Matthew says. "He does the engineering
work on our toys." Harold says nothing, but there's such hunger in
his eyes that Matthew, for the briefest instant, sees Harold as he
must have been as a boy. He can see the face of the little Harold, fat,
like the little Matthew, a boy without playmates, hungry for a
friendly word, and he feels a sudden compassion for him.
"Frankly," Matthew says, "he's a genius. He came up with a brilliant design for this brick maker I'm presenting in a couple of
weeks—"

"Now really, it was your idea, Matthew."

"Oh, but it was just an idea. You made it work. And with a
design of—well—elegant simplicity."

"I stole it."

Matthew stops breathing. He has certain hopes pinned on the
success of this toy. This is stunning news. "What?" he asks.

"It's nothing we're going to get into any trouble for. I took it
from—the truth is, I took it from a comic book."

Blank looks.

"When I was in the Peace Corps—"

"You were in the Peace Corps?" asks Matthew.

"Yes indeed. I built housing; that is, I taught people how to build
housing. Rammed-earth housing. We had wordless comic books
that showed how to build a ram to make mud bricks and then build a
house out of the bricks. Your sandcastle brick maker is the grand-
child of that ram."

"It makes bricks out of sand," Matthew says to Gwen, who seems
never to have heard anything about it before. "I thought I invented
it. Or came up with the idea for it, anyway."

"Oh, ours is much better than the Peace Corps version," says Harold. "The bricks interlock, for one thing. And you can make six different shapes. Much better."

Matthew's enthusiasm for the brick maker has suffered a blow. So has his self-esteem. He turns to his menu. "The food is supposed to be extraordinary here," he says.

"I can't decide what to have," says Gwen. "What are you leaning toward, Harold?"

Harold inclines a little toward his right. "I'm leaning a little toward the right," he says.

Gwen laughs and says, "Oh, Harold."

Matthew chuckles to be polite. The moment of compassion has passed; he hates Harold for having sabotaged his brick maker, for having diminished the value of his idea. Belinda smiles, but she too has come to despise these people; for a moment she considers simply getting up and asking Matthew to take her home, but their waiter returns.

"Shall I take your orders?" he asks.

"Let me ask you something first," says Harold. He twitches on his seat with the pleasurable anticipation of being amusing. "Does the cuisine match the decor?"

The waiter smiles indulgently. "No, sir," he says. "Our cooking is essentially Italian, but with the personal innovations of our chef."

"Oh, good!" says Harold, and with an elaborate expression of relief he telegraphs the approach of the punch line. "I was afraid the special was going to be 'crust of bread and day-old water.'"

The waiter smiles but shows no likelihood that he will laugh.

"Would you tell me about the *pappardelle Toscana*?" Belinda asks.

"*Pappardelle alla Toscana*," he says with no hint of reproof, "is a traditional dish. *Pappardelle* is a wide egg noodle, very nice. Typically it's made with ham and livers of chicken in a tomato sauce with mushrooms. Our chef uses a little *pancetta* in place of the ham, and *porcini* mushrooms. It's very nice." Since it is entirely proper to look at him while he is speaking, Belinda does look at him, closely. He speaks well, beautifully, in fact. Belinda listens to his recitation as to a poem. *A student*, she thinks, *intelligent, dark, handsome, brooding mouth, but laughing eyes. Too young for me, alas.*

"Would you like me to describe any other dishes?" the waiter asks.

Harold says, "I think Belinda would like you to go right through the menu."

Gwen laughs. Belinda reddens. She smiles, but the smile doesn't cover her embarrassment or annoyance. She gives Matthew a poke with the toe of her shoe, and he glances at her. He sees the most fleeting of sneers on her face, but she quickly turns toward the waiter, and her look turns seductive. In a throaty voice she says, "I certainly would."

The waiter chuckles at this. "Perhaps you would like to know something about the *tagliatelle con fruitti di mare, signora*?" he says as if he were a Venetian gigolo inviting her to enjoy the moonlight with him from a gondola on the Grand Canal.

"Mmm," says Belinda, "it sounds—very interesting." She raises a shoulder coyly, and the strap of her dress slips beguilingly off it. She catches it, just in time, it seems to Matthew, bats her lashes, and says, correcting him, "But it's *signorina,* not *signora.*"

He says, "*Scusi, signorina,*" and from the way he says it, it might be Italian for "Later, when you finally manage to get free of these tedious people, why don't you drop by my palazzo?" He begins to describe the dish, but Belinda stops him. In fact, she reaches out as if to touch him by way of stopping him but reaches only partway and says, "That's all right. I'm familiar with it."

They order, and Gwen orders the *tagliatelle con fruitti di mare,* though she hasn't the faintest idea what *tagliatelle* is.

"I don't really know what I ordered," she confesses when the waiter has gone. "What is *tagliatelle*, anyway?"

"I think that's just the Italian word for linguine," says Harold. Belinda hesitates for only a moment, to decide whether he's making a joke, and when she concludes that he isn't, she laughs heartily.

The food is absolutely wonderful. It ought to be enough to make the evening magnificent, and for a while it is. Eating is such a great pleasure that the four of them speak very little, and when they do they talk only about the food. Were it not for the persistent whining of the boy at the next table, they might be in paradise. When they have finished they lean back, contented, regarding one another with the generosity of spirit a full stomach brings. This lovely moment doesn't last, though, for Harold has complaining on his mind. Eating always reminds him of his childhood, and his childhood shames him because as a boy he resented his parents for working so hard and having so little time for him. As he grew older and began to see what all that work had cost them, and to admit that they had really thought they were doing it for him, he became ashamed of his childhood self for misunderstanding them. He has become a tireless champion of his parents, whom he now considers self-sacrificing, quietly suffering, wronged. Whenever he feels especially content, after a meal, and particularly at the end of a fine evening when he has not only eaten well but supposes he has been clever, then, as Lucretius put it, "in the midst of the fountain of wit there arises something bitter, which stings in the very flowers." In Harold's case it's the memory of the injustice he did his saintly parents, and that bitter memory must be sweetened with praise of them, at the expense of anyone in his vicinity.

"You know," he says with a sigh, "it's a shame you can't deal with people on the basis of trust."

Since Matthew and Belinda do not recognize this as the preamble to a story about Harold's self-sacrificing parents, the remark seems to them to have come from nowhere. Gwen, poor Gwen, recognizes it very well—not the specific words, perhaps, but the tone. She too sighs. Her sigh might be taken for endorsement.

"I used to think you could," Harold goes on. "That you could deal with people on the basis of trust. I was very trusting."

Belinda has figured it out now, not in the specifics, but she's recognized the tone. She knows he's going to expound some personal philosophy. Something cynical and annoying. She's had about all she can take. She's wearing a mocking look, though she isn't aware of it. Harold's a jerk, she has decided, and some part of her no longer cares whether he or anyone else knows how she feels.

"It used to be that someone told me something," says Harold, "and I believed it. Someone gave me his word, and I took it. I got this from my father. My father loved everybody, trusted everybody. He was a truly kind and generous man. He ran a model shop—sold model trains, kits, magazines about model railroading, things like that."

"Sounds like a dream world," Matthew says, hoping to change the tone. Harold, thinking of the terrible injustice to come in the story, almost glares at him. "I mean," says Matthew, "it must have been fun, hanging around the store when you were a kid. I know I would have loved it."

Harold raises a hand. "That's beside the point," he says. "I want to illustrate something about human nature. So, my father had a shop, and he was a friend to all the children in town. The shop always had kids in it—"

"And they stole from him," says Belinda. Her voice, her look, her attitude, say that this is an old story.

"Yes," says Harold. "That's right. They did. They would slip tubes of glue in their pockets. Magazines under their shirts. Somehow they would get whole model kits out of the store. You're not surprised, are you? It doesn't seem to matter much, does it? Boys will be boys, right? The petty thefts of children aren't particularly significant. Who knows, maybe you're right. But that's not my story. Permit me to tell my story."

Belinda spreads her hands open, palms down. "Tell your story," she says, too polite to permit herself to add, "You pompous asshole."

"My father and mother did all the work in the shop themselves, except for one part-time assistant. A widow."

Matthew looks down at his plate. He busies himself poking a bit of food around. He's reminded of his own mother, widowed by the Second World War.

"A charity case, actually. She had one child—"

A small, fat boy, thinks Matthew. *An object of ridicule. A boy with no father to stand behind him, lend him strength against the taunts of bigger, powerful boys, boys with fathers.*

"She had almost nothing, and a child to support. So my father gave her a job. He made her his assistant. It worked out quite well. She was very thorough, a hard worker. Because she was so good, my father got the idea of opening a second shop a couple of towns away. The widow could run the first shop while my mother and father got the new one going, and if it was successful they'd hire another manager for the other store, and they wouldn't be mere shopkeepers any longer, they'd be running a chain. A couple of magnates, for God's sake. Well, that's just what they did. The widow took over the shop. Her boy used to come in after school and sit at a table in the back, doing his homework."

By himself, thinks Matthew.

"Harold, you know what?" says Belinda.

"What?" asks Harold.

"Today is the official celebration of my birthday, and I would rather not hear the rest of this story."

"Why?"

"Because it is not going to be a happy story, Harold, and as the birthday girl I would like to hear only happy stories today."

"Gwen is a 'birthday girl,' too, I might remind you," says Harold.

"And I'll bet she doesn't want to hear any unhappy stories today, either," says Belinda. She doesn't look at Gwen.

"Well," says Harold. He does look at Gwen. Gwen looks into her plate.

Something brushes Matthew's foot. *A rat? Belinda's foot? Gwen's foot?* Matthew glances under the table and is amazed to find the child from the next table investigating the glass-covered section of the wall. He can understand that it would be an object of curiosity for a child but thinks that this child should not have been permitted to crawl over his feet to investigate it, should not, in fact, have been brought to this restaurant at all. The parents, a glance tells Matthew, don't seem to care what the boy is up to. Matthew leans across the table and says to his companions, in a voice of steely calm, "I don't want to alarm any of you, but there is something *crawling* under our table. It's—a *child.*"

Belinda leaps up from her chair. She looks terrified. At first, Matthew doesn't connect this behavior with what he has said. His first thought is that Harold has kicked her. "A child! A child!" she nearly shrieks. Matthew can't believe what he's hearing. Harold and Gwen snap upright.

People turn their heads. Waiters hustle over. Belinda cries, "A child is under our table!" She puts a hand to her forehead as if she were about to swoon. Matthew isn't at all sure whether he's amused—and therefore pleased, or embarrassed—and therefore annoyed. He is certainly astonished.

Harold lifts a corner of the tablecloth and peeks underneath, wearing a look of apprehension and disgust and making such a good job of his performance that Matthew can't tell whether he's actually revolted by the idea of a child under the table or just playing along, playing, perhaps, an elaborate game of flirtation with Belinda. "Oh, how revolting!" he says, and with this one patrician utterance, all his snobbery is redeemed as far as Matthew is concerned. *You can't just improvise that tone. You have to have been putting it on forever.* Harold squares his shoulders, takes a deep breath, and reaches under the table as if he were performing an act of heroism. He brings out a terrified, red-faced boy, draws himself up to full height, and demands of the room at large, *"Who* is responsible for this?" He holds the boy at arm's length. *As if he stank,* thinks Matthew.

The boy's mother rushes over to claim him but doesn't say a word, in the hope that the whole embarrassing affair will end at once and dissipate like an odor; but Harold has the audience he's always longed for, and he isn't about to let it go so easily. "Allow me to suggest," he says, plummily orotund, "that you get the little deviate some good psychiatric help before he makes a career of molesting women in restaurants." The mother almost slinks away. Gwen, her mouth hanging open, wonders if she hasn't been wrong about Harold. Perhaps there is a vigorous, even outrageous, man beneath that pompous skin; perhaps she should have encouraged him more.

To the waiter, standing nearby, looking aghast but struggling to keep himself from laughing, Harold says, "I think you'd better bring us a round of drinks. We're pretty shaken up. The women have been through quite an ordeal."

"No. No, thanks," says Belinda. "Nothing for me." She has remained standing.

"You're not going?" says Harold.

"Yes," says Belinda. "I think so."

"The evening's young. You can't be tired."

"No." She smiles a freezing smile. "Not at all. It's just that I want to go back to Matthew's and screw."

The waiter laughs out loud.

On the way out, Belinda pauses at the door, throws the collar of the coat up, spins around to look at the room again, the details of artificial decay, the peeling plaster, the water stain, the tipsy safe, the open wall, and says in her best Bette Davis voice, "What a dump!"

Matthew thinks he may be falling in love.

As soon as they're outside, Belinda says, "That's a straaaange pair." She puts her hands in the pockets of her coat. In the right-hand pocket, she feels a small card. She pulls it out, glances at it, puts it back.

"They are, aren't they?" says Matthew.

"They're nuts, you know."

"Well, I wouldn't go that far."

"I would. I can't stand him."

"Sorry. I should have said no when he asked us to join them."

"He made me so uncomfortable. In fact, I can't think of anyone who has ever made me more uncomfortable. He finds fault with everything. Even if he doesn't say anything about it, you can see it. There's a look on his face as if he smells something rotten."

"You're right. He's a lot like BW, isn't he?"

"Yes, he is! Was he the model?"

"No, at least not consciously."

"The difference is that BW can actually be funny. Harold has the weirdest sense of humor I've ever encountered."

"You liked that business about the kid under the table."

"Yes, I did. *That* I liked. It was quite insane, but completely appropriate. I definitely liked that, and for a minute there it almost made me forget the rest. Well, not for a minute. More like a second. And it may only have been because it got us out of there. But when he called the little woman a Luddite I decided right then that I despised him and nothing could make me change my mind. The wife thinks he's a scream, though. There's *another* weird one."

"She's not getting something from him that she wants," he says.

She may not even know what it is, he thinks. *Liz didn't. Or claimed not to. All she said was, "It's not this."*

"The next thing you know," he says, "she'll be going to some kind of counselor. And it won't be long after that before she starts telling Harold that she's discovered she never loved him. It's a short step from that to complete lunacy." Matthew is awfully close to telling more of the truth about himself than perhaps he ought to. "I've seen it happen before. People start cleaning up their lives and before you know it they're left holding nothing but the pieces. It was only ignorance that held the whole thing together. A brick of compacted sand. It comes crumbling apart."

The brick that is me wouldn't last two weeks if I admitted all my anxieties, my disappointments, my wishes—I'm sure of it.

"God!" says Belinda, still on the subject of Gwen. "Those clothes! And she was out to *celebrate*, for God's sake. I think I'm going to go home and burn every sensible piece of clothing I own. I'm going to start going to work in leather dresses and big boots. I am *not* going to become like that woman, *ever*." She runs her hands up the lapels of the coat, pushes the collar up. "I don't know," she says, apparently subdued. "I may not keep the coat." A long pause, and then suddenly she flings it open. She takes a deep breath and says, "But I am sure as hell keeping this dress."

"I haven't seen a single cab," says Matthew. "Maybe if we walk a bit."

"We could take the T."

"In that coat? Besides, I'm just not a subway person."

"Oh, come on. There's a stop up here."

They walk to the subway in silence and start down the steps. At the foot of the steps, a janitor is stolidly and ineffectively mopping something. Matthew is immediately certain that it's blood. Belinda and Matthew stop, and the janitor looks up at them. He stops mopping and steps back to let them pass, but to continue downward they will have to walk through the blood or ask the janitor to move. They exchange looks. Belinda shudders and pulls the coat tighter around her. They turn and walk back up the stairs.

"God!" Belinda says when they're outside again. "Was that blood?"

"I think so. Let's start walking and hope we find a cab."

"I look like a pretty obvious target in this coat, don't I?"

"For muggers, you mean?"

"Yeah."

"Maybe not. Maybe they'll figure that any guy walking with a woman in a white mink is probably armed."

"There's a cab," Belinda shouts. She runs into the street, waving her arm. The coat falls open, and the wind presses her dress against her body, taut with effort and fear. The taxi stops, and they get in. Matthew gives his address, and Belinda huddles against him, chilled and disturbed.

"I'm going to take the coat back," she says.

"Don't do that," Matthew says. "You like it, don't you?"

"I like it, but it's too much for me. It's just too much." She puts her head on Matthew's shoulder and doesn't say anything more for the rest of the ride. In her pocket, she flicks her thumb across the edge of the card.

When they reach Matthew's apartment, the fare stands at one of those awkward amounts that doesn't allow easy keep-the-change tipping. Matthew hates asking cabdrivers for change. The cost of a cab ride, he reasons, is cheap compared with the cost of a meal in a restaurant, and the tip a cabdriver gets is tiny compared with the tips Matthew gives waiters. He doesn't like to seem to be the kind of guy who counts nickels when he reaches his destination, and he doesn't want to hold the driver up, delay him from going on to reach his next fare, so he usually calculates the tip as he approaches his destination, continually recalculating as the fare changes, and then always rounds the tip up to the nearest dollar. He hasn't been paying attention on this ride, and when they reach his building he reminds himself that he is the companion of a woman in a white mink. He hands the driver a ten and says, "That's fine, thank you," calculating, as he climbs out of the cab, that he has tipped more than fifty-two percent.

The concierge barely looks up when Belinda and Matthew enter the lobby. This one, a student at a nearby music school, is wearing a headset and tapping drumsticks on an electronic drum pad. The tapping makes only the softest sound in the lobby, like the scuttling of small rodents in corners, but in the headphones it makes the sound of a full drum set, at a level likely to induce premature hearing loss and certain to mask the sound of any request or demand a resident might make. The elevator door opens. Belinda steps in, and then she squeals when the car hops upward suddenly. Matthew, in the act of stepping into the car, strikes his toe against the rising lip of the floor. He lurches against the back wall, catches himself on the grab rail, and exclaims, "God damn!" The doors close. Through the narrowing space Matthew can see the concierge, still drumming.

"Are you all right?" asks Belinda.

"Yeah. Sort of. I hurt my toe." Belinda presses the button for Matthew's floor. "I stubbed my toe," Matthew says with something like astonishment. "I don't think I've stubbed my toe since I was a kid."

The hole in Matthew's living room wall now reaches from the window at the far end of the room to the window near his audio equipment, nearly half the length of the room. There is a distinct downward thermal gradient in its vicinity. Belinda hasn't taken her coat off; she snuggles into it while she squats to inspect the hole.

"Any leads?" she asks.

"None," says Matthew. "I was out here this morning for nearly an hour, sitting on the floor, hoping I'd smell it while the sun was coming up. I had a theory that the sun warms the cavity here and releases—well, whatever it is. Guess what? Not a thing. All I could smell was coffee. I'm sure the guys working on this think I'm nuts, and this morning I almost agreed with them."

"Will you be able to have this carpet repaired?"

"I don't think so. I think all the carpet in here is going to have to be replaced."

"You're not going to embrace the *esthétique du mal*?"

"No, I guess not. It's tempting, though. Anyway, I asked about just replacing the section they pulled up, and the guy from the carpet company claims that the edges would never match. You'd always see the seam. Do you want a drink?"

"Yes. I want cognac. Lots of it."

It will give her a headache, but Matthew can see that she wants it, so he doesn't say anything. He pours cognac into snifters, puts them on his black tray, puts the bottle on too, and carries the whole thing to the glassy end of the living room, where Belinda is waiting, in the dark, looking out over the rooftops. He gives her her glass, and she clinks glasses with him.

"Happy birthday," Matthew says. Belinda smiles. She drinks her cognac determinedly, in four swallows, and holds her glass out for more. Matthew pours, and she turns away, looking out the window again.

"When I was a girl," she says, "I wanted a fur coat, and not just the way you think a girl might want a fur coat. Not just some abstract fur coat. And not an ordinary fur. I wanted something really glamorous. I wanted *this* coat. A white fur coat. I'm not quite sure where I got the desire, or why it became so strong, but I think it might have been Smirnoff ads. Some liquor ad, anyway. I'm almost sure it was Smirnoff. They used to have tall blondes in white fur coats, sort of wrapping themselves around enormous bottles of Smirnoff."

"Sex sells again."

"Mm. You're right. But who thought about that then? Come to think of it, who cares? I don't, and I sure didn't then. I didn't want the vodka—I wanted the coat. I wanted to be a tall blonde in a fur coat. You want to know something about me, Matthew? I didn't have *anything* I wanted when I was a girl. Nothing. I used to get

hand-me-down clothes from the family next door. It was so humiliating. You don't know."

Matthew is about to sympathize. He's about to say that he does
know and tell her an anecdote to show that he understands. It's
about a model sailing ship he wanted when he was a boy. His
mother had an enormous model in her junk shop for weeks; someone had left it on consignment. It was dusty and damaged, the spars
hung askew, and bits of broken rigging hung down like cobwebs,
but to Matthew it was magnificent, just wonderful, and he wanted it.
He felt that he had little enough, much less than other boys, no normal house, no yard, no bicycle, not even a father. Circumstances
had brought this ship model virtually into his home, all but forced
him to look at it every day, and yet it wasn't his and couldn't be his.
He couldn't even touch it, because his mother couldn't afford to buy
it if he damaged it more than it already was. Matthew means to tell
Belinda this, to show her that he does understand the way the pain of
deprivation can endure. She sees that he intends to speak.

"Don't," she says. "Don't say anything. Just don't say anything.
I know you were a miserable boy, Matthew. But this is *my* story. *I*
want to talk now."

Matthew nods. He has recalled, against his will, the time when
Liz pointed out to him that he was making up for the deprivations of
his childhood by working at Manning & Rafter, making the toys he
never had. It seemed so obviously true that he couldn't believe he
hadn't realized it, and he resented Liz's understanding him better
than he did himself.

"We weren't starving," says Belinda, "I know that. I know how
much worse off everyone else in the world was or is or whatever. I
know that life was basically pretty comfortable, but for a girl, *then*
anyway, for a girl to go to school in clothes that everybody recognized weren't hers—I mean, I knew they were looking at me, and
they knew I was wearing what Elaine Toomey wore last year. It was
horrible."

Matthew nods his head.

"Today it probably wouldn't be. Today it's a completely different story. Leila would be happy if all her clothes were in tatters.

Most of them are. But I wanted clothes, nice clothes, new clothes. And when I got older I wanted a fur coat. A white fur coat. And you know what? It was *all right* for me to want a fur coat. Completely all right."

"Mm-hm," says Matthew.

"I didn't have to feel *any guilt* about wanting a fur coat. I was poor! When you're poor you're allowed to want anything you want."

Matthew smiles. Belinda almost does.

"You know what I mean. It was okay to want *anything* when I was poor, but now it's not, because I'm not poor anymore. I'm almost rich. By my parents' standards, I *am* rich. And now I can't want this coat. It makes me feel—I don't know."

"Guilty."

"Yes, guilty. It makes me feel guilty. And you know what it is? Exactly? How can I walk past a woman who's poor enough to have the right to want a coat like this? You see what I mean?"

"Yes," says Matthew. *It would be pretty hard getting past that gumdrop woman, too,* he thinks. *"Animals suffered agony to make your coat."* He's reminded of the gay guy's retort again, and he almost grins, but he keeps a sober look on his face. He decides to save the story of the gumdrop woman until later, when Belinda isn't upset.

Belinda spins, making the coat flare around her. She's getting good at it. "It's too much for me," she says. "I'm going to return it tomorrow."

"Belinda," Matthew says, "let me buy it for you. As a birthday present. Then you wouldn't have to feel guilty about it—"

"No." She shakes her head. "Thanks, but it wouldn't work. I'm going to take it back."

She stands there for a moment. Then she holds her glass out for Matthew to fill.

"Besides," she says, "if you really wanted to give it to me as a present, if you really wanted to take the guilt off my shoulders, you'd just go ahead and do it. You wouldn't ask me to approve the idea."

"Well," says Matthew, "I didn't think of that."

"Sure you did," she says. "You have to have. You're not stupid. Somewhere in the back of your mind you must know that I couldn't say yes to that proposal."

"Come on, Belinda. I swear I didn't think of it." He honestly doesn't think that he did, but he can't imagine how to convince her of that.

"Forget it," she says. "It doesn't matter. It's my problem, anyway, not yours. Excuse me a minute." She walks the length of the room, spins around in the coat, and then turns down the hall. Matthew hears the bathroom door close. He sits in silence. In a couple of minutes, Belinda calls him. "Matthew? Matthew, come here."

He wonders if she's sick. She doesn't drink cognac well. "In here," she calls, from the bedroom. Only the lights of the city light the room. Belinda has spread the coat out on the bed, fur side up, and she's lying on it, naked, stretching, enjoying the fur against her skin, almost writhing. For her the foreplay has already begun.

She's so aroused, so—charged. This is going to be better than the night she changed her name. Matthew climbs over the end of the bed, slides his arms under her legs, pulls her toward him by the hips, and puts his lips to her clitoris. He loves the musty odor of her down here, the acid taste of her. She's abundantly, extravagantly wet. He laps at her clitoris with his tongue, like a cat, so that the bumps and dimples will make her tingle. Belinda is silent, as she usually is during sex, but Matthew can tell how much she likes being licked from the way she runs her fingers through his hair, grabs his head in her hands and pulls him tighter against her, the way she rises and pushes herself harder against his tongue. Liz was silent, too, completely. Belinda sometimes murmurs when Matthew's licking her. Matthew supposes that the pleasure of sex embarrasses her, as he supposes it embarrassed Liz, so he considers the occasional murmur a big concession, the shy acknowledgment that his lapping, the tingling of those bumps and dimples, is working. Tonight, however, he hears more than murmurs—moans on top of murmurs—and quite suddenly Belinda thrusts herself so hard against him that he cuts his tongue on his teeth, and then she cries

out, one short, sharp cry, as if she were the one hurt. Matthew starts
to pull away. "No," she says, clutching the back of his head.
"Please don't. More." Matthew obliges, bending to the task with
relish and pride. *No mere adequacy here,* he's pleased to be able to
tell himself. *This is a first-class effort.* Matthew's so glad to be
pleasing her, so proud to be the engineer of this transport of bliss,
that he begins to suppose that she loves him.

When Belinda runs her hand over the coat, she can feel, through
the soft fur and supple skin, the hard card inside, and when she
touches it she can't help smiling, wouldn't be able to stop the delightful shiver that ripples through her if she tried. She read the card
in the bathroom, before she came into the bedroom and undressed.
It says:

> Bèlla signorina—
> Will I see you again?
> Massimo
> 555-2162

"Now I want you in me," she says.

Matthew undresses. Actually, since he pops a button from his
shirt in his eagerness, it might be fair to say that he rips his clothes
off. He's naked. He's erect. He's ready. He remembers the condoms.

"Just a minute," he says, starting for the kitchen.

"Oh, forget that," says Belinda. "I'm not going to give you any
diseases."

Throughout what ought to be an ecstatic act, Matthew is nagged
by the feeling that for months he has appeared foolish in her eyes,
that she saw through him, understood that he was afraid of her, not
for her, or that perhaps Belinda knows that he isn't likely to impreg-
nate her. *Did Liz tell her? Would she do that to me?*

When Belinda has gone, and Matthew's in bed, he lies awake,
wondering what he ought to do. Should he buy the coat for her? He
could have it delivered to her. It could arrive with a clever note.
"Because I loved you in it and loved you on it." *Not bad. How*

much does a coat like that cost? Maybe it would be better not to
have it delivered to her, but to have it here in the apartment the next
time we go out. Spread out on the bed. Fur side up. Maybe she'd be
as aroused as she was tonight. How would I get her to go into the
bedroom to discover it without being obvious? "I want you to look
in the bedroom." No. Spread it out on the living room floor. There
it would be, like a fur rug. What a gesture. Would it look as if I'm
trying to buy her? As if I think she can be bought? How much does
a coat like that cost? Would it look as if I'm proposing? I should
find out how much a coat like that costs first. Then I'll decide what
to do.

In the morning, when he sits down to write his notes, he'll remind himself to find out what the coat costs, and, sitting at his dining table, he'll chuckle over the resemblance between the decor of Dolce Far Niente and his ripped-apart apartment. He'll recall his thought that the only thing missing was one of the messages of the Neat Graffitist. He'll page through his notebook, looking for one that seems appropriate, and when he finds it he'll copy it on the wall, beside his notes on the odor, just as a joke. Why not? The wall obviously has to be repainted anyway, and writing on walls, he's discovering, can be satisfying.

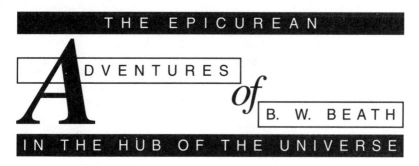

THE EPICUREAN ADVENTURES *of* B. W. BEATH IN THE HUB OF THE UNIVERSE

Dolce Far Niente

Are we the last to notice the assimilationist trend among ethnic restaurants? In the days of our youth, we could tell one from another. Crystal, white linen, supercilious maître d'—it's French, *naturellement*; red and gold—Chinese; downstairs—Indian; and so on. In this orderly scheme, Italian restaurants generally projected a working-class or peasant image. We could count on candles in chianti bottles; huge, cheap meals of pasta and tomato sauce; lots of garlic; fat loaves of bread; simple, zesty food in Brueghelesque settings. Tuck the napkin into your shirt collar, talk loud, bring the whole family, let the kids run around, and give them a good smack if they get out of line. Now—all, all is changed. In the last year we have dined in an Indian restaurant that looks like a wood-and-white fern bar, a Chinese restaurant that looks like an art-deco lounge on the *Normandie*, a French restaurant with hatch-cover tables and exposed brick, and no fewer than four restaurants in which the walls are paneled with ash, there is a brass railing in every spot where there might conceivably be a brass railing, and everything is bright,

light, and shining, including the diners, who are well scrubbed and blond. One of these ash-and-brasseries is Thai, one Italian, one Nouvelle melting-pot, and one Indian. What's happening here? Is the tendency toward an American mush so advanced that not even the newest immigrants retain or want to retain any of their home-country stereotypes? Whew! Excuse us. We may have gotten a little carried away.

Dolce Far Niente is an example of a kind of ethnic restaurant that has sprung up in the last couple of years; it turns its back on moldy old-fashioned ethnic stereotypes and embraces fresh new ideas. In this case, the dominant idea seems to be that nothing in the décor should suggest that the place serves Italian food, or that it serves food at all. It is turned out in some damned style or other, but since we are a mere food critic we are unable to say just what style it is. It is one of those styles that know no boundaries, within which tin is as good as gold—*l'esthétique du mal*, perhaps, or *langue-en-joue*. For all we know, it may be International, or postmodern, or neo-something, or retro–something else. Whatever it is, it includes jokes: a safe tipped on one corner, artfully peeling plaster, and trompe l'oeil water stains. One literal-minded diner within our eavesdropping range, recognizing how much effort had gone into making this place look like the aftermath of a disaster, announced, "I'll have the crust of bread and the day-old water," expecting, no doubt, that disaster décor called for mission cuisine.

There are no chianti bottles here, but if there were, they would be broken, deliberately, just so. There are definitely no checkered tablecloths, but if there were, they would be artificially stained. We are dealing with a new order here, for new citizens of a new world, with inverted notions of trash and taste.

Perhaps the neighborhood has influenced the décor. Once a truck paddock, the area is now a spooky center of high-tech shenanigans. Bustling by day, it's echoing and empty at night, as if neutron bombs fell at five. The buildings have been saved, but for whom? Or what? For little liberated animalcules crawling from their agar? It gives us the creeps, or the willies, or the creeps *and* the willies, and we're man enough to admit it.

Ah, but here's the surprise: despite the ridiculous interior and bleak neighborhood, we'll be back again and again. Why? Certainly not because we were charmed by our waiter, a cheeky pup, presumptuously familiar, who clung to the obsolete stereotype of the Italian Lothario and seemed to be laboring under the impression that the name of the place is the motto of the staff. No, we'll be back for the food, the glorious, glorious food. When food is this good it can be all an evening needs to be great.

It can make the most pompous and tedious companions tolerable, can even make them seem clever, amusing, charming—well, almost. The food here is of that transcendent quality, from the crusty, chewy, twisted loaves of peasant bread to the tart sphere of lemon ice that comes unbidden but oh-so-welcome as an accompaniment to one's espresso. Most of the dishes are interpretations of Italian classics, which is to say that they have been altered at the whim of the chef. Constant readers will know how wary we are of these chefs' whims— often they mean that the "chef swims" in water over his head and, too often, drowns. But not here. The substitution of goose liver for chicken in an otherwise conventional *ràgu Bolognese* produces a richness of flavor and aroma so sensual it nearly makes us blush. The surprising bite of the chicken filling in the tortellini comes, we learned after persistent probing, not from the cayenne we had expected, but from the Chinese hot oil, *làyóu*. And oh-oh-oh those *supplì al telèfono*! We figure that a half hour a day on the rowing machine will allow us to eat these lusciously gooey mozzarella-filled risotto balls once a month. *Scusi*—time to row.

—*BWB*

Dolce Far Niente
13 Bascomb Street, 555-3993.
American Express, Diners Club, Visa, MasterCard. No checks.
Handicapped: easy access.
Parents: leave the kids at home; this is a post-stereotype restaurant.
Dinner 6–1 Tuesday–Sunday.
Reservations required.

4

Superior Indian Cookery

Matthew is at work, in his office, two floors from the top of a two-year-old building in the section of Boston that was once the garment district and is now the financial district, where construction has been booming for the last several years. At the former location of Manning & Rafter, the executive offices were actually within the factory. Now the factories are in Hong Kong, Korea, and Mexico, and Manning & Rafter doesn't own them. The company has become a client of a contractor based in Hong Kong who delivers toys at a specified time, for a specified price, and farms the work out in a baffling international shuffle that meets his deadlines and maximizes his profits. When the last of the domestic manufacturing operation was eliminated and the factory became an echoing space, management moved into this tower, where there is no evidence of the manufacturing side of the business at all. By day, the building is full of executives and their clerical help; at night, vanloads of Haitian women arrive to clean it. Matthew's office, it has occurred to him, faces the wrong way; the view extends beyond the harbor and the airport, out over the Atlantic, but he spends much of his day in telephonic conference with Hong Kong. When he first came to Manning & Rafter, he liked to spend part of each day mixing with the workers, watching the toys move along the line, finding out whether the workers' children played with the toys they made, and if so what they thought of them. On his first trip to Korea to conduct an unnecessary inspection of the plant there, he asked all the questions he used to ask the men in Boston. The answers he got, filtered through translation, were cautious, polite, subservient, and useless. Now, on these inspection trips, he spends most of his time in meetings, in restaurants, or in his hotel. He used to be proud that he understood the technical aspects of production—materials, manufacturing methods, and so on—but now he sometimes doesn't know what the new toys are made of until he reads the trade names for plastics on spreadsheets.

It's one of those pellucid winter days that Boston gets in January, when details that usually go unnoticed shine crisp and bright, and ordinary things seem to flaunt themselves, demanding attention. On such days, the eye can see so much farther than usual that one's context is enlarged. The world seems more complex, overwhelming, packed with things that demand attention, a daunting heap of tiny bits of information, like the mound of sand that Matthew was asked to try to comprehend as individual grains rather than a mound in a session at an executive retreat in the fall, in New Seabury, on the Cape. "See the grains," said the session leader, "and you're overwhelmed. See the mound, and you're missing the details. Learn to switch between visions, and you control your perception of reality." Matthew sat and listened and did the exercises. He did not take notes. He emerged from the session with a pounding headache. When it was time to write the required evaluation, he summoned BW for help:

> Throughout the session, we had the feeling that the company had been bilked by a charlatan in a rumpled tweed jacket. In fact, we were convinced that the jacket, a disguise, a costume

worn to meet our expectations of what a psychologist ought to wear, was proof that the charlatan *was* a charlatan, a crook in psychologist's clothing.   Upon emerging from the session, however, we were astonished to find that as a result of the training we had received in perceiving a mound of sand as individual grains, we were able to perceive the staggering fee the company had paid this tweedy fellow as individual dollar bills! Not a *stack* of bills, mind you, but individual bills. With just a little more effort, we were able to see the fee as a mound of quarters, and then as individual quarters. We are forced to admit that we really must have learned something. It may take a great deal of company time for practice, but we think that eventually we will be able to perceive the fee as individual pennies, and then we will know that each and every one of them was money well spent.

Nothing was ever said about this evaluation. Matthew has been surprised to find that, since the session, he tries the technique every now and then; he's playing with it now, trying to grasp the view from his windows all at once, as a whole, and then shift to the details and try to perceive them all at once, and then shift back, and so on. When he gets the shifting to work, he can't seem to stop himself. It's dizzying, but he can't stop. He seems to feel the building move.

The intercom on his desk burbles and ends the experiment, just as he is shifting from the whole to the details. "Yes?" Matthew says.

"Mrs. Barber?" says his secretary. There is a question in her voice, and Matthew focuses on that detail. She's new, and she has never had any contact with Liz. Matthew can imagine her disbelief when the woman on the phone claimed to be his wife, a wife she never knew existed.

"The *former* Mrs. Barber," he says, in just the way he would have corrected any other small error, the mispronunciation of the name of a colleague, for example. "I'll speak to her."

"Hello, Matthew."

Suddenly he shifts to the big picture. It's Liz! Liz is calling him! She must be miserable without him! She must want to get together to see if she can't talk him into forgiving her for not understanding her own heart! He breaks out in a smile. "Hello, Liz," he says. He hopes that she can't tell from his voice that he's smiling.

"How are you, Matthew?" She sounds lighthearted, relaxed, pleasant, not the way he would expect her to sound if she were going to beg him to take her back. He goes on the alert for any sign that she's teasing him or wants something from him.

"I'm all right," he says. "How are you?"

"Oh, okay," she says. "I'm in town."

"You are?" He would like to ask her if she'd like to get together. They could have a drink. They might even have dinner. Matthew would be happy to see her, quite happy. He finds it easy to admit this to himself but couldn't begin to admit it to her. He lets the silence hang for a moment.

"Just for some shopping," she says. "And a check-up."

A check-up? he thinks. *Cancer. Oh, my God, cancer. A mastectomy. A hysterectomy. Death.* "Everything all right?"

"Sure."

"Sure?" Does she mean it? Or is she hiding something? He's terrified for her at once. His heart accelerates, his tongue tastes of metal, and that reminds him of the time, one fall, years ago now, when she fell in the bathroom. She was wearing panty hose for the first time since the previous spring, she wasn't used to the slipperiness of them, and she slipped on the tile floor. When he heard her fall and she cried out, he was so afraid for her that he began to sweat and shake, and all the time he was tending to her, cradling her in his arms, she couldn't stop laughing at her clumsiness, exclaiming how funny she must have looked when her feet whooshed out from under her and repeating, "Well, it's fall, so I fell," but he was crying from terror and relief, and he had had the same metallic taste of fear in his mouth that he has now.

"Yes, sure," Liz says. "Look, um, how would you like to have dinner with me?"

"I'd—" He almost says what is true, that he'd love to have dinner with her, but he catches himself and puts some distance in his voice, trying to make himself sound as if he were speaking to a pal, the way he would have spoken to Belinda before he began having sex with her on the living room floor. "I'd be delighted to have dinner with you. Where would you like to go?"

"How about the Black Hole?"

"Sure! The Black Hole it is. Do you want to have a drink somewhere first?"

"I'm meeting someone."

"Oh," he says. *Was she smiling when she said that? What does she mean, exactly? Who is she meeting? Should I ask? No. You're indifferent*, he tells himself. *You're a pillar of indifference.* "Why don't we just meet there, then?"

"Okay. Seven?"

"Good."

So he's going to have dinner with Liz at the Black Hole. Showering, dressing, getting ready—it all feels comfortingly familiar. For a while, before they moved out of the city to Lincoln, he and Liz must have eaten at the Black Hole once a week. It was a time when they were eating out nearly every evening because they were both so busy. They'd finally given up on the idea of children, had even abandoned their halfhearted investigation into adoption, and Liz had thrown herself into work at John Hancock, determined to impress people and to rise, and succeeding at both. They kept returning to the Black Hole because it was comfortable in the way that old corduroys are. There was the added comfort of feeling anonymous: even though they ate there so often, no one connected with the place ever gave any sign of recognizing them. How pleasant it is to be no one now and then. They could just sit, talk a little if they were in the mood, or barely talk at all if they were too tired or stunned from work, hiding their silence in the business of eating an Indian meal— tearing bread apart, scooping rice up, transferring curries from bowls to plates. Those were wonderful evenings, it seemed, but after Liz left, Matthew began to wonder. Maybe what he'd taken for silent contentment was to her just silence, or worse. *No. All that is*

over. Fourteen years of marriage. Fourteen months apart. It's
over. She's coming back.

Now he's on his way to the restaurant, walking, aware of a certain lightness in his step, in his heart. He's smiling. If he could
carry a tune, he would probably be whistling. He feels as close to attractive as he ever manages to feel now, since he became convinced
that he had passed the best point in his appearance, peaked without
ever having been aware of it. Now in the morning, when he's getting ready to leave the house, he seems to see only bad news. Perhaps he looks too closely, but he knows that if he doesn't examine
himself carefully before going out into public, his body is sure to
embarrass him: hideous hairs, to choose the first example that presents itself, would sprout from the bridge of his nose if he didn't
pluck them with the tiny tweezers Liz gave him as a stocking stuffer
one Christmas. Ah, but tonight he has no thought of that—hardly
any thought. All offensive hairs have been plucked or clipped. He
feels fine. Having Liz call and suggest that they have dinner together has certainly made him feel better. He put some mousse on
his hair and combed it straight back, in a style he picked up from ad-
vertisements for Italian suits.

The Black Hole has no liquor license. He and Liz always used to
stop at the liquor store across the street and get some beer before
they went in. Now Matthew stops there, intending to get some beer,
just as he would have in the good old days, but when he steps across
the threshold the rush of old familiar feelings is strong, and it makes
him realize that by bringing beer he's likely to seem to be trying to
re-create an evening from the past, to recapture something. Even if
that weren't the case, and he admits to himself that it is the case, Liz
might interpret his bringing beer that way, and if she has no interest
in rekindling anything, then Matthew might look pathetic. He
stands in front of a refrigerated case trying to decide what to bring
instead of beer. There are some chilled wines. If he brought some
cheap wine, it might evoke the spirit of former evenings at the Black
Hole without seeming to be an attempt to duplicate them. It might
be just the right lighthearted and subtle thing to do. However, he

reasons, things have changed since the days when he and Liz drank either beer or cheap wine. He really should bring something better, something that speaks of his present situation, something that will divorce this night from the old nights and force Liz to see how different he is now from what he was. Champagne? No, that says other things, suggests hopes for the night that he doesn't want to reveal, at least not at the start. Maybe he *should* bring beer; it's the obvious thing. No, not beer. Something more interesting, something clever, amusing. Vodka? Red-pepper vodka? Ginger brandy? Tequila? Tequila. Tequila and Indian food. That seems amusing, almost clever, at least different.

He buys a bottle of tequila and two limes. Across the street, the line of people waiting for tables in the restaurant extends beyond the door and onto the sidewalk. The temperature is about twenty degrees. People are stamping their feet and passing bottles in brown bags. Everything is as it was. Liz isn't in the line outside, so Matthew squeezes through the door.

"Excuse me. I'm meeting someone, excuse me. I think someone is waiting for me inside. 'Scuse me."

He stands on the tiny landing at the top of the stairs. Liz is a few steps down, laughing, her head tossed back, her hair falling in waves over the collar of her coat. She has her hand on the shoulder of another woman, to whom she is apparently telling a hilarious story. The other woman is Belinda. Matthew turns to go. This is an involuntary reaction, as if he were still married to Liz, had been having an affair with Belinda, and feared that Liz had found him out. Then he realizes that there is no reason for him to go and no reason why Liz and Belinda shouldn't be together. They've been friends for years, after all. He turns back. Belinda sees him and waves. Matthew wonders whether they have been discussing him all day, comparing notes, giggling girlishly as they are now. Liz turns toward him. Quite possibly she has never looked better. Matthew has the sinking feeling that she must have fallen in love with someone. Some other man must be making her glow like that. She smiles. His heart leaps and drops, leaps and drops. She really is everything he has ever wanted.

He squeezes down the stairs.

"Hi, Matthew," says Liz. She kisses him.

"Hi, Liz." He turns to Belinda. "Hi, Belinda," he says. He kisses her.

"Have a drink," says Liz. She hands him a bottle of champagne, Perrier-Jouët, without a brown bag. Matthew drinks from the bottle.

"Is this an occasion?" he asks.

"It sure is," says Liz. "I didn't quite tell you the truth on the phone. There's another reason for my being in town. I have been promoted. And I mean spectacularly promoted."

"Congratulations," says Matthew.

He's pleased for her, but he hopes the promotion hasn't been all that spectacular. After she decided that she wasn't going to be a mother, she decided she was going to be a success. She spent months looking for a business where, she said, "anybody with half a brain can shine." She chose insurance. Matthew was grateful to her for not choosing toys. He still hopes that she'll tire of business and drift back to him. God knows he gets tired enough of business himself. There are days when he sits at his desk and feels encased by work, as if it were a transparent wrapper, something too tough for him to break, like the stubborn vinyl packaging on the compact discs he buys. It isn't only business that has him wrapped up, though, he realizes; it's the whole set of his habits, his ways of thinking about himself and about what seems to him to be the narrowing cone of his future, fewer possibilities every day.

"I'll be coming back to Boston," she says. "As head of group sales and underwriting. An office in the tower. Windows. The whole thing."

"No kidding," says Matthew in as flat a voice as he can manage. He passes the bottle to her. If he raised it to drink from it, his hand would surely shake.

Padded with winter coats, most of the people lined up along the staircase that twists down into the restaurant occupy about twice their summer volume, but first in line is a lightly dressed couple of a type that Matthew and Liz used to snicker at.

"Colonials to your left," Matthew mutters.

Liz looks without seeming to, turning her head only the minimum, shifting her eyes as much as she can. "Oh, but definitely," she says, raising her eyebrows.

"Hmm?" says Belinda. "Colonials?"

"The people at the bottom of the stairs, the first ones in line," says Liz. "Just take a look at them." Belinda does. "A little fancy for this place, wouldn't you say?" Belinda smiles and nods. The man is wearing a double-breasted suit and shoes that look like dancing pumps, the woman a straight black skirt and a halter that seems to be made of chain mail, with gloves and reticule to match. Belinda and Liz snicker and chortle, lean against each other like impudent schoolgirls. "How does it happen to people?" Liz whispers. "How do they wind up thinking that a place one flight below the sidewalk is a place for fancy clothes? Matthew and I always used to call this the Black Hole, did I tell you that already? I told you that already. Anyway, we used to call these people colonials."

"Right," says Matthew. "They make me think of a colonial attitude, somehow." He's struck by this thought: he has a condescending attitude toward these people and their ilk, and this attitude is very much like the one he supposes them to have toward everyone foreign and dark. He wonders why his thinking about history, about international politics, nationalistic attitudes, hasn't become more sophisticated as he's aged. He still holds the attitudes he had as a boy, a naïve sense that fair play for all is the obvious best condition for the world—but perhaps he's changing. He used to think that he didn't understand condescension, real condescension, not the kind he affects for BW's reviews, but the condescension that's born of contempt. Now, however, recognizing his attitude toward the colonials, who fidget at the bottom of the stairs uneasily, speaking furtively, in the way that cautious schoolchildren might pass notes under their desks, he wonders how long he has misunderstood himself, failed to recognize what his attitudes have become, the contempt he feels for the people at the bottom of the stairs, a contempt he feels for many more people and types of people than he is quite ready to admit.

"We probably weren't being fair," he says.
Liz gives him a look. "Probably were," she says.

Just behind the fancy couple is a big man in an enormous parka,
unzipped, his barrel chest bulging from it. On the wall behind him is
a board on which the day's specials are listed and described in several colors of chalk. The big man is speaking animatedly, gesticulating broadly, putting his whole body into an address to the others
in his party. When he makes a point, he rises on his toes and
bounces, and with each point he erases a little more chalk. His
group might be four or six; it's hard to tell which of the people listening to him are actually with him and which are listening only
because they're too close to be able to choose not to. All these
people are drinking discreetly from whatever they've brought with
them. Some have glasses and pour wine or beer into the glasses,
small amounts at a time, because of the likelihood of being jostled
on the stairs. Others drink from bottles, and Liz and Belinda and
Matthew pass their Perrier-Jouët around, like prosperous bums in a
doorway.

"God, this is good stuff," says Matthew.

"We bought it for the bottle," says Belinda. She and Liz dissolve
in giggles again, like kids drinking illicitly before a dance.

The big man in the parka is saying, "A lot of this is just rhetoric-
of-gesture stuff."

"Oh, certainly," says a short, round, gleeful man, gesticulating
with his bottle-in-a-bag, "but not all of it yields to hermeneutics."

"Of course not," says the big man dismissively. "You have to
remember that much nonverbal language is not *made* for understanding."

Belinda snorts with a suppressed giggle, and she and Liz huddle
closer together.

"But you have to ask yourself," the big man continues, "if there
isn't an underlying grammar of motives in all gesture."

"All human *endeavor*," suggests a small woman beside him. She
twists a strand of her hair around and around her right index finger
and nods enthusiastically. She holds a bottle of beer by the very top

of the neck, and after she speaks she raises the bottle in that way and manages somehow to drink from it without dropping it.

"Of course," says the big man. "It's politics as poetry—poetry as politics. There really is no distinction, none at all, if you accept the premise of a pan-human substructure for all thought." The heads of all those in the big man's party bob, making it possible to distinguish them from people who are simply standing nearby.

"A genealogy for all thought," says the gleeful man, "starting from some primordial construct and arriving at the present, when madness is the first cousin of reason."

Liz taps the bottle against Matthew's shoulder, and he takes it and drinks from it.

"When you look at the intersubjective schema, you see that we make sense, *when* we make sense, because there is only one way *to* make sense, is that it?" says a tall man whose head is a bald dome with long, thin gray hair around the rim.

"But what *is* that way?" asks an attractive matron, tall, sturdily constructed, energetic, as bouncy and full of verve in her way as the big man in his. She strikes Matthew as the sort of woman who is involved in her children's education at every level, baking cookies for class parties, writing letters to the editor of the local paper castigating the board of education for its hidebound practices, busy, always busy. "I mean, is it because our brains are all alike? But they're not, are they? Wouldn't we all think alike if they were?"

"Well, that's the point, really," says the big man. Is that condescension in his voice now, or is it just the deceleration of a teacher who knows when to downshift to a more elementary level? "That in the most fundamental ways we *do* all think alike, that the mediation of structural regularity produces consensus, so—"

A tiny, smiling Indian man calls from the foot of the stairs, "Are you a group of four?"

Matthew turns at once to look at Liz, to share the pleasure he feels upon seeing the little man, whom he and Liz thought of as "the grandfather," supposing him to be the patriarch of an extended family that ran the restaurant. Matthew's delighted to see that the grandfather is still here, still playing host, still—the thought strikes him poignantly—alive. Liz and Matthew grin at each other, and Liz begins an explanation for Belinda, in whispers. "That little man was always here when we used to come—"

The group that includes the big man declares itself a group of six. The grandfather nods and smiles as if to say that it is a very fine thing to be a group of six, even though, as it happens, there is no table available for a group of six just now, and then he asks of Matthew, "Are you a group of four?"

"We are a group of three," says Matthew.

"Oh, that is very good," says the grandfather, and his glowing smile indicates that, however good it may be to be a group of six, it is wonderful indeed to be a group of three. "Come with me, you Group of Three."

The restaurant is tiny and entirely below ground level. At the foot of the stairs is a cubicle for the cashier, a waist-high enclosure, and opposite it is an opening through which a narrow snapshot of the kitchen is visible. Matthew can't help smiling when he passes this opening and hears the voices coming from it, striking exactly the note of frantic urgency that he remembers, a tone that used to make him wonder whether he and Liz visited only on nights of crisis. To the right, after one has passed the register, is a row of tables along the street side, under a row of small windows through which one can see the legs of passers-by. A lightly padded bench runs along this wall, and beneath the bench runs a pipe that is the heating system. On the coldest nights, a seat along that bench is worth waiting for, but Matthew's favorite spot is one of the tables in an el to the left, a little room of its own, apart from the larger room, but with the rest of the diners visible, the perfect spot for eavesdropping, always one of Matthew and Liz's favorite occupations when dining out. The grandfather leads them there.

"Our favorite spot," says Liz.

They sit, and Matthew looks around. At one of the tables in the center of the room, four conventioneers are seated, wearing plastic convention badges that identify them as Specialized Librarians. Most of the tables under the windows have been pushed together, and a dozen large young men are sitting there. They have cases of beer on the floor at each end of the table. They're boisterous, and likely to grow more so as they work their way through the beer, but there's good humor in their voices, and good humor always softens Matthew, who otherwise finds loud young people disturbing, even threatening. The camaraderie among these loud young men is appealing, though. They're members of a fraternity that Matthew was never invited to join, the fraternity of sport.

"What would you say?" he asks Belinda and Liz. "Hockey players? I'm willing to bet they're hockey players."

He's right. They are members of the Boston University hockey team and a group of Russian hockey players on a goodwill tour.

"Are they ogling us?" asks Liz, making a point of not looking toward them. "Belinda and me, I mean. Are they ogling us?" She puts a hand behind her ear and pushes her hair up in the manner of a starlet posing for a cheesecake shot thirty years ago.

"Mm, no," says Matthew. "They're pretty completely occupied with beer drinking."

"Well!" says Liz.

Matthew hears foreign accents, but he can't tell what accents they are. He's struck by the similarities among the hockey players. They all speak with the voice of the athlete: deep, self-possessed, hearty. *Those athlete types, those coach types. They resound. They boom. Boom like hollow logs. It's international, that booming. It knows no boundaries.*

"They might be *foreign* hockey players," says Matthew.

"They can't be *that* foreign," says Liz, tossing her hair.

"They might be *blind* hockey players," says Belinda.

Liz raises the bottle of champagne as in a toast and tips it to drink from it, tips, and continues tipping. "Hey," she says. "Gone."

"Ah! I can fix that," says Matthew.

Reaching for the bag with the tequila and limes, Matthew notices, sitting at a tiny table beside them, a gaunt man who is clipping something from a newspaper. A mirror fills the wall on the man's left. He is duplicated there, and beyond the image of the man, Matthew sees himself observing the man, frozen for an instant with his bag of tequila and limes, staring. Opposite the man, on the table, where his companion's food would be if he had a companion, is a stack of newspapers and magazines. The man has a stubble of beard, evenly dark. His hair is cut short. The temperature outside must be below twenty, but he's wearing nylon jogging shorts, yellow, and a matching nylon jacket, zipped and snapped right up around his neck. He's cutting one frame from a comic strip in the paper, muttering to himself while he works. Matthew can't make out what he's saying, but it's clear that he disapproves of something. It might be a line in the comic strip, the whole comic strip, the concept of comic strips, anything. He puts the single frame onto a stack of clippings to his right and tosses the paper onto the opposite chair. Still muttering, he eats some curry, directly from the boat-shaped metal dish in which it is served. He mutters as he chews and swallows. He puts a couple of spoonfuls of basmati rice in his mouth and chews that while he chooses another section of newspaper from the pile. Instantly, outrage registers on his face, but he doesn't mutter any louder for it. He picks up his scissors and begins clipping the headline from an article in the middle of the page.

Matthew has to force himself to stop looking at the man. He turns away, leans across the table, and says very softly, "Don't be obvious about it, but take a look at the guy on your left, the one in the little yellow shorts." Matthew pulls the tequila bottle out of the bag and pours some into the empty glasses that are brought to each table as a matter of course. He takes a lime from the bag and hacks it into wedges as well as he can with his table knife. He distributes the wedges. He removes the top from the salt shaker and pours a cone of salt onto the tablecloth in front of each of them. This business gives Liz and Belinda a chance to observe the paper clipper without being obvious about it.

Liz licks her index finger and dips it into the salt. She takes a sip of tequila and then licks her finger. "Is this right?" she asks. "Oh, the lime." She nibbles a bit of the lime. "This is fun," she says. "I've never done this before. It's kind of—raw. You know what I mean? Crude. Like eating with your hands, gnawing on a hunk of raw meat. Anyway, the guy is clearly a nut."

Matthew has a twinkle in his eye. He sips his tequila. "I think he's not just *a* nut," he says. "I think he is a very singular nut." He pauses and turns the twinkle toward Belinda, enjoying the idea that he and Belinda know something that Liz doesn't. As soon as he says what he's about to say, Liz will understand that he has a life without her now, has had experiences that she hasn't, knows things that he didn't know when they were together. She will see that there are mysteries about him now, and there's the possibility that she might want to probe them. That possibility thrills him. "I think he might be the Neat Graffitist," Matthew whispers. "The guy who writes those odd messages we see all over the place." Though he delivers this explanation in Belinda's direction, it isn't for her; she doesn't need it. It's for Liz.

"What messages?" asks Liz. "Ooh, tell me." Matthew doesn't hear the note of jealousy he'd hoped to hear, just curiosity. He's disappointed.

"Well, first of all, I have to tell you he's not the one," says Belinda. "I saw him. I meant to call you, Matthew. I'm sorry. I can't believe I forgot. I know what a fan of his you are."

"That's all right, but tell me about it," says Matthew.

"And tell *me* about it," says Liz.

"Okay," says Belinda. She leans inward, conspiratorially, and Matthew and Liz do likewise. "Basically," Belinda says, "he's a guy who writes graffiti."

"Very neat graffiti," says Matthew. "You see them in particular places. Smooth, flat places. Like the side of a mailbox. Or those silver boxes you see on corners—I think they're some kind of telephone switching box."

"Or on newspaper boxes."

"Uh-huh," says Liz with great seriousness, as if they're telling her about a network of spies that they've stumbled upon.

"Very neatly lettered," says Belinda.

"In Magic Marker," says Matthew. "No spray cans or anything like that. He writes little philosophical statements."

"But not all the time. Some of them are more like *headlines*," says Belinda. Matthew raises his eyebrows and jerks his head in the direction of the man in the yellow shorts. All glance at him. He's clipping another headline from the newspaper.

"Right, but this isn't the one," says Belinda. "I saw him on State Street, near the Devonshire. He's shorter, and he has a round face, and he's a happy guy, crazy but happy, nothing like this one."

"You're sure the guy you saw was the one?" asks Matthew.

"Yes. I'm sure. He had about three garbage bags full of possessions, and he had a cardboard sign propped up against each one. The signs were more of his statements. The same printing. It was the guy. No doubt about it. And he was talking, just going on and on. Not loud, just talking, but *to* people, to the crowd. And as I went by, he said, 'I did what they told me to. I took the medicine and fell asleep.'"

"Well," says Matthew. He shrugs to show that he's not convinced, but to Belinda his shrug says more than he intends. It says that he isn't willing to believe that the man she saw is the Neat Graffitist. She realizes that Matthew's jealous. He wants to keep the Graffitist for himself. She's surprised to find that this makes her feel weary, not annoyed.

"So, anyway," says Belinda, explaining for Liz, "he'll write something like 'Arab terrorists supply drugs to typists in the State House.' Or one of them, his biggest work so far—it covers most of a sheet of plywood—is about some group that he accuses of killing—pigeons, is it?"

"Ducks," says Matthew.

"Killing ducks in New Jersey," says Belinda. She wonders, without caring very much about the answer, how much longer she'll bother seeing Matthew.

"Right," says Matthew. "But the main thing is that he always makes some kind of comment. He doesn't just make a statement. He always draws a conclusion about it. He almost has a sort of philosophy. Like the one about the terrorists supplying drugs to—actually it's 'word processors in the State House,' not 'typists.'"

"You're right," says Belinda. How much longer will she care to go on drifting with him through these nights of dinner, drinks, and drunken conversation?

"The full text is: 'What makes Arab terrorists supply drugs to word processors in the State House? Nobody deliberately chooses to do an evil thing.'"

"Matthew collects these writings," Belinda explains to Liz. She drains her glass. Her time with Matthew seems to have added up to nothing. How much more time will she be willing to spend on him?

Matthew shrugs, grins. "A little weird, I guess," he says. How much weirder Liz and Belinda would think it was if they knew that he has copied his entire collection onto the wall of his apartment, above the open section, imitating the neat printing of the originals, or that he has added some of his own, counterfeits, indistinguishable from the others?

"Could I please have some water," calls the man in the nylon shorts without looking up from his work on the papers.

Liz and Belinda respond by giggling like children at a family gathering, convulsed by the bizarre behavior of their intoxicated elders. Matthew sits upright and says, "Shhhh." A gust of fear has disturbed his fun. He wants to go on, but he doesn't want the man in the nylon shorts to realize that they're talking about him. He is certainly a crazy man, and he's sure to be enraged if he finds that they're talking about him. Matthew doesn't want the women to know that there is fear behind his wanting them to be quiet, so he pours more tequila into the glasses and tries to assume the sardonic tone of B. W. Beath. He leans inward and whispers, "Maybe there's more than one. Or maybe he has assistants. This guy might be part of a vast conspiracy." He makes the gesture of lettering on an imaginary wall between them, in small, neat block letters, and says as he writes, "'Ectomorphic joggers observe diners in Indian restaurants, take notes. Watch what you say.'"

Belinda begins to giggle. She tries to stifle it, but it breaks out, and it infects Liz and Matthew, and they begin giggling and stifling their giggles, and tears run down their cheeks. Matthew hasn't laughed like this for a long time. He glances around the room. The noise level is so high that no one has particularly noticed their laughter. The hockey players are shouting stories at one another. The academics are not quite shouting, but they are making emphatic points in loud voices.

"Another one," says Belinda, "is, 'Mail handlers at South Street Annex have nurses in their union.'"

"So what?" asks Liz.

"Just what I wondered when I saw it," says Matthew. "And the next day someone had written under it, very neatly, almost in the same style as the original, but in a different color, 'So what?'" Only after he has said this, and Liz is laughing at it, does he realize that he took Belinda's line from her. "Sorry," he says.

She grins a mirthless grin and makes an it's-nothing gesture with her hand. "Anyway," she says, "a couple of days later he added— how did it go?"

"'Happy people don't cause trouble,'" says Matthew.

"Yeah," says Belinda. "He must have seen the note and realized that he forgot to add his comment. So he made a comment on the comment."

Liz makes no response.

"I guess you had to be there," says Belinda. "*But*," she says to Matthew, "I have a hot piece of information for you." There is drama in her voice—some sarcasm, too. "He calls himself the Culture Guerrilla," she whispers.

"The Culture Guerrilla?" asks Matthew. "How do you know?"

"Well, when I saw him, I—" She is about to say, "I was with three guys from MIT," but she decides against it and says instead, "I stood in a doorway for a little bit and—observed him. And there were three young guys there who were watching him, too. Two of them were real experts. They knew more about this guy than *you* do, Matthew." *Now why did I say that?* she asks herself. *That wasn't fair.* "Well, probably not. You are his biggest fan, but they could quote dozens of his sayings, and not only could they quote them, but they knew where each one was. They had a *chart*. They were from MIT." There! She said it, and what a delightful thrill it gave her to say it. It's a wonder that she can keep herself from saying that she has become the darling of a small set of graduate students at MIT, a wonder that she doesn't tell about the hours she spends talking, talking, talking with them, about the way they took at once to Picture Frame, sitting at the computer for hours, without caring whether there was a dead body in it or not, about the way they seem to her to swagger, their confidence and the way it electrifies her, or the amazing sexual energy of Massimo, the leader of the pack, whom she calls, as all his American pals do, Max. "Anyway, according to these kids, one of his messages says, 'Culture guerrillas eat at Ike's,' and they figured that he was giving himself away. Deliberately. That this was like a signature. Like a painter signing a painting."

"No, I don't think so," says Matthew. "In fact, that doesn't even sound like one of his. Did they say there was a second part? Is there a comment?"

"Yeah. There is. 'They stuff themselves, but their souls are hungry.'"

"No, that's not him. It's too pat. It doesn't have that twisted quality. These MIT guys probably wrote it themselves. You know, I wouldn't be surprised if they did! I wouldn't be surprised at all. I'll bet he's spawned imitators, and now he's even inspired parodies."

The grandfather arrives to pour water for them. He has the same bemused look that Matthew remembers. On nights when the restaurant was quiet, nearly empty, he seemed puzzled, as if pondering the mysterious behavior of his absent customers. *Where might they be on this night if they are not in my restaurant? What can they be up to? What are they doing that is keeping them away from us? Are they eating somewhere else? Are they fasting today? Is this a day of family feasts, when everyone cooks and eats at home?* On nights when the restaurant was full, and everyone was bustling around, trying to keep up with the orders, putting on their circus show, he seemed puzzled still. *What brought all these people here? Why are they all in such a hurry to eat? What can they all be talking about? Is it possible that they were all at one gathering, and someone said, 'Now our business is over here, and we must all go to Superior In-*

*dian Cookery'? How are we managing to cook and serve food for
all these people? Why are we not throwing up our hands and telling
everyone to go home and rest?*

"What shall we order?" Matthew asks the grandfather. He
glances at Liz, and she smiles, just a tiny smile, but a pleasant one.
They had gotten into the habit of asking the grandfather this question after one evening when they realized they'd fallen into a rut—
chicken *tikka masala* for Liz, always, and *bhoti kabob* for Matthew,
always. That evening they asked the grandfather what they should
order, and he told them. From then on they had asked him every
time, and they had ordered what he suggested every time.

"Well," says the grandfather, "I think you will like the chicken
tikka masala for you and you"—nodding to Liz and Belinda—"and
for you"—turning to Matthew—*"bhoti kabob."*

Matthew stares at him for a moment without speaking, and then
he turns to Liz, but she seems not to see anything remarkable in
what the grandfather has said. *Was I wrong about what we used to
order, or has Liz just forgotten?* "Fine," Matthew says. "We always take your advice."

The newspaper clipper has nearly finished eating, but he's still
muttering and clipping. Now he's cutting something from a copy of
Newsweek. Matthew pours more tequila.

"I wonder how many people have wondered who he is," he says.
"The Neat Graffitist, or the Culture Guerrilla, or whatever. You
know what I mean? All of us who have read these things of his have
something in common, and we don't know it. It's interesting. It's
interesting to think about the ways that people in a city can be bound
together without their even being aware of it." Liz and Belinda just
nod. "Or, maybe not," Matthew says. It is interesting, too, to think
about the ways in which he and Belinda and Liz are bound together,
by the past, now that certain experiences he had with Liz have been
duplicated in ways that, it pleases Matthew to consider, neither Liz
nor Belinda is aware of, and by the present, by this moment, the
tequila, the noise in the room, their conversation, their conspiratorial

huddle, and, possibly—oh, what a titillating thought—by some as-yet-undefined elements of their future.

Their food arrives, and they fall to with gusto. They've reached that point of intoxication when the best object of drinking has been achieved: their inhibitions have been lowered, their tongues have been loosened, a warm well-being has suffused them, a puckishness inhabits them. They smile continually. They talk freely. They are, at a low and manageable level, in a state of constant sexual excitement, just that level that makes one flirt without embarrassment and respond to flirting without seriousness.

The academics are being served, and their being served attracts the attention of the entire room, because three waiters are required to bring their food to the table, and when it arrives it will not fit. There is a panicky conference among the waiters, and a folding table is produced and unfolded, requiring the diners at two neighboring tables to rise and wait while their tables are shifted and the folding table is wedged between the academics' table and the one where Matthew, Liz, and Belinda are sitting. Onto this appendix is placed dish after dish. The academics seem to have ordered wildly, with no notion of how much food they'd be served, but if they're surprised to see so much food, they don't show it. They go on talking animatedly, apparently unaware that everyone is watching them. Perhaps they wanted all this food. The big man must put away big meals, but the others aren't big. One couple is almost miniature. Is that concern in the expression of the little man? Chagrin? He looks at Matthew suddenly. He raises his eyebrows. Matthew grins. The hockey players stand simultaneously, face the academics, and applaud.

The academics look up, face the hockey players. The big man raises his hands above his head, clasps them, and waves them, as in a victory salute. He grabs a round of bread, *nan*, tears a piece off, and with it scoops up a mouthful of whatever is in front of him. The others at the table seem surprised by this. They glance at one another, hesitate, and then all begin eating in the same way, and all resume talking at once. Matthew can make out bits of their remarks between mouthfuls, thus:

"—surrealist constructivity of *objets trouvés*—"

"—metalinguistic maze without any pretext at historical absoluteness—"

"—defines the intersubjective level *tout court*—"

"—with the destruction of language as the protagonist—"

"—although when perceived totally, it is nonexistent—"

"—entirely autoreferential—"

"—precipitating the crisis of language—"

"—descending to an adversarial reductiveness—"

"What on earth are they talking about?" asks Liz, leaning into the huddle again.

"You mean right now?" asks Matthew. "Or generally?"

"Either."

"—permit syntax to overgenerate profusely," emerges from the little man.

"Well," says Matthew, "the little man is proposing to permit syntax to overgenerate profusely."

"No kidding," says Liz. "Are the others for it or against it?"

"I don't know. Want me to take a survey?"

"Nah. But see if you can get them to stop eating with their hands. It may be authentic, but it's quite disgusting." Belinda and Liz are getting a little out of control, snickering, laughing out loud.

"Do you know where the ladies' room is?" asks Belinda.

Liz looks at Matthew immediately, and they smile but somehow keep from laughing. A warmth spreads across Matthew's back, through his stomach, and into his scrotum; it's the physical manifestation of happy memories. He and Liz have laughed about the bathroom here many times, on many happy visits. Of course, if it's true that Liz never loved him, then she couldn't have been as happy as she seemed to be. She must have been faking it sometimes, maybe all the time. No, that couldn't be so. They *were* happy times. Liz's not loving him didn't make them less happy, not at the time. Later, when she decided that she didn't want to go on living with someone she didn't love, yes, but not earlier, not always. There were many happy moments, there must have been.

"Go around this corner," says Liz, pointing, "and go through the door that leads into the kitchen. Turn left at the dishwasher and then go straight toward the door that leads to the alley. Just before you get to the alley, there's a door on your right. That's it."

Belinda wrinkles her brow and grins. She puts on a good-sport look and shrugs. She leaves. Matthew pours tequila. He and Liz raise their glasses and burst out laughing.

Through the door that leads to the kitchen, Belinda sees, directly ahead of her, the dishwasher, a wiry Haitian, stripped to the waist, laboring at a huge pile of dishes in a trough of galvanized metal. Water is spilling in a thin stream from one corner of the trough. The man turns as soon as Belinda comes through the door. The look in his eyes is wild, almost terrified. Belinda has the impression that he may be in fear for his job. Clearly he's falling behind the diners; they are dirtying the dishes faster than he can wash them. Panic, that's what she sees in his eyes. How can he keep up with the pace of eating? Where have all these people come from? Why must they eat so fast?

"*A gauche, à gauche, allez à gauche,*" he says. He seems to try to smile, but the expression he produces looks more like a grimace.

"Thank you," says Belinda. She takes a step and feels her feet sliding out from under her.

The dishwasher's eyes widen. "Careful! Careful!" he cries.

Belinda, though she feels herself falling, tries to smile, tries to reassure him that everything will be okay. She grabs the edge of the doorframe and catches herself. She notices the marks of her slide on the floor, watches her feet scribing arcs in the soapy, greasy water. Helpless to stop herself, she rotates backward, out the door, into the dining room, stopping when her feet strike the carpet. She catches sight of Matthew, looking at her over Liz's shoulder, surprised. She launches herself back into the kitchen. Does she hear laughter behind her? She picks her way across the floor, holding her hands in front of her in case she begins to fall again. She turns the corner and is now in the kitchen. It seems to be about twelve feet square. She tells herself that it must actually be larger, that it only appears so small because of the clutter. Five people are trying to cook in this tiny room. Here the tile floor has a coating not of soapy water, but of oil so even and glossy that it seems deliberate. Two men are laboring at a tandoori oven, shouting ceaselessly while they work. They seem to be exhorting the oven to cook faster. They glance up at Belinda for the briefest of instants and shout at her in much the same manner as they have been shouting at the oven, but with smiles. They jerk their heads in the direction Belinda has been told to go and go back to shouting at the oven. Three other men seem to be running foot races from one corner of the kitchen to another. Surely they must be engaged in some useful occupation. Ahh, they are. They're making up plates, mounding rice on platters, scooping curries from enormous black pots, shouting among themselves and occasionally at the tandoori bakers, lifting scorching bread from pans of hot fat, and while they are doing all of this they don't fall down. Belinda is amazed. Why don't they fall down? She can barely make forward progress across the floor. *This is a friction-free floor*, she thinks. Little by little, taking mincing steps, she makes her way to the alley door. It's wide open, but the heat of the kitchen is so great that Belinda barely feels the cold air. An enormous white Lincoln is parked in the alley, right beside the open door. An Indian woman is sitting on the back seat, watching a small color television. At Belinda's right is a wooden door, faded green. She knocks, softly. The men in the kitchen call out at once:

"It is free."

"It's all right."

"Okay!"

"Go right in."

"No one is there."

She realizes how closely she has been watched. She smiles at the men and nods, opens the door, closes it, latches it, raises her skirt, pulls her panty hose down, and squats over the toilet. She's in a tiny room, once a closet. There was barely room for the toilet, but a sink was installed by cutting a hole in one wall and building a niche that must, she realizes, project into the kitchen. The door doesn't close

BOOKCITY
501 Bloor Street West Toronto 961-4496

8:43 pm 04/07/97
36896
X HUMAN CROQUET   1 @ 19.95   19.95
X SINGAPORE WINK   1 @ 6.99   6.99
X IMPERFECT SPY   1 @ 6.99   6.99
X MAGAZINES   2 @ 7.75   15.50
SUBTOTAL   49.43
TAX - GST   3.47
TAX - Province   1.24
TOTAL TAX   4.71
TOTAL   54.14
CASH PAYMENT   54.14

gst # r 100581552

...n hear the bustle of the
...ar her urinating.
...ew and Liz try, for just a
...in themselves.

...oup comes to their table,
...voman, wearing layers of
... the White Mountains.
...asks. Matthew has been
...ound the room, trying to

... ordered," says Matthew.
...h you then?"

"No," says Matthew. "Thanks, but we really aren't interested."

The woman looks at the man in the nylon shorts. He's still muttering and clipping. The woman hesitates and then turns away,
though he's certainly a good candidate for surplus food. He has
cleaned his platters completely. He's terribly skinny and would
probably welcome another dish. *People would be willing to help the
poor if only they were more attractive*, thinks Matthew. He thinks
of saying this to Liz and Belinda, but they have their heads together
and are laughing like schoolgirl pals again, watching, while trying to
appear not to watch, the big woman's efforts.

"Oh, Jesus," says Liz. "Get a load of this. She's going to try to
give it to the colonials."

The colonials are listening while the big woman offers her food
to them. They are polite, but nervous.

"Now those are good manners," says Liz. "Those people are
willing to listen to this woman without ever telling her that they
think she's nuts. That's breeding."

"Listen to her," says Belinda. "Now she's describing the dishes."

"They probably think she works here. She goes around displaying the dishes that are available."

The colonials refuse the food, politely. When the woman goes away they put their heads together and begin whispering about her. Matthew sees their eyes dart in her direction, and he can imagine their conversation.

"Who on earth would want her leftovers?"

"Do we look impoverished to her?"

The waiters and busboys descend on the academics' table en masse and begin clearing it, as if they have decided that enough is enough. If there is food to be served, it will come directly from the kitchen. There will be no food bought once and served twice.

The woman turns to what should have been the most obvious group, the hockey players, who are singing. They accept the food eagerly, and the woman begins ferrying platters and bowls to their table. Some of them she has to snatch from the hands of the busboys. The hockey players offer boisterous thanks. One rises and kisses her.

The big academic in the down jacket tries to communicate with them in Russian. He elicits only shrugs and mocking laughter. The academics go through some animated confusion over the check, gather their coats, and make their way out. As they leave, one of the hockey players makes a joke at their expense. Matthew, Liz, and Belinda can't make it out, but when all the hockey players, American and Russian, laugh in the way that only young men who think they have the world by the balls laugh, Matthew understands.

"You hear that laughter?" asks Matthew.

"Are you kidding?" asks Belinda.

"What did they say?" asks Liz.

"Oh, I don't know," says Matthew. He doesn't say what he wants to say, because it would diminish him in their eyes; he wants to say: "I mean, do you hear what *kind* of laughter that is? It's cruel. It's the cruel laughter of big, stupid guys, and it turns out to be international."

Belinda and Liz begin speculating about the sexual abilities of Russian hockey players, in voices much louder than they realize. Matthew urges them out.

"Good-bye," says Liz as they pass the hockey players. "It's great to see you having such a good time."

One of them rises immediately. "Please to sit down," he says, stepping aside from his chair unsteadily and gesticulating elaborately.

"Oh, no, no. We have to go," says Liz. "Good-bye. Good-bye. *Do svedanya.*"

"Oh, no. Please don't say '*do svedanya,*' *krasivaya zhenshchina.*"

"*Da—krasivaya,*" says another. "*No ona tebe v materi godit' sa.*"

There is laughter from everyone at the table. Matthew's sure that Liz is the butt of some hockey player humor. He doesn't understand the language, but he recognizes the tone.

The standing hockey player reaches for Liz's hand, and she gives it to him, almost involuntarily. He raises it to his lips and kisses it. "*Krasivaya zhenshchina,*" he says. "*Nemnogo stara, no krasivaya.*"

Liz leans toward him and loses her balance enough so that he has to put his arm around her to steady her. She kisses him, on the mouth, in, Matthew tells himself, a parody of passion. "Bye-bye," she says with an air of youthful coquettishness, a twinkle in her eye. She turns and scampers up the stairs—yes, scampers—without an unsure step. "Good-bye! *Do svedanya!*" she says, again and again, up the stairs.

Matthew holds the door for her, and she lurches through it into the cold air. She throws her arm across Belinda's shoulder for support. "Boy, am I drunk," she says, and laughs.

"We'll get a cab and take you to your hotel," says Matthew.

"Noooo. Not yet. I'm okay. The air will bring me around. I don't want to go back to the hotel yet. Let's go to your place, Matthew. I've never seen it. Linda's seen it. I mean *Belinda.* Belinda's seen it, haven't you Belinda?"

"Yes, I've seen it."

"See? Belinda's seen it. I want to see it, too."

"Sure," says Matthew. "You're a little D-and-D, you know."

"Well, good," says Liz. "I haven't been D-and-D for quite a while. That means," she says, turning to talk into Belinda's ear, "'drunk and disorderly.' That was what we used to call ourselves when we'd had just enough to drink to make us loose, you know? Kind of lighthearted, and a little outrageous. Sometimes Matthew would call home from work and say, 'What do you say we go out tonight and get drunk and disorderly?' Doesn't he still say that?"

"No," says Belinda. "Not to me, anyway."

"Not at all," says Matthew. Now Matthew seems to be on the edge of being drunk most of the time, but he never gets disorderly, never loose, lighthearted, outrageous.

"Well, let's go," says Liz. She takes Belinda's arm and Matthew's and marches them off. Matthew has the odd sensation of being with his mother, as if he were showing off a new girlfriend for her. He's thrilled to be taking Liz to a place she doesn't know, a place where he has entertained other women, made love to other women—one other woman, anyway—and how exciting to have that other woman along. *What*, he wonders as they walk along, *has Belinda told her about us?*

Across from the Public Garden, outside the Katherine Gibbs Secretarial School, they pass a young man leaning against an iron fence, sobbing like a child. He stands with his arm against the fence, resting his head on his arm, and sobs. His shoulders shake, and he can barely catch his breath between sobs. Liz slows, seems to want to stop. Matthew clamps her arm against him and moves her along, firmly.

"He was crying," whispers Liz. "Just standing there crying."

"I know."

"He was a young guy."

"I think he's just drunk," says Matthew.

"He probably is, but he was just standing there, crying."

"Maybe his sweetie left him," says Matthew, and he doesn't regret saying it. Let her draw her own conclusions. Let her know how much she hurt him. She should know.

"This isn't at all what I would have expected, Matthew!" Liz exclaims, exactly as Matthew had hoped she would. He brought her into the living room in the dark. Under these conditions, the place never fails to impress a visitor. There's so much glass that one seems to be floating, and the manifold illumination of the city, uneven and intriguing, picks out details at random and stipples the chrome and glass with color. "I mean, this is nothing like what you used to like," Liz says.

"I wanted a change. I think part of me always wanted to be Fred Astaire."

Liz gives him a look, and then she gives Belinda a look. She decides not to ask whether part of her always wanted to be Ginger.

"How did you put this together? Did you design this yourself?" She looks at Belinda again. "Or did you have help?" Belinda smiles and shakes her head.

"Nope," says Matthew. "I did it myself. Picked everything out. I just kept looking. I went to every furniture store in the city, every lighting place, every place that sells home furnishings. I knew I wanted it to be black and white and chrome. I didn't think I could go too far wrong if I stuck to that idea. It really worked, I think."

"This stuff must have cost a fortune."

"Well—some of it was expensive." The thought crosses his mind that he shouldn't be giving Liz the impression that he has money to spend. "But not that expensive." Now he's ashamed of the thought. "It's amazing, though, how much I could have spent if I'd been willing to—or if I'd been able to afford to. There were some chairs I fell in love with. Dining chairs. Armchairs. Designed by Richard Meier. You know who he is?"

Liz shakes her head.

"An architect. Anyway, he designed some chairs that I saw in a magazine. So I went to Knoll to sit in one and find out how much they cost."

"Mm."

"They had one in the window. Exactly the chair I wanted. I went right in and sat in it."

"What? In the window?"

"Well, yes, but it's just kind of an extension of the display area. So I sat in the chair, and I liked it. How often does anybody get excited by a chair? This was the best chair I'd ever seen. It wasn't all that comfortable. It's not upholstered. It just has a wooden seat."

"No cushion."

"Certainly not," he says with an indulgent smile. He's never spoken to Liz like this before, never felt so sure of himself. "One would not put a cushion on this chair. Anyway, a beautiful woman came up to me and said hello. The perfect clerk for Knoll. Definitely this year's model. Sleek, understated. Smooth hair, you know, cut short. A simple dress. Gray, I think. But snug, and—"

"Get back to the chair."

"Okay. 'It's beautiful, isn't it?' she said. Something like that.

"'It certainly is,' I said. 'I want it. In fact, I want four.' I really wanted eight, but I knew I wouldn't have room. Four were all I could fit. 'How much?' I asked.

"'Are you an architect or decorator?' she asked.

"'No,' I said. 'I'm just a normal person.' She didn't even laugh at that, just smiled.

"Well. She flipped through a book. She poked at a calculator. Nice calculator. Braun. She looked up and smiled again. Nice modern smile. 'Thirteen hundred dollars,' she said.

"Well, that didn't seem too bad to me. It was up a notch from the kind of money I'd been spending, but what the heck. Then she showed me this matching table. While I was drooling over that, trying to decide whether it would fit in the apartment, she poked the calculator again, and she said, 'So that would be seventy-two hundred for the four.' Are you awake?"

Liz is asleep.

Belinda snickers, almost silently. Matthew turns toward her and shrugs.

Belinda gets up. "I'll get a blanket for her," Belinda whispers. "Where are they?"

"I'll get it," says Matthew.

Carefully, with exaggerated efforts at silence, walking on tiptoes, Matthew and Belinda cover Liz with the blanket. Then Matthew removes the folding screen that he uses to hide his television set—a small, three-panel screen, like a shoji screen, white paper panels framed with wood, painted black, with black wood grilles that make a pattern of rectangles over the paper—and sets it up so that it hides Liz.

Here is what Matthew would like to have happen now.

Belinda snaps the light off, turns toward Matthew. There's mischief in her eyes and a wobble in her walk. She puts her finger to her lips. On her way to Matthew's side, she seems about to lose her balance a couple of times. She giggles soundlessly, holding her finger to her lips. Matthew smiles. He's intrigued. Why is she behaving so secretively? She squats beside his squashy tub of a chair. It swivels when she grabs it for support. They snicker and giggle and hush each other. With the smallest and briefest of smiles, Belinda begins undressing. She removes her blouse and drapes it over the chair, in just the way she has so many times on evenings when she and Matthew have returned here after dinner.

Matthew rises from his chair and begins undressing, with the same false attitude of familiarity, though in truth he is amazed. He would never have imagined that Belinda would do anything like this, never. There seems to be an unspoken pact between them that they will treat this as if it were perfectly normal, as if it were just another evening when they make love on the carpet in the living room. He wonders whether he has ever been so excited in his life. His heart is pounding. He is thrilled to his fingertips, exactly that: his fingers tingle, and his sense of touch is heightened.

They make love like furtive teenagers, the familiar flavor of sex spiced tonight with the danger of discovery.

Belinda has so astonished him that he feels he's making love to someone he doesn't know, or, to be accurate, that he is being made love to by someone he doesn't know, since Belinda's in charge, definitely. She knows what she wants, and she's making sure she gets it. She's abundantly wet, and she moves as if she doesn't have full control of her muscles, all twitches and tics and shudders, with no rhythm that Matthew recognizes, like a piece of modern music. This is unlike any other time they've made love. Now and then Liz stirs, on the sofa, about two feet from them, and the slightest sound from Liz sends a shudder through Belinda. The whole thing is so delicious that Matthew can't help smiling. It's adventurous. There's that thrill of fear—and of guilt, too. They're using Liz, using her presence for their own purposes, and it makes them feel—it makes Matthew feel, anyway, and he's pretty sure it must make Belinda feel—naughty. Naughty. That's just what the delectable feeling is. He feels naughty.

Belinda collapses on him, exhausted. Her arms and legs seem to be quivering. She feels that she couldn't lift them if she tried. She feels as if electrical currents have been sent through her, as if she's undergone a kind of sexual shock therapy. She lies there, limp on him. He's still in her, still partially erect, a condition that is not usual. Ordinarily, when he's finished, he is quite finished.

Later, when she's finally able to pull herself away, Belinda leaves, with a sense of slipping off into the night, still flushed with the pleasure of their love and deception.

It does not, however, happen that way. It happens this way.

Belinda snaps the light off, turns toward Matthew. There's fatigue in her eyes and a wobble in her walk. She puts her finger to her lips. On her way to Matthew's side, she seems to lose her balance a couple of times. She squats beside his chair and has to grab it to steady herself. "I'd better go," she says.

"Mm," says Matthew, but he puts his hand behind her head and pulls her toward him, kisses her. He runs his hand over her back, tugs her blouse from her skirt. She pulls away. With the smallest and briefest of smiles, she shakes her head.

"Uh-uh," she says.

"Why not?" says Matthew. He reaches for her, tugs her toward him by the front of her blouse, begins unbuttoning it. "It's an exciting idea."

"Not for me," she says.

"Oh, come on," he says. He doesn't want to plead. He wants her to give in to him. He doesn't want to have to say "please."

"I'd feel very weird, Matthew."

"But incredibly sexy," he suggests.

"Maybe," she admits. "But quite possibly just weird."

"Please," he says.

Liz stirs, on the sofa, and Belinda shudders.

"No," she says. "No."

She takes his hand and leads him toward the door. "Hey," she says, passing the section of wall where the hole ought to be, "it's all back together. I was going to say something, but I thought you wouldn't want Liz to know." She rumples his hair. "I know you," she says. "You don't like to let on that anything is less than perfect."

"Thanks."

"So it's all fixed?"

"No. Afraid not. I just put the bookcases back so that it wouldn't show." He wonders whether she understands what that means. He went to a great deal of trouble to hide the wall and his graffiti, to make himself and his apartment look good for Liz. When Liz is gone, he'll have to pull it all apart again.

At the door, they say good night. "Sorry about—you know," she says.

"Forget it," says Matthew. "It was a stupid idea. Childish. I should never have suggested it."

"Cut it out. Don't go being so hard on yourself."

"I won't. We'll just forget it."

In the elevator, on the way down, Belinda feels anger at first, resentment that Matthew would try so hard to put on a good front for Liz, moving those bookcases. She feels a sinking feeling that she takes for falling out of love, but then she reminds herself that she has never been in love with Matthew, nor he with her, and she decides, when the elevator bounces uncertainly and comes to rest a few inches above the lobby, to cut herself loose from this drifting hulk and let him sink without her if he will.

Matthew tiptoes into the living room with a pillow for Liz. He slips it under her head. For a moment he stands beside the couch, looking at her. He thinks of caressing her while she sleeps, then feels ashamed of the thought and goes to bed.

Matthew is drifting off to sleep, wearing a grin, feeling oddly self-satisfied, not at all disappointed. Though he didn't make love to Belinda while Liz was in the room, he did kiss and caress her while Liz was right there, and that's something. He has tasted exotic, unfamiliar pleasures, and he's content with that. Thunk. *Now what's that? A small sound, a hollow thunk.* It's Liz, bumping into his bedroom door. *Liz.* She slides into bed with him, making an odd sound, deep in her throat, that might be a growl or might be a chuckle. Matthew's too besotted to be sure which. *Liz.* She approaches him without coyness or reticence, hungrily, even roughly. She throws the covers off him and straddles him. She grabs his testicles and squeezes them, grabs his penis and pokes it into her. She makes love to him with unfamiliar vigor, pushing at him, thrusting at him almost violently, and she doesn't say a word, doesn't make a sound. *She's acting as if she has something to prove. Was she really asleep in the living room, or did she hear me and Belinda? Did that excite her?* When she's finished, she rolls off Matthew and falls asleep against him, lying on his arm. He snags the sheet and quilt with his toes and pulls them up until he can grab them with his other hand. Carefully, so that he doesn't wake her, he pulls the covers over both of them. He kisses her, just below her ear, settles back, and is soon asleep.

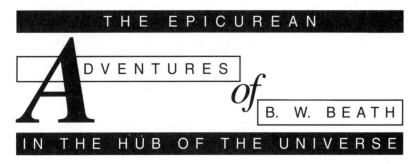

THE EPICUREAN

ADVENTURES *of* B. W. BEATH

IN THE HÜB OF THE UNIVERSE

Superior Indian Cookery

Let us explore together this question: why are people at a certain stage of life—when they begin to feel like weary rowers who have gone too far, forgotten where they were going and why it was supposed to be worth the trip, when they begin to drift and mope and regret having departed the shore—drawn to ethnic restaurants?

Consider us. How are we to explain the warm spot in our heart for **Superior Indian Cookery**, the subterranean agglomeration of grottoes that we call—affectionately, very affectionately—the Black Hole? Something comes over us whenever we stoop to pass through the low door and make our way down the narrow, winding stairs, lined with others waiting for a table. What is that something? An *otherness*. We always feel a little odd, a little displaced, when we visit: we are somewhere we do not quite belong, doing things we do not ordinarily do. We do not ordinarily drink from a bottle concealed in a brown paper bag, for example, but here, waiting on the stairs, we do. Everyone does. We must bring our own drinks, since there is no liquor license. Pouring drinks from a bottle in a bag, even if the bottle holds

a decent wine, makes drinking seem like an illicit activity, exactly like the illicit activity it was when we were young. "Ahha!" we said to ourselves. "Perhaps we're on to something here. Being here returns us to a time when so much of what we wanted from life (alcohol and sex, to name two) was forbidden and, being forbidden, more alluring, possibly, than it has ever been since. But is that all? Surely it can't be just that?" What, then?

The décor? Probably not, even though some of the fabric hangings on the whitewashed walls seem to depict erotic scenes, perhaps even orgies. We are not sure because the hole is so black that we find it hard to separate fact from imagination.

The other diners? Possibly. We wonder, we marvel, when we observe the clientele. We see such diversity: scions of old colonial families, pale and myopic from too many years of breeding too close to the good old stock; a good sampling of the offspring of the ruling classes of emerging nations, sent here to study at BU or BC or any other school beyond the indigenous terrorists' range; and, most exotic of all, citizens of MIT and Harvard, in their intriguing garb,

speaking a curious patois that sounds
much like English.

The service? We don't think so. We
watch the waiters go about their work.
Is it only paranoia that makes us think
the staff is talking about us? We confess
that we have this feeling in all ethnic
restaurants. When our waiter calls out
something in Hindi or Urdu or Canton-
ese—or Italian, for that matter—we can't
help wondering whether he's saying, "I've
got some people here who are most
certainly insane; come and take a gander at them," or, "If a moment arrives
when you can make an observation
without being observed yourself, you must
not fail to notice the ludicrous socks on
the man who has ordered the *kima
masala*." It has occurred to us that, for
the staff at Superior Indian Cookery, the
place must seem to be filled with exotics
all the time—people of bewildering
customs, speaking a baffling lingo, pursuing inscrutable goals. When we leave,
where do they imagine we go? Certainly
they must suppose, since their imagina-
tions must be as good as ours, that we go
somewhere much more interesting than
we actually do. If they imagine lives for
us that are more intriguing than ours are
in fact, doesn't some of that rub off on
us? Don't we, seeing a curious look in
the eyes of our waiter, bask in it? Aren't
we glad to be thought exotic? The grand-
fatherly host, smiling, always smiling,
probably thinks that whenever we do not
come to his restaurant of an evening, it
is because we are indulging in bizarre
sexual practices. Perhaps we are. And
what about that nice-looking trio on the
stairs, the ones drinking the tequila—
what will they be getting up to after
they've finished the last sweet spoonful
of their *mitha bhat* and disappeared into

the dark, into the mysterious nighttime
Boston that only the natives know? We
can't speak for you, of course, but as for
us, we know that we feel a darn sight
more intriguing just knowing that the
paterfamilias here might be thinking about
us along such lines.

The food? Possibly. Most of what we
eat here is stew of one sort or another,
and that's fine with us. Stew is the international dish of comfort and consolation.
When a French *maman* sees that the family
is *un peu triste*, we're sure she makes
bœuf bourguignon or *cassoulet*. Our own
mom made chicken stew (with, unfortu-
nately for the quality of our childhood
memories, lima beans). It's the spices
that make stew different around the world,
and here we find that there is always a
flavor we can't quite identify.

It must be something else, then, but
what? We scan the room to see what
people are drinking. Most are having
wine or beer; however, there is that intriguing threesome (a man and two
women, attractive, fortyish, giggly)
passing a bottle of Cuervo Gold. Tequila with Indian food? A surprising idea.
We ask if we might try it and, since the
answer is "Please do," do. A couple of
swallows later, we make a couple of discoveries: first, that the combination is
surprisingly good; and, second, that that
is exactly why we have come here—we
have come in hope of finding something
surprisingly good. We always come here,
we realize, expecting to be surprised,
hoping that the surprise will be good.
Isn't *that* really why we want to go back
to youth, after all? We are not talking
about nostalgia now. Forget the cozy
fires, your mother's kisses, your father's
pipe tobacco—what you really long for
is what you found in your first olive, your

first drink, first kiss, first whatever: surprise. When you went home for the holidays looking for some remembered flavor of youth, you expected to find it in the old house, in the remembered things, places, and people, and you were disappointed, weren't you? Of course you were. Only the echoes of the past were there, diminished and disappointing. You were looking for the wrong thing! You were looking in the wrong place! What you miss most from the past, from your youth, is novelty. You have lost the capacity to be surprised, and you wish you could regain it. Well, we have found it! We have found it here, in the Black Hole. Here, we now understand, something scrumptious from our past awaits us, waits for us to descend the narrow stairs, bottle in hand, and claim it. It's a taste of the naïveté that made life more interesting when we were young.

We learn here, with each bite of something unfamiliar, that it *is* possible to recover something of the past—not to repeat the experiences that we remember fondly, we know that wouldn't work—but to recover the capacity to experience anew, to be surprised, to be pleased when we weren't expecting to be pleased, to take great pleasures from small things, like a stew or a piece of bread, to find in the smallest experience, the touch of a hand we've touched a thousand times before, something fresh. We are rejuvenated. That's it. That's it. And if we have restored to us the ability to be surprised and pleased, then the future is promising, and we are hopeful. We see how much wider the world is than the circumscribed little dog run we've been inhabiting! We see how much there is still for us to learn, see, do! Strange

people to meet, strange things to eat! Now that we have recovered the capacity to be surprised, anything may happen. We may fall in love. Oh, sure, we've been in love before, but this time it will be different. How many moribund marriages could be revived simply by adding a pinch of an exotic spice to a familiar dish? (Maybe that's what those wall hangings are about.)

Perhaps we now know the secret. We've been rowing the damned rowboat of life for a long time. Our hands are sore, and we're tired body and soul. We stop rowing. We drift. We say, "I can't go on." A voice from somewhere says, "But you must go on." We say, "Why? What lies ahead but death? Why row toward death? Why not just drift and let it come to us?" But here, in the Black Hole, that little voice, speaking with an outlandish accent, says, "Taste this. See? There are surprises ahead." "Well, then!" we say, and we take up the oars and row with the vigor of youth.

And that, *nôtre lecteur, nôtre semblable, nôtre frère,* is why so many people, when they reach what our dedication to frankness forces us to call middle age, are attracted to ethnic restaurants.

—BWB

Superior Indian Cookery
1991 Brahmin Avenue, 555-0202.
American Express, Visa, MasterCard, Diners Club. No checks.
Handicapped: steep stairway, tiny toilet.
Lunch 11–3, Monday–Friday.
Dinner 5–11 daily.
Reservations not accepted.
BYOB.

5

Café Zurich

Matthew's proud that he didn't throw himself at Liz's feet and beg her to come back. He feels that he can be patient now, wait for her to come to him, and now he believes that, eventually, she will come.

I wouldn't have been so—cool before, he tells himself. *I've really changed.*

In the past he has sometimes thought of himself as having changed, but usually for the worse. Perhaps now he has changed for the better, become the man his suits suggest: cool, sophisticated, urbane, chock full of je ne sais quoi. Perhaps he'll find that he can say a mental good-bye to his old self and win Liz as a new man, not the one who bored her, the one she couldn't love, but this new someone, more like BW. If sex with Belinda was electrifying after she changed her name, think what it could be with Liz after he has, in effect, changed his. *Belinda. What about Belinda? I'll have to say something to Belinda. I can't just stop seeing her. I'll have to make a good-bye.* The thought that she may love him enough to be sad, even to cry, gives him a delicious thrill, which shames him. He picks up the phone at once and calls Belinda to make a date for dinner.

"Hello?"

It sounds like Leila, but he isn't quite sure, and he's been mistaken before. He's learned to avoid committing himself until he's sure, so he simply says, "Hi. It's Matthew."

"Hi, Matthew. How are you?"

It's Leila.

"Fine. How are you, Leila?"

"Fine."

"Good." *Why can't I ever think of anything to say to her?*

It's because he doesn't know what she thinks, what she knows, what interests her, or how she spends her time. He hardly ever talks with her, after all. Perhaps if he and Belinda had become more serious about each other, if they had thought of getting married someday, he would have found the time, opportunity, and inclination to really get to know Leila. Perhaps, but wouldn't he have been likely to find that his lust kept getting in the way?

"May I speak to Belinda?"

"Mom's not home. She's still at work, I think. There's some kind of push on. She's been working a lot lately."

"Oh. Sure, of course." This is a false reaction. Matthew doesn't know anything about what Belinda's been working on lately. He's surprised and a little embarrassed to realize how long it's been since he's thought about her. It had been their habit to talk on the phone together nearly every evening, even though they didn't see each other more than a couple of days a week. After Liz's visit Matthew let a day slip, and then another, and with his mind on Liz he has ignored Belinda for more than a week. "I've been horribly busy myself," he claims. "It's a busy time of year."

"Yeah, I guess so."

"Well, I wanted to ask her to have dinner with me."

"Sure. Okay." A pause. *What is that in her voice? Lack of interest? Just distraction?* "I can take a message if you want."

"Okay. Well, how about Friday? This Friday. Since she's been working so hard, Friday should be the perfect day, right?" There is no response from the other end. *Why do I feel like such a jerk when*

I talk to this girl? "It's traditional," he says. "TGIF."

Matthew, Matthew, says the voice of BW, *calm down. Stop thinking about her breasts.*

"All right," says Leila. "I'll tell her."

"We'll be going to Café Zurich, tell her. She'll want to dress up."

"Matthew? Hold on a minute, okay? I want to check the calendar."

A longish wait, and then Leila is back, a little breathless. "That's great. That should be fine. Friday. Café Zurich. That should be neat. What time?"

"Oh, seven."

"Okay. See you."

On Friday, Matthew buys the white mink coat. In the evening, before leaving home, he opens the box, removes the coat, spreads it on the living room rug, fur side up, and considers the effect.

Too—I don't know—cold, somehow, he thinks. *It seems to say the wrong thing.*

"Hooker," for instance, says the voice of BW.

You may be right, Matthew admits. *Maybe the bed.*

He takes it to the bedroom and spreads it on the bed, just as Belinda had.

That seems better, says BW. *It's what she did, so it ought to say whatever she wanted it to say.*

It might, but I don't know exactly what Belinda might have wanted to say when she invited me to make love to her on the coat. I'm starting to think that this whole coat business is the wrong gesture—completely wrong. It's not a good-bye gift; it's a payoff.

But think of Belinda's surprise and pleasure, and your own, when you reenact that sex scene on the coat later this evening. Even if you have told her good-bye—especially if you have told her good-bye—that's no reason why you shouldn't have one last fling. All the more reason, really. Leave it there.

When he arrives at Belinda's, Leila greets him. She's wearing a robe. She looks as if she's made up for a date. A martini is waiting for him. Leila pours it and says, "I'll be back in a minute." Matthew takes no particular note of that remark and drinks his drink. After a while Leila comes down the stairs, in a black coat, wearing high-heeled shoes and black stockings, carrying a tiny bag that Matthew has seen Belinda carry before. Matthew wonders if she's going to a prom or something. He's surprised to find how touched he is by her appearance.

"You look as if you're ready for a big night," he says.

"Well, I am," she says. "Look—I," and then, in a breathless rush, she says, "Mom couldn't go, you know, work and all, and I figured that you had to go to the restaurant because you're going to review it—right?—and I wanted to go instead, but I was afraid that if I suggested it, you might not think it was such a great idea, so I thought I would just spring it on you, and I hope you aren't annoyed."

"Annoyed?" he says. "I'm delighted," and he is, but he's surprised to notice how avuncular he feels. He calls a cab, and finishes his martini, and wonders whether he'll be able to think of anything to say to her.

At Café Zurich they sweep through the revolving door and into the foyer, and the bowing and scraping begin almost at once.

Showtime, says the voice of BW.

Leila stops just inside the door and turns toward Matthew. Her eyes ask him to lead. She's a little breathless, and he's amazed. He says, "Let me help you with your coat." She turns, and he slips her coat from her. She's wearing Belinda's backless dress. Her shoulders are white and smooth and perfect. Almost involuntarily, Matthew looks into the mirror in front of them, and there he sees her, looking at him or, more probably, looking at them, judging the effect.

Quite a charming couple, really, BW seems to say to him. *Who is this handsome, rather European-looking man slipping a coat from the shoulders of his young, full-breasted mistress?*

More like a father out with his daughter.

Possibly, says BW. *Or a businessman from Cleveland with a child rented from an escort service.*

Depends on how you look at it, I suppose.

Matthew hands Leila's coat to a lackey, who nods when he receives it. Another lackey materializes behind Matthew and, with a murmured "Allow me, sir," assists him in the removal of his coat. Matthew's beginning to feel as if he's in an operetta. Leila stands with her hands clasped in front of her, waiting for the next marvelous thing. She looks as if she ought to be holding a corsage. Matthew offers her his arm, she puts her hand on it, both flunkies push double doors open, and Matthew leads her inside, observing their progress in yet another mirror, directly ahead of them, revealed only when the doors are open. He tells himself that he ought to think they look ridiculous, but he doesn't believe it. He thinks they look quite nice.

Matthew gives his name to the maître d', who says, head bobbing, hands rubbing, "Oh, yes. Mr. Barber. Your table is not quite ready. Would you care to have a seat in the lounge, and we will call you? It will be just a moment."

"Certainly," says Matthew. He knows the lounge here. *Designed to impress. Certain to impress Leila. She ought to get the full experience.* "We'll have a drink in the lounge," he says to her, though there's no reason in the world to think that she hasn't heard the maître d' as well as he has.

"Oh, good," she says. They take the few steps to the lounge, Leila always waiting to be led, to be shown or told what to do. Matthew glances around the room. There are quiet corners that he would ordinarily choose, but he doesn't want to look like a seducer of young girls, trying to conceal his illness in the dark, so he suggests a banquette near the door, near the bar, in the most brightly lit part of the room, where his intentions will appear aboveboard.

Two waiters arrive immediately, as soon as Matthew and Leila have made a move in the direction of a table. One pulls the table out from the banquette, too quickly, too far out into the room, with too much brio. The other bows, says, "Good evening, sir, madam," and deposits a plate with a crock of pâté and a ring of Ritz crackers on the table in front of them.

Ritz crackers? cries BW.

Before they have had a chance to get settled, the waiter asks, "Would you care for something from the bar?"

Matthew is, for a moment, about to ask Leila what she'd like to drink, but when he glances at her he sees a note of panic in her eyes, and a resonant note of panic runs through him. *Good God,* he says to himself, *I'm out with a child. Can she order a drink? Can I order a drink for her? Are they going to ask for her ID? Are rules like that overlooked here? Why the hell didn't I take her to a dark corner?*

Champagne, says BW. *Surely they won't refuse her a glass of champagne. Ask for the wine list anyway—it will give you a chance to stall.*

"May I see the wine list?" Matthew asks.

"Certainly, sir."

The wine list appears without any apparent lapse of time. It's bound in leather and resembles a photo album of the sort usually embossed with the words "Our Wedding." The waiter presents it to Matthew, opening it as he does so, and then stands, waiting, while Matthew looks through it. *How much does she know about champagne?* he wonders, and then hates himself for it.

Good question, says BW. *It would be ridiculous to go overboard with this. Domestic, I think, but good domestic.*

"We'll have a bottle of the Domain Chandon Brut," Matthew says.

"Certainly," says the waiter, taking the list and, at last, disappearing.

Matthew turns toward Leila and she toward him, and both try not to giggle. "Do you have an ID or anything?" Matthew whispers.

"No," she says. "I never even thought of it. I probably could have gotten one. Are they going to ask for it?"

"I haven't the faintest idea," says Matthew. "I don't usually go out with underage women."

Leila can't help herself. She snickers. For one thrilling moment Matthew feels about sixteen. "Look," he says, the moment past, "if they make any fuss, you're my daughter. It's your birthday. They'll look the other way, I think."

The waiters are back, moving with the exaggeration of actors playing to the last row in a big house. One places a wine bucket in a stand on the opposite side of the table. The other begins twirling the bottle as soon as the bucket is in place. Matthew raises an eyebrow and glances at Leila, but she's watching the business happily. He smiles at her pleasure. She catches sight of him, turns slightly, grins and blushes, embarrassed that she should be caught being naïve and avid. *Already,* he thinks. *Even at her age, it's already embarrassing not to be sophisticated.* Then she touches his hand, and his heart leaps. It's a conspiratorial touch, perhaps her way of asking him to make allowances for her, of saying, "Remember, I'm just a girl." The cork pops. Matthew turns back to the performance.

Of course they would pop the cork, sneers BW. *No subtleties here. Every little luxury, every bit of service, has to be announced, has to be given an exaggerated flourish, has to have its fanfare, so that you don't miss it, so you know that you are in a luxurious setting, so you know that you're really getting service, by God.*

Matthew wonders whether the waiter saw Leila touch his hand and whether, if he did, he can be convinced that she's his daughter if the need arises.

The waiter pours a little champagne in Matthew's glass and waits. Matthew sips. It tastes all right to him. He smiles and nods, extends the glass to Leila, and says, "What do you think?"

She sips and says, "Delicious." Matthew nods to the waiter, who pours and, mercifully, leaves.

Before Matthew can begin to sweat about what to say to Leila, she leans toward him and says, "So, give me your professional impressions."

"Well, let's see," he says. He surveys the room. Nearby a group is loudly reminiscing about Joseph's, a restaurant sadly missed, one much better than Café Zurich, closed long ago for reasons Matthew has never known. *Boors,* says BW. *Why is it that boors seek out the most expensive restaurants? The waiters are the best-dressed people in the room. Why can't people dress themselves decently?*

Some couples look very nice, Matthew objects. *They're out for a big evening. It's kind of touching. Their freshness. Their awkwardness.*

Yes, well, that is the effect the place is after. This is supposed to be taste of the luxe life. It's more like a stretch limo than a restaurant. These people are supposed to feel that they're out of their league, says BW. *See them whispering to each other, the little couples. "This is the life, eh, sweetie?" No, it's not, kids. All the people around you are just like you, and all of you are glancing furtively at one another, wondering if any of you is anybody.*

"Well," says Matthew, stalling. He spreads some pâté on a cracker and gives it to Leila.

"Mmm, this is good!" she says.

Oh, for God's sake! Ritz crackers! says BW, but Matthew's delighted by Leila's delight, and he says, answering her question at last, "I think it's very nice." For a while they sit there happily drinking their champagne and eating the pâté and amusing themselves by trying to decide whether anyone in the lounge is anybody.

Too much time passes. Matthew begins to wonder why their table isn't ready. He excuses himself and goes to speak to the maître d'.

The maître d' isn't at his station. From somewhere nearby, Matthew hears an animated conversation, in hushed, tense tones. In the mirrors that line the room, he sees two men in an alcove to his left, lit by the glowing light of a cigarette machine, kept discreetly out of sight behind a grove of potted ficus trees. He can see only the backs of their heads, but he's sure one is the maître d', who seems to be trying to calm one of the waiters. For a moment, Matthew, emboldened by the fact that he's Leila's escort, is about to walk right over and inquire about his table, but he thinks better of it.

The tone of voice. Something's wrong.

"I want you to call the police," says the waiter.

"I will," says the maître d'. "I told you. I'll call the police. But I want you to calm down. Just carry on with your work, and I'll handle everything."

"He's not getting out of here tonight. I know he did it. If the cops don't take him, I'm going to take care of this myself. You hear what I'm saying?"

"I hear what you're saying. Put that away."

"Put that away"? What? A gun? A knife?

Probably nothing worse than a knife, BW tells him. *It isn't likely that waiters are carrying guns yet. Although it certainly isn't impossible, if preadolescent drug couriers are packing Uzis. One might want to rethink one's tipping policy if the practice becomes widespread.*

"You ask anybody," the waiter is saying, beside himself and yet restrained, perhaps by some professional code, from raising his voice above a whisper. "This guy is no good. I'm not the first one. Things are missing from there all the time. From the lockers. Nobody says nothing. Nobody wants to make trouble."

Jesus, it's just like my building, thinks Matthew. *You can't get enough water for a shower some mornings, but nobody complains. At the owners' meetings everybody just shrugs as if there's nothing anybody can do.*

"Nobody has the nerve," says the waiter.

That's it. Nobody wants to make a scene.

"Hey. Let me tell you something. That's not the way I am." Matthew can hear a fist thumping a chest. "I'm not taking it."

Maybe this guy would like to move into my building.

"Somebody hurts me, I'll hurt him. I'll hurt the guy, you know? You know what I'm saying? I'll hurt the guy if I have to."

"Look," says the maître d', "let me give you the sixty bucks, and you calm down."

"What? What? What are you telling me? Why are you going to give me the sixty bucks? Then what happens to him, nothing?"

Matthew would like to hear more, but there is the possibility that they'll come out from the alcove and find him eavesdropping. He walks to the maître d's station, where he stands and looks into the dining room, as if he has just arrived there, has heard nothing. He expects the maître d' to be watching that spot, expects to be seen, and in a moment he is. The maître d' comes bustling across the floor.

"Ah, yes, sir, yes," he says. "Did you have a reservation?"

"Yes," says Matthew. From the corner of his eye, he sees the waiter emerge from the alcove and disappear into the dining room.

He's small and thin. He doesn't look dangerous. Matthew wonders whether he really does carry a knife—or a gun. "Yes," he repeats. "Barber. We've been waiting in the lounge? You said our table would be ready in a moment?"

"Oh, of course, of course. I was just going to come to get you. Your table is just ready now. Would you care to go in?"

"I'll be right back," says Matthew. He's annoyed. He suspects that he was parked in the lounge so that he'd spend more on drinks, a second-rate trick. He thinks of telling Leila about his suspicions, but she looks so pleased, sipping her champagne, that instead he just touches her shoulder (there goes his heart again) and says, almost in a whisper, "Our table's ready."

On the way to the table, Matthew takes a professional gander at the room, without being obvious about it, and notes that many tables are empty.

Well, they're probably reserved, he tells himself.

Whether they have been reserved or not, there is no reason why you and Leila could not have been given one, BW insists. *You were parked in the lounge, and you fell for it, permitted it.*

Oh, what does it matter? I'm not going to let something like that bother me.

Well, you are in a forgiving mood. Exactly the mood they're relying on. Like the other rubes, you have arrived here wanting to be pleased. You don't want to notice the shortcomings, you want to be happy, and if you must be deceived to be happy, you are willing to participate in your own deception. Hope does not come easily or naturally to you, Matthew, but tonight you're hoping for a wonderful evening, for yourself and for Leila. You would love to be enchanted, and you're willing to go halfway.

At least. And you leave me alone, BW.

I shall try.

Booths, tricked out in wedding-cake baroque, plastered and gilded, are arranged along two walls, one near the lounge and the other at the far end of the room; tables fill the vast center area; and a

long banquette runs along the far wall, curving at the near corner
and sweeping back toward the door. All the upholstery is purple
velvet. At the time of decoration, gold braid must have been too
good a buy to pass up. The table to which Matthew and Leila are led
is one of those along the banquette. It's a table for four. The maître
d', with a great snapping of fingers, summons a gray-haired
busman, who, with bustle and clatter, begins removing the two su-
perfluous settings. Matthew is pleased to find that he's removing
the places set on the outside, assuming that Matthew and Leila will
sit side by side on the banquette.

*Well, he doesn't think she's my daughter. A man of the world,
this one.*

It may merely be a subtle form of flattery, suggests BW, *a technique acquired from years of serving aging men who buy dinner for
girls who are not their daughters, men who, this hoary-headed
busman has learned, tip well when they are given any little nod to
their virility.*

Fuck you.

The captain yanks the table out from the banquette; Leila slides
in, and Matthew slides in beside her. A waiter sets their champagne
bucket down and goes through more of the pouring business, with
flourishes and arabesques, ornaments aplenty. Matthew resolves to
pour subsequent glasses on his own. The waiter backs away, bowing, and at last Matthew and Leila are alone again. Matthew looks
up and seems to see heads turning aside.

*They are. It's not my imagination. People have been looking at
us.*

*Well, of course. She is striking, Matthew, and this dress really
does not cover her adequately. On Belinda it was one thing, but on
Leila quite another. Frankly, when she walks across the room one
finds it quite difficult not to stare.*

They're all whispering.

*Well, it's possible that they are just praising the food, making
excuses for the excesses in the decor, pretending to be pleased with
the service, trying to reassure one another about the stability of
their relationships, that sort of thing.*

I think they're speculating about us. Me and Leila.

Yes, that is more likely. I was just trying to calm you.

Matthew turns toward Leila, clinks his glass against hers, and says, "I think we've become a conversation piece."

Leila looks around. Then she turns back toward him, inclines her head close to his, and says, "You may be right."

The waiter arrives. "How are we this evening?" he asks.

Matthew's tempted to make a mockery of this question, but Leila responds immediately, "Fine, thank you." She answers so plainly, and her voice speaks so eloquently of her pleasure at being here, her disposition to be pleased, that Matthew finds himself unwilling to sneer. The waiter hands, first to Leila and then to Matthew, menus even larger, heavier, and more elaborately bound than the wine list, another copy of which he sets on the opposite side of the table. He asks Matthew, "Shall I pour more champagne for you?" Their glasses are still nearly full.

"No, thank you," says Matthew. There isn't a hint of sarcasm in his voice; he has been charmed, not so much by Café Zurich as by Leila, by her ingenuousness. He discovers that he's able to see the room as he supposes Leila must see it, to find there what she finds: well-dressed people, drinking from cut-crystal glasses, eating from gilt-edged plates, the quiet clatter of their tableware, the murmur of conversation, the pageant of service, the grandiloquent gestures of the waiters, the maître d's show of obsequiousness when he ushers a couple to a table, the business of opening and pouring wine, all the little performances that are supposed to add up to a classy place. The lighting is very good, soft and warm, incandescent, not fluorescent, and the people are flattered by it. The men look rather handsome, on the whole, and the women, dressed for this night in elaborate dresses, their shoulders bare, look—at a distance, at least, under these soft lights—alluring and intriguing. *If these people look this good under these conditions, then maybe,* Matthew allows himself to think, *I look as good to them. And the glances I'm getting may be admiring ones.*

Leila looks into the menu she has been given. Open, it hides her from the other diners completely. Matthew could reach his hand down the front of her dress, run his hand over her breast, caress her, and no one would be able to tell. He tries to tell himself that he's not actually thinking of trying to fondle Leila behind her menu. *I'm not thinking about that.* He tells himself that he's merely amused by the size of the menu and that the idea that it would be possible for him to caress her secretly behind it is just a form of mental note-taking, for his review. *I mean, I may be thinking that it would be possible, but I'm not really thinking of doing it.*

"Do you see anything you like?" he asks Leila.

"I can't even pronounce most of these things," she says, staying out of sight behind the menu.

"Don't worry," says Matthew. "The waiter probably can't, either." Leila laughs, and she pokes him under the table, on his leg, high up, almost at his hip. This seems remarkably intimate to him; it's not a part of his body he would have expected her to touch.

It's probably nothing more than the playful gesture of a kid, he tells himself. *Chummy. Devoid of sexual importance.*

Not necessarily. Not necessarily. I think she meant something by it.

Regardless of its intended significance, Leila's poke has had quite an effect on him. He has begun to feel clever and charming.

"Besides," he says, "most of these dishes are misspelled." She giggles again. Can he do no wrong?

"They could have fooled me," she says.

He leans conspiratorially close to her, behind the menus, standing like a stockade fence between them and the rest of the room. "They've fooled most of the rest of the people in here, too. Don't worry."

She's about to say something, but both are suddenly aware that a waiter has slipped up on them and is replenishing their glasses.

"Uh-oh," says Leila. "They're on to us." She bumps her shoulder against his. A pleasant warmth begins to spread through him, beginning at that spot on his shoulder and ending in the center of his chest.

"Here, let me—" Reaching for her hand, he hesitates.

Oh, go ahead, Matthew, says BW. *Be daring.*

"—take you by the hand," he says, taking her hand, "and lead you through this maze of a menu."

No laugh. That was pushing it. Relax, he tells himself. *Be yourself.*

He releases her hand. "The problem," he says, "is that in Switzerland three cultures meet—four, if you count the Swiss themselves."

Belinda would have laughed at that, he thinks, *but it's lost on Leila.*

Yes, well, I think I ought to point out, says BW, *that Leila's ignorance makes her the perfect companion for the particular type of male fantasy that you find yourself living. She is young and pretty and bright, but she is ignorant. You are supposed to teach her. That is supposed to be part of the fun.*

"There are the French," he says, "the Germans, and the Italians. The Swiss have sort of taken whatever they like of those cuisines and made them their own. Americans have done the same thing, of course. Think of pizza, right?"

"Or croissants."

"Right. The doughnut of the eighties. Anyway, some of the traditional Swiss dishes have little stars next to them. I'll tell you what—why don't I order for both of us? I want to get a range of stuff for the review. We can swap dishes back and forth, and if there's anything you don't like, just skip it. Okay?"

"Great."

Matthew looks up, and a waiter comes scurrying over. He orders. Leila watches.

"What do you think of our fellow diners?" he asks when the waiter has gone.

"I don't know. I'm afraid to look. I don't want to get caught."

"Oh! You have to know how. Here, turn a little so that you're facing toward me more. Okay. Now we'll pick up our glasses and clink and lean in a little toward each other and take a sip and set the glasses down and lean in toward each other again, and now you look

into my eyes and put an expression on your face as if you're listening to me say romantic things to you."

She makes a burlesque of it. They laugh.

"Be serious. At least look as if you're paying close attention to
me. Okay, now, while I'm still talking, keep your face turned just as
it is, and let your eyes wander around the room. Riiiight. Now tell
me a little something about what you see."

"Well, right behind you there's a man who's about, oh, sixty, I
guess, very fat, with big cheeks hanging down—"

"Jowls."

"Jowls?"

"Those big cheeks that hang down. They're jowls. Or—no—
they're wattles. Wattles because that's what they are on a turkey."

*Is that right? No, it's not right. Wattles isn't right. Wattles are
nearer the neck, not like jowls.*

He thinks he ought to correct himself, but he doesn't want to. He
doesn't want to appear uncertain. He decides to let it stand.

Oh, good, says BW. *You've taken an important step here. You
are now officially leading the girl astray. She's going to go around
calling jowls wattles. I hope it's not on the college boards.*

"Wattles is perfect," she says. "He has these big *wattles.* And
he's eating, I don't know what he's eating, but he like doesn't seem
to like it? He looks like a guy who doesn't like much of anything.
And he has a teeny little wife with him who just sits there and eats
but doesn't say anything. Oops, I take that back. She's saying
something now. And he's shaking his wattles."

She goes on, making comments about the diners she can see, and
Matthew begins to feel blessed.

*It's as if I've been given a chance to go out on my first date all
over again. But this time I know how to behave. I know what to do.
Somehow I even know what to say.*

"If you lean in close, I'll tell you about the couple right next to
us," says Matthew. She leans not merely close to, but against him.
Certainly it can't have occurred to him, before he asked her to lean
closer, that if she leaned this close, with their heads bowed and

nearly touching, he would be looking right down the front of her dress.

She wants me. The way she leaned against me like that. She's trying to show me that she wants me.

That may be so, it may really be so. The only other explanation for all of this—her coming out with you in her mother's place, the dress, this leaning against you—is that she's a heartless tease, who will make you ridiculous.

"Maybe another sip of champagne," says Matthew, "just to keep up the illusion that our little tête-à-tête is not an excuse to talk about them." They sip, and after they replace their glasses on the table she leans right back up against him again.

"He's wearing a gray suit," says Matthew. Matthew's wearing a gray suit, too, but the young man's is better tailored. It drapes in a relaxed way that Matthew has always admired but never achieved, though he fusses over the fit of his jackets for months after he begins wearing them, and again and again he trots them over to a seamstress—a Swiss woman, as it happens—to have buttons shifted and reshifted, sleeves shortened or lengthened, or to have the linings, which have an infuriating habit of hanging below the back, shortened.

Perhaps, Matthew, whispers BW, *this relaxed drape is more a matter of attitude than fabric and tailoring—insouciance, friend, insouciance. When you don't care how it hangs, then, and only then, it will hang with that careless perfection you pursue by shifting buttons.*

Leave me alone.

Then, too, adds BW, *the fellow is considerably younger than you are, and in better shape. That would have something to do with it.*

"How old?" asks Leila.

"What?" says Matthew, startled. *Jesus! I'm going nuts. I'm starting to talk to myself. Leave me alone.* "Oh, not that old. I'd say it's this year's model. Armani, I think." A nice recovery. He's rewarded with another of those exciting punches to the leg. "Oh. Oh. You mean the guy. Probably—"

How old is this guy? Twenty-five? Thirty? Thirty-five?

"Twenty-eight? I don't know. Thirty-two?"

"Close enough."

Of course. It is close enough. Twenty-eight, thirty-two, forty-three, there's no difference for her after twenty. I wonder how old the geezer she pegged at sixty really is.

"He's a 'laid-back kinda guy,'" says Matthew. "Doesn't want anybody to think that he's impressed with this joint. He's got his tie loosened, you know, his collar unbuttoned. I can't tell what he's thinking. He doesn't have any strong expression on his face, but he's tending toward a scowl." Matthew imitates. "He has longish hair, thin, fine. She's a blonde. One of those blondes who gets a tan right away, you know the kind I mean? They turn the color of teak sometime late in May and they stay that way on into October. She's attractive."

"Mmmm," says Leila, pursing her lips, knitting her brows, performing a parody of jealousy.

Oh, wonderful, wonderful.

"But not my type," says Matthew. "Too stiff. Too cold. She's like—well—"

"I know. Cashmere sweaters and loafers."

"You've got it. She has a fur coat over her shoulders, a mink. But there's something the matter. She's pissed about something. She keeps poking at the tablecloth with her fork. Let's tune in, shall we?" Leila smiles.

The blonde asks the young man, "How come you don't like Victor when you don't even know him?"

Matthew raises an eyebrow to ask, "Did you hear that?" Leila nods her head, just enough so that he can see.

"I just don't like him," the young man answers. "I just don't see anything there to like."

"That's a stupid attitude, you know."

"Stupid. Fine. It's stupid."

"You should see the way they're sitting," whispers Matthew. "They've twisted around so they aren't really facing each other anymore. She's turned more toward us, and he's looking toward the door."

"I'm just saying you shouldn't make up your mind in advance," says the blonde.

"Why are you so interested in my liking Victor?" asks the young man.

"It isn't Victor, it's people," says the blonde. "You don't like anybody anymore."

Leila and Matthew exchange looks.

Their soup is served.

"Mmm, this is delicious," says Leila, sampling hers. Matthew hears the relief in her voice and realizes that she must have been worried that everything she would be required to eat in order to play sophisticate would be yucky.

So young, so young, he thinks. *In the context of her life, this is an adventure. She's vulnerable here. She's put herself in my hands. I'm her guide through unknown territory. She trusts me.*

However, says BW, *to put the plainest face on it, Matthew, she has the most exciting body you have ever been this close to, and if you let scruples keep you from fucking her, you'll regret it forever.*

On the other hand, I might feel guilty forever.

Grow up, Matthew.

"I've never had this before," she says. Immediately she frowns, raises her eyebrows, and rolls her eyes. "What am I saying? Of course I've never had this before. I've never tried anything weird." That's a broader statement than Matthew would have liked to hear, since it raises the question of just how much of the evening she catalogues under the rubric "weird." Just the food? Or the whole idea of being taken out to dinner by an old guy like Matthew?

"Am I acting like a jerk?" she asks.

"What? Not at all." *You're wonderful. You make me feel wonderful.* Does he dare to say what he thinks? If he dares, can he say it without, on the one hand, making it sound like a move in a seduction gambit or, on the other, having it sound as if he thinks of her as a specimen? "You're wonderful," he says. He doesn't get it quite right, erring, out of timidity and indecision, in the direction of specimen.

"Oh, yeah," she says with that frown again. "I'm a great kid."

"Oh, shit," says Matthew, to his surprise. "I didn't mean it to sound that way. That isn't what I meant."

"I'm acting like a kid. A jerk."

"No. You're being honest, and—"

"Yeah?"

"Oh, I don't know. I don't know how to put it." *Yes, you do. Try "naïve," or "touchingly naïve," or perhaps "unaffected," or "refreshingly unaffected."*

"I think *jerky* is the word you're looking for."

"Leila," he says, dropping his voice and speaking with the flat tone we use to show, or pretend, that we have dropped all pretense, "if you were ten years older, I'd be falling in love with you."

Leila gets it. She doesn't say anything. She goes back to her soup.

"Maybe I am anyway," Matthew says, speaking so softly that she just hears him, and then bending to his soup.

A fine job, Matthew, says BW. A very fine job indeed. I think you've really turned a corner here, and I couldn't have done a better job myself.

I just told her the truth.

Yes, yes, you did. You used what is sometimes the best ploy of all: the honesty ploy.

It wasn't a ploy. It was the truth.

It was a ploy, Matthew. You're using the truth to win her. You've found your technique. You've got your line. It happens to be the truth, but it's still a line. The pitiful part, from where I'm standing, is that it really is the truth. You'd rather fall in love with her than go to bed with her. I correct myself: you'd rather have her fall in love with you. I think it's your greatest weakness, Matthew, this need to be loved.

The gray-haired busman removes their soup bowls, and two waiters arrive. One delivers their salads and operates an enormous pepper grinder over them. The other places a small casket beside each plate. They bow and scrape away.

"What's that?" asks Leila.

"It looks like a coffin," says Matthew.

"You're sure you knew what you were ordering?"

"Gee, I thought so. 'Grilled Lilliputian.' I thought that was—"

She giggles. *She got it. She got it.*

"All right," she says. "I'm taking a look." Slowly she raises the lid of the casket. Inside, reposing on velvet, is a salad fork. She removes it. "It's cold," she says.

"Oh, boy," says Matthew. "Chilled salad forks." He's about to add something acerb, but Leila says, "They really know what they're doing, I guess, huh?" and he just smiles and nods.

They eat their salads, then their entrees are served, and they eat in silence for a while. Then, suddenly, as if an idea has just occurred to her, turning on the banquette, so that Matthew has a passing worry that she may jar the table and spill everything, she says, "Matthew?"

"Yes?"

"Could we go out after dinner?"

"Sure. Where would you like to go?"

"Could we go dancing?"

Matthew likes to think of himself as a pretty good dancer, but he knows he's not. He never learned to dance when he should have, in high school. He was barely able to get up the nerve to dance at all then, and he was terrified of the fast dances. He knew all the words to rock 'n' roll songs, but he couldn't carry a tune or tap his feet in rhythm. At a dance he was tapping a paper cup in what he thought was time to the music, when a girl sitting next to him, a wallflower like him, said, "Will you stop it? You're not even on the beat, you know," and he never risked dancing again. He began listening to old pop music of the thirties and forties, that led him to jazz of the same era, and that's how he discovered the saxophonists with the big sound, Ben Webster, Coleman Hawkins, Chu Berry. In college he discovered that drinking made him a better dancer—not good, exactly, but good enough so that he dared to dance. For a few years he enjoyed it, but he never progressed. He had a couple of steps that he could do, and he did the same steps, at different tempos, across a

decade of shifting fashion in rock music. Then, presto, he felt too
old for rock 'n' roll. Liz loved to dance, and every now and then she
would get a group together to try one new club or another. Inevitably, on these outings, Matthew would catch sight of himself and his
friends in a mirror, surrounded by the kids who were the other patrons, and see a bunch of aging men and women who should, it
seemed to him, have stayed home. Matthew hopes that Leila
doesn't want him to take her someplace where he'll feel like a
chaperone at a high school dance.

"Where would you like to go?" he asks.

"I don't know. Someplace grown up. Like an old movie? You
know, 'out together dancing cheek to cheek'?"

Am I in the middle of some kind of miracle? Am I awake?
"Heaven, I'm in heaven—"

"Of course we can," he says. "I know a couple of places. I
haven't been to any of them, but you know what we can do? We can
try them all."

"Great."

"How are you enjoying the *Züri Gschnätzlets*?"

"Is that this? God, I love it. Is yours good?"

"Wellll." He shrugs. "It's a little overdone. I don't mean over-
cooked. It's got too much of everything. The sauce is too rich. Too
much cream. Too much seasoning. I think they used dried herbs,
and to make up for the loss of flavor they threw them in by the hand-
ful. And then they used too much flour to thicken the whole thing.
So—"

"Oh." She pokes her fork into the food on her plate. "I wonder if
this is any good. Or am I just too dumb to notice?"

"Cut it out."

"Here. Try some."

She forks a bite from her plate. The champagne must be getting
to her a bit: this is far too big a bite. She laughs at the sight of it,
holds it over her plate, letting some of the sauce drip off, bounces it
a couple of times. "Open up," she says. She swings the fork toward
Matthew, and the whole gooey load falls into his lap. It misses his
napkin, placed as he habitually places it, uselessly over his left leg,
and lands on his crotch.

Very softly she says, "Oh, shit."

The fastidious Matthew is mortified. He doesn't say so to Leila, but the fear that rushes immediately to mind is that people, seeing the stain, will think he has wet his pants, as he used to when he was a boy, and the second fear, which quickly supplants the first, is that they will think he has ejaculated, an aging lecher who couldn't contain himself in the overstimulating presence of his young victim. He scoops the food up with his hand and pulls his napkin over the spot.

"I'll go get some paper towels in the ladies' room," says Leila. "Where do you suppose it is?"

"Off the foyer? Just ask the maître d'."

"He scares me to death."

"They're trained to do that. Just picture him with his clothes off."

"That never works for me. Mom tells me to do that, too."

"Then imagine him picking his nose or something. He's just a flunky."

"Okay." She goes off on her quest, and when she approaches the maître d' she looks back over her shoulder, rolls her eyes, and makes a comical grimace for Matthew's benefit.

She's adorable.

Yes, says BW. *And what adorable expressions she'll make when you possess her, Matthew. If she's a virgin—and I think it's highly unlikely—you may even see a real grimace. Perhaps, though, she'll try to give it a comical twist, like this, so you won't feel that you're hurting her. What do you think?*

Leave me alone.

You don't really want me to leave you alone, Matthew. You want me to egg you on. Just look at her, watch her as she walks. You would come in her with such force! Like a cannon! Such pleasure! It would be better than that night with Belinda, the night she changed her name.

I can almost feel it.

Yes. You can, you can. Your testicles ache. Isn't it delightful? You ache for her. How long has it been since you've felt that much lust? She could make sex new again, and I think she's willing to do it, to do it for you.

I don't know. I don't want to think about that any more right now.

The maître d' begins his routine: a small bow, pursed lips, a murmured something, probably "Madame." Leila bows back, poor thing. Now she's speaking to him, he's answering, he's directing her with a wave of the hand when words alone would have been quite enough. Leila turns toward Matthew, sees that he's observed it all, smiles, and touches her nose, just barely. Matthew applauds, discreetly. Leila disappears around the corner.

The blonde on Matthew's right scoots along the banquette as well as anyone can scoot on velvet. She leans toward Matthew and touches his arm. "She's gorgeous," she says. Matthew's annoyed. This is a trespass, a violation of the notion of personal space, which may be the essential civilizing principle of modern urban life. Matthew smiles and says nothing, hoping that his bland smile will make clear his unwillingness to hear anything more from her. It doesn't work. "We just drove back from New Hampshire," says the blonde, "just now."

She must be curious. She wants to know what the story is, he thinks. He ought to end this, he knows. He ought to say, "I'm not interested," or, "I don't care," but he can't bring himself to be that impolite, and he's flattered by her curiosity. "Oh," he says.

The blonde takes this as an invitation to proceed. "Skiing," she says. "Have you ever been skiing in New Hampshire?"

"Cross-country," he says. He's struck by the fact that this is really an attractive woman: excellent clothes, fine hair, smooth skin, perfect teeth. *Is it just curiosity?* he wonders. *Or has my being with Leila made her interested in me?*

"Oh. Cross-country," she says, as if to one of the benighted. "I've never tried that. I've heard it's fun. We didn't think much of New Hampshire, I'll tell you that."

"Really? Parts are very pretty."

"I mean the people. The worst. Where do the beautiful people ski in New England? Do you know?"

Matthew can't believe what he's heard. *"Beautiful people."* She said *"beautiful people."* He thinks of answering with the truth:

"No. I have never wondered where the beautiful people go to do anything." *Has she been trying to find them? Does she want to enroll in the club? Or is it just that she expects the skiing to be better wherever they go?* Matthew shrugs. "Maybe they don't ski in New England at all," he says. "They're probably all in Gstaad."

"Mm," she says vacantly.

"You can probably get some good Swiss cooking there," says Matthew. This remark raises not even a smile, neither from the blonde nor from the young man, who is smoking and paying close attention to his cigarette. *Does she know that Gstaad is in Switzerland? Does she know that she's eating Swiss cooking? Does she know that she's in what is supposed to be a Swiss restaurant? Does she know that what she's eating isn't very good? Does she know that I was trying to make a joke? Is she awake?*

"Well, we went to some ridiculous little place, an inn, supposed to be charming, according to a little write-up we read. 'Charming' turned out to mean 'crude' and 'cold' and 'uncomfortable.' I walk in wearing my fur coat, right? People look at me like I'm some kind of freak. And when I wore high heels—I wore high heels to dinner. The looks. And of course, the place was freezing. There I am shivering in a silk dress."

"I think I broke my toe," says the young man in the pleasantest tone Matthew has heard him use.

The blonde laughs. "Not skiing," she says, "fucking." They both laugh.

Matthew wonders where Leila is. He'd like to get cleaned up as well as he can and get out of here. *And where's the waiter? I want the check.*

"The bed was so short that Jasper jammed his toe against the footboard—"

"Just as I was about to come," offers Jasper. He smiles at Matthew as if at an old pal. His mood is much improved now that he's discoursing on a subject he likes. "What was I going to do? I was between a rock and a hard place." If Matthew were sitting nearer to him, without the protection of an intervening table, he would, Matthew's quite certain, poke him in the ribs with his elbow.

"Thank you, darling," says the blonde.

"It's an expression, what do you want?" says Jasper. "I decided to go for the pleasure, worry about the pain later."

For a moment Matthew thinks of asking whether it was worth it. "Is it really broken?" he asks instead.

"Oh, I don't think so," says the blonde. "It's swollen, but it's probably just sprained or something."

Leila returns to the table; Matthew forgets himself for a moment and stands to push the table away from the banquette to allow her to get in, but he remembers in time and only half rises, with his napkin still on his lap. A waiter rushes over and yanks the table out, with flourishes and bows and incomprehensible murmurings.

Leila's carrying a book printed on beige paper, about the size of an atlas. She slips in beside Matthew, lays it on the table, leans up against him, and whispers in his ear, "Look what I've got."

"Hm?"

"A menu. It's a souvenir. I got it from Pick-nose. You'll have to pay for it, I think, but you can carry it in front of you when we leave. Nobody will see the spot on your pants."

"You're a genius," he says. "You know that?"

Ah, says BW. *There's a charming bond between you now, and the time is certainly right for a kiss, I think.*

Why not?

He kisses her. It's hardly a kiss at all, really, but for an instant his lips touch her cheek.

"I have paper towels, too," she says. "In my bag. But I don't think they're going to do much good. There's probably a lot of fat in that sauce. It might not even come out when you get your suit cleaned, I'm afraid."

"I don't care. I just want to get out of here without feeling like an ass."

They rise from their seats. Matthew's astonished to find that he doesn't feel in the least embarrassed. He doesn't feel like a middle-aged man hiding a stain on his pants; he feels like a young scamp running out on the check. He laughs, in spite of everything, possibly at himself. The man he usually thinks of himself as would be mortified, but right now that man seems like a fool. Matthew even dares to draw attention to his predicament, tapping the menu against his front while he waits for Leila to slide out from behind the table, flaunting his coolness in the face of adversity.

"'Bye," says the blonde. She's looking at Matthew over her coffee.

"So long," says Matthew. "Be careful of his toe next time you're"—he pauses a worldly pause—"skiing." She smiles, and Matthew wonders whether there's any way he could get his phone number to her without alerting the young man. He can't think of any. It interests him to note, however, that he abandons the notion because he can't think of any way to put it into effect, not, as would have been the case on another evening, because he's hit by the feeling that it would be stupid even to think about trying to start something with her because she wouldn't be, couldn't be, interested in him. She is interested in him. He can see that, and he knows that he has Leila to thank for it. Leila, meanwhile, is trying not to snicker. She squeezes between the tables, and Jasper, watching her, draws a long breath. The blonde looks again at Matthew, waits until she's caught his eye, and smiles an intriguing smile.

Matthew, says BW, *don't you see it now? Don't you see what Leila can do for you? Fuck her, and the legs of women all over Boston will open for you. The blonde wants to go to bed with you now, right now. She wants to prove that she's a better lay than Leila. What an opportunity you've got here. Fuck that kid! I'm telling you, Matthew—fuck that kid and you'll be a changed man.*

Matthew gives Leila his right arm and holds the menu in front of him with his left hand. "What are we going to do about coats?" Leila asks.

"We'll just carry them out. Put them on outside."

"Got it," she says as if she were in a spy movie.

Matthew picks up the routine at once. "Once we're over the border, we'll be safe."

"Yes, my darling, I know."

"Be brave."

"I will. I will."

As it happens, the maître d' himself holds Leila's coat for her while she slips into it and then offers to hold Matthew's for him.

"No, thanks. I'll just carry it," says Matthew. He extends his arm, and the maître d' drapes the coat over it. Matthew and Leila pass through one set of doors, nod to the flunkies there, and pass through the second. Everyone looks at Leila, not at Matthew. She's much better camouflage than the menu.

"Free!" shouts Matthew, still in spy-movie character.

"My brave darling!" says Leila. She puts her arms around his neck, very much in mock-movie style, and kisses him. It seems to be a real kiss. *Was it? Or is that just wishful thinking?* She helps him into his coat. There's a cab waiting just up the street. Matthew flags it, and the driver pulls up to them. They get in. Matthew gives his address.

"We'll go to my place," he says to Leila, "and I'll change. Then we can go dancing."

"Okay. Great."

Matthew's sure that going to his place to change must sound like a pretext. He's also sure that the taxi driver heard him, even though he knows that he ordinarily has to shout to make himself heard through the plastic partition.

In front of the Ritz-Carlton, the cab comes to a stop in traffic. Matthew looks out and sees a couple standing under the canopy: a short, round, balding man of fifty something, wearing a brown suit composed primarily of unnatural fibers, accompanied by a long blond drink of water in the area of twenty, wearing a dress composed entirely of tiny reflective panels; it leaves one smooth shoulder bare and is gathered at the hem on one side to bring it a long, long way up her long left leg. Her hair is pulled to one side, caught in a clip. These two stand together, she talking animatedly but without facing him, he with his arm firmly around her waist, as if in fear that if he let her go she'd run screaming into the night, her dress scintillating. The cab moves on, and Matthew glances at Leila to see if she's noticed this couple. She's looking out the opposite window.

They are not far from Matthew's apartment, driving along Huntington Avenue, when Matthew remembers the white mink.

Thank God I didn't leave it on the living room floor.

In a way, says BW, I'm rather sorry you didn't. It would have put you on the edge; it would have been exciting, Matthew. And another thing; it has occurred to me that one reason the kid is interested in you—who knows, it might be the only reason—is that she's curious about just what, exactly, her mother experiences on those evenings when she's out with you. Quite probably she has been curious for some time.

That's repulsive.

You can use it, though. You really should use it.

Matthew pays the driver, overtipping. He's amused to see that his hand shakes a little when he hands the bills over. The driver gives him a mock salute. Perhaps there's a hint of a wink in his eye.

Matthew and Leila walk past the concierge. Matthew feels a twinge of regret that the girl who lives down the hall from him isn't on duty. She might discover an interest in him if she saw him taking Leila up to his apartment.

He nods at the concierge, mumbles a greeting, guides Leila toward the elevators, though it must be obvious to her where to go; the lobby's small, and the elevators are nearly directly ahead of them. *She's seen elevators before, Matthew. She knows what they are. She knows where she's going. She knows what she's getting into.* The elevator repairmen, the Hardy Boys, are standing at the door to one of the elevators. They have a plastic out-of-order sign propped in front of it. When Matthew and Leila approach, one of them says, "All set here. All set." He snaps the enormous repair manual closed, and the other whisks the sign out of the way. Matthew and Leila step in. Matthew presses the button for his floor. The elevator rises smoothly upward for a couple of floors and then stops. Matthew and Leila stand for a moment, waiting for it to begin moving again. Nothing happens.

"Great," says Matthew, nodding. "Great." He presses the button again. Nothing happens. Nothing at all. There is no distant clicking or whirring to offer hope that the box might begin moving again. Just nothing.

"What's wrong?" asks Leila.

"God only knows," says Matthew. "These elevators haven't

been working right since I moved in." He presses the alarm button, and a bell, very like a school bell, rings somewhere below them. "We shouldn't be here long," he says. "The repairmen are right in the lobby."

"Is it safe?" asks Leila.

Matthew's touched. She's asking him for reassurance.

"Oh, sure. There are half a dozen safety devices in these things. We're just going to have to wait until the Hardy Boys come and get us out." Matthew leans on the alarm button.

"Can you use that phone?" She points to a little door labeled PHONE.

"Ha!" says Matthew. He has opened the little door before. He opens it for Leila. Nothing's inside but some gum and candy wrappers.

"This is too bad," he says. *It's going to break the mood,* he thinks. *What can I do about that? Should I put my arm around her? Should we sit down? Damn, this would have to happen. I deserve this, I suppose. This is my luck. This is what I get for thinking— well, for thinking what I was thinking. Maybe I should ask her to dance. That would be kind of cute.* Suddenly, the doors begin to open. A thin crack appears between them, and the voices of the comical repairmen come through it. Fingers, dressed in red gloves, reach through, a pair of hands, then two pairs of hands, prying the doors apart. Their emancipators send up a cheer for themselves, and suddenly the doors pop open. The elevator repairmen are standing there grinning, pleased with themselves. Matthew and Leila have to hop several feet to the floor, Matthew wondering as they do how much of Leila is visible to their rescuers when she clambers down.

They shake hands all around, and, fearlessly, Matthew and Leila take the other elevator.

"Well, that was a riot," says Matthew once they're inside his apartment. He sniffs. The odor is back. *Damn. It's in its rotten-banana phase. And there's some other smell, too. What is that?* He takes Leila's coat, watching her nose. He sees nothing to suggest that she smells anything that offends her, no flaring of the nostrils, no wrinkling. "I'm going to make myself a drink," he says. "Would you like something?"

"I would, yeah. But I don't know what. Daddy taught me how to make all those drinks, but I don't really like the taste of any of them."

"I'm going to have a Scotch. Do you like Scotch?"

"No."

"I'll bet you'd like a Black Russian."

"I don't know."

"I think you'll like it."

"Whatever." She wanders past the kitchen and turns the corner. The view has its usual effect. "Oh, wow," says Leila. "This is beautiful."

"It's nice, isn't it?"

"It's *amazing*. This is the most beautiful apartment I've ever seen." She's standing as close to the windows in the living room as she can, as if she were standing outside a shop window, looking in at something she wanted.

Matthew starts his favorite Coleman Hawkins tape, the bluest, throatiest. Leila doesn't respond to the music, as far as he can tell. He returns to the kitchen to make the drinks. He hesitates over Leila's.

You know, Matthew, says BW, *it is possible to get a lot of alcohol into a girl pretty quickly through a well-concocted Black Russian.*

I'm not going to descend to that.

He puts lots of ice into a lowball glass and pours less than a shot each of Kahlúa and vodka. He carries the drinks to the living room. He understands for the first time ever just what *seething* means when it is applied to emotions.

"You'll like this, I think," he says. "But don't let it fool you. It's stronger than it tastes. Go slow. I'll be right back as soon as I change."

While Matthew's changing, Leila wanders around the living room, reads his graffiti, inspects the demolition of his wall. When Matthew returns, he stands a moment in silence, watching her.

I don't know what to do with her.

I know what to do with her, says BW. *One look ought to tell you. She looks so desirable standing there!*

But I feel like a pathetic figure when I think of touching her or— anything.

You're just afraid. It's not scruples—it's fear.

You're right. I am afraid. I want to touch her, but I'm afraid that everything will go wrong. I don't want to startle her.

"Hi," he says. He sounds like an adolescent. He has no idea what else to say.

"This is pretty wild," she says.

"Oh, that. Well, there's a mysterious odor."

"Yeah, I know. Mom told me. I sniffed around, but I didn't smell it."

You didn't? I can smell it right now. Rotten bananas. And— what? Motor oil. Bananas and oil. "Well, it comes and goes."

"I meant the sayings."

"A little crazy, I guess, but I figured what the heck, the wall has to be repainted, so—"

"It's like that writing you see all over town."

"The Neat Graffitist. Right. He's my inspiration. Would you like to write something?"

"Mmm, no. I wouldn't know what to write."

"You're sure you don't smell anything."

"Yeah."

"Well, write that. I've got all my sniff reports there. On the right."

She takes the marker and writes, "I don't smell anything. Leila." Matthew watches her write and wonders why she can't smell it. The oily odor is so strong right near the hole that he has to breathe through his mouth.

"What is this music?" Leila asks.

It must sound like schlock to her.

Mr. Paranoia's first reaction, says BW. *You think she's going to ridicule it, don't you?*

"It's Coleman Hawkins." He's ready to shrug it off, to pretend that it doesn't really mean anything to him, that it's just a curiosity, if that seems to be the way she feels about it. If she says anything against it, anything at all, or snickers, he's ready to tell her that he put it on because he thought it would give her a laugh. He might hate himself for his weakness in the morning, but right now he's prepared to say anything about his beloved Coleman Hawkins that she might want to hear.

"Great saxophone," she says. "Really great."

Great saxophone? Great saxophone?

He laughs a little, involuntarily. "Yeah," he says. "It is. That's Coleman Hawkins."

"Ohhh. Of course. I should have known that, right?"

"No. No. Not necessarily. Why should you?"

"Do you want to dance?" she asks, just like that.

Matthew, says BW, *there must be a God, or at least a devil. Don't just stand there. Didn't you hear her?*

She might be teasing me.

That would be the first thing that comes to your mind! Maybe she is teasing you. Maybe she's laughing at you, you and your stupid old music, your obvious desires. So what? You can use that. Let her tease you. Let her tease you right into her sweet little cunt. Who'll have the last laugh then?

She's not teasing me. Look at that smile. There's nothing in that smile that says she's laughing at me. There isn't an ounce of nastiness or deceit. It's just a smile.

All right, all right. Who cares? Dance with the kid, will you? She's standing there.

Maybe she just wants to dance. Maybe that's really all there is to it.

"I'd love to," he says at long last. In an instant she's right up against him. He wasn't prepared for this. He had expected that she would take his hand, and he would put his arm around her waist, and they would shuffle around the room a little, but her idea of dancing is apparently completely different. It's an embrace with music. Matthew isn't sure whether this is a style or she's in love with him. *Well, not in love with me, but that she has a crush on me.*

That she wants you, says BW.

She lets her head rest on his shoulder, she puts both arms around him, down around the small of his back, and she presses her pelvis against him, but it's not passionate. It's dancing. Matthew is so excited that it's beginning to get embarrassing, but she's just dancing. He presses her against him. *Not really. I'm just squeezing her a little, just a little.* He can't detect any response.

The song ends. "Thank you," he says, thanking her for pressing herself against him, not for dancing with him.

"Thank *you*," she says, and he cán tell that she hasn't thought of their dance in the same way he has, that they're not playing the same game. If they were, she would have said something like "You're welcome," with a twist to it, a hint of a leer, so that he'd know that everything she'd been doing was deliberate, and that it was meant to lead somewhere. *She's just too young. She doesn't even understand.*

Nonsense, says BW. *Even you would have to admit that for much of the evening you haven't been thinking of her as a child. Nor have you been thinking of yourself as some gray-haired lecher taking advantage of a girl. Maybe you are, technically, but you haven't been thinking of yourself that way. Admit it. In this dark room, wearing that dress, lit only by the light of the city, she's a woman. Look at the two of you, taking a sip of your drinks. You're just like a pair of grownups.*

"What was that tune?"

"'Angel Face.' It's pretty, but the next one's a real classic. 'Body and Soul.'" He takes her in his arms again, and they go back to hugging to music. This time, though, he's holding her differently, in a way that, he tells himself, he shouldn't be holding her, both arms around her, running his hands slowly over her bare back. He's getting carried away.

I am. This has to stop.

Oh, come on. This is pretty tame. Your hands aren't exactly all over her. Please don't stop now, Matthew. For your own sake, don't stop now.

He kisses her neck, low, near her shoulder. Again he cannot detect a response. She doesn't hug him, she doesn't turn her face up to him, she doesn't push him away, she doesn't scream and run for the door. He kisses her shoulder, and the song ends, but she doesn't end their embrace, and all at once, with the truth of their embracing out in the open, he does feel like an old lecher, and he says, "I think I'd better take you home," but only part of him means what he has said; another part is just using the remark to tell her that he's excited by her, that he wants her, and he's inviting her to say something like "Oh, not yet."

I don't believe this, Matthew.

I don't, either. I'm trying to get her to approve of what I want to do with her. A fifteen-year-old girl. I'm trying to get her to tell me it's all right to fuck her. What's wrong with me?

And what does she do? She kisses him. It's a real kiss, warm, promising, provocative. He loves it, loves it, returns it, holds her tighter and tighter, and in the middle of it all, he says to himself, *Belinda's sure to find out. And if Belinda finds out, Liz will find out. And on top of that it isn't right. I'm going to have to take her home.*

He ends the kiss, and he says, "Thank you. And now, I'm going to take you home."

Coleman Hawkins is playing "I Love You," a tune with a poignant and lovely lyrical line, deep and penetrating, that goes right to your heart and makes it tremble.

On the way to Belinda's—Leila's, that is—riding in the cab, Matthew hardly knows what to think of what he's doing.

I'm doing the right thing. The stupid thing, maybe. But I'm protecting myself.

From Belinda and Liz. I know. But think of what you're giving up. You'll never get another chance like this. It's not just this girl, it's this one last chance. Are you sure Liz or Belinda is worth it?

It's not just them. I'm protecting myself from—Leila.

How so?

Well, there's the possibility that she was just playing with me.

Oh, God, let up, will you?

No. The possibility was there, it was always there. I mean, ask yourself, why would she be interested in me? Why would she be interested in a middle-aged man?

Matthew, there might be any number of reasons. She might admire you, for God's sake. She might be intrigued by your way with words. She might be charmed by your money. You might remind her of her father. A lot of these girls are nuts about their fathers, you know. Or she might merely be curious.

Curious.

Certainly. She might simply wonder what it would be like to be in her mother's shoes for a night. Taste the dishes her mother would have tasted. Dance the way her mother would dance. Fuck the man her mother's fucking.

See? There you are. She isn't interested in me in a normal way, the right way. She's curious. I'm a curiosity.

Matthew, you are going to drive one of us nuts.

But, you know, there's also the possibility that none of that is true. There's the possibility that she has a crush on me.

How sweet.

Yes. How sweet. How very sweet. There is the possibility that, in her eyes, I'm—well—charming. Interesting. A handsome older man. Maybe a little frightening. A forbidden adventure. Fascinating, in a way.

Always a possibility. A possibility that you might have exploited.

Yes. At least a possibility. Maybe only a possibility. But while it was still a possibility, it was at least something. And I guess I want to leave it as a possibility. When she gets home, and she goes up to her room, maybe she'll cry over what might have been.

You're a dreamer.

But, you know, I feel wonderful. I feel good. I'm being good to her. Very good to her.

He reaches out for her, puts his arm around her shoulders, pulls her toward him, holds her close to him, and strokes her hair. He speaks into her ear, softly.

"I had to take you home," he says. He sighs, enjoying the melodrama he's creating. "I—wanted you. You know what I mean. You're beautiful, Leila, and—well—I wish that— Maybe I'd better not go into what I wish. You made me wish I were sixteen again. In fact, for a while there, you almost made me feel that I was sixteen again."

The cab pulls up in front of her house. Matthew helps her out, asks the driver to wait, and walks her to the door. There he kisses her good night. He makes it a first-date kind of kiss.

"Thank you for letting me taste sixteen again," he says.

Sounds like regurgitation, says BW.

Matthew feels wonderful, just wonderful, buoyant with the possibility that Leila loves him and would have gone to bed with him, ennobled by the feeling that he has done something to be proud of, a truly adult thing.

He walks down the steps and across the sidewalk to the waiting cab, still savoring his nobility. He's working awfully hard at ignoring BW, but he can hear his voice in the back of his mind, telling him that he has been a sap, that he had a ripe peach in his apartment, his for the plucking, virtually asking to be plucked, and he has put her in a cab and taken her home so that he can feel like a worthy character in a sentimental old movie. *You sap!*

He's about to get into the cab when the thought strikes him that this is the perfect night to walk home, slowly, chewing on his goodness till the flavor's gone. He raps on the driver's window. The driver winds it down.

"I've changed my mind," says Matthew. He's about to add, "I've decided to walk home," but in his mind this sounds like a criticism of the earlier trip. So he says, instead, "I'm going to be staying for a while." He leafs through the bills in his wallet, pulls out what he thinks is right, hands it to the driver. When the driver fans the bills to see how much is there, Matthew sees that one of the bills he had taken for a one is a ten.

"Hey, thanks," says the driver. He pulls his wad from his pocket and places the bills in the appropriate sections, with the same denominations, lining them up just so. Matthew has hesitated beside the window, wondering if there's any way he might point out to the driver that he hadn't intended to include that extra ten. "Have a good time," says the driver. He twists himself around, getting comfortable. For a moment, Matthew's flattered. He doesn't mind at all that the driver has assumed that he's staying, that he is Leila's lover. However, the driver goes on. "You want to be careful, though. These young ones can be expensive, know what I mean?" Up goes the window, quickly.

Matthew slams his fist on the cab roof as the driver roars off. He feels cheap. The driver thinks of him as an old lecher, Leila as a girl who would exploit an old lecher.

Damn.

There goes that warm, noble feeling, says BW.

Back comes the feeling that he's ridiculous.

It wasn't that way at all; it was nothing like what he was thinking. Damn. It was tender, it was sweet.

Matthew begins striding toward home, seething. Suddenly, he stops.

Why go home? What's the point of going home? Why be a good man if you're perceived as a bad one? he asks himself. *Why be a sap? If Leila was teasing me, why not call her bluff?*

Right! says BW. *If she's curious about what it would be like to make love to her mother's lover, why not satisfy her curiosity?*

Why not satisfy my own?

Why not, if it comes to that, just please yourself?

He begins walking back, stops across the street, hesitates, crosses the street, nearly rings the bell, but thinks about the possibility of Belinda's returning, and the possibility that Leila would reject him anyway, that as far as it went was as far as she was willing to have it go, and he turns around and walks home.

Near Huntington Avenue he passes a darkened doorway; he is peripherally aware of a figure within it. Startled, he turns, and he sees a man standing there, a short man surrounded by garbage bags. Matthew walks to the corner, where there is a sports bar, stops, and looks back. The man in the doorway looks out, looks up and down the street. Matthew steps back, out of sight. *What's he up to?* he wonders. The man gathers his garbage bags, moves across the

street, sets the bags down beside a traffic signal control box, takes a
marker from his coat, squats, and begins writing.

*It's him. The Graffitist. Belinda was right. He's short, with a
round face. And he's smiling. He's happy.*

That's no smile, says **BW**. *That's a grimace. He looks as if he
smells something foul.*

Matthew watches while the Graffitist writes. When he's finished, he caps his marker, gathers his garbage bags, and shuffles off.
Matthew waits until he's halfway down the block before crossing
the street to see what he's written.

> CHEER UP—NOBODY LIVES FOREVER. YOU'LL
> ENJOY DEATH. NO WORRIES, NO PAIN, NO
> HUNGER, NO WISHES, NO REGRETS, NO WIND.
> ARTIFICIAL SWEETENERS AND TANNING
> BOOTHS ACCELERATE THIS PROCESS.

When Matthew gets home, he writes this on his wall. Then he
throws his clothes on the floor of the closet, gets into bed, and mas-
turbates with Leila in his mind's eye, like an adolescent after a date
with the best-looking girl in school.

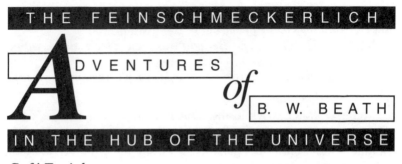

THE FEINSCHMECKERLICH ADVENTURES *of* B. W. BEATH IN THE HUB OF THE UNIVERSE

Café Zurich

Are we going soft? We have thought about this review for hours, and though we know what we ought to do, we cannot quite bring ourselves to do it. We ought to mock the vaulting pretentiousness of **Café Zurich**, its burlesque theatricality, the grotesque vulgarity of its patrons, and so on, and so on, and so on, but something awful has happened to us. We've been stricken by something very like a disease, its symptoms a debilitating tenderness, even compassion, that seems to have had a peculiar effect on our judgment, something analogous to a portrait photographer's forgiving and flattering soft-focus lens. Somehow, when we look back at the evening we passed at Café Zurich, a rosiness suffuses all, the viscous sauces seem luscious, the flunkies' fake performances seem quite genuinely deferential, and the puffing fatties dining around us seem somehow charming. Was there Valium in our water? *Was das einege Zaubertrank?*

Wait a moment. The effect is fading. It comes and goes. There, that's better. We can see clearly again. Yes, it's all coming back to us now, warts and all. We seem to be in a barn decorated by a pastry chef. The effect is supposed to be grand, to take our breath away. Café Zurich is—let's get this straight at the start—a dinner theater. These people aren't really in the restaurant business; they're running a theme park. The implicit promise when one walks through the studded leather doors is not tasty food but a taste of luxe. Since we are assumed not to be able to recognize this flavor, we must be told when we are tasting it. The background music tells us as soon as we arrive, inspiring as it does thoughts along these lines: *Say, I recognize that music in the background. It's classical. Renaldi or Baldy or something like that. You hear it in all the classy malls. You know—"The Four Seasons." Jeez, this is some swanky place, huh?*

If it weren't for the fusillades of corks, rubes like us wouldn't realize that people are drinking champagne, right? Nor would we realize that we really ought to order some ourselves. If our waiter opened our bottle gently, without that happy pop we've seen on TV, how would we know we were getting the real stuff? This is not a subtle place, reader. Every little luxury, every bit of service, has to be announced, has to be given an exaggerated flourish, has to have its fanfare, so that we won't miss it, so that we will be assured that we are in a luxurious setting, so that we will believe we're really getting service.

If Café Zurich had wheels, it would be a big white stretch limo, with a bar, TV, VCR, and European sex videos—dubbed. To come here is to relive the big date, prom night, your wedding reception. Just look at the people around us. They can't read the menu, so they have no idea what to order. They can't make conversation about anything they haven't seen on television. They glance furtively around the room, wondering if anyone is anybody. No one is.

Ordinarily, we hate to dwell on, or even bring up, the sorry work of age upon our fellow diners, but we find that we must in sketching this scene for you, for the diners come in all ages and stages, and the differences count. At many tables are men whose pink pates show beneath longish strands of white hair, whose ruffs of fat hang over their white collars, dining in silence with women who scowl, who seem always to have scowled. At others are couples still in middle age, in from the 'burbs for the night, mangling those odd foreign phrases on the menu, wondering aloud what gustatory trials they conceal, offering one another solid misinformation, passing on errors that have gone uncorrected for so long that they are now almost as good as true. At still others are much younger people, starry-eyed, timid, cautious in choosing their utensils; he's uncomfortable in his tie and tight collar, and she is wearing the dress she wore in her sister's wedding. Oh, here's something a little out of the ordinary: a graying man with a slip of a girl, tête-à-tête, but separated by nearly thirty years. Father and daughter? Lounge lizard and victim? *Fille de joie* and client?

Uh-oh, it's happening again. We're slipping into that state of enchantment. Now, when in memory we look around us, we see bedazzled couples with stars in their eyes, couples who quite evidently love the evening arranged for them, the performance mounted for them, even the indifferent food served to them and the phony brio on the side. We have to ask ourselves: "If they are made happy by all this, even for an evening, doesn't that redeem the place? It can't be completely contemptible, can it? One night of bliss—surely that's worth something, even if we have to surrender to illusion to achieve it."

We're fighting to regain our objectivity. Just give us a moment. There. That's better. Let's be rational about this. Certainly every restaurant is a theater, and every meal is a performance, but this is really much too opéra bouffe. From the moment of our arrival, the staff began bowing and scraping and performing outré rituals designed to make us feel like jejune rustics still wet behind the ears connoisseurwise.

Allow us to describe for you the outstanding fault in the whole *verschwenderisch* display, the one that towers above all the others, the crowning achievement in this temple of *übermässigkeit*, the food. The pâté we were served in the lounge was entirely acceptable, but we were expected to convey it to our epicurean maw on those round orange crackers called Ritz. Call us "snob" if you will, but we felt as if we were at one of those food barns in the country where one is expected to tuck into a "full-course" meal of New England cookin', course one of which is inevitably some dreadful cottage-cheese spread, with the very same round orange crackers called Ritz. Just what are these Ritzes doing in Café Zurich? Is their presence supposed to be a nod to the sometimes simple tastes of the sophisticated, or to the unalterably vulgar tastes of the nouveau-riche? We can't say. We left the lounge and went on in to dinner, where our breathtaking companion began with the *Bündner Gerstensuppe*, a vegetable soup with barley and *Bündnerfleisch*, the air-dried beef that the enterprising Swiss use for soling shoes. We chose the *Busecca alla Ticinese*, a vegetable soup with small strips of tripe or something. We both ate a wedge of iceberg lettuce topped with some paste flavored with garlic; this was listed on the menu as *insalata mista*—perhaps our Italian isn't all it should be. Essaying the *Zuger Rötel*, a trout poached in white wine with herbs, swimming in a soapy sauce, we found that the herbs had been laid on in wholesale quantities to compensate for their not being fresh. Since she was in a forgiving mood, our charming companion ate her way bravely through—well, nearly through—her *Züri Gschnätzlets*, thin slices of decent veal, veal kidneys, and mushrooms in a tenacious and mucilaginous goo quite possibly developed to benefit the Swiss dry-cleaning industry. The *Gschnätzlets* (by the way, aren't you proud of us for not having made a single joke about the fact that all of these dishes sound like sneezes?) were served with *Rösti*, grated potatoes fried in butter, then stamped with a

cholesterol warning from the Swiss surgeon general. In the breadbasket were tiny *Zwiebelwähe*, the onion tarts that the inventive Swiss use as doorstops. Each of these dishes so admirably restated the theme of Café Zurich that we feel compelled to seize the opportunity to restate it ourselves; it was—how shall we put this?—*de trop, de trop, de trop*. There must be someone in the kitchen screaming "More fat! More flour! More salt!" We watched with ghoulish fascination while each dish collapsed under its own unbearable weight. Apparently we consumed quite a bit of this ponderous meal, for, upon our return home, we were disturbed to find that our elevator couldn't quite lift us all the way to our exalted floor, stopping instead, exhausted and wheezing, between two inferior floors. We swear to you, trusting reader, that this actually happened.

Let's try to forget the food and return to the operetta, the *rivista frìvola*, shall we? If you have been paying close attention, you will already have guessed that when entrées are served, diners are treated to the old synchronized-lifting-of-silver-plated-hemispherical-lids-from-dishes routine, second cousin to that most bizarre of sports, synchronized swimming. For those of you fortunate enough never to have witnessed this routine, I will describe it. A troupe of minstrels—sorry, we mean waiters—gathers. A platter bearing a hemispherical dome is placed before each diner. A waiter stations himself at each diner's side, grasping a handle at the top of the hemispherical dome. At a signal, all covers are raised at once, with a flourish. The first time we saw this, we watched with sinking dread, sure that the encircling waiters were going to sing "Happy Birthday to You" in French, German, and Italian. They did not, thank God, though we heard them exclaim, ere they bowed out of sight, *"Godo! Savourez! Erfreuen Sie!"* Oh, but wait. That pleasant fuzziness is coming over us again. Where were we? We had eaten, and in rosy memory it seems we were content. We found ourselves intrigued again by the graying man and flowering girl whose relationship continued to puzzle us. In the name of research, in duty bound to you, dear reader, we permitted ourselves to overhear their conversation, and we found that their alliance was something sweeter than what we had suspected, something charming and harmless, as close to innocent as such things can get these days, that he was not the drooling wolf we feared he might be but—how terribly old-fashioned, nearly obsolete—a gentleman. Watching them—surreptitiously, in a mirror—we were touched, we really were. When he bought her a souvenir menu, we understood, at last, the point of Café Zurich: it isn't the evening that counts, but the memory of it. We're sure it works for everyone, that it will work even for us, that in time only a fluffy, insubstantial sweetness will remain, masking even

that terrifying moment when, with the swift precision of a Swiss cutpurse, our waiter whisked large sums of our money into Café Zurich's numbered account.

Glossary
de trop: too much
Erfreuen Sie!: Enjoy!
feinschmeckerlich: epicurean
fille de joie: working girl
Godo!: Enjoy!
nouveau riche: rich but still ignorant of major European languages
opéra bouffe: a farcical comic opera
outré: overdone, fulsome
rivista frivola: extravaganza
Savourez!: Enjoy!
übermässigkeit: excessiveness
verschwenderisch: lavish, wasteful
Was das einege Zaubertrank?: Was that some kind of magic potion?

—*BWB*

Café Zurich
22 Canton Street, 555-1648.
American Express, Visa, MasterCard, Diners Club, American money. No checks.
Handicapped: easy access.
Lunch 11–3, Monday–Friday.
Dinner 7–12 Tuesday–Saturday, 2–8 Sunday.
Reservations required.

6

Two-Two-Two

Matthew is in his office, standing at his window, bouncing on the balls of his feet, full of the success of his brick maker. He presented it this afternoon, and it was accepted for production, unanimously, with applause. He had, he allows himself to realize now, been fearing the presentation for weeks. He had feared that his star was dimming at Manning & Rafter, and he had begun to think about what he would do if—he almost thought of it as *when*—the brick maker was rejected. He really couldn't afford to quit. He supposed that the only thing he could do would be to endure, to suffer whatever blows his ego would have to take, and stay on, go on, show up every day and do whatever was left to him to do, until he was dismissed, with salary continuance and health insurance and the vested portion of his retirement fund, or until he could afford to let himself be pushed into an early retirement. How long could he wait? Ten years? Could he survive so strong a daily dose of humiliation for that long?

Fearful though he was, he knew that he had reason to be hopeful. Christmas sales had been a surprise. With some exceptions, the electronic games and tricky toys that Matthew despises had not sold as well as everyone had expected and he had feared. Parents had bought simpler, familiar toys, and in most of the country the products of Manning & Rafter had sold out. Retailers wanted more for next year. Already they were calling for toys that would last, not only in the sense of enduring the mistreatment that kids were likely to give them, but in the sense of sustaining a child's interest. Matthew hoped that the brick maker was the right toy at the right time, and so unfamiliar was he with hope that he didn't recognize it: he thought he actually knew that the brick maker would succeed, and this self-deception made him confident, so confident that he made plans for the evening—dinner, a very special dinner, at a restaurant newly reopened, a place called Two-Two-Two, with Liz, who would be meeting him there.

The presentation went beautifully. The board, convinced that simpler toys will make a comeback, expects the brick maker and many other toys that Matthew has championed in the past to succeed handsomely.

A smile forms on Matthew's lips when, as always happens when he thinks about his brick maker, he's reminded of the summer when it was conceived. Quite possibly this memory is the reason he's drawn so often to think about the toy. According to the version of the story that he told at the presentation, Matthew was visiting some friends at a cottage they had rented in Westport, near Rhode Island; he saw some children making a sand castle at Horseneck Beach, and out of their improvised play came the idea for this toy, a set of molds for sand and, most important, a ramming device that packs the sand into the molds to make bricks that will interlock. With the bricks, a child can build elaborate and sturdy castles. Matthew feels a paternal pride for this toy: he's proud of having had the idea that led to inventing it and proud of having, in the terminology used at Manning & Rafter, "mentored" the gadget through its development, and he gets a secret thrill each time he recalls the castle that inspired the idea, because in truth it wasn't

children he observed building it, but a woman, a blonde who was
sitting on the wet sand at the water's edge, molding bricks of sand
in an empty juice container and building with the bricks she made.

It is Matthew's habit at the beach to take long walks and think.
The sound of the waves rolling in, the rhythm of that sound, makes
him feel less confused. Perhaps it merely muffles or regularizes
the sound of confusion, but the effect is the same: he can let his
thoughts roam, sometimes quite productively, while, subtly, he
ogles the women. In the summer we are considering here, the most
daring women were wearing bathing suits cut startlingly high on
the hip, sometimes even above the hip, their legs bare right to the
waist. When these women—or, more frequently, girls, since the
most daring suits were usually worn by girls of an age Matthew
couldn't guess with certainty—walked past him, he would try to
take them in without appearing to notice them, his eyes apparently
on something far ahead, thoughts roaming productively to the
soothing shuffle of the surf, while his peripheral vision was working like mad. So narrow was the bit of fabric at the crotches of
these suits that he could sometimes see a bulge of soft skin pro-
truding from either side of it, and the miracle fabric clung so
closely and thoroughly to the flesh beneath it that it sometimes
formed an inviting crease at the center, a Spandex dimple.

There he was, that summer day, walking along the water's edge,
when he spotted, from quite a long way off, the woman making the
sand castings. She wasn't a girl; she must have been somewhere in
her thirties, but she was wearing one of the daring suits, a black
one, cut low in front, high on the sides. She had abundant blond
hair, and it was blowing in the wind. She sat with the awkward
unconcern of a child, bent to her task, apparently thinking of nothing else, careless of her appearance. Her legs were open, thrown
out to the sides as a child would throw hers out to the side, and pubic hair fringed the skimpy crotch of her suit, golden, like a girl's
hair in a fairy tale, catching the light and Matthew's eye, so that he
couldn't help looking. In memory, it seems to him that he saw that
narrow band of black fabric from far away, as if that alone had
caught his eye from far down the beach, the curlicues of hair, glis-

tening with oil and salt, gleaming like a frame. As he passed her, she looked up for an instant and smiled at him, and he smiled back and nodded, but he hadn't had the nerve to stop and speak to her because he had been staring at her cunt, after all, and he suspected that her family might be nearby—parents, an ancient grandmother, a loutish husband—sitting on aluminum chairs, watching him with vague concern. There were some children nearby; they might be hers. *Besides*, he told himself after he had walked by, *she was enjoying herself. She was having such a fine time being a child at the beach that it would have been rude to interrupt her, to have stopped, attracted by her quite adult legs, her woman's breasts, her grownup's pubic hair, when she was playing there as if she were a child.* After he'd walked a good long way beyond her, he turned around and headed back. Well before he reached her a little girl ran to her and began tugging her, and she pulled her legs in, rose quite gracefully, brushed the sand from her bottom, and walked off, an attractive, graceful woman, not the gangling girl she had seemed to be when she was playing in the sand.

The idea for the sand molds didn't come to Matthew that day, but days later, one night after he had gone to bed, when he had brought the memory of the woman to mind and was masturbating. He remembered the way she was playing, and though he meant to concentrate on her mouth, her breasts, her spread legs, the hollows where the muscles in her thighs were stretched, the pubic curls, his perverse intelligence turned the spotlight of memory on the juice container and the bricks of sand. He went limp in his hand while his mind raced along, diverted against its will from sensuality to ratiocination. Thus, perhaps, are more ideas born than the circumspection of inventors permits us to know.

Matthew buys a bottle of champagne, in the hope that after dinner he'll be able to get Liz to come home with him to drink it. He puts it into the refrigerator and takes two glasses from the cabinet and puts them on a table in his living room. Then he decides that the effect seems too calculated, shows his eagerness too much. He puts the glasses away.

But maybe the champagne itself is too much, he thinks.

No, BW tells him. *It shouldn't be. You'd keep champagne on hand for other women, wouldn't you? She'll think you use it for seductions.*

Would she think that? Matthew wonders. *No—she'd see through it.*

You're right, BW admits. *She would. She'd see everything if you have champagne. She would know that you've wanted her back all this time, that you're trying to celebrate her return. You mustn't give so much away. You must be cool. You must not seem to have thought too much about this evening. No champagne. Definitely no champagne.*

Yes. That's it. I mustn't seem to have anything at stake.

That's right. Even though you really think that all your future happiness is at stake. If you knew that there was something—anything—you could do to make Liz come back, if you knew what that something was, you would do it.

No, it isn't that. That wouldn't be enough, making her come back. If I knew that there was something I could do to make her love me, that's what I would do.

Yes, of course. That's it.

But, maybe I've done it. Maybe I've already done the thing that's needed. I've changed. I'm not the man I was. I'm different. I'm not even aware of all the ways I've changed.

Or how few they really are, says BW. *How insignificant. How unremarkable.*

Matthew makes himself a martini, sips it, thinks, and lectures himself. *What made Liz come to my bed? What made her make love to me so eagerly? So well? Did she know that I tried to make love to Belinda, right there in front of her? Was she awake? Not likely. It was the idea that I was different. Novelty. It must have been that. Her thinking that I had changed, that I wasn't the same old Matthew, the one she wasn't able to love. It was all of it, all the differences—the apartment, and Belinda, the idea of Belinda, the idea that I've had other experiences, other women. All right.*

That's what I have to work on. I have to be different from what she remembers. And I mustn't seem to have anticipated this evening too eagerly. I mustn't give myself away. Why not get there late? Take my time getting ready.

He takes his martini into the bathroom. He shaves. It is, he tells himself, one of those days when his face seems to be aging well. The wrinkles around his eyes make it look as if he laughs a lot. His jaw has become stronger over the years, he thinks. His hairline has receded suddenly, in the last year or so, after having held steady for a decade and a half, following an early recession in his twenties, but it doesn't look so bad today, and he's noticed that many men younger than he are losing their hair more quickly. *Maybe it's because they use blow dryers.* He brushes his teeth with his rotary electric toothbrush, a gadget that claims to remove more than ninety percent of his dental plaque. He rinses his mouth with hydrogen peroxide; several months ago, an article about trends in cosmetic dentistry convinced him that peroxide might bleach his yellowing teeth. He rinses a couple of times, and then inspects his teeth in the mirror. He holds a scale to them, a narrow plastic card with gradations of color from white to brown printed on it. Are his teeth getting whiter? He can't be sure, but he thinks that they might be, and he's heartened by the thought that he's doing something to reverse the yellowing process, fighting it, not just lying there and taking it. He undresses and places his clothes in piles for the laundry, the dry cleaner, his own washing. He inspects his body in the mirror. He's secretly proud of his middle-aged body; he works at maintaining it at a health club, Back Bay Bodies, three mornings a week, even though he feels like an old man there, especially when one of the women hopping about in the aerobics room catches him watching her—but when he notices the globular middles and fleshy necks of men his age, he feels all right. *Then I think I'm not doing so bad. Not so bad at all.* He's annoyed that hair has started growing on his back, though. *It's really getting thick. Well, not that thick, but thick enough so it's noticeable.* When he was a boy, the hair on the backs of old men dis-

gusted him more than any other sign of aging. He was sure it
would never happen to him. *But I secretly feared that it would.
I'm not sure how bad it is, really. I'm no judge. I try to tell myself
that it isn't as bad as I think.* He has thought of going somewhere
to have his back waxed. *One of those places where women get
their legs waxed. Or bikini waxings. Liz used to get that done.
Probably still does. The woman making the sand castle, though.
She didn't. That golden hair. I can see it gleaming. The little
droplets of oil on her hair, suntan oil. Or water. Salt. The sea-
salt taste of her if I licked her there. Sure.* He once checked the
Yellow Pages for hair-removal salons and found three right in his
area. He walked past each one of them but didn't have the nerve to
go in. *If Liz comes back, she might be willing to go with me. How
old were those men, the men with hair on their back that I saw as a
kid? I wonder. How old did I think was old then?* He showers.
He dries himself. He rubs styling gel into his hair. He's not really
sure whether he likes what it does to his hair or not. It seems to
stiffen it, and it makes him feel affected, but it straightens those
unruly white hairs, and that's what he was after when he began using it. He sits on the toilet seat and cleans his toenails. He examines his penis for hairs. They began growing in a year or so ago.
*That was when I noticed them, anyway. When I started using con-
doms. The hairs got stuck when I was rolling the thing off. Not
really painful, but they disgusted me. A hairy penis. It seemed
bestial.* He began plucking them. Now he checks for them after
every shower.

He chooses a gray shirt with a spread collar, a gray silk tie em-
bellished with what look like brush strokes of white here and there,
as if applied by a hasty, impassioned artist. *A bold tie, graphically
bold, but quiet, just gray and white.* He wears a charcoal-gray suit
that fits him better than any other he owns, black silk suspenders,
wool-and-silk socks in a pattern that resembles herringbone but
with one side of the V about half the length of the other. *Bold. But
quiet. I look good. I really do look good, and none of what I have
on is what I would have worn when Liz lived with me, when we*

*were married. I have changed, see? I'm not the same as I was
when we were married. I hope she'll see it. I hope she'll like it.
Hell, I hope I'll sweep her off her feet. Hope is a wonderful thing.
It makes you about ten pounds lighter. Actually, I only need to be
about five pounds lighter. Then I'd be right where I want to be.
Seven pounds. That would give me a little buffer. Seven pounds.
Eight pounds.*

He finishes his martini, standing in the living room, looking out
over Roxbury. He tries the effect of leaving his jacket unbuttoned,
observing his transparent reflection in the window. He tries the effect of one hand in his pocket. By taking tiny sips, he makes his
martini last until exactly the time when he should be at the restaurant, meeting Liz. *I like this, stretching the drink out, making it
last. Maybe I could cut down on drinking this way. I used to make
a bag of candy corn last all the way through "Suspense" on the
radio. When I was a boy. Candy corn. A secret passion. Liz used
to kid me about it. That will have to go. Let her think I've out-
grown it. I can keep a bag at work. Back in the drawer, next to
the Jiffy bag with the spare underwear.*

The feeling that he's late makes him walk faster than normal,
but when he sees the cabs at the corner, he hesitates, reminding
himself that he wants to be late.

*I want her to see that I'm different now, right? I don't keep
such close track of time. I'm indifferent about being on time for
her. But she'll be annoyed if I'm too late.*

The thought that Liz will be angry if he keeps her waiting is too
much for him. He doesn't want the evening to begin with her angry. He steps up to the lead cab. The driver spots him and turns
back to unlock the door. Matthew changes his mind.

*No. I'm going to be late as it is. If I'm going to be late, then
I'm really going to be late. I'm going to be good and late. Late
enough to make a statement.*

He shakes his head and waves his hands to show the driver that
he's changed his mind. The driver gives him the finger and locks

the door again, and Matthew walks to Two-Two-Two.

"Hi," he says when he steps through the door, full of secret self-satisfaction. "I made a reservation for seven o'clock, but I'm afraid I got delayed." He doesn't sound like himself, and he likes it that way.

I'm changing, he tells himself. *You see it?* he asks BW. *You know what it is? I'm on the verge of becoming a happy man. Confident. Confident and happy. Apparently all it takes is the love of a woman. Isn't that amazing?*

"The name is Barber," he says. "I think someone's probably waiting for me."

This statement is acknowledged with an expression that has the approximate shape of a smile. "Barber," says the smiling host. "Seven o'clock. We still have your table for you."

A little ice in the voice there, he thinks. *Well, fuck you.* He smiles but offers no thanks for their holding the table.

"You're the first to arrive," says the smiling host, with, perhaps, just a little more ice. "This way please."

The first to arrive? thinks Matthew. *Where's Liz?* He follows the host to a table in the back. In the past, whenever he was shown to a table in the back, he felt that he'd been judged and found wanting, because he knows that the better-looking, better-dressed customers are seated in the front, in the window, as advertising, but he's glad to be seated in the back this evening. He wants privacy.

It's a long, narrow room, with green velvet banquettes along both sides and a partition, at chest height, running lengthwise, dividing the room into halves with the dimensions of a bus. Matthew has found this linearity straitening and annoying, the exaggerated perspective making him feel uneasy from the moment he sat down. Tonight, however, sitting in the rear corner, he feels that he's at the focus of the room, where all sightlines converge, and he likes it.

This really is the preferred seat, he tells himself. *Funny that I never realized it before. You have a good view—the best possible view—of people as they enter. And entering Two-Two-Two has always been a performance.*

The room is just as Matthew remembers it. He's pleased, since it suits his mood to have things as they were, but he can't help wondering about the wisdom of the new owners' decision not to redecorate.

They haven't even touched up the paint.

The furniture and moldings are black lacquer, nicked and knocked and scarred by blows from chairs, trays, and customers out of control. Several years ago, Two-Two-Two was the liveliest spot in town. The bar was so crowded, even on weeknights, that the drinkers spilled into the dining room and turned the place into a party. Everyone seemed to like it that way—even Matthew, once he got used to it. He and Liz used to drive in from Lincoln for dinner fairly frequently for a while; it was an adventure, and anecdotes about Two-Two-Two were important in suburban conversations at the time. The Barbers invariably found that their table wasn't ready when they arrived, but they soon came to expect that (indeed, it was the commonest anecdote about Two-Two-Two), and they would get a drink at the bar and watch the party. They never joined it, but it amused them to watch. When they began recognizing people, they were able to follow the intricacies of the table-hopping dance that went on there. In all their many visits, Matthew and Liz never noticed, or never allowed themselves to notice, that nearly everyone in the place was drugged to one degree or another, on one substance or another. Two-Two-Two was the first mainstream place in Boston where cocaine was sold and consumed openly in the rest rooms, and the drug trade was a part of the place's cachet, but Matthew and Liz weren't part of it, and didn't want to be part of it, so they let themselves fail to notice it. It took a long time before anyone realized that the party was killing the place. The regulars were making it too much their own. Night after night, the people there were the same people who were always there. They had begun to bore themselves. When total collapse finally came, the space remained vacant for months. After

Liz left Matthew and he moved into the city, he would see, more often than he could have believed possible, a former regular standing at the door, peering in, blocking the reflections with his hand, apparently mystified that the place should be closed, hoping that there might be someone inside who would open up for him. Only much later did Matthew learn how many people had been going there not for the food or conversation, but to make their connections.

And where's my connection? he asks himself. *Where's Liz?*

He wants to order a drink, but he isn't certain who might take his order. He suspects that the young woman walking past his table is connected with the restaurant in some official capacity, since she has been walking around since he arrived, but she isn't dressed as a waiter, and she seems to have no idea what she should be doing with herself beyond walking around. She has the hair of a waif, uneven strands that fall in ringlets, damp, as if she has just come in out of the rain. This apparent dampness is, Matthew knows, a look, probably expensive to achieve.

"Excuse me," he says, not in the tone that signals a request or an order to a waiter or waitress, but in the tone he would use if he were going to offer to help someone. The woman stops and looks at him. She seems, at first, startled to have been accosted by a stranger, but then, perhaps because she's relieved to find on his face the smile of someone who seems to want to help her, she smiles herself and says, "Yes?"

"Are you lost?" Matthew asks. To his delight, he realizes that he's flirting with this girl, who is, if not obviously attractive, desirable for her vulnerability. He glances at the door, thinking how wonderful it would be if Liz were to come in just now and see the girl smiling at him.

"In a way, I am," she says. "My boyfriend and I just took this place over, and I'm like, 'What do I do now?' I just walk around trying to make sure everything's okay, but to tell you the truth, I can't even *tell* whether everything's okay. Does it show?"

"A little," says Matthew. "You do look a little overwhelmed."

"Believe me, I am. *Is* everything okay? Is someone taking care of you?"

"Well, not yet."

"I'm sure someone will be over in a minute. We never expected crowds like this."

"I think a lot of people have been waiting for you to reopen."

"Oh, yeah. I know what you mean. The place had quite a reputation. But we're not going to be like that. We kept the same name, the same look, but everything else is going to be different. We have a wonderful chef, completely different menu, and a different approach. You know what I mean? It was like, everybody who used to work here wanted to come back? And we go, 'Uh-uh. Wronnnnng. We're not running the place that way.' So, can I get you a glass of wine?"

"Actually, I'll have a Bombay martini, straight up, with an olive."

She winks and goes off to the bar.

She winked, thinks Matthew, feeling buoyant, hopeful, confident. *Winked.*

A band of mirror runs around the room, at eye level for a seated diner. In it, Matthew observes himself, tiny at the end of the room, where he sees himself straight on, a little larger in the band on the room divider, full-size in the band right beside him.

My face looks thinner than it has recently, he thinks. *Could be this shirt. A dark shirt is a good idea.*

Or it may have been that wink, BW suggests.

Is that really all it takes—the attention of a woman? Am I that—hungry?

Perhaps, Matthew, says BW. *Perhaps.*

Go to hell, BW, he thinks. *Where on earth is Liz? What's keeping her?*

He can't see the new arrivals the moment they enter, because the door is hidden from him, but he can observe the reactions to their arrivals. Each brings a gust of cold air, and Matthew can see its effect on the people at the bar. As the draft advances, heads turn toward the door. There's a delay, a rippling effect, like the effect of a breeze on a field of grass or, Matthew supposes, on a field of wheat, though he has never seen a field of wheat.

Or, suggests BW, *like that annoying wave people produce at football games when they are bored by the game itself or simply overcome by an irresistible need to act in mindless concert with other yahoos.*

Some arrivals get no more greeting than a blank glance, the worst sort of rejection, utter lack of interest. For others there are elaborate displays of pleasure.

Most of it false, of course, says BW. *Entirely fake.*

Again there is a ripple of turning heads. For this person, whoever it may be, there is a collective lingering glance.

It must not be somebody they know, thinks Matthew.

The looks are pleasant.

No recognition. But the beginnings of smiles. Somebody happy. It's somebody happy. Happiness holds people's attention. Happiness is attractive.

It's Liz, blowing in fresh as the air she lets in with her, peeking around the corner, looking for Matthew in the back room, nearly bounding down the steps, saying, "Hi, hi, hi," when she reaches his table.

Matthew has been expecting an apology when she arrives, and he has concocted a script for their exchange, giving himself lines that make it clear he hasn't been forlornly waiting.

"Sorry I'm late," Liz will say if she follows his script. "Everything that could go wrong did go wrong. I hope you haven't been waiting here for half an hour."

"No, no," he'll say. "Not at all. In fact, I just got here. Somehow I lost track of the time."

Liz, however, doesn't cooperate. She makes no excuse, simply throws her coat onto the banquette next to Matthew and takes the chair across from him. "God, what a day, what a day, what a day I've had," she says, beaming. "Did you order a drink?"

"Yes, I did. And here it comes now, I think."

The waif is making her way down the three steps from the bar, carrying Matthew's martini, holding the glass by the stem. The glass is filled to the brim, and she's concentrating fiercely on keeping it level, taking her steps with exaggerated care.

Like a mime pretending to carry a full cocktail glass down three steps.

She glances in Matthew's direction, sees that he's watching her, and smiles. She spills a little of the drink.

What about that smile? Is she flirting? Or is she just happy, happy to be running this restaurant?

She delivers the drink.

"I'll have one of those, too," says Liz.

The waif shrugs. This isn't really her job, after all, but since she isn't certain what else she ought to be doing, she might as well serve cocktails. "Okay," she says.

Matthew smiles at her. "Good luck," he says. He thinks of adding a wink, an echo of hers before.

Liz would be likely to notice. Not a good idea.

Oh, go ahead, says BW.

No. Not a good idea.

"This place hasn't changed at all," says Liz, looking into the mirror behind Matthew, using it to look around the room, then twisting on her chair to look into the lounge. "Not at all."

"I was so late getting here," says Matthew, "I was sure you'd already be here."

"Oh, I'm sorry, Matthew. You've been waiting here. I'm sorry. I lost track of the time." She puts her hand on his arm. "I found a condo."

She's buying a condominium. She doesn't intend to come back, then.

"In the South End."

Oh, great. We'll be neighbors. I'll be able to look into her windows with my binoculars.

"I love it. I just love it. I'm going to buy it. I just decided. Just this minute. Just this *instant.* I saw it in my mind, and I decided. Do you mind if I use Ralph for the closing and all?"

"Why would I mind? He's our lawyer, not just mine."

Why does she ask that? Was it Ralph? Was something going on with Ralph?

"Well, okay. Anyway, I looked at condos all afternoon, and then I went furniture shopping. Just browsing, but I lost track of the time."

What does she have in mind? Why did she have to come back to Boston at all? Why couldn't she have left me here in peace?

"Actually, you know, I was thinking maybe I'd get some stuff like yours. Really modern. What do you think?"

I think that was my idea. You ought to come up with your own.

The waif delivers Liz's martini, and Matthew uses the moment to decide whether to say what he wants to say. He does: "I think you should think for yourself."

"Whoa! *You're* in a bad mood," says Liz.

"I am not in a bad mood," says Matthew.

For a moment, he's enraged by this accusation. *You were always accusing me of being in a bad mood, of being a grouch.*

You're right, BW tells him. *And how you hated it, remember? How you hated being told that you were annoying, that you were a source of irritation to her. A shame I wasn't around then.*

"You know," Matthew says, very calmly, "I always hated it when you informed me that I was in a bad mood. Always hated it."

And fuck you, anyway. When I was in a bad mood, what makes you think that you hadn't put me there? You were annoying, you know, very annoying. But I never complained—never complained about your annoying habits. Went along with whatever you wanted to do.

How true, how true, says BW. *And you got no credit for it. No credit for putting up with her. You know why?*

Why?

This will be hard for you to hear, Matthew, but I think it quite likely that she mistook your tolerance for timidity—

What?

—and that timidity made you boring to her, even annoying. You should have told her what you thought. Exactly what you thought.

"Anyway," Matthew says, "are you sure you want to do that? Buy a condominium? I know you're taken with it and everything, but aren't you rushing into this? Neighborhoods have been changing a lot, you know. Maybe you should get a feel for the city—as it is now. Get to know different neighborhoods before you buy something."

"Ah, the voice of caution."

You see? says BW. *I was right. You're probably annoying her right this minute.*

"No, no," says Matthew. "I know it sounds that way, but that's not it. That's not what I'm saying. It's not timidity—or caution. I just don't want you to find out six months after you move in that you've bought a place you can't stand. You could wind up with a place that—stinks. Literally. Dead rats rotting in the walls."

"Matthew."

"Old garbage fermenting in the disposal. Who knows? Why don't you rent something for a while? Look around a bit."

Two fire trucks pull up outside the restaurant, lights flashing, but without sirens. Red light sweeps the length of the restaurant, again, again, again. The waif leads a beautiful young couple into the dining room. The woman is slender and extraordinary. She has the kind of cool beauty that has always attracted and intimidated Matthew. She's dressed in the thinnest of silks, surely no more than an ounce and a half in all. The man is of what Matthew considers the same type, elegant and slim, even beautiful, apparently moneyed, quite at ease. The waif seats them and they look around the room, insouciant, mildly curious, apparently blind to the pulsing red.

Beautiful, BW remarks. *Thinner than what you usually like, probably bulimic, but a beauty of the highest order. Beyond your reach, I'd say.*

"What's going on?" asks Liz.

Firemen in rubber suits enter the restaurant, occasioning the same ripple of interest in the bar that Matthew observed earlier, no more.

"Well," says Matthew. "The restaurant may be on fire."

The firemen look around quickly, and the bar crowd watches, interested, but not terribly.

"Should we leave?" asks Liz.

"Well," says Matthew, "that would probably not be hip. We'd look kind of stodgy. You know—uncool."

The firemen dash down the steps, trot the length of the dining room, and disappear through the door to the kitchen. The slim beauties look at the waif, who shrugs and, wearing a puzzled look, follows the firemen into the kitchen. The beauties pick up their menus.

"Apparently," says Matthew, "everyone has decided not to give a shit, or at least not to appear to give a shit."

"Well, what the hell," says Liz. "You've got to go sometime."

The firemen emerge from the kitchen, at a slower pace, on their way back to their red trucks. The waif follows them.

"Um, excuse me," says Matthew.

The waif stops, spins around. "Two more?" she asks brightly.

"Sure. Why not? But actually I was going to ask you what's going on."

"Oh, you noticed the firemen? There's no cause for alarm." She spins around again, and off she goes.

"So, what do you think?" asks Matthew.

"Probably blackening some snapper or something. Do they do that here?"

"No, I mean about the wisdom of renting for a while. Look things over, check things out."

"Check things out"? Did I hear you say that? asks BW.

"Oh, I don't know. I'd wind up stuck in a lease—"

"Hey," says Matthew. "I've got an idea."

"Oh, no."

"What?" *What does she mean, "Oh, no"?*

She reaches across the table and takes his hand. "Matthew, I don't want to move in with you, you know."

Shit. I ruined it.

"Oh, no. Of course not. I didn't think so. I—"

"I thought maybe you were working your way around to asking

me to move in. Move in with you. Move into your place."

"Huh? Oh—no. No, no." He chuckles. "No, no. I don't mean that you *couldn't* stay there. If you had to. Until you got settled. But, no, I wasn't going to suggest you move in. That wouldn't work." He chuckles again, in a fair imitation of a man who finds it surprising that she would think such a thing possible, now, when so much has changed, when his life is so different. "You know—well—things are different for me now, and—"

"You're not expecting Linda to move in?"

"Belinda."

"Belinda. Right."

"No, I'm not expecting Belinda to move in. I'm not expecting *anyone* to move in. It's just that my life is quite a bit different now." He smiles. He hopes this smile suggests that his bed is rarely empty, that Belinda is only one of many.

"Well, that's good. Belinda's—she's kind of up in the air, I think," says Liz, letting the remark dangle. Back in her smoking days, she would have taken a puff now and let the smoke out slowly, making visible the teasing thread of her remark.

It's a shame she doesn't smoke anymore. She used to handle that tantalizing interruption very well. Now she has no real substitute for it.

She glances around the room, to give the appearance that she has no intention of speaking further, but her glance falls on the angular beauty and she discovers that the angular beauty is looking at her, so she turns back to Matthew in self-defense. She finds him staring at her. He's wondering whether he ought to tell her that she doesn't play the game of waiting to be asked what she means as well as she used to when she smoked.

"How long has it been since you quit smoking?" he asks.

"How long since I quit smoking? Wow. I don't know. Years. It was right after we moved to Lincoln, wasn't it? What made you ask that?"

"Oh, I don't know. Just popped into my mind. Once upon a time, we both would have been puffing away here. That's all. Just struck me."

Good, Matthew, says BW. *Quite good. You didn't give her the satisfaction of asking what she meant. I'm proud of you.*

"I hope I haven't hurt you, Matthew," says Liz, but the way she purses her lips and puckers her brows makes it seem a lie. "I just didn't want you to get the wrong idea. The other night was just— the other night. I was curious. That's all."

"Why are you telling me this?"

"I don't want you to misunderstand."

"I don't think I'm misunderstanding. Let me see if I've got it. You were just curious. You saw the snappy furniture I bought, and you wanted to find out if my furniture had made me a little snappier, too."

Good, Matthew, says BW. *This is good.*

"Come on—"

"Sorry. Just kidding. I really do understand. Of course you were curious. You wanted to find out if Belinda had taught me any tricks."

Oh, excellent, says BW. *I like the way you got her off guard there and then hit her with Belinda.*

"Let's order some food, okay?" says Liz. "I don't like the way this is going." She looks around, trying not to let her eyes rest too long on the beautiful couple. "Who's our waitress, anyway?"

"We don't have one. The waif will take our order if we ask her to. She can't figure out what else to do."

He twists around, looking for the waif. In a moment she drifts around the central divider, her eyes vacant, her mouth in a goofy, unfathomable grin. "Excuse me," he says as she passes. His tone suggests that something is wrong, not with the restaurant or anyone connected with it, but with him. He seems embarrassed.

"Yes?" says the waif, warily.

"I'm hoping you can help us. We have a question."

"I'll try to help you if I can. What's the question?"

"Have you noticed that couple just over there, the ones—"

The waif begins to turn around to look.

"No, no," says Matthew. "Don't look at them. Just glance in the mirror beside me. You'll see who I mean. The beautiful couple."

"Oh, I know the ones you mean. Of course I've noticed them. You're kidding, right?"

"What I want to know is, are they plants?"

"Plants?"

"I mean, did they just happen to come here, or did you hire them to sit there and look beautiful?"

"No, they just walked in."

"I see. Well, that settles that, then." He folds his hands. The waif turns aside. "Oh," says Matthew. "Just one more question."

"Yes?"

"Could someone bring us menus?"

"Oh. I'll get them."

"Did you notice them?" Matthew asks Liz after the waif has gone.

"I don't want to talk about them. I don't want to think about them. Already I'm starting to feel thick."

For a moment he stares at the couple, in the mirror, unnoticed.

They are probably the scions of a couple of the first families of Argentina, to take the first example that comes to mind, suggests BW. *The streets of Boston are full of them these days, also Peruvians and such, rich, haughty, and gorgeous, all of them. What do you suppose these families do with their unattractive children? One shudders to think.*

Matthew looks down at his glass. The drink does not quite cover the olive. "I should have ordered another martini," he says.

"Here, have some of mine," says Liz.

"I don't want some of yours. I want one of my own. A full one."

"You know something, Matthew? You drink too much."

"This from the woman who passed out on my couch a couple of weeks ago?"

"That was an isolated thing. I was celebrating, and I got carried away."

"So? I'm celebrating now, and I'm getting carried away. Where's the waif?"

"She's on the other side of the room. Just sort of wandering around."

"Oh, yeah, I love that. The way she walks around, failing to notice that anything needs doing."

"She's heading toward the back of the room, and in just a moment, if nothing goes wrong, she'll turn at the end of the booths and head our way. Get ready. She's reaching the end. She's turning. Here she comes."

Without looking, Matthew holds his glass out in the aisle, blocking the way of the waif as she passes, and says, "Please, ma'am, may I have some more?"

That was nice, he thinks, *that little bit of cooperation. We were always good at that. Liz ought to see that we were good at that.*

"You're not yourself," says Liz.

Ah, at last. She's noticed some of your verve, your dash, says the voice of BW, heavy with sarcasm.

"That's right," says Matthew, using BW's tone, "I am not myself. No. No. I *am* myself. I was not myself when you knew me. Or rather, when you thought you knew me."

"Let's not fight."

"Are we fighting? We're not fighting." *We never fought. Almost never fought. Maybe we should have. Maybe things built up. But what? Nothing built up. Isn't that what she decided, that there was nothing, just nothing?* "There's no cause for alarm. We're just telling each other what we think."

"Let's not."

"Why not? You started it. You said I drink too much. Don't I get a turn? Hm? I should get a turn."

Liz says nothing.

"Let's see. Here's something. This always annoyed me. You always had an idea about the way you wanted something to go. You know what I mean?"

Liz still says nothing.

"And you disapproved of any deviation. It had to go just your way. The way you wanted it. No deviations from Liz's plan. Of course, you never used to tell me what those plans were. But God knows you used to let me know when I wasn't following them. Not that you used to *tell* me, of course. Nothing as direct as that. You used to make sure I knew, though."

"Hey."

"Notice how nicely I'm modulating my voice? No cause for alarm. There, wasn't that refreshing? Go ahead. Now it's your turn again."

Please do go ahead, thinks Matthew. *I have so much more to say. Like this: you made me think that women hate sex. You know that?*

Right, says BW. *Nearly fourteen years of marriage without an orgasm.*

My God, thinks Matthew. *That's right. How humiliating.*

She did it on purpose, of course.

What?

She hid them. She was having orgasms like crazy. Coming in colors. But she hid them. Hid them behind a kind of indulgent tolerance: "Let the huffing slob climb onto me and relieve himself. I'll put up with it, but I sure as hell won't enjoy it. At least I won't let it show."

That couldn't be. I can't see how it could be possible. Still, you're right that she always made me feel she was doing me a favor. I believed it. I still believe it.

The waif delivers Matthew's martini, carrying it on a tray this time. On the same tray are two wineglasses and a bottle of Lynch-Bages.

Where is that going? Matthew wonders.

Watching in the mirror, he sees the waif carry it to the beauties. She opens it at their table, clumsily, resting the bottle on the table and fumbling with the corkscrew, giggling at her own ineptitude, while they watch with something like noblesse oblige, making not a single negative comment, raising not an eyebrow.

Who could scold her? She's so adorable.

The adorably incompetent waif, tugging at the reluctant cork,

loses control of the bottle just as the cork pulls loose, spilling about
two glasses of really excellent wine on the female beauty, who
gasps, half rises, then recovers. She sits again, so composed, or
apparently so composed, that she smiles. She laughs. A spilled
glass of wine—

Lynch-Bages, moans BW.

—is too trivial to upset this beauty and her beautiful companion.

"Squid-ink pasta?" says a voice.

"Hm? Oh. There," says Matthew, nodding at Liz.

"And the bouillabaisse stir-fry."

"Yes, here."

"I can't believe you ordered that," says Liz. "It sounds weird."

"Smells good," he says.

"Is this the half portion, do you think?" asks Liz. She stares
doubtfully at the mound of pasta. "I wanted the half portion."

"Well, just eat half."

"Didn't I say 'half portion'?"

"I didn't notice."

"Of course not."

Liz doesn't begin eating right away. She looks at the plate, and
her shoulders drop. Her hands drop into her lap, her face falls.
She looks at Matthew for a moment, but he's distracted by the crisis at the other table, entranced by the beauty in the bordeaux-
soaked silks, now clinging to her tiny breasts so that he can see her
nipples. Liz looks around the room and says, just as Harold's wife
did at Dolce far Niente, "Everyone here is so *young*," but in the
voice of someone who has lost a contest. Matthew is scarcely
aware that Liz is talking. The soaked beauty conducts the briefest
consultation with the male beauty, and he pulls his sweater over his
head. He hands it to her and runs his hands back along his hair,
smoothing it into place so perfectly that it seems never to have
been disturbed. She pulls the sweater on but leaves her arms inside
it. She performs some invisible hocus-pocus, and one hand pops
out of a sleeve, with a ball of silk, held like a trophy, then the other
pops from the other sleeve, and with both hands she wrings the silk

into her wineglass. Matthew can't see whether a drop falls into it, but, oh, how he'd love to drink from that glass.

She stands, all grace, and pulls the sweater down. It comes about halfway down her thighs, but the wine stain on the skirt still shows. She shrugs, and the slightest frown appears on her lips. Then she sits and begins removing the skirt. She reaches under the sweater and unbuttons or unzips it or whatever.

Liz talks on. She's saying, "Didn't you think, sort of unconsciously, that as you grew up, the world would grow up with you?"

Matthew's trying to listen to her, and would listen to her, would at least give her the attention she deserves, but he's captivated by the performance across the aisle. He's still turned toward Liz, in an attitude of attention, but his eyes are focused past her, at the reflected image of the beauty, the image of aplomb.

This ability to rise above what's happened to her. It's magnificent. No crying over spilled bordeaux. That's what I like about her.

That may be, says BW, *but it's more likely that you're just lustful. I know what you're thinking, you know.*

Yes, I know.

You're wondering whether this is the type of woman who wants something from sex, who takes something from sex. Pleasure.

The beauty leans across the table and takes her friend's chin in her hand, pulls him toward her, rises slightly off her chair, leans farther across the table, and kisses him, but at the same time, with her other hand, whisks her skirt down her legs and lets it fall around her ankles. She sits again, raises the skirt on the point of her shoe, takes it in her hand beneath the table, compresses all her silks into a ball, no bigger than a baseball, and thrusts them into her bag. It's a balletic performance, worthy of applause.

Why can't I be like that? Why can't I shrug things off? Matthew wonders, and he frowns.

That frown, that note of regret, alerts Liz. It isn't quite the appropriate response to what she's saying at the moment. She notices that he's paying attention to something, someone, other than her. She looks at his eyes, and a quick, unconscious application of the principle that the angle of incidence equals the angle of reflection tells her where he's looking.

"You know, Matthew," she says. "That's another thing I couldn't stand."

"Hm?"

"You were always looking at other women."

She's got you there, Matthew, says BW. *You were. You are.*

"Just looking," says Matthew. "Just looking—and wishing."

He's quite surprised at himself. In the past, if Liz had pushed him, he would have said what was true, that he loved her, that he enjoyed looking at other women, even though he loved her, but that his feelings for Liz kept him from pursuing them. That would have been true. It would have been the truth, but it wouldn't have been the whole truth. There would also have been his timidity to take into account. He always suspected that he'd be rejected if he pursued any of the women who attracted him. The most attractive women attracted him most, and he didn't consider himself a package that the most attractive women were likely to want. He supposed that attractive women were attracted to attractive men. He considered himself someone who became attractive only in time, as people got to know him. On first sight he was forgettable. He knew that. Nicely dressed, nice enough to look at, but not outstanding. It seemed to him—and it was something he thought about, a thought that popped unbidden even into his sexual fantasies—that Liz, certainly an attractive woman, found him attractive only because she loved him. When, after so many years together, she told him that she had never loved him, he couldn't imagine why, in that case, she had ever been attracted to him. When his bluest period had passed after her departure, he discovered a compensating factor in her declaring that she never loved him: if she had never loved him, then she must have found him attractive, not in some love-blinded way, but in a way that other women might find attractive. That's when he began to flirt.

I was loyal to her, though. Faithful. Completely faithful—
Not completely.

Virtually completely.

Faithfulness is not a condition that admits of degrees.

Cut it out. My point is that Liz never, well, she never thanked me for being faithful to her. So faithful to her.

Yes, you're quite right. She was not sufficiently appreciative of your loyalty. She did not understand how much you were giving up by being pretty faithful to her, how much you wanted other women. You know something, Matthew? This just occurred to me. You're still essentially faithful to her. You still expect her to come back, hope she'll come back, and it keeps you from really trying your luck. That and fear of rejection, of course.

For a while Liz and Matthew sit in silence and eat, but Matthew is annoyed, and he's letting his anger build because he wants the boldness that anger will give him. To let the anger build, he has to fight the effect of the food, for he's eating something really delicious, a concoction of the chef, identified on the menu as "bouillabaise stir-fry over angel-hair pasta." He ordered it partly out of incredulity, but he's finding, to his surprise, that the chef swims very well. Topping the pasta is something like bouillabaise—with shellfish, saffron, all that good stuff—but what would have been broth is a sauce, so insistently delicious that it keeps diverting Matthew from his anger, nudging him toward a happy contentment. The chef has had the good sense not to serve too much of this wonderful stuff, and Matthew wants every bit of what there is. What's needed is a spoon. There's none at his place setting, none at Liz's, either, and the elegant sauce barely clings to the tines of his fork. "My God, this is good," he says.

"This is awful, really awful," says Liz. She pokes the squid-ink pasta with her fork.

For a moment Matthew feels the old guilty feeling: he shouldn't be enjoying himself while Liz isn't. In another moment, though, new feelings drive the guilt away. "Too bad," he says. He looks at her heap of black bands, with shreds of something orange and something green threaded through them. Inwardly, he grins.

She got what she deserves, says BW. *It doesn't look edible at all: it looks like display food from a Japanese supermarket.*

"This is simply incredible," Matthew says. He looks around for the waif; he really would like a spoon.

"Don't gloat."

"Why don't you send that back and get some of this?" he suggests, knowing that it's the sort of thing she would never do.

"No, I don't want to do that." She picks at the dish, eats a strand.

"Don't be a martyr. Here, try a bite of this."

"No. You hardly have enough for yourself."

"Jesus Christ, Liz, will you just try a bite? I want you to try a bite of this."

"Oh, shut up. I don't want to try the damn thing."

"You don't want to try it because I'm offering it."

No response. Before this moment, Matthew hadn't really been aware that he was in a contest, but now, like a wolf running its quarry down, he senses that he's gaining, that he can win if he doesn't let up, and now that he knows, he wants to win, winning seems to be everything.

"It's tainted because I'm offering it to you," he says.

No response.

"It's tainted because I like it."

The waif cruises by. Matthew catches sight of her in the mirror, just her hips and legs as she walks past, but he's learned to recognize her from that slice of view. He turns, but her back is toward him and she's drifting off elsewhere. Matthew gets out of his chair and walks after her. When he catches up to her, he says, "Excuse me," and puts his hand on her shoulder. It's a nice shoulder, just poking out of the wide neck of a nubbly sweater.

Nice in the hand. Wonderful to the touch. Smooth. So smooth.

He dares to give the smooth shoulder a squeeze when the waif turns her head and smiles her blank, all-purpose smile at him. "Would you bring me a spoon?" he asks. "The sauce on that bouillabaise stir-fry is so good."

Smooth as your shoulder. Sauce as smooth as a woman's shoulder. I can use that.

"I want to get every bit of it, but I don't want to offend the other diners by licking the plate." She doesn't laugh. "And, I tell you what, bring another order of it for the woman with me, okay?"

"Sure. A spoon and another order of bouillabaise stir-fry."

That smile. What teeth. My crooked yellow teeth.

He returns her smile with closed lips. He feels wonderful, for just a moment, and even considers that it might be possible, if he were to begin patronizing Two-Two-Two regularly again, that she'd get to know him, and that once she got to know him she might fall in love with him. That is really what he imagines, that she might fall in love with him.

Why not?

Then she asks, "Where are you sitting again?" and he realizes that he has made no impression on her as an individual, none at all. Perhaps none of the diners has, no one in the room. Maybe she sees only a congeries, not a single face or voice or desire.

She should sign up for a course with that tweedy faker. Learn to see the grains. Not just the beach.

When he tells her where he's sitting, she says "Okay," and when he says, "Thanks," he touches her hand. Why not?

Maybe if I always ordered the bouillabaise stir-fry, nothing else, she would eventually remember who I am. Maybe.

"Are you doing this just to annoy me?" Liz asks when he returns. He knows what she means.

Picking a fight, touching that girl. Woman. That's what she means.

"Doing what?" he asks. "I asked her for a spoon, and I told her to bring you some of this bouillabaise stir-fry." He seems to be so very obliging, as if he really did want her to be happy.

"Oh, you didn't."

"I did. You'll like it. You don't like that stuff. Why should you have to eat something you don't like?"

"What are you trying to do—impress her?"

I suppose I am. Is that stupid? Is it impossible?

"I'm not trying to impress anyone, my dear. Not even you."

"Well, I don't want the goddamned bouillabaise stir-fry. So tell her that when she brings you your spoon, which she's about to do."

"Here you are," says the waif. "Here's your spoon." She holds it out to him, by the handle, the bowl toward Matthew.

"Tell her," says Liz.

Matthew grasps the handle of the spoon and the hand of the waif. With a smile, he says, "You'd better cancel that second order of bouillabaise stir-fry." He doesn't quite dare to give the dear little hand a squeeze. He's pushed Liz about as far as he can, and he doesn't have any idea how far he can go with the waif.

Besides, there's still a possibility that this will pass, Liz will want to come back to my place. No telling. All of this may thrill her. I plucked those hairs from my penis.

The waif employs her shrug. What, after all, does any of this mean to her? The stupid restaurant was probably her boyfriend's idea anyway, and she'd be just as happy doing anything else with any other boyfriend, as long as he was cute and treated her okay and didn't get angry or blue. "Okay," she says, and she's off.

Did she notice that I was holding her hand? Practically holding her hand?

"Well," says Liz, "I've probably spoiled your chances there. She must think you can't make up your mind."

"I'm sure she thinks that *you* can't make up your mind."

"Well, she can't think much of you anyway. You couldn't convince me to eat the damned bouillabaise stir-fry."

"I can't see why that should make a difference. I'd say my chances are still quite good." In fact he thinks nothing of the kind, but he's putting on a good act, and he feels the nasty satisfaction one can get from being cruel when being cruel is a way of fighting back.

"Oh, come on, Matthew. She's a child."

"Not from what I've seen."

"This is becoming insulting. And grotesque."

"Insulting? Insulting?"

Careful, Matthew, whispers BW. *Don't lose it now.*

"Do you remember what you said to me two years ago? Huh? *That* was insulting. The most insulting thing I can imagine. And why the hell are you back now? What's the idea, anyway? Why suggest that we get together? Adding insult to injury? Did you just want to poke at the wound a little to see if it was still open? Huh? You're the one who started all this. Why?"

"Oh, I don't know."

"You don't know? Sure you know. You must know."

"I did *not* mean to hurt you."

"Oh, you didn't. What did you have in mind?"

"I knew I was going to be coming back to Boston, and I knew I was going to have to tell you sometime, so I thought I might as well tell you right away."

"All right. All right. I believe that. But why the hell did you have to make it that kind of evening? A reunion. The Black Hole and all. And why the fuck did you have to get into bed with me? I mean, shit, Liz. Why did you lead me on?" He laughs at this, in spite of himself. Liz laughs, too.

"I told you. I was curious."

"Yeah—but. You knew it would make me think that you—you must have known it would make me think you wanted to come back."

"I didn't think. I was bombed."

"Yeah, and curious."

"I'm still kind of curious."

Uh-oh, you're getting an erection, says BW. *Don't fall for this, Matthew. This is a power play.*

"What?" There's a smirk on her face. Is that a parody of a come-hither look? Is it the real thing? "Your curiosity wasn't satisfied?"

"Not entirely."

"So you might like to drop in from time to time for further investigations?"

"I might."

"Well, fuck you. Or rather, I won't fuck you. What do you

want me to do, provide dinner and drinks and dick until you find someone you can fall in love with?"

Excellent! Excellent! says BW. You don't sound like yourself at all. "Dick"? You never say anything like that, Matthew. Where did you pick that up? I have to tell you, I was sure you were going to give in. You surprised me. You really did.

"Why not? Wasn't that your arrangement with Belinda?"

A waiter is suddenly at their side. "One of you wanted an order of bouillabaise stir-fry?" he asks.

"Oh, God. What jerks," says Liz. Matthew has the fleeting impression that she's about to cry.

"We did order it, but I canceled the order," says Matthew. The waiter stands looking at him with no expression.

Is he thinking this over? Is he going to come to some decision, or is he paralyzed in the face of a novel situation?

"You don't want it, then?" asks the waiter.

Matthew almost laughs. Liz explodes. "Of course we don't want it. That's why we canceled it. We only ordered it because I couldn't eat *this* crap."

"Was there something you disliked about the squid-ink pasta?"

"There was a great deal I disliked about it," says Liz with the sneer she'd like to turn on Matthew. "It was too peppery, for one thing. You shouldn't put so much pepper into a dish like this. I've had this dish in many restaurants, including restaurants in Italy—"

She has? When?

"—and it's never as peppery as this."

She likes spicy food. This isn't about the food. This is about me.

"Well, this is our chef's preparation," the waiter explains, adopting now the gentle, falsely helpful tone the young like to use with aged people who appear to be bewildered by the exciting changes in the modern world, a tone equivalent to a helping hand. "He tends to create dishes that are more highly spiced than others."

"Well, I think you should let people know that, then, don't you? You should print it on the menu. A warning. 'Beware: Chef is an idiot.'"

Matthew is surprised by this.

I've never heard her talk like this before.

I didn't realize she had such a fully thought-out philosophy of food, says BW. *Apparently she's in favor of bland food, to be seasoned to taste by the people who will eat it. Is that a democratic attitude, would you say? Democratic versus the autocratic attitude of the chef, who prepares a dish one way only, his way, and tells the diner to take it or leave it? There might be something we can use in that idea.*

This isn't the time for that.

The waif has come over. She wears a look of concern, but secretly she's delighted. Here's something for her to do. She can intervene in this situation, whatever it is.

"Is something wrong?"

"Would you just bring us the check?" asks Matthew. He's had enough. He'd like to leave. He's begun to think fondly of his bed. He'd like to go home to it, alone. *Or at least,* he corrects his thought, looking into the eyes of the waif, *without Liz.*

"And don't put this plate of bouillabaise stuff on it," says Liz.

"You don't want it now?"

"We told you to cancel the order, don't you remember?" says Liz.

I told you, thinks Matthew. *Don't you remember me? I held your hand while I told you. Practically held your hand.*

"Oh, sure. I remember. I just didn't get around to telling them to cancel the order in the kitchen. We've been so busy, you know? It's no problem, though. You won't be charged for it. I'll get your check."

Liz sits in silence, fuming. She looks around the room. Matthew sees defiance in her eyes, as if she were daring anyone to look at her, to register any acknowledgment of the little scene. In the mirror, he scans the room himself, to see if anyone *is* registering any acknowledgment. All eyes are down, on food, except those of the beautiful couple, who are smiling tight controlled smiles and glancing their way. Matthew smiles into the mirror and is rewarded by seeing their smiles relax and broaden. *Are they aware that I was aware of their difficulty earlier? They must know. There's a bond between us now. I've relieved them of some of the weight of their embarrassment. Maybe I should introduce myself.*

"What are you smiling about?" asks Liz.

"Oh, nothing. It's too complicated to explain."

"Was that some kind of indulgent smile? You're hoping everyone will think you're putting up with me? I'm the bitch and you're putting up with me? Is that it?"

Perhaps in some corner of his mind Matthew has been hoping just that. The waif returns with the check; Liz begins berating her as soon as she arrives at the table: "You know, we used to come here very often, and the service was always a little distracted, but this is ridiculous. We had to wait about half an hour to get our order taken, and then I didn't get what I wanted."

"You got the wrong dish?"

"No, it was the right dish, but I didn't want so much of it. I wanted the half order, not the full order. Our waiter should have asked me which I wanted, not just brought the full order without giving me an option."

My God, she's really getting irrational.

Matthew looks the check over. The second order of bouillabaise stir-fry is on it. Matthew hesitates for an instant, then decides not to bring it up; he even includes it when calculating the tip.

Liz says, "You know, I don't know how many times we've eaten here, but something always goes wrong."

Never as wrong as tonight. It's true, though. She's right, really. If she would only shut up, I could agree with her.

"Oh. Well, the restaurant is under completely new management now," says the waif.

"I wouldn't brag about it," says Liz.

"Liz," says Matthew. "Please." The waif takes the check and walks off.

Matthew and Liz are at the door, Matthew helping Liz into her coat, when the waif comes bounding up the steps from the dining room, calling, "Sir! Sir!" and waving his check at him. "I'm terribly sorry," she says, "but I forgot to take the bouillabaise stir-fry off your bill. That second order. Let me make out a new charge slip for you."

"Never mind," says Matthew. *Shit. She's been in a daze the whole time we were here. Why did she have to wake up now?*

"It will only take a minute."

What should I do?

Basically, says BW, *you're facing a choice between the waif and Liz. I suggest you choose the waif. Frankly, I don't think you have a ghost of a chance there, but—*

But it's Liz I want.

Still?

Still.

"Forget it," he says to the waif. "Just forget it."

Wet, sloppy snow is falling, and Matthew regrets having left his umbrella at home. Stepping out onto the sidewalk, walking toward the corner, he can't help hoping that it might be possible to reverse what has happened. Now, how could he do that? He might say, as he used to say so often, "I'm sorry," or he might claim that he was only kidding, or—

I could fall apart. Throw myself at her. Tell her I've been behaving so miserably because I've been trying to save face. Tell her I was trying to hide my feelings because I want her back so much. "I know it's impossible, Liz, but still, I—"

"Oh, Matthew."

"I'm sorry. I didn't want to do this. I didn't want you to see me like this. I was fighting it so hard that—I guess the only way I could keep from showing my feelings was to pick a fight."

Drop to my knees. Put my head between her legs. She'd smooth my hair. Grab her bottom. Nose between her thighs. It might work.

They reach the corner in silence. Then Liz stops and turns on Matthew a look he takes for sadness. Actually it's the look that people employ when they have to convey bad news to someone toward whom they feel bottomless enmity. "Listen, Matthew," she says, "I guess I'm kind of on edge. You know? It's an unsettling period for me. Exciting, but unsettling. I'm a nervous wreck, to tell you the truth. And then seeing you again—and everything."

"I can understand that." Hope is revived.

"Well, look. There's something I have to tell you. I wish I didn't. It's—oh, look, I have to tell you this. Belinda isn't interested, you know. I mean, she isn't interested in—well, she has something else going on. Something else entirely. She's got this boy. This Italian boy. I mean he's just a kid, and—gorgeous. I mean absolutely gorgeous."

Matthew is speechless with anger and fear. He's certain that what Liz is saying is true. He couldn't say why he's certain, but he is. He's hearing the corroboration of his fears, and that's something he is prepared to believe. But still there is a flicker of hope: *Why is she telling me this?*

Let's see—to make you miserable, to demonstrate that she can make you miserable, to shatter your fragile hopes for a happy life, to bring you to your knees—

No. No. It's because she wants to clear my life. Get Belinda out of it. To make room for herself.

You can't be serious.

"She didn't tell you, I know," says Liz. "She told me. I met him. I can't wait to meet his friends, let me tell you." This is said with such lust that it snuffs that flicker of hope. *Where did this come from? Where did she get this kind of desire? What's she been up to?*

"I'm sorry. I shouldn't have said that. Come to think of it, you know him. Well, you don't know him, but you've seen him. She met him in some restaurant, when she was with you. He was a waiter."

"Taxi! Taxi!" It's Matthew. He has run partway into the street and is hailing a cab. He wants Liz away from him, now, right now. He's afraid he'll hit her. He knows he isn't a violent person, but he's terrified that he's about to hit her. The cab pulls to the curb and Matthew grabs Liz by the arm, pulls her to it. Her eyes are wide. He looks like someone she doesn't know, someone whose next act she can't predict. She's too surprised to resist him. He yanks the door open and pushes her into the cab. "Take her where she wants to go," he shouts at the driver, and he slams the door, putting his body behind it, and he pounds on the roof, again, again, and even in his fury he's amazed to see that he dents it, surprised and pleased to see how much strength he's built at Back Bay Bodies.

"Hey!" screams the driver, and in a second he's out of the cab. "Hey!" again, but Matthew's face is twisted, his teeth are clenched, his hands are bent like claws, and to the driver he looks capable of anything, eager for trouble, out of control. "Shit," says the driver. He gets back into the cab and drives off in a hurry.

Matthew stands there for a moment, suddenly exhausted, drained. Then the snow, melting on his head, begins running down his neck. He shudders, and he begins walking home. At the corner of Dartmouth and Boylston, he pauses at one of the writings of the Neat Graffitist.

> WHEN YOU COME TO THE END OF SOMETHING,
> BE CONTENT. YOU CAN'T UNDO WHAT'S BEEN
> DONE. THE BEST MARKER FOR THIS KIND OF
> WORK IS THE RUNZNOT® WATERPROOF
> MARKER. IT'S INDELIBLE.

The wind is driving the wet snow against the signal box on which this is written, but the letters are not running. Matthew stands at the writing for a couple of minutes, memorizing it. *I'll switch to Runznot,* he tells himself. *You can't beat a testimonial like that.*

At night, deep in the night, Matthew hears cries, in his sleep, as if in his dreams. When these cries wake him, he realizes that they come not from his neighbor, but from himself. From this horrific discovery he takes a tiny satisfaction. At least it's possible that his neighbor's cries didn't mean that he was leading a better life.

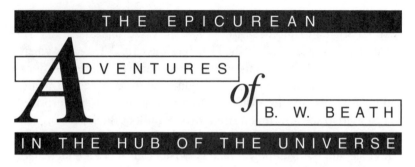

Two-Two-Two

Once upon a time, we knew a couple who seemed quite content in their life together, but read on. After fourteen years of marriage, they began a little game, something the husband discovered in his idle reading. The Romans, he learned, had a custom of marking each day as happy or unhappy by dropping a white or black pebble into an urn. To the husband this sounded like fun. He bought, at a florist's shop, smooth white stones and smooth black stones. He placed them in a dish beside a vase on a dresser in their bedroom. The idea was that at night, before going to bed, they would drop a stone into the vase. At the end of a month, they would spill the stones from the vase and see what kind of month it had been. They tried this one March, which, in Boston, was probably the first mistake. At the end of the month, they spilled the stones out onto their bed and separated them. There were twenty-nine white stones, seven black. "But that's only thirty-six stones," said he. "There should be sixty-two—thirty-one each."

"Is that what you thought?" she asked. "That we'd put a stone in every day?"

"Sure."

"I didn't see it that way at all," she said. "That way, we'd have to call every day either good or bad. Days aren't like that. Don't you agree? I mean, I can see that if we had gray stones, we'd put a stone in every day, and at the end of the month most of the stones would be gray, but we don't have gray stones, so we put in a white stone if we have a really great day, and we put a black stone in if we have a really lousy day."

So, they tried it her way, and at the end of April there were only six stones in the vase: three black, three white. The husband shrugged this off. "Well," he said, "that's pretty good. They balance out." For the wife, however, the month was a revelation, since none of the stones were hers. For her the month had been entirely gray. In fact, since she hadn't had any actual gray stones to deposit, it had been worse than gray: her month had amounted to nothing, nothing at all. This set her to thinking. She began a month-by-month stepping-stone excursion into the past, curious to see how far she would have to go before she encountered a month that might fill a vase. She went far enough to see that her life no longer aroused her. It no longer pleased or angered her enough to warrant a stone, no longer made her feel much of anything. It was a level plain, a windless sea, an empty vase. She blamed this sorry state not on herself, of course, but on her husband, and so, after explaining all of this to him as gently as she could ("It's not that there's anything wrong with you—I mean, I really think you're okay—honest—I mean, you never really did anything wrong—it's just that—"), she left him.

He hoped that after a while she would find the world at large even more disappointing than life with him, and she would return. When she did, he imagined, everything would be different—white stones in heaps. Time passed, and she didn't return, but still he believed that eventually she would. Even as it became less and less likely, he told himself that it still wasn't impossible, and he couldn't cure himself of the habit of wishing.

Now his troubles are over. He's free. He understands how foolish it would be to try to get back together. You can't raise the dead, he knows now. You can't undo what time has done. It's too late to choose another route when you're at your destination. How did he learn all this? It happened in a single evening spent in the dining room here, observing this ridiculous attempt to revivify the stinking corpse of **Two-Two-Two**.

—BWB

Two-Two-Two
222 Clarendon Street, 555-2222.
American Express, Visa, MasterCard, Diners Club. No checks.
Handicapped: three steps down to entrance, three steps down from lounge to dining room.
Lunch 11–3, Monday–Saturday.
Dinner 7–12 Tuesday–Saturday.
Brunch 12–4 Sunday.
Reservations recommended.

7

Ike's

For some time now, Matthew has had the mistaken idea that margaritas don't make him drunk. That is why, sitting at the bar at Ike's, he's getting drunk on margaritas. He began the evening at the bar at the Alley View, where he had a frozen Bombay and, since it tasted so good, another. Now, sitting here, he's trying to decide, first, whether or not to review this place, and second, whether or not to continue living.

It's really not worthy of a review, says BW. *Why don't we move on?*

And I'm not suited to this world, this time, this culture, and never will be, thinks Matthew. *Why not check out?*

Matthew isn't aware of it, but his lips are moving. It wouldn't be quite accurate to say that he's talking to himself, since no sound issues from his moving lips, but he's awfully close.

I'd really rather you didn't, admits BW. Perhaps it is to Matthew's credit that his lips do not move with BW's thoughts, only with his own.

It doesn't have to be painful or messy, you know, says Matthew.
*I'm not exactly sure how I'd go about it, but I'm sure that with a
little research I could come up with an acceptable method.*

Before you go that far, says BW, *why not try something else?*
Yeah?

*Try surrendering to me. Just think of the advantages if you let me
guide you. There are pleasures for you in my world, Matthew. I
guarantee I can teach you to have a good time. There will be no
more of these seizures of the spirit, no more anguish of the soul. Put
yourself in my care and you will nevermore stumble into despon-
dency. I'll hold you up.*

Sure.

*Matthew, don't you deserve some pleasure? I mean, really,
aren't you owed? Consider this: you took Leila home untouched.
Don't you deserve something in return for that? You were faithful
to Liz all those years.*

Virtually.

*Shouldn't there be a return on that? Why not start collecting
what you're owed?*

You mean—

*I mean why not start doing as you've been done to? What's hold-
ing you back? You owe nothing. Nothing to anyone. The balance of
payments is in your favor. Why do you keep making deposits in this
account of goodness?*

You want me to go into banking?

*Very good. Be amusing. After all this time, be funny. But you
know I'm right. When are you expecting to collect? You don't believe in heaven or hell. Start collecting now. Listen, let's take just
one example. Effie.*

Effie.

*Ah, I knew that would interest you. Let's suppose there actually
is something wrong between her and Richard. Don't you think you
could get in there? Of course you could. She likes you, you know
she does. Use that. Use it. Take. Take her. You can have her, you
know.*

Well, maybe, but—

But what? She wouldn't love you? She wouldn't love you, is that

it? To hell with that. Nobody loves you. Nobody ever has.
  Oh, shit.
  So, what do you say—should we review this place?
  Who cares?

Ike's is a large, hard-edged room, formerly a firehouse, now a restaurant selling a version of fifties prosperity and complacency. The smiling face of the eponymous Ike is everywhere, in black-and-white photos and framed magazine covers on the walls, interspersed with artifacts of the era, chosen with no apparent theme or requirement other than that they come from the period and that they appear, from the exalted vantage of the present, odd and amusing, as do, in this context, the improbably jovial Ike himself and the beaming Mamie so often beside him. The other gimmick is bulk. The quantity of food served here is enormous. Order a drink, and it's served to you in a glass the size of a cocktail shaker. It isn't a good drink, but there's plenty of it. Spaghetti is served in a bowl that would have sat at the center of the fifties table, full enough to feed a family of four. The burgers start at half a pound; a full pounder is available.

It's quite revolting, really, says BW. *A paltry, tawdry kind of bounty. What do you think?*

I'm not going to do anything stupid, Matthew is thinking. *I'll keep my mind occupied. I won't think about myself so much. I'll lose those five—well, seven—pounds. I'll make it work out. I'm an intelligent man. I was the smartest kid in high school. I have courage. I'm brave. I'll find a woman. She'll help me out of this phase I'm in.*

Why do you think a woman will save you? asks BW. *Why a woman?*

Maybe it's only wishful thinking. I'd rather be saved by a woman than, say, religion, or by a passion for work. I hope it's Effie. I think it might really be Effie. I'm sure something's wrong between her and Richard. She's too much for him, and he's too dull for her. He doesn't look into things deeply enough. He doesn't get into the details enough, doesn't see and consider all the ramifications and possibilities. I do. Oh, I do. It's part of my problem. But if I had somebody to say it all to, well—we could be very interesting to-

gether. There's a real possibility that she might call me, you know. There is, really. Just to get together to talk. We could go out to dinner. The Black Hole—that would be good. A simple place, and they get a thinking crowd. Kind of offbeat. No, no. I should shake her up a bit. Take her to—the Ritz. And then come right out with it. "Effie, you want to know something funny? I think I'm in love with you. I think I've been in love with you for years. How would you like to leave Richard and come to live with me? I have plenty of money. We could take a couple of years off. Buy a boat. Cruise up and down the intracoastal. Think things out." No, that's not what she'd want to do. That's what I would want to do. Or is it? Maybe. Could be dangerous, of course. But she wouldn't want it anyway. She'd want to stay involved in things. I could get involved, too, couldn't I? I could do something, something for kids, maybe. Set up a fund or a foundation. Get toys to poor children. Educational toys. Develop some games to teach physics. Computers—computer games. Belinda might be interested in that. She could get the Zizyph people interested. I should call her about that. She can't really be so interested in that waiter. We could get together and talk it over. Things could work out. They will work out. I really think they will.

A group of students arrives at the bar.

Now look at that, Matthew thinks. *That's the sort of thing that makes me think there's reason for hope.*

What Matthew finds heartening about them is the fact that they are a racially mixed group of students, quite thoroughly mixed, exhibiting skin tones ranging from his own sandy pink to the rich brown of a good strong cup of coffee, the step from one tone to the next quite a narrow one, so that, if they were to line themselves up properly, they would resemble the flexible plastic scale Matthew holds against his teeth to assess the success of his whitening efforts. There seem to be no strong pairings within the group. They seem to be a group of friends, not pairs of lovers.

You know, he thinks, *this could be the salvation of the world. Groups like this.*

It helps your perception of them, BW suggests, *that they are all young, attractive, and beautifully dressed. I'm certain it also helps that one of them is an eye-catching little girl, dressed entirely in black, who glanced at you when she arrived.*

She's looked this way a couple of times since then.

Perhaps she's trying to guess your age. It may be a contest among them.

She really is quite attractive, a tiny thing, wearing a skirt of some elasticized material, so short that the hem, drawn in by the elastic additive, cups her buttocks precisely along their nether curve.

I thank you, God, thinks Matthew, for this most amazing fabric. And that I should have the good fortune to live in the age of miracle stretch fibers.

That is a gorgeous little ass, says BW.

You don't have to put it that way.

Others join the group. As it grows it spreads along the bar, and the girl with the elasticized bottom shifts closer, closer to Matthew, whose upper lip begins to sweat.

You know, Matthew, says BW, you ought to consider the possibility that you're nuts.

What do you mean?

Well, let's look at your catalog of symptoms. At the top of the list we have—a mysterious odor. You've had your apartment torn apart as a result of what may be—let's face it—an illusion.

It's not. It's no illusion. And it's getting worse. It's getting into my clothes. I can smell it now. This jacket smells of it. It's—oily. Heavy smelling. Sickening. When I was a boy and sick with something or other, my mother brought me books to read in bed. Used books from her shop. One of them was—I don't know—a guide to trees or something. It stank. It must have been mildew or something. I opened it, and it made me sick. Made me vomit. This is like that.

Mm.

Oh, cut it out. I don't mean it's just like that. I mean it has that effect. It's starting to make me sick.

Mm.

You don't smell it because you don't want to. You ignore it.

Let's go on. Next on my list is your obsession.

My obsession.

Your lust, Matthew. You are obsessed with the idea of sex with young girls. It really is time you admitted that. Why do you bring those binoculars to the ballet? You examine the dancers, the young ones in the corps.

Hey.

You forget that I'm privy to your thoughts, Matthew. I know what's going on in here. I know the way you look at their breasts, focus on their crotches. I know you're looking for something to suggest that slit you can't get out of your mind—a dimple of cloth, a wet spot. And I know the fantasies you concoct. The one with that ballet student? You remember the girl, the one you saw walking along Newbury Street, with her headset on, bouncing to a rhythm you couldn't even hear. Oh, yes, she was lovely, quite lovely.

Mm. She was.

How does the fantasy go? Oh, yes. The poor thing is impoverished. She'll have to leave the ballet school because her parents can't afford to maintain her in Boston. But she stumbles across you somehow! She pours out the whole story. Lucky thing! You have an extra bedroom. Food in the fridge. Plenty of spare cash. No strings, you assure her. You'll be pals. She moves in. Ahh, but that night, the lonely, frightened, grateful child taps at your bedroom door.

Mm.

Let me ask you something, Matthew. Why do you always make them fall in love with you—in these fantasies? I mean, excuse me, but what difference does it make? If the point of the fantasy is that you wind up fucking the girl, why do you go through all that preliminary bullshit? Why not just cut right to the fucking?

Listen, you, maybe I'm not after fucking, as you insist on calling it. Maybe I'm after something more. Did you ever consider that?

I considered it. There's something to it. But this—nobility you're claiming is a fake. It's really just timidity. Timidity in disguise.

Timidity again.

It's not one of the deadly sins, but it's killing you, Matthew.

Timidity and, I would say, loyalty. Misguided loyalty.

To Liz, you mean?

No. Well, partly, perhaps. But mainly to an idea. Some stupid idea of goodness or something that I don't understand. Let's have another drink.

I ought to get some food. Some food would be a good idea.

Fine, but get a drink. Buy one for the girl, too. You know the one I mean. The one in the skirt. The one with the ass. Don't hesitate, now. Just do it. You don't have to talk to her, just ask the bartender to give her whatever she's having. You may have a chance there. If you ask me, you don't deserve it, after sending Leila home, but as I said, you're owed, and I think you're getting another chance. Take it, will you? Take it!

I don't know. I—

All right, I'll take it. "Excuse me."

"Excuse me," says Matthew, lifting his hand, catching the eye of the bartender.

"Yo."

"I'll have another margarita."

"I'll have another margarita."

"And give the beautiful girl in black another of what she's having."

"And—some nachos."

Deadly, deadly timidity.

"And—give the beautiful girl in black another of what she's having."

One of the handsome lads in the group of students is saying, "My father has this thing about getting the whole family together, right?" He pauses to take a pull at a bottle of Anderson's Denver Beer, pauses again to savor that Denver cachet, and continues: "Like he thinks we all really want to be together, but circumstances keep us apart?" Pause. "Right."

This is well received. Even Matthew finds himself smiling. He's listening quite openly; he has no companion to conceal his eavesdropping. The girl with the elastic bottom is served her drink, looks up, and catches sight of Matthew in the mirror behind the bar. Matthew catches sight of her catching him.

Uh-oh, I'm discovered. Glance away? No, that only makes it worse. Hide it somehow. Notebook. Take notes. Disguise myself as a restaurant reviewer.

I'm not certain you can carry that off, BW says. *We restaurant reviewers are, as a rule, on the suave and self-possessed side.*

"So this year, he calls and goes, 'We're spending a week in Brazil.' I'm like, 'Brazil? Where *is* it?'"

"Oh, I went to Brazil," says one of the girls, not the one who has caught Matthew's eye. "Or not Brazil exactly? Peru? I had this roommate who was from Peru? And she was always like, 'Come visit me'? So I go? And I found out that in Peru, if you eat at a café, you know, on the street? The beggars, they come right up to you while you're eating and go, 'I'm hungry, can you give me your food?' It's terrible. I can't stand it. They should wait until you're finished eating—it makes you very upset."

Ah, yes, says BW. *I see what you mean now. They do give you cause for hope, don't they?*

Well, the little one.

I know your hopes for her.

"Macho Nachos?" A waiter has arrived at Matthew's elbow, holding what looks like a tray that must, surely, hold several orders of nachos.

"Oh," Matthew says. "Yes."

The waiter smiles and places the entire platter in front of Matthew, on the bar. It is so large that it reaches beyond what, observing the informal boundaries civilization provides us in settings where we are forced to be side by side with our fellow humans, would be Matthew's space. He looks down at the platter and is immediately reminded of the town dump in Lincoln. It too was a large mound, irregularly massed, with a segregation of toppings such as this, the discarded washing machines ganged in one area, furniture in another, as the pepper rings, sour cream, and salsa each have their own areas on this mound.

The group beside him has turned, as a group, as if geared to a common shaft, to look at Matthew and his heap of chips. They're smiling, curious to see how the old guy will handle this.

"Looks like a map," says one of the girls, but not the right one, not the right one.

Looks inedible, says BW. *That's processed cheese, you know. I wouldn't touch this if I were you. Give it to the kids.*

"I think you've got all of the basic food groups there," says one of the boys, not the girl in the elastic skirt.

All the food groups and one of the deadly sins, says BW.

"All the food groups and one of the deadly sins," says Matthew.

Very good! says BW. *Now that's wit.*

"Huh?" says the boy, indicating that, among the responses he had expected to hear, this wasn't one. "Oh, yeah," he says, brightening. "Um, gluttony, right?"

"Right." Matthew pushes the platter along the bar, toward the kids.

"The seven deadly sins are—" He pauses to give any of them a chance to supply one. They regard him with restrained curiosity, as if he were their teacher; he's struck by the notion that he is. "Gluttony, pride, covetousness, anger, envy, sloth, and—" He pauses again, and he marks the pause with a sip of his drink, as Liz would have marked it with a puff on her cigarette, when she was smoking. "Lust," he says, turning quite frankly toward the elasticized girl.

"Whoa!" says one of the group, and the others burst out laughing, some even applaud. Matthew isn't quite what they expected to find here at the bar at Ike's, and surprise is one of the things they're after.

To the girl Matthew says, "My name is—" *What name? Matthew Barber? These kids wouldn't give last names. That would make me seem hopelessly antique. Or maybe that would have its charm.*

Remember what I said about these girls being in love with their fathers.

No, I want to meet her in her idiom.

Impossible.

Well, something close to it. Matthew. No. Not that asshole. Matt?

She's smiling at him, waiting.

"—Bert."

"Bert"! screams BW. *I would never permit myself to be called "Bert." "BW" if you must, but never "Bert."*

"BW—that's what my friends call me."

"Hello, BW," she says. "I'm Tracy."

Well, well, says BW. *Is this my chance, then? Am I on? This may prove to be an interesting evening. I think chumminess is called for here. Make them think I'm interested in all of them equally, that I want to be their pal, not that I merely want to get into Tracy. Stand aside and watch this, Matthew. You may learn how to live.*

"Help yourself," says Matthew, prompted by BW, indicating his nachos. "God knows there's enough here for a crowd."

The boys accept this invitation at once, in the manner of guys, reaching over and around the girls and taking a chip or two at once, jostling for positions that give them better access to the garnishes they prefer, and the girls are only slightly more reticent; they all join in, even Tracy, who pivots on her stool to take a chip (just a chip, one with nothing at all on it, probing beneath the crust and toppings to find one), so that she is now turned toward Matthew, not toward her friends.

I don't believe it, Matthew thinks. *I'm getting a second chance. Maybe you were right. Leila wasn't for me. This is what I need. This is what we need. She's adorable.*

That ass of hers, that ass. Two piglets in a sack.

Cut that out. You know I don't like that.

"So, what do you do, BW?" asks one of the boys.

Make toys? Review restaurants?

"I design computer games." *Where did that come from? Belinda. Of course.*

"No kidding?"

The right choice. The right choice. "No kidding."

"Like what?"

"Well, the one I'm working on now is called—Picture Frame.

It's—it's not one of those games that involves shooting helicopters down or killing dragons—it's a game that takes some thought—a mystery."

"Sort of like Where Am I?"

Uh-oh. What's that?

"Similar, I suppose, but—well, the premise here is that you're in someone's apartment, and you wander around in it."

"Hm."

"You listen to the messages on his answering machine, read his mail, browse through his books, and so on."

"Mm."

"And—this is the best part—he has a computer. So you can get into his computer. And you find out a lot of interesting things about him that way."

"Why?"

"Hm?"

"Why do you do it? I mean, why do you wander around the guy's apartment? Are you looking for clues? What's the mystery?"

Shit, thinks Matthew. *It's the same question. I should tell Belinda about this.*

"Well," says Matthew, defending Belinda and her game, "the real mystery is just finding out what the guy is like. Getting into his life. I mean, how far do we ever penetrate—"

Oh, I like that, but you're on dangerous ground here, tricky footing, thrilling, though, quite thrilling.

"—into someone else's life, thoughts, heart, you know?"

That won't do, Matthew, says BW. *They want more than that. Allow me.*

"To tell you the truth," says Matthew, "I wanted to leave it that way—a pure intellectual exercise. But I had to take the practical view, you know? I knew that the half-witted video slaves who are going to buy this thing are not looking for pure intellectual exercises."

Smiles. A chuckle or two.

"They want the highest goal of modern life, the thing that everyone's looking for—they want to be entertained."

More chuckles.

"So, of course, I knew it had to have a mystery. A little violence. A little sex."

Nods and uh-huhs from the kids, suggesting that they share BW's attitude toward the base tastes of his audience. *How do you like that for improvisation?* asks BW. *And the little assholes don't even recognize themselves.*

Come on, BW. They're being nice to us, aren't they? Treating us nicely?

Shut up, Matthew. Leave this to me.

"I mean," Matthew continues, in a voice he hardly recognizes, "otherwise who gives a shit about this guy, right?"

Laughter.

See? That's their idiom, says BW.

"But he is kind of interesting on his own, I think," says Matthew, pushing his true self back into the conversation. "I mean, isn't everyone? Or, if not everyone, this guy anyway." *You're making a mess of this,* says BW. "There are surprising things as you go through his apartment," says Matthew, a little desperately.

"Like?"

"Like one wall is all torn away—partly torn away. You can see into it—you see the framing, the insulation, some foam cups the builders left there. And you wonder why this should be—why is this torn apart?"

"Something was hidden there."

"A body."

"Or money."

"Well," says Matthew, "you can find the answer in his filing cabinet, a lot of memos to the condo board about an odor, but skip that for now. The thing is that, around the hole, where the wallboard is still in place, he's written these sayings. Kind of intriguing."

"And the sayings are clues."

"Right."

"But to what?"

To what he is. To his state of mind. To his past. What else? Isn't that enough?

Obviously not. They want to know what the point is. What's the mystery?

"Ahhh," says Matthew, surrendering. "You want to know what the mystery is. Well, at some point, clever player that you are, you notice that a window in the living room is open. Mouse your way over to the window, click on it, and you're looking out. Click down, you look down. And there he is. Lying on the pavement, flat on his face. There's a crowd around him."

"Checked out."

"Apparently."

"Why?" It's Tracy this time. At last.

"Hm?"

"I mean, why would he do that?"

"Oh," says Matthew, "any number of reasons. Just disappointment. Regret. Hopelessness." He knows, even as he lists them, that they are diseases she doesn't understand. "Middle age," he adds, and feels himself sinking into a slough.

Shut up, will you? says BW. *You're going to lose them, lose her.*

"I don't think he did it," she says.

"Ah!" says Matthew, under BW's control. "Neither do the police."

"Oh, so that's it," she says, brightening, pleased. "That's the mystery. 'Who killed—whatever his name is.'"

"Matthew Barber. 'Who Killed Matthew Barber?'"

Shit. Why me?

"So, listen, BW," says the tallest of the boys, "would you like to go to a party with us?"

BW is suspicious. *I don't like it,* he says. *Why would these kids be interested in having you come along with them?*

"Why don't you come?" asks Tracy. Matthew almost says yes at once.

Don't do it, warns BW.

Why not? asks Matthew. *They like me. I think they're flattered that I should be their pal. Well, not pal, exactly, but you know they probably never get to talk to anyone my age, without all the interfer-*

ence that age brings. Do you see what I mean?

Matthew, you're dreaming, says BW. *I'm telling you to be suspicious of this offer. We're just going to shrug it off. We're drunk, you know. Getting drunk, anyway. And it is not a good idea to go off with people you meet in bars. We're just going to get Tracy's phone number and call—call it a night. We'll work on her in a couple of days, on our own terms.*

"No, thanks," says Matthew, with a grin and a chuckle to show that he's taken the invitation as a joke, wouldn't have thought of it as anything but a joke, and has other, better things to do.

See? says BW. *That's cool. You showed them you were flattered but you knew the invitation was only for the sake of politeness.*

"Oh, come on," says Tracy. "It'll be fun. You'll have fun." It sounds like a promise.

"Well, all right," says Matthew, bedazzled and hopeful. "Why not?"

Hey, says BW. *What's happening here?*

I'm going to get everything I've always wanted.

"Say," says one of the young men to the bartender, tapping him on the arm to take his attention away from the drink he's mixing, "would you pack all of this up?" He waves his hand over the remains of their snacks—Matthew's nachos and some ribs and a huge pick-up-stick tangle of fries.

"I'll send a busboy over," says the bartender, too busy and too cool to be annoyed.

"What are you doing?" asks one of the girls. "We're not going to take all this with us."

"I'm going to send this out as a contribution to the homeless. You see the guy out front?" They turn, as one again. Outside the restaurant, in front of one of the windows that now fill the openings through which fire apparatus once drove, is a man Matthew has seen on the streets before, often, in fact, since he lives in Matthew's neighborhood, in the lobby of an automatic teller machine installation on Boylston Street, near Fairfield. Matthew has seen the man in Copley Square, sitting on the steps of the library, and sometimes wading in a reflecting pool inside the entrance to the Westin Hotel, scooping pennies, watching for the security guards, but most notably and most often he has seen him on Dartmouth Street, between Boylston and Newbury, where, as he is doing now, he performs a drunken version of a dance that, it seems clear to Matthew, is meant to please, perhaps some dance he did as a child, when it earned him a caress, a treat, a quarter, just what he's after now. Always drunk, he slips and staggers as he dances, and people avert their eyes, change course to avoid him. Once when Matthew saw him in the pool at the Westin, though, some children were riding up the escalator, trying not to look, as if they thought it must be impolite, but they couldn't keep themselves from looking, from giggling. The man became aware of them, turned, waved in an oddly endearing way, as if he had had training in this gesture, this endearing wave, as if he had once been a clown. He went into his dance, fell down in the water, and sent the children away laughing openly, gladly. Outside, he's doing his dance now, stumbling as he does.

"The clown," says Matthew. Tracy gives him a questioning look. "I think of him as the clown. I see him around. See the little dance he's doing? He's like a clown. Maybe he really was a clown once, but there isn't much work for clowns these days, and that's why he's out of work. What do you think?"

Matthew, shut up. You're going to ruin everything.

The bartender pushes the check across the bar, toward Matthew. There is no ambiguity about this. There is only one check. Matthew's expected to pay it. The students do not even seem to realize that it exists. Matthew hesitates for a moment, a moment during which he suspects that he's being played for a sucker, and then he puts his American Express card on the check and pushes it back across the bar.

"Well, I'm giving this stuff to the clown," says the munificent lad. "It's nacho night on the streets."

"Oh, wait a minute," says the girl who once visited Peru. She reaches under her skirt, brings her hand out with the middle finger extended, wipes it along one of the chips. "My contribution to the homeless," she says.

Matthew is disgusted. For an instant, he thinks of acting. He could simply remove that chip and deposit it on the bar, saying nothing. *What would Tracy think of that?* Or he could grab the girl by the wrist and tell her what a revolting little pig he thinks she is. Or he could slap her, hop off his stool, and storm out of Ike's, never looking back.

Oh, cut it out, says BW, *are you disgusted or just envious? You want that chip for yourself?*

What a bitch. They're disgusting, these kids, all of them.

I thought they were the salvation of the earth.

A busboy arrives with foam containers. He dumps the leftovers into the containers. In this state, jumbled, inverted, the food looks like garbage.

"Take it out to the clown on the sidewalk."

"Hey, I'm not going to do that."

"Twenty bucks." The bill emerges as if from nowhere, as if the boy were performing a trick his doting father taught him.

The busboy takes the money quickly, pockets it, and takes the containers outside.

The group follows, and when they pass the clown, now balancing foam boxes, they salute him, call out to him, whistle, laugh. Matthew worries that the clown will forget himself and wave, drop the boxes, make himself ridiculous, or, worse, that he'll spot Matthew and make some sign of recognition, making Matthew ridiculous. He passes with his head down, like a racketeer on the evening news.

Most of the group gets into two BMWs that are double-parked on Boylston Street, in front of the restaurant. Matthew watches, hanging back, tempted just to drift away, down the street, home, but Tracy's beside him, and she's a stronger temptation. He hopes she'll stay where she is and not join the others. His hopes seem to be answered; she stands by his side, close enough to touch. She seems to want to stick with him. A cab turns the corner, and one of the boys flags it down. Six of the revelers, including Matthew and Tracy, pile into it, five in the back. Tracy's elasticized bottom, nestled in Matthew's lap, promises a taxi ride to heaven, but something's wrong: the boy who has taken the front seat is rapping on the partition, and the driver's calling out, "Hey. Four's the limit. Four's the limit."

Matthew knows what to do now. He's been in this situation before. He has his wallet out at once. For a moment he feels the familiar fear that he has no money, a fear that strikes whenever he has to pay for something in public, but he has money, of course he has money, he can relax, he got plenty of money from the machine this afternoon, it's okay, it's all okay—but where's his American Express card? He's left it inside.

Shit. I'd better get it.

Are you kidding? Leave now and you'll never see her again.

But the card—

It'll be there. It'll be there in the morning.

"I'll take care of this," Matthew tells his new pals. He pushes a ten through the flap in the partition, slaps the flap closed, snaps his fingers.

That's the way. What a sport. What savoir faire.

Off they go. Matthew rides in a happy fog, mystified by the chatter of his chums, who seem to speak a dialect he doesn't understand. He has the feeling that, if he made the effort, he could understand them, but he's content to be out of it, quite happy to sit back and go along for the ride, holding Tracy in his lap, wearing a goofy smile, like a happy child. He can hardly resist the urge to announce his happiness, give thanks for this unexpected companionship, confess that he's thrilled to have a lap full of Tracy, whose amazing bottom makes every bump and pothole a delight, but there's no opening in the conversation for him: everyone seems to be talking at once, even the boy riding in front, who's talking to the driver, laughing as he talks. Matthew can't tell what he might be talking about, but he envies his talent for talking with cabbies. It's quite an animated discussion, with the boy doing most of the talking, the driver shrugging now and then, nodding, shaking his head. The boy laughs and slaps the driver on the shoulder.

Telling a joke? Matthew wonders.

The boy lights a cigarette, still talking, talking. He glances toward the back. His eyes meet Matthew's and he smiles. Matthew nods and smiles. The boy raises his eyebrows, tilts his head toward Tracy, and winks, slyly, surreptitiously; Matthew glances at Tracy, sees that she's looking away, glances at the boy again, tilts his head back, rolls his eyes upward, grins.

Two guys in wordless understanding, says BW.

Yeah. I wonder if this guy and Tracy—

Sure. Of course. You saw that wink.

The boy has turned away. He's talking to the cabdriver again, slapping him on the shoulder again, but there's money in his hand this time, a folded bill. He taps the shoulder of the driver's leather jacket a couple of times before the driver acknowledges him. The driver takes the money, frowning, shaking his head.

Is he paying him? Are we there? Maybe they were arguing over the tip.

The ride is making Matthew dizzy; he's begun to feel a little crapulent; he'd like this trip to end. He hasn't been paying attention to where they're going, and now when he looks out the window he doesn't know where they are. They've left the North End, crossed the Charles, and are now in Charlestown, in an area torn apart to build new approaches to the Mystic River Bridge. They turn off the main road, and the cab dips and lurches and stumbles along a side street, a path through fields of rubble, its surface pocked and pitted, nearly impassable.

The driver stops the cab. They seem to be nowhere.

"Okay, everybody out!" calls the boy in the front, in high spirits, pounding the plastic partition.

"Where are we?" Matthew asks. He doesn't see any buildings when he looks out the window, just the steel uprights that support the bridge approach, some heavy equipment lined up under the roadway, enormous, bulky, dark, and looming, mounds of earth and rubble, stacks of something shrouded in tarpaulins, nothing more.

"We're headed up there," says the boy in front, pointing through the windshield. "This fuck won't go any farther. He's worried about the cab. He says the road sucks."

Matthew can see some buildings ahead. He can't really tell how far away they are.

"Cabdrivers," says Matthew, loudly enough to be heard through the partition. "They're my favorite people."

The driver twists around and looks at Matthew. His head is nearly spherical. It's the only part of him that projects above the back of the seat. "This is it," he says. "No more. I'm not bustin' the fuckin' cab in this shit."

"Fuck you," says Matthew, perhaps assuming that he's found his new friends' idiom at last. "We'll walk."

Matthew levers the door open and gives Tracy a squeeze, as if he were merely telling her to slide out. She gets out, Matthew gets out, everyone is out, then everyone is in, whooping, howling, laughing, everyone but Matthew. The doors slam. The cab drives off, roaring, screeching.

At first Matthew feels only astonishment, disbelief, something like the shock from a blow. As if he'd had the wind knocked out of him, for a moment he can't seem to breathe. In another moment he's sucking air into his lungs fiercely but can't seem to get any oxygen from it. Then he droops, all his energy gone at once, and feels like a fool, that he's been played for a fool and deserved it. They saw everything, these children, understood everything about him, his desires, his clumsiness, his fakery, his vulnerability, everything.

His anger begins to rise. It overwhelms his embarrassment, replaces it with fury. He cries out, and it's a fine, furious cry, wordless, horribly eloquent. He turns, turns, turns again, searching for something. He doesn't realize, honestly doesn't realize, that he's looking for a weapon. He stumbles over something, bends and grasps it, raises it, and sees in the wedge of light that falls across his arm and hand that it's a piece of concrete paving. He hefts it. *The cab, where's the cab?* He turns, turns, turns, hunting. The cab is moving away, to his left. *Fucking shits.* He hurls the piece of paving in the direction of the cab, but it's too heavy, and the cab is already too far away. The chunk falls humiliatingly short. *Shit. Shit.*

He looks around for something else to throw, picks up other, smaller chunks, and hefts them, until he finds one he likes. He straightens up to throw it, and he sees the cab's brake lights come on. The cab is stopping. Fear chills him. He steps into the shadows, against the bridge abutment, and watches, holding his chunk. The cab makes a left turn, and in the light of its sweeping headlights, Matthew can see the reason: the road ahead is closed. Only when the lights sweep around and light up the opposite side of the bridge abutment does Matthew realize that the driver has had to turn completely around and will, in a moment, pass within a few feet of him. He feels the rush of a thrilling emotion. Recalling the instruction of one of his badgering gym coaches, he glances at the chunk, adjusts his grip, draws a breath, takes a stance, coolly, planting his feet. The cab pulls into view, moving slowly, dodging potholes. He winds up and throws. The chunk strikes the driver's window squarely and smashes it instantaneously, the glass bursting into the bright pebbles Matthew sees in the gutters every morning after the nighttime radio harvest. The driver shouts, the cab swerves, a wheel drops into a pothole, the frame shrieks against the pavement, and the cab comes to a wrenching halt, tossing the kids around inside.

Holy shit! says BW. *That was great! Amazing!*

The driver is out of the cab at once, looking around, turning as Matthew turned when he was hunting for a weapon, in the same half squat. Matthew is terrified, sweating, shivering, unable to move, but thrilled, thrilled.

"Yo, shithead!" he shouts. "Fuck you!"

The driver reaches into the cab, grabs from the floor the jack handle he keeps under his seat, turns, and runs toward Matthew, brandishing it. *Oh, shit.* Matthew turns to run, falls. Down, he turns and turns about, trying to run and rise at the same time. Is he running? He can't tell whether he's running or crawling. He seems to hear the sound of the driver's running feet, his breath. *That can't be. It must be me.* He has no real sense of what his arms and legs are doing. *Somewhere to hide. A place to hide.*

Not to hide, to strike. A place to strike from.

Hide in the shadows.

Strike from the shadows.

Fury owns a part of him, an anger forty years old and more. He's looking for another weapon, though he isn't conscious of that, won't allow himself to be conscious of that, is only half-aware that he grabs something, rejects it, grabs something else, a short length of reinforcing bar, bent at one end, hefts it, decides that it will do, and hurls himself, all without thinking, toward the darkest area he sees, a complex of shadows farther along the abutment, where dark tarpaulins cover stacks of paving blocks. He squeezes into a gap between two piles as high as himself and tries swinging his weapon. When he finds the space too confining to allow him to swing well, only then, and only far back in his mind, does he realize that he's been looking for a place to strike from, not to hide. It may be that he has been looking for a place to strike from for a very long time. He peeks around the corner and sees no one, though he can hear the cabdriver calling out, "Where are you, you fucking bastard?" and hears the kids blowing the horn of the cab and calling the driver to come back. He slips out of the confining space and moves farther along, slides into a wider gap, where he can swing the weapon easily, and takes a stance, waiting.

All his emotions, all his thoughts, have found their common thread in fury, but they've brought him something new, another emotion, this thrill he feels, crouching there, elementally alive, thrilled by the thought that he can be doing this. He's not afraid. For the first time in a long time, he realizes, he's not afraid. Part of him wants the cabdriver to come this way, and that part of him is in control now. He wants to strike out at him, he wants to be forced to strike out at him in self-defense. He wants to hurt him, to hurt *some-one.* He can imagine himself hitting the driver, and his imagination takes a tactile form: he can imagine his arms swinging, imagine the resistance when his weapon hits the driver's head. He feels the strength in his arms, and he admires it, he's proud of it. What has all that time at the health club been for, after all? To make his suits hang better on him? To lengthen a life that disappoints him again and again? To make him more desirable sexually? No. Here is the reason. Now he sees, feels, the reason: to make him better able to take revenge, revenge on the big, stupid boys who ruined his youth, who smeared shit on his underwear, revenge for his unrewarded loyalty to Liz, revenge on all the gorgeous creatures who smile indulgently when they catch him looking at them, those knowing, tolerant smiles, revenge, revenge. Look at his posture, his expression. He's standing upright, not cowering; smiling, not whimpering; eager, not anxious; aggressive, not defensive. He was never good at sports, but in this angled light, in these cinematic shadows, he looks like an athlete: confident, capable, cool.

No, no, says a smaller, weaker, fearful part of him. *Don't do this. Hide, just hide.*

Shut up, says BW.

There he is, the cabbie, squat, thick, muscular, holding his bar.

His is smaller than mine.

Get back, get down.

No. It's now. Now.

Matthew feels cold suddenly. The sensation surprises him.

It's the wind, that damned wind! He smashes the rod against the ground, since he cannot strike the wind.

It won't leave you alone. It intrudes on any emotion, any time.

Even now.

It won't let you be.

Won't let you be happy.

Won't let you be blue.

Won't even let you be angry.

"It's always *there!*" he cries, and swings the rod again. *Always drawing attention to itself.*

Like the thrilling little bodies of those girls you can't ignore. Like Tracy.

It takes a moment for him to realize that he has hit the driver, that the man has stumbled backward, is leaning against the steel upright, is staggering, has dropped to his knees. Matthew steps out from hiding. He looks in the direction of the cab. The kids are still calling out, one or two are outside the cab, but they have their hands on it, are holding it, for its protection, and don't seem to be interested in leaving its shelter.

He shivers, turns, and looks at the driver. He's bleeding from his ear. Blood runs down his chin. His mouth is open. He looks confused. Hate made Matthew swing for his head, and hate makes a part of Matthew want to hit him again. The fury is still there. The one blow was not enough to quench it.

Go on, hit him. Hit him again. I had no idea this would feel so good. Hit him, Matthew. Go on. Hit him. Don't let the fucker get up. It's the voice of BW, the part of Matthew that wants to strike again, the part that has made him forget that he's not the sort of man to do something like this.

No. No, says Matthew. *Leave him alone.* He backs away from the driver. The man puts his hand to his ear, pulls it away, and sees the blood. His eyes widen, and his mouth begins to move, soundlessly.

His eyes! says BW. *Look at his eyes! Look at that, Matthew, look at that. That's terror! This man is afraid of me. Afraid of you. Oh, I like that. I like that fear.*

Matthew raises the rod and takes a step toward the driver. He enjoys the way he feels his muscles tightening—in his arms, his back, his neck, his jaws, too, tightening, clenching. The driver tries to back away, but he's against an upright and doesn't dare take his eyes off Matthew to look for an escape. The wind rises, the vicious wind, cold and dusty, and the driver shudders. So does Matthew, and it makes him feel a kinship with the driver, two foolish aging men, fighting on this forsaken landscape, while children watch.

What fools.

But he is so fucking afraid of me, Matthew. Let go of me. Let me hit him again. Once more. For the kids who smeared shit on your underwear back in high school.

All right, yes. No. No.

Come on. Once more. For Liz. One more for Liz. One for Liz. One for Tracy in the elastic skirt. She was laughing at us, Matthew. She's not laughing now, I'll bet. One more. Let's give it to her, one more. One for Leila. You should have fucked her. You know that, don't you? I told you you should have fucked her. One for Leila, come on, one for Leila. One for the little kid from the ballet. Who will never come tapping at your bedroom door. One for her. So many blows to strike, Matthew. One more, at least. Just one more.

No. No.

Matthew backs away, dragging BW with him, and the driver takes his chance as soon as he sees it, gets to his feet, backs around the upright, turns, and runs. Matthew turns, begins walking in the opposite direction, and then begins to run, runs without knowing where he's running, until he's out of breath. He's reached the edge of the cleared area, where buildings still stand. He stops, leans against a wall, breathes deeply.

I should have—spent more time—on the rowing machine—at the health club, he thinks.

I could have killed him, says BW.

I don't think so. I don't think I would have let you go that far.

I would have. There was a point there—when I—when I didn't want to stop.

I know, I know. I felt that.

That was the best part. Exciting. So exciting.

Keeping a hand on the wall, he walks along, slowly, dragging his feet, until he comes to a darkened doorway. He settles onto a step and sits there, hoping he'll be able to breathe again soon.

Everything's changed now. I have to go away. I have to get out of this city.

Don't be ridiculous, says BW. *You're just being dramatic. This will never come out. You're not the sort of person a witness remembers, remember? Those kids won't remember you. Neither will the cabbie.*

I told the girl about being—I told her to call me BW.

Ah, yes. Well, that could be a problem. But, let's face it—she probably wasn't really paying attention. And she isn't likely to read my reviews. Most of these kids don't read anything, you know.

But I want to go anyway. I want to get out of here.

Where? Where will you go?

Somewhere, anywhere.

Well, make it somewhere warmer. Somewhere where that damned winter wind isn't always moaning.

I feel it now. I feel that wind.

Of course you do. It blows in one day in the fall, and then for months everyone's wearing galoshes and trudging, heads bent against it, that goddamned wind.

It makes you wonder—how many of us will make it to spring? I'm going to go. I'm going to change everything, change my life.

But you already have, Matthew. You're someone now. You're really someone. Someone to fear. Be careful, be careful of this man. He's not the man he used to be.

I'll disguise myself. Maybe I'll change my name. We're going to have to keep a low profile. Lie low, they used to say in the movies. Film noir movies. That old black phone at the Alley View.

We'll be in hiding. We won't be what we appear to be. Watch out for this man. He's capable of violence. He will only take so much. There is some shit he will not eat. Hide your daughters—he has no scruples. Say, Matthew, that brings up an idea. We really should see Leila again before we go. If you let me handle it, we can still get in there.

I wonder what she'd say if I told her what I'd done.

Suppose you stopped there now? Suppose you showed up like this, bloody, on the run?

Do I have blood on me?

Well, no, but you might just smack your hand against this wall. Scrape it up a bit. It would be good if there were some blood, I think.

She'd assume I was the victim. She and Belinda.

Good. That's good. You can use that. They'll want to comfort you.

But I don't want that. Don't you see? They're locked into one idea of me—just like Liz. Liz would call an ambulance right away if she saw me like this. Then the police. She'd assume that I lost. Somebody had beaten me up, mugged me, robbed me. She'd have me down as the victim.

Shit, Matthew, you're really hopeless. I ought to call Liz, show you how to operate. Tell her I need an alibi. Tell her I'm going to get out of town. Tell her I'm sure I killed the guy.

Sure. But when she found out I hadn't, there I'd be again, diminished. God, is that true? Would she be disappointed if I hadn't killed someone? Would it take that much to change her mind?

How about this idea—don't talk to anybody. Pretend that nothing has happened. Everything, everything has changed, but only you know it. Don't let anyone else know it. Continue on. Do everything just as you would if nothing had happened. Stay right where you are. Don't even change your name. The name's the same, but everything else is different. Now you know what you can do.

Now I know I'm no better than anyone else. I'm as bad as everyone else.

If you want to put it that way. I could have killed him, you know. I could have killed him. I am capable of that.

Shit, I left my American Express card at Ike's.

He hears a voice, close to him, then shuffling footsteps and someone sniffling, and he shifts farther back into the shadowy doorway. A man dressed in rags, bent, his hair wild, is making his way along the broken sidewalk across the street, at the edge of the zone of destruction. He's surrounded by garbage bags. He's carrying them, but there are so many, so full and so round, that it seems impossible he could be carrying them. They seem to be moving with him, like creatures in an animated cartoon.

Matthew remains in the shadows, watching, waiting. The man, in a businesslike manner, with no rush about him, shuffles along with his garbage bags, muttering all the while, moving purposefully along the sidewalk, and in a moment Matthew realizes his objective. Standing alone at the edge of the leveled landscape is a traffic-control box entirely free of graffiti.

It's him again. The Graffitist. He's everywhere.

When he reaches the box, he sets his bags down, takes out a marker, squats, and begins writing. Matthew crosses the street and takes a position behind him, near enough to note, with pleasure, that

he's using a Runznot, the brand of marker he recommended in the
message Matthew read in the rain weeks before, the brand Matthew
himself uses for writing on his wall. The graffitist writes this:

> IF IT'S ANDERSON'S IT'S PURE AND STURDY
> AND TASTY—
> AND IF IT'S PURE AND STURDY AND TASTY IT
> MUST BE ANDERSON'S!

It's Jack's ad, says Matthew.
Stolen from Pabst Blue Ribbon, if you ask me, says BW.
It's funny that he should write an ad.
He's probably being paid. It's a new breakthrough—commercially supported graffiti.
The Graffitist goes on writing:

> IF YOU'RE HAPPY YOU'RE WISE AND GOOD AND
> JUST—

Ha! says BW. *That lets us out.*
The Graffitist finishes:

> AND IF YOU'RE WISE AND GOOD AND JUST, YOU
> MUST BE HAPPY!

What bullshit, says BW.
It's something to think about, says Matthew. *Those ifs, though.
Which way do they point? Does he mean that you can't be wise,
good, and just unless you're happy? Or does he mean that if you're
wise, good, and just, you can't help being happy?*
Who cares?
*I just wonder whether he's saying that you have to be happy to
start with. Is this a message of hope? Or—or is he telling me that—*
He is not writing this for you, Matthew. He is writing this because he is a crazy person.
I think he must be saying that the ingredients are enough.
*Matthew, this is a philosophy based on a beer commercial. A
plagiarized beer commercial.*
But it's intriguing—

Are you kidding? This is sentimental claptrap.

"Maybe not," says Matthew, aloud.

Hearing these words, the Graffitist turns and sees Matthew. He draws back like a frightened animal, cowering, huddling down against the switching box, bringing his hands up to his face as if he were preparing for a blow.

"Don't be afraid," says Matthew. "I wouldn't hit you."

You wouldn't?

No. I wouldn't do anything like that.

Oh, no?

No. He holds his hands out, as if to show that they're empty, but in one he's still clutching the bar.

Shit. You're right. I hit someone.

"I hit someone," says Matthew. The Graffitist draws away, but he's against the control box and can't retreat any farther.

I hurt someone. I hit someone. How could I have done that? I wouldn't hurt anybody.

"I wasn't myself."

I'm not the kind of person who would hurt someone.

"I'm sorry."

Stop it, Matthew. Stop it. You are not sorry. I am not sorry.

"I—I've seen a lot of your writings."

Oh, this is wonderful. This is a fine thing. This is great. Get chummy. Maybe he'll take you on as an apprentice. Invite him up to the apartment. Show him your own work on your own walls. You can drive each other nuts. Is that what you want? God, he stinks.

You smell him? Why do you smell him all of a sudden? Why can't you smell that stink at home?

Matthew drops the bar and pulls out his wallet. The Graffitist watches every move, apparently terrified. Matthew looks into his wallet.

Twenty? he thinks.

Twenty? says BW. *Nothing! Let's get out of here.*

You know, I never made good on that promise I made the night I lied to Effie. I never gave anything to the guy who mumbles, the one outside the health club every morning.

I knew that was rattling around in the back of your mind. So what? Come on.

Matthew takes all the bills from his wallet, folds them once, and holds them out to the Graffitist.

The Graffitist makes no move to take the money, so Matthew presses the wad into his hand.

"Keep up the good work," Matthew says.

What are you doing? How much did you give him? asks BW. *You must have given him a hundred dollars. You're crazy, you know that?*

The Graffitist holds the money without looking at it, looking at Matthew.

Look. Look around you. You are standing in the middle of nowhere. You are alone. Do you get the message? Listen, will you? Do you hear that wind? Do you hear that damn wind moan? What else do you hear? What do you hear besides that wind? Nothing.

The Graffitist clears his throat.

Nothing but this asshole. Don't you get the message? Nobody gives a shit about you, Matthew. The world doesn't care what you do. The universe doesn't care what you do. You are alone. Your only friend is me.

The Graffitist says, "Listen. I want to tell you something."

I'm right, says BW. *Stick with me and things are going to work out. I'm much healthier than you are, Matthew. I'm not going to kill myself. I'm not going to become an alcoholic. I'm not going to give up. I'm going to get what you've always wanted.*

"Let me tell you something," says the Graffitist. He's still holding the money in front of him, as if it means nothing to him.

I see a great future for us. I am going to keep you from falling apart. You don't have to worry. Trust me. I am your better self.

The Graffitist, still wary, straightens up.

Come on, says BW. *There's a wonderful world out there, Matthew. It belongs to guys like me. Not to guys like—this.*

The Graffitist says, "I've learned that—"

Matthew snatches the money from him and begins to walk away.

The Graffitist is stunned. He hadn't expected this. "Wait!" he calls.

Matthew stops and turns around. He looks at the Graffitist and his shoulders drop. "I'm sorry," he says, but he turns away and trudges on for a few more steps.

"Wait!" the Graffitist calls. "Listen to me."

Matthew stops again, turns, and stares at the Graffitist with a puzzled expression. For a moment he seems about to return, but then he looks at the money in his hand, shoves it into his pocket, and shouts, "Fuck you, you asshole!" He spins around and begins to walk with something like conviction, begins in fact to stride, like someone with things to do, someone who knows where he's going.

The Graffitist, hurt, furious, glances around for something to throw at Matthew, sees the bar, grabs it, hefts it, but thinks better of it. He's not the sort who would do something like that. He drops the bar, gathers his trash bags, and goes off in search of shelter from the wind.

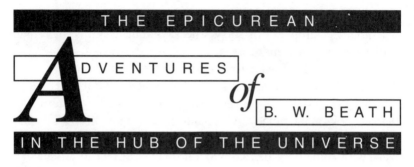

THE EPICUREAN

ADVENTURES *of* B. W. BEATH

IN THE HUB OF THE UNIVERSE

Ike's

Seated at the bar at **Ike's**, we watched, fascinated, while an aging fellow (possibly only our age, come to think of it, but so bent by care and conscience that he seemed much older) tried to pick up a lovely little girl, shrink-wrapped in a tiny skirt. You can guess the type: an old poop with yellowing teeth, so *derrière garde* that he ordered a martini without irony, wearing a suit so nondescript that we hardly remember it, enlivened we must admit by snappy socks that we wouldn't have rejected ourselves but which, frankly, did nothing for him but betray a pitiful struggle against age.

In the interest of bringing you the fullest possible account of Ike's and its denizens, we consumed a few quite awful margaritas and as many "Macho Nachos" as we could stomach as an excuse for lingering to watch the poor fool fail. He did, of course. When at last he left, frustrated and humiliated, we couldn't help wondering something: Whatever had made him think he might have succeeded? Why had he

thought he had a chance? What cruel disease infects a pathetic fellow like this with such impossible dreams? We thought that the gorgeous girl herself might have the answer, so, for the sake of this review, we bought her another of those lousy margaritas and engaged her in conversation. We learned, as, to be honest, we had suspected we would, nothing from her that we didn't already know, but quite suddenly, this morning, after we had sent her home, in that tranquil time when we jot our notes, it came to us. It was the food, the terrible food. Here the food is not merely bad; it's paradigmatically poor, and it's served in enormous quantities, so that we have a case of too much of nothing, by half. Now reason along with us. How does any of us determine where he belongs in the scale of worthiness? By comparison. We measure ourselves against something else. Ahha! Now we see why the food made our pathetic friend try to pick up the toothsome cutie. It offered an unrealistic comparison. Consumed in the quantities Ike's

provides, food this bad would make a
cipher feel adequate to anything life
might send his way. Think what this
miserable muck does to the mediocre.
It makes them feel like us. Over-
reaching themselves, they may fall.
Falling, they may be hurt.

—*BWB*

Ike's
5050 Boylston Street, 555-1953.
American Express, Visa, MasterCard.
Handicapped: read the review.
Lunch 12–3, Tuesday–Saturday.
Brunch 12–3, Sunday.
Dinner 6–12 Tuesday–Sunday.
Reservations recommended.